MISSISSIPPI FLYWAY

MISSISSIPPI FLYWAY

Nel Rand

iUniverse, Inc.
New York Lincoln Shanghai

Mississippi Flyway

Copyright © 2005 by Nel Rand

iUniverse books may be ordered through booksellers or by contacting:

iUniverse
2021 Pine Lake Road, Suite 100
Lincoln, NE 68512
www.iuniverse.com
1-800-Authors (1-800-288-4677)

This is a work of fiction. Any resemblance to actual persons or events is coincidental. While some of the places are real, I have taken liberties with the settings for the sake of fiction. I hope the good people who live in these locations will forgive me.

ISBN-13: 978-0-595-35762-8 (pbk)
ISBN-13: 978-0-595-80235-7 (ebk)
ISBN-10: 0-595-35762-8 (pbk)
ISBN-10: 0-595-80235-4 (ebk)

Printed in the United States of America

For my sister, Joann, who remembers everything. Thanks for the road trip Sis.

To my gracious and loving mother, Dorothy, who is not Louise in my story.

To my children Lisa Rand, Jay Rand, and Mona Tucker-Rand. Thanks for being such amazing human beings.

Last, but not least, to my dear friend, Jacque Duncan.

Acknowledgements

First and foremost I would like to thank my dear friend and mentor, Meg Jensen, who taught me how to write a novel and guided me through the maze of what to do with it after it was written. Also, thanks for being so gentle with the first draft.

Immense thanks to Sue McGhee, Susan Pasarow, Andres Berger-Kiss, Linda Chaplik, Elizabeth Bunker, Ellen Saunders, Stephanie Baldridge, Darlene Key, Pearl Wright, Mel Parks, Olga Anderson, Darlene Harkins, Beverly Bean, Pam Patrie, Robin Lawton, Aline Bradford, Pat Wagler, Margaret Rand, and Bill Rand for reading the manuscript in its many incarnations and providing thoughtful critiques. Thanks to Jan Brattain for her artistic efforts. Thanks to Ben Tucker for rescuing my manuscript when the computer ate it for breakfast, and to Norm Duncan for all of his technical help setting up my website, and being there when my computer took on a mind of its own. Thanks to the research librarians, Linda Minor and Carolyn Gates at the Forest Grove library, and to all the librarians at the Banks library for putting up with me. Thanks to George and Pearl Wright for keeping a roof over my head in such sylvan style. Thanks to all of my friends and family who encouraged me to stick with it.

Finally thanks to all the gracious people who displayed such an abundance of southern hospitality on my trip back home: Sandra Robine, Pat and Jerry Piper, Frieda and Larry Rickman, La Quita Fox, Phyllis Wagner, and Mary Barlow.

The reprint of the verse from Rainer Maria Rilke, "Ah, Not to Be Cut Off" is reprinted from *The Enlightened Heart, an Anthology of Sacred Poetry*, Edited by Stephen Mitchell, published in1989 by Harper&Row, page 144. The reprint from the poem *Renascence*, by Edna St. Vincent Millay, was published as *Collected Poems, Edna St. Vincent Millay*, 1956, page 13, published by Harper&Row.

CHAPTER 1

▼

Ah, not to be cut off,
not through the slightest partition
shut out from the law of the stars.
The inner—what is it?
if not intensified sky,
hurled through with birds and deep
with the winds of homecoming.
—Rainer Maria Rilke—

—Owl, Cairo, Illinois, 1948—

I could run as fast as the wind or fly like a bird, and it wouldn't make a whit of difference now. I'm going to be late for Mass no matter what. Sweat stings my eyes and lips. I grab my book bag by the leather strap and sling it over to the other side. The stitch in my side eases up a little as I stop to catch my breath. I'm going to bypass purgatory and go straight to hell.

"You ain't going to no hell, Owl, just quit cryin', comb your hair, and start runnin'," I could hear Rose say. She murders the King's English the way Tiny and Louise do because she hates English class and always skips it. It's my favorite class. I could diagram sentences and parse verbs till the cows come home, and I love to learn new words and use them right away in a sentence. I love words about as much as I love the birds that follow the river on their endless migrations. Rose never seemed to worry much about being late for Mass. Half the time she never even goes. She doesn't have to worry about it now. She's a sophomore at Cairo High public school, where nobody makes you go to church. Next year I'll be there with her.

I light out again when the stitch goes away. Almost there. I see the steeple of the Sacred Heart Church, its sharp metal stabbing up into an innocent slate of blue. As it mounts the sky, the sun hounds out the subtle yellows and pinks of sunrise, the time of day I love most, except for nighttime.

Owls fly at night and they're my favorite bird. Tiny started calling me that when I was little 'cause he said I was wise and never missed a thing, and the name stuck. Everybody but the nuns calls me by my nickname. If the Indians were right about us being animals before we were humans, then I was an owl.

I once called a great horned owl out of hiding, in broad daylight. I'm not proud of what I did, but I tricked a female into thinking I was a male, and that there was a juicy mouse to eat over where I was hiding behind the willow tree up on the levee. I made muffled squawking sounds that tried to hide my excitement about finding food, and then, starting way down at the back of my throat, I let out a breathy sound that rounded itself through the tunnel of lips, and out came a "whoo-hoo-ho-o-o" in a low deep voice. And, sure enough, the female answered the call with a higher pitched "whooooooo-hoo-hoo." She flew over close to me and stared with big, phosphorescent, disappointed eyes. I felt ashamed of myself for having tricked her and stopped calling owls after that.

To my left, behind Commercial Street, a low fog rides the surface of the river like a surfer hell-bent on staying with the wave. Flotsam and jetsam of yesterday's flood upstream rushes by on the swift current like gray ghosts, the river impatient to dump its contraband into the sea.

I can make out what looks like an old baby carriage drifting in an eddy close to shore, and then the current catches it again and heads south. I hope to jiminy the baby isn't still in it, hope it's been rescued. I sigh at the thought of being a sweet baby again, untouched by the taints of this imperfect world. It's too late for me. The best that could happen would be for me to sink like a rock down to the quiet bottom of the muddy Mississippi and bury my sins in the cool sludge, never to resurface, a more tolerable solution than burning in eternal hellfire.

I stoop to pull up my knee socks that have pooled down around my ankles during my marathon run (a good three miles). The weight of the book bag nearly topples me head first when I bend over.

I begin the final sprint to what for sure is trouble I don't need from others: I'm an expert in the art of self-torture. I can still hear Father McDill through the screen of the confessional blowing his nose and making those scolding noises, like an old blue jay about to bother some poor bird. He'd made a bigger deal about being late for Mass than about what I told him that Tiny and I did together.

The sun, hot on my back, chases me up the wide stone steps. Sweet relief as I retreat into the perennial twilight of the foyer. The holy water is cool on my fingertips and forehead. I wish I could throw my whole body into the big marble font and swim around there until time for English class. I make the sign of the cross. In the name of the Father, Son, and Holy Ghost, in a mumble, invoking the all-powerful male trinity. You can never understand…never forgive me. I cup both hands into the basin of water and let the cool water drip down my face…rub it on my lips and swallow some as if to erase the blasphemy in my heart. God have mercy on my soul. To make things worse, I started my period yesterday. Louise called it "the curse" and sent me to Rose to deal with it. I can tell Rose anything. Well, almost anything.

"Am I really cursed?" I asked.

"No, you ain't cursed. Don't listen to a word Louise tells you. She don't know nothin'. Every woman, (she called me a woman) starts doing this about your age. It's just natural. Ain't no curse from God or nobody else." She gave me some Kotex and an aspirin for the aching and after school let me hang out with her and her friends at Poppy's. She even bought me a chocolate ice cream soda, and she and Wilma and Darlene lifted their Coca Cola glasses and toasted my womanhood.

Now that I've caught my breath, I put on my head scarf I had stashed in the book bag and tie it under my chin in a double knot as I grit my teeth and launch myself down the long central aisle. Sunlight sifts through the tall stained-glass windows, throwing kaleidoscopes of rainbows in cross-sections along the rows of wooden pews. The familiar smells of frankincense and myrrh waft up the aisle from the sanctuarysweet smells filled with images of far away lands, invoking not the triune God for whom this church bell tolls, but antediluvian kin, gracious parliaments of feathery beings for which I am named.

Along the stone walls, cradled in giant egg-shaped niches, stand life-sized statues of saints and angels, hands pressed together in prayer, with eyes turned toward heaven. The angels sport great white carved wings. If only I had wings.

It's Monday, and the church is deserted except for the nuns, the students, and the usual scattering of bent, devout old women with black scarves covering their heads. In a way I admire the old faithfuls their constancy, and wish I could just jump headfirst into belief in something greater than myself. I guess the things I have the most faith in are birds, words, and music. I have silly daydreams of being a concert pianist. I like to sit at Granny's old player piano with my hands hovering over the old yellow ivories as they dance up and down to piano rolls of Scott Joplin rags and Sousa marches. With low E and high C missing, the keyboard looks as if it's grinning. I pretend I'm playing for the queen of England, who rises in applause and pronounces me the world's greatest pianist. I haven't felt much like playing in the last few weeks though, ever since Tiny left.

The nuns are on their knees, a row of blackbirds perched in the front pews. My eighth grade classmates are directly behind them, girls dressed in white blouses and navy skirts, boys in knee-high navy pants, white shirts, and bow ties. All are wearing navy socks that end mid-calf, exposing adolescent kneecaps, reckless prompts that the human body is not to be taken seriously. Running legs in the playground look like sock puppets with bulbous heads, laughable, skeletal reprimands against vain thoughts. The only empty seat is mine. I can feel all eyes on me as I genuflect and slip into the pew, causing a noticeable shuffle of bodies like dominoes falling. I push the book bag under the pew.

Father is already into the Offertory. The congregation kneels.

The little altar bell rings softly three times. In his robe with gold brocade, Father McDill is transformed from the red-nosed, beer-drinking priest who goes fishing with Tiny out on Kentucky Lake into the magician-priest of the Mass as he consecrates the bread and wine. He raises the gold chalice high above his head and leans toward the statue of the crucified Christ hanging above the altar.

"Hoc est enim Corpus Meum." "This is my body," he chants in Latin. "Whosoever eats of my flesh will have eternal life."

I strike my sore breasts hard with my fist three times, reciting the prescribed words of repentance. With clenched teeth, "Through my fault, through my fault, through my most grievous fault." The round flat wafers inside the gold chalice are transmuting into the body of Christ.

The striking of the breast is repeated with the chalice of wine.

"Hoc est enim Calix sanguinis." "This is my blood," the priest chants. He looks directly at me.

"Through my fault, through my fault, through my most grievous fault," I repeat, in chorus with the other participants, as he holds up the communion chalice.

The alchemy is complete.

I rise on wobbly legs with the other students at the nod from Sister Lothaire to proceed to the communion rail. I kneel and try to keep my fluttering eyelids closed so I don't have to look into the face of my confessor, open my mouth, and stick out my tongue. Father McDill had absolved me in the confessional last Friday so that I would be able to receive communion, but I feel unredeemed. He had given me a penance of reciting twenty Our Fathers and fifteen Hail Mary's. He'd even interrupted my confession and told me it was a family matter, that I should not place temptation in Tiny's way. I shouldn't dress provocatively. Men were highly excitable about those things. And besides, since there had been no penetration, he'd said, I was still intact: a virgin. Then he'd made a big deal about me being on time for Mass.

I pretend that the dry, thin, sour wafer that sticks to the roof of my mouth is peanut butter. I wonder how many calories are contained in the body of Christ as my stomach growls. I forgot to bring the hard-boiled eggs and apple I'd packed to eat after communion. The nuns always had cinnamon rolls and hot chocolate ready for us after Mass on communion days, ever since Betty Lou keeled over at the communion rail from lack of food, as it was a venial sin to eat before receiving the body of Christ. Louise had told the nuns not to feed me anything because I was on a special diet. She'd have me starving to death if it were up to her. She'd gotten a prescription from Dr. Snyder for dextroamphetamine for both me and Rose, so we wouldn't get fat like Tiny. Louise had been horrified when Rose started developing breasts. "It's not natural for a young girl to mature so quickly," she'd said.

"Well, hell's bells, I'm a girl ain't I? I got titties, and they ain't gonna disappear no matter what." Rose was good at sassing back at Louise. At the first hint of pubescence, I just took the pills to get her off my back. To tell you the truth, at first I sort of liked the jolts of energy they gave me, the way my pupils dilated, making my eyes look dark and mysterious, the hunger pains, an affirmation of my existence. But now I just want to be done with it: the sleepless nights, frazzled nerves, and constant hunger.

We walk back to the pew with bent heads, eyes directed downward. After communion, the priest places the silver and gold chalices away in the sacristy, above the marble altar. He genuflects, turns to the congregation with arms outstretched, gestures a symbolic cross in final blessing.

All stand as he plows down the torso of the church, swinging his ball of smoking incense as if to clear his way of any earthly trash as he exits, with an altar boy at each side, and one behind.

A drift of silvery smoke from the passing incense finds me and nestles in the crescent of my ear, cooing dovelike, in a language that I almost, but not quite, remember. I cup my hand over my left ear to capture it as I lean down to pick up my book bag. We stand and face the central aisle, my row last to file out to form impeccably straight lines, the girls behind the boys, as we march out into the blinding brilliance of a sunny April morning.

*   *   *   *

Alone in the classroom, the smell of cinnamon rolls twists up like strong vines through the floor register, fierce tendrils wrapping around my body, squeezing the breath out of me. My mouth puckers, and my stomach growls like a hungry lion being teased with raw meat. I keep going out to the fountain in the hall to fill my empty stomach with water and to get away from the creaks and moans in the classroom that sound like poor souls crying out from purgatory. When I hear marching feet on the stairs, I run back into the room and open my catechism.

The students scurry to their seats and stand at attention as Sister Mary Lothaire follows them into the room. I begrudge them their full bellies.

"Good morning, Sister." In singsong voice with the others, I stand, and the room starts a slow spin around me.

"Good morning, class, you may be seated." I watch Sister walk. She looks hobbled in her shiny black Oxfords. I cringe at the memory of a newsreel I'd seen at the Tivoli last Saturday about women in China limping around on bound feet. Sister Lothaire is a shadow shrouded from head to foot in folds of heavy black muslin. The presence of a real body beneath the copious drapery seems dubious. Does she get the monthlies like other women? There is an astringent smell about her, like the witch hazel Louise puts on my chigger bites in the summer when the buck grass grows tall enough to harbor the almost invisible, jumping red dots of fire. Sister's pumpkin face, swollen and choked by an ill-fitting wimple and bib, changes colors like a chameleon, betraying her moods. She blushes the color of Granny's prize roses, nervously fingering the polished black beads of her rosary whenever Father McDill pays unexpected visits to the classroom. When she is angered by incorrigible (one of her two favorite words) behavior from her students, her face puffs up all green and bruised. Even while seated she appears to be in constant motion, looking in all directions at once, a mythical Janus, guarding unseen gates against any blasphemy (her other favorite word) that might emerge in the classroom. Her lips forever recite silent prayers as she fingers her rosary. Her jaws chew nonexistent gum. She has troubles with her dentures. They fell out one morning during choir practice. The getaway teeth rolled under a pew, and we all laughed, relieved to see that Lothaire was human. Billy Buxton crawled after the fleeing chompers, an unexpected adventure in an otherwise long and tedious day.

Billy Buxton is a bad boy. Louise warned me to stay clear of him. She said he has a dirty mind and a filthy mouth and would never amount to anything. She would have a fit if she knew that Rose used to hang out with him, but he got held back three years in a row and didn't make it to high school with her, so that put an end to it. He got in trouble last week and was sent to Father McDill for writing F-U-C-K on the sidewalk of the playgrounds with red chalk. Joan Marie said he tried to look up her dress once.

The cooing in my ear starts up again as the shuffling of students taking their seats reverberates like an ocean wave, first crashing, then soft. I just want to get up and run...get away. Wish I were up on the levy counting snow geese, watching them land like patches of snow in the marshes down by the river. I'm a volunteer bird counter for the Audubon Society during peek migration seasons, a job I take very seriously.

"Now, pupils, you may take out your catechisms and turn to page sixty-four."

Sister Lothaire's voice sounds like a rapidly receding train whistle. People are shuffling pages, dropping books, and slamming desk lids in order to delay the inquisition for a few minutes. The central aisle that separates the boys from the girls opens up like the river, a saving oasis, rolling wide with hot chocolate, foamy with melted marshmallows. I dive down deep to the bottom and gorge myself. Objects and people in the room take on a blue hazy glow when I surface.

Thank God. Sister is beginning the daily interrogation on the boys' side of the room.

"John Paul, what is the Holy Trinity?" I can barely hear Lothaire's question over the persistent cooing in both ears now.

It's warm for April. The window is open to the smells of freshly cut grass and the constant river, oily and fishy, in its perennial migration. The smells are the river's way of saying, "Hello! I'm here!" I can't imagine life without the presence of the river smell—of decay, hinting of our mortality, binding us as one in that certainty.

I give myself over for a moment to the pull of the cooing and the other birds singing in the big oak tree framed by the window. I know almost every song I hear. I earned a Girl Scout badge in bird song identification when I was ten.

"The Holy Trinity is three divine persons in one divine substance." John Paul's voice is changing. It starts high, and then cracks into a husky croak that makes for muffled giggles around the room.

The monotone voices spitting back rote answers to Catholic dogma are now in female voice.

"Jacqueline, what is the Paraclete?" The petite Italian girl's desk sits directly in front of mine. Jacqueline rises to her feet with a fleetness. She always has the right answer.

"The Paraclete is the third person of the Holy Trinity…the Holy Ghost, the Holy Dove sent on earth to comfort us and ease our sorrows."

It's my turn. I struggle to stand on noodle legs. I can't feel them beneath me. I barely hear Sister's voice through the outraged roars in my stomach and the sweet trilling in my ears. I never have the right answer. Suddenly my new secret power kicks in, and I don't even care anymore. Recently, I discovered the ability to shrink people and even make them disappear. I used it on Tiny before he left. Maybe I made him disappear for good.

"Ellie Mae! Wake up child! And stop grinning like a Cheshire cat!" I squint, and Lothaire shrinks to the size of a cat.

"Ellie Mae Moon, I'm talking to you!" The nun's feline face turns strawberry red and then purple. Her voice sounds like a record playing at slow speed.

Betty Lou sits behind me and whispers the question to me. "What is the attitude we take toward the Blessed Virgin Mary?"

"We adore the Blessed Virgin Mary," I say out loud. I'm thirsty. My parched voice sticks in my throat.

A heavy silence fills the room, like a blow from Lothaire's pointer. I hear only the singing in my ears as my winged suitor courts me away from the world.

The outraged vulture with the pointer flies at me.

"You incorrigible child!"

I feel the sharp sting on my bare legs and across my back and shoulders only for a moment. Then the pain is gone. I hear the swishing, but it no longer hurts as Lothaire delivers the blows harder and faster.

"Blasphemy! We never adore anyone but God the Father," the nun shrieks. "We only venerate the Blessed Virgin Mary."

I reduce Lothaire to the size of a tiny black ant and wonder why she is so angry about words that hold no meaning. The hollow tenets of a religion that haven't helped me at all with my problems are perplexing. I, who have tried so hard to arrange my life into separate little boxes marked before and after.

I feel only the soft tingling that start in my toes and undulates upward, taking away my hunger: warm waves in harmony with the love song my suitor sings full voice.

The shrill siren sounding recess startles Lothaire into self-composure. The pointer drops limply to her side. I restore her to her full size.

"For your punishment you will go to the church instead of taking recess this morning. You will recite ten Hail Marys and fifteen Our Fathers." Lothaire looks old and tired after the tirade. She takes out a handkerchief from her sleeve and wipes the sweat from her brow.

At her signal we all rise and form two perfectly straight rows, one for each gender. I'm behind Jacqueline as we march out into the glaring mid-morning sun.

Weightless, I float across the playground and into the shadow of the church, feeling my face tighten into a smile.

"This is my body. This is my blood," a voice insists as I climb the wide stone steps. The world is wrapped in a radiant blue. I fly into the protection of the dark. It is, after all, my natural habitat.

The altar bell rings three times, swelling in crescendo, exalting me.

Strong currents of energy wash over me.

As the song of the dove takes form, the alchemy is complete.

I hold tight with my fledgling wings to the feathery back of the Paraclete, as he extends his great wings to full span and flies with me high above the rafters to a place deep within the forested canyons of Ellie Mae's mind—to a place where no one can touch me anymore.

CHAPTER 2

▼

—Ellie, St. Louis, 1967—

In the dawn's light the old sycamore tree in the backyard throws its shadow onto the lace curtains that hang over the long, south-facing window. Its limbs are gossamer dancers, reflections that will be lost as the sun rises. The tree towers the four-story brick house.

I plant myself here at my desk every day at daybreak to drink the cherished first cup of coffee and listen to the multitude of birds in the sycamore tree sing the sun up. The robins are in good voice this time of day. They ask vital questions in four/four time of all who would listen. Throaty sparrows and chattering wrens sing duets amidst a background of other birdsongs. Finally, as the sun mounts the sky, the scolding jays and cawing crows join the chorus, drowning out the melody. I surprise myself at times by singing with the birds in their own songs, a skill I learned as a child, although I don't remember the learning of it. I can be myself around the birds. I don't have to aim to please anyone. It seems I've spent most of my life trying to do that. With the birds, it's like stepping through a looking glass where everyone speaks a universal language, one I was fluent in since birth, and no one stands in judgment.

Owl: *You once conversed with rivers and oceans, each in their own singular tongue as they flowed to the sea, breaking the codes of impervious reefs, and soothing in hushed voice the fires of molten volcanoes. You chanted with stony meteorites, soared and screeched with birds of prey, and chattered with gentle sparrows. You prattled on and on with bees and were spokesman for majestic forests. You keep the memories deep within you, forgotten.*

There was an urgent pungency to the smell of overripe tomatoes carried in from the garden on a slight breeze, mixed with a hint of jasmine and mint, awakening my senses to the start of a new day. I'd special-ordered the jasmine from a nursery in Atlanta, a night-blooming, intensely fragrant variety. A moment after the sun infused the sky with coral glow, the exotic flowers closed their petals in protection from the heat of another hot, muggy day in the city. Smart plant. Wish I could do that—just close up against all irritants.

In the promise of a new day, I feel almost safe here, even a bit smug. I gather my bare legs and feet up on the oversized Stickley oak chair, a steal I'd found at a garage sale, and hug myself. This is the largest room in the house, with a high, oak-beamed ceiling and an oak-paneled fireplace, a corner room with long windows facing out on the north, south, and west. It is a privilege, a victory, to be sitting here in my study. I'd fought and elbowed my way here, through my ex-husband's surliness and my mother's tyranny.

Since Ted's departure last spring, my one decisive act has been to move my desk from the cramped, dark, upstairs guest room down here into the library that he had claimed as his without discussion. This one room was the main reason I wanted to buy the house three years ago. I knew I could write here, sustain a focus, make a plan of action, and follow through with it. There was a sense of diligence about the space, as if someone had courted the muse on a daily basis here, over the better part of a lifetime, perhaps. I once read about a village by the sea in Ireland where all the women made lace. In the province of Manabi, Ecuador, were special caves where craftsmen wove, by hand, fibers of dried palm leaves to create the first Panama hats—the environment playing a crucial role in excellence of craft. Perhaps repetition of the practice of an art or fine craft in a particular place chinks away at stone walls of resistance; perhaps it makes an easier passage for the creative to enter. I don't have the courage to plunge into deep waters yet, but I come at dawn everyday to sit and drink coffee, marking trails with breadcrumbs so the muse will one day find me.

I was disappointed but hadn't argued the point when Ted claimed the space as his. After all, his was the more important job. But resentment, hard as a diamond, slowly formed itself in my heart. Now the room was mine; the whole house was mine.

If only I could keep Louise at bay. Even the anticipation of her intrusions breaks my peaceful mood. Why did I let her and Ted talk me into moving just three houses away from her? The DO NOT DISTURB sign on the closed door in bold black letters does not deter her. She'll be along soon enough to harass me about getting my life in shipshape and ready to face a world of dull, meaningless routine, a world she would thrust upon me—one that would define my life in terms of commodity and physical appearance and reflect her values, not mine.

I take inventory of the bare room. I like it this way: uncluttered. The rest of the house is in shambles. I haven't felt like cleaning since Ted moved out. Cardboard boxes full of books that have passed the test of time are stacked on the floor next to the wide built-in oak shelves. They've been there since last April, patiently waiting for me. A carved wooden statue of three monkeys, "See No Evil, Hear No Evil, Speak No Evil"—the one memento I'd been able to retrieve from Granny's house after she died—stands on the bookshelf next to the few books that demanded to be unpacked: Rachael Carson's Silent Spring, a yellowed, tattered paperback of The Bhagavad Gita, Song Birds of North America, and a first edition of the I Ching, Book of Changes that I picked up in San Francisco's Chinatown before I married Ted. I'd been drawn to the book with magnetic force, although at the time, I hadn't a clue as to what any of it meant. I used to fondle and smell the book everyday as if the familiarity would unlock the mystery hidden within the leather bindings. Only lately have I started throwing the coins and reading the hexagrams. I consult the Chinese Oracle as people read from the Bible everyday for wisdom and direction. Through daily use, an order to the hexagrams can be discerned but not easily described. They are like songs without words. As I open to number fifty-six, Lu, the Wanderer, above is Lu, the Clinging Fire. Below is Ken, the Keeping Still Mountain. The image is that of a wild fire sweeping over the mountain. "Strange lands and separation are the wanderer's lot." The image sends shivers up my spine. It resonates with something deep…

"Yoo-hoo. Oh yoo-hoo. Ellie are you home? I'm here."

A streak of dread and guilt shoots up my spine, hot and icy. I look at the clock…six fifty-five. Why does she have to get up so early?

"Ellie, are you in there?"

The timbre and cadence of Louise's voice twists around my eardrums like tightly plied thread. The shrill, cracked voice with metallic undertones creates a sour, tinny taste in the roof of my mouth. I think if I should ever look down Louise's throat, I would not find vocal chords but a vast wasteland, a desert, not of sand, but of hard, cracked mud—like the soil in the bottomlands down near the river in the dry season.

I knock over my half-full coffee cup in an effort to throw a wadded up Moon Pie wrapper into the wastebasket where I had missed a dunk shot yesterday. Usually her entrance is announced by the wheezy sound of the wheelchair as it rolls up the ramp onto the front porch, but I'd been lost in the image of the hexagram and hadn't heard a thing.

"Yoo-hoo. Ellie, are you home? I'm here," the voice insists, as if her presence will save the day. My left eye begins twitching beyond control. "I should have known you would be in here." Louise stops at the door to glance at the DO NOT DISTURB sign and then butts through the archway in her wheelchair, like a bull encountering the color red.

"Why do you always have to be so secretive? After all, this is your home now. You're the only one here." She exaggerates the *your* with a flat, nasal sound as she rolls in with her newly hired companion and housekeeper trotting close behind. He won't last long: none of them ever do.

"This is Jeremy. Isn't he a doll? With all his good looks, he can cook too." Louise rolls her eyes like a movie queen in a silent film. Awareness of the presence of a handsome man softens the shrillness of her voice.

"Jeremy, this is my daughter, Ellie. I'm sure you're not surprised we're related, although she carries more meat on her bones than I do." She says this with delight, as she bats her mascara-encrusted eyelashes at the embarrassed-looking man.

"Good morning to you too, Ma." I pretend I didn't hear it. I forget how to breathe. The day that had started as a promise of renewal has ended. In its place is the consuming anxiety that seems to rule my life when Louise is around. Every time she hurls hurtful words at me, I want to shed my skin and crawl under something dark and cool. Jeremy stands behind the wheelchair staring at me expectantly. I want to protest, but I can't put words in proper order to form a sentence.

"Where's that wonderful poster of Twiggy that I gave you? I thought it would look good right over there." Louise points with conviction to the north wall. "This room is like an empty tomb now that your husband's gone." She shakes her head from side to side as she inspects the sparse study, frowning.

"Ex-husband, Ma."

She'd better stop with the Twiggy thing. I follow Louise's eyes around the room as she takes in the bare walls and empty bookshelves in obvious disapproval. A new book of song lyrics and poems by Leonard Cohen lies like a sleeping prophet of protest on its side on the desktop. I ease open a drawer and push the book in, hoping Louise hasn't noticed. She has a way of cheapening anything dear. She would denounce the lyrics, labeling them unintelligible, subversive.

Ted took all of his thick, important-looking medical books bound in heavy leather that smelled like glue and cod liver oil and, thank God, the two oil paintings. One was of a man fly-fishing, standing in the middle of a stream landing a big walleye bass. The fish had put up a good fight. His haunting eyes had always followed me around the room, pleading for mercy. The image seemed to embody my plight. Hooked by marriage to a man I had stopped loving, perhaps had never really loved, and bound by duty to a spiteful mother I had never stopped loving, despite all of the nagging. I'd been reeled in by love and the promise of love and thrown into a frying pan of hot oil. It was the fish in the painting that led me to file for divorce.

The second painting had been a portrait of Ted's father, sitting stiff and proper in his favorite Morris chair. The painter had exaggerated the patriarch's stature and rendered him aristocratic by the use of gold leaf in strategic places. The large canvas had dominated the room. Ted Frolick Sr. distinguished himself in the field of orthopedics by writing the definitive book on the subject. Ted Jr. followed in his father's footsteps and became a well-respected orthopedic surgeon in St. Louis. The father's eyes were not soft and gentle like the fish's; they'd glared at me with cold disapproval whenever I entered the room. The real-life eyes had been worse, examining me as if I were a specimen of some little-known and undesirable species. He'd always felt that his son had married beneath his social status. Ted had acquired the same look of contempt toward the end of the marriage. I plan to hang the Audubon print of a heron landing on water, when I get around to it, where the portrait of my disapproving father-in-law had hung.

I think of Ted's mother, who toughed out her marriage until her son had completed medical school. Having outlived her usefulness, she locked herself in her bedroom and overdosed on Valium while her husband was busy at the hospital tending to other people's broken bones instead of his own wife's broken heart.

"You didn't answer me. Didn't you like the poster of Twiggy? She's all the rage right now," Louise says, her eyes running down and then up my body, inspecting for any new portly protrusions. Louise had gifted me with the poster of Twiggy in hopes that it would inspire me to lose weight. I both despise the waif and am sympathetic to her plight, with her huge raccoon eyes staring out from a shiny world of black and white. She looks ghoulish in her tight little miniskirt with her toothpick legs sticking out, no bulge in the front where her breasts should be, dwarfed by her fur mini-coat by Mr. Fred. A few days ago I'd drawn words in a bubble above Twiggy's head with an arrow pointing to her mouth: "Starve me to death you bastards! I'll do whatever you tell me to because I want you to love me." I wrote 'bullshit" across her body in a diagonal slash of red lipstick and tore the poster to shreds, setting the pieces on fire in the waste can and dumping the ashes in the trash pit in the alley. The ritual had been therapeutic.

"I've come to cheer you up." Louise seemed to know that she had pushed the Twiggy issue as far as she could, at least for now. "I know things look bleak right now, but you've got to pull yourself together. When life gives you lemons, you make lemonade."

I wasn't sure I could survive the clichés and insults this morning. Sympathizing with Lot's wife, I feel, first, nervous spasms, then the protective, familiar numbness in the limbs, and, finally, hardening of all soft tissue as I turn into a pillar of salt.

"You just need to fix yourself up a little bit. You could win him back. You need to go out and buy yourself one of those nice three-piece polyester suits like I wear. They're so slenderizing, and everybody's wearing them this season. Get with the program—it's 1967. And go get your hair cut and permed." Louise touches her lacquered hair with her long, red, manicured fingernails. "Look at me. No man ever left me. You know why? Because I fix myself up everyday. I wouldn't be seen without my makeup in the morning. Remember when you girls would bring your boyfriends home, and they were always attracted to me? That's because I take pride in how I look and…"

"Ma, don't start with tha…"

"You girls need to have more respect for yourselves." Louise always speaks in the present tense when referring to Rose. She'd been found dead from a drug overdose in the Mississippi River ten years ago at the age of twenty-three.

"Ma, you're the queen of de Nile." Louise doesn't listen to the words above her monologue, nor do I remind her that, indeed, her husband did leave her. Tiny had walked out of our lives one day when Rose was fifteen and I was twelve.

Jeremy stands silent behind the wheel chair, his arms at his side. He looks embarrassed at being caught in the middle of this mother/daughter imbroglio. It's up to him to save himself. I'm not going to.

Why did Louise automatically assume that Ted left me? I'd been the one to end the marriage, but Louise couldn't bring herself to believe that a daughter of hers would give up the security of being married to a prominent doctor from such a wealthy family. No matter how high I tease my hair or how many neat little polyester suits I wear, it would never please Louise or patch up my broken marriage. It is over.

"You're not on an eating binge again, are you?" Louise's eyebrows flutter in launching position as if ready to take flight when she spies the Moon Pie wrapper under the desk. She strains her neck to see it.

A slow burn slithers up my spine, precipitating a dangerous thaw. Jeremy smiles and gives me a thumbs up behind Louise's back as I start to open my mouth. The only sound that comes out is a low croak. The sun has turned traitor. The air is hot and stagnant. Jeremy rocks the wheelchair back and forth in tiny jerks as if to fan and soothe Louise into silence.

"You seem to blame me for all of your faults." Louise looks offended. She shrinks to the size of a dried pea.

"I'm not blaming you, Ma." That's a lie. I blame Louise for just about everything that has gone wrong in life. I identify the twitch in my left eye as self-loathing. When in hell will I ever grow up and take responsibility for my own life? My ears are ringing.

I restore Louise to normal size. She looks older than her fifty-four years, embedded in her wheelchair. She'd been a great beauty in her heyday, dancing across nightclub stages from St. Louis to New York as a showgirl. She'd even performed in a Broadway production in a chorus line. I think of my favorite photo of her as a girl of seventeen posed in a scanty costume with enormous headgear and spiked high heels, smiling out, confident and gutsy. How did she go from fan dancer to matron with such a rigid code of morality? Dancing had been her passion. Tiny used to call her Cyd Charisse. Her heart was broken when she could no longer walk or dance after the accident. I look at my mother's face. The soft roundness of youth had been replaced by a harsh, angular look. Ever since the accident, Louise has reverted to wearing stage makeup to hide her disappointments in life and the premature onslaught of old age. Her penciled-on eyebrows—exaggerated black arches—look like blackbirds flying across the greasy white sky of a child's drawing. The dark eyes thick with mascara and lips overdrawn with apple red lipstick are accents, fresh flowers in an otherwise dying bouquet, placed among the wilted blossoms to save the day—a last encore before the bunch will be casually discarded by a world enchanted by youth. Her once-long black hair is now cropped, dyed a glaring orange to hide the gray, teased, poked, and prodded twice a week at Sassy's Beauty

Parlor to a height and span unbecoming to her now craggy facial features. Her hair looks like the spread-out, scraggly wings of an exhausted old bird of prey, frozen in place, struggling to lift into flight, protesting the certainty that she will be grounded for the rest of her life.

"How are you feeling today, Ma?" I feel somehow responsible for the accident. If I hadn't left her alone and moved to Oregon, maybe this wouldn't have happened.

"I brought the newspaper with me…thought we'd get an early start…go through the want ads together," Louise says, ignoring the appeal to communicate in any reciprocal way. "You've moped around long enough. It's time to get back on your feet, show the world the mettle you're made of. Face reality and stop burying your head in the sand. Get a real job. Nobody earns a living writing stories unless they're really good."

Louise is the size of a pea again.

"After all, art ain't gonna' put food on the table." She says this in an almost-lilting voice, like she enjoys inflicting pain.

That's enough. My throat is closing, jaws tightening—tongue and lips are in lockdown position.

"Uh huh."

"You'd still have that great job at the newspaper if you'd kept your mouth shut and just done your job. Any woman would kill for that job. You have to decide what you want to do with your life. You're thirty-one years old. I can't make that de…"

The ache in my chest becomes a stabbing pain; the room spins. I haven't inhaled for a long time.

Jeremy looks at me with concern. Louise is reduced to a monologue with no corporeal form. The loss of body somehow gives new force and volume to the voice.

I retreat toward the bathroom, aiming one stone foot in front of the other like the gait of the living dead. Finally I'm out of Louise's sight but not quite out of earshot.

"Look at me, for example. I could have been a Rockette in New York City if I hadn't married your father. I could kick higher than any of 'em. Still could if I wasn't in this damned wheelchair."

The air is stifling in the bathroom. The mirror reflects back an oxygen-deprived face, a rotten ham with maraschino cherry eyes. "Eat shit and die," it says, sounding remarkably like the voice in the other room that is now booming—the last sound I hear before losing consciousness.

CHAPTER 3

▼

Looking in all directions to make sure no one is watching, I unlock the backyard gate and lope stiffly across the alley to the vacant lot. The left side of my head throbs where it hit the hard porcelain of the toilet bowl this morning. Jeremy had heard the thud, rescuing me with a glass of cold water in my face.

It's almost twilight and cooling down a bit. Dried thistles and cockleburs scratch my bare legs as I wade through the weeds—sharp little stings—an antidote to the numbness in my limbs that still persists but is easing.

Contentment washes over me as I blend with the dry weeds. No one knows who owns this abandoned lot. When Ted and I moved in across the alley, I appointed myself guardian of the place. I'm surprised to see a lone monarch butterfly this late in the season. He lands on my outstretched hand.

Owl: *One summer day when you were an infant, before your body knew how to walk, Louise wheeled the buggy out into the early morning sunshine. A fluttering mass of orange hummed round you—Monarch butterflies, passing through on their journey to the mountaintops of Mexico to winter, longing for news along the way. You, the town crier, reported in their native milkweed dialect. You've forgotten, but I guard these memories in clenched talons, waiting for you to one day remember and set me free.*

I make the rounds to see what fruits have ripened in my absence. The old apple tree bore a few gnarled sour fists last month, but they are all gone. I wade through tall grass over to the fig tree. Every day for a week I've gorged on brown pithy teardrops as they ripen, sticky and sweet. A praying mantis is stretched out and pressed flat, clinging to a branch; he looks to be part of the tree. I wonder if this amazing stick creature eats figs. Does he crave the sweet treats—overindulge—drunk in his addiction to the earthiest of all fruit? He's lucky to live at the source of his craving. He doesn't have to make excuses to anyone for his habit. A twig snaps under-foot, and the mantis assumes a praying position. I fill my shorts' pockets and hands with figs, leaving the rest to the praying addict and the yellow jackets buzzing around the rotting fruit on the ground.

The loamy perfume of the vacant lot soothes me; it baptizes me anew into the family of wild, growing things. There is no absence here, rather a palpable presence, a thickening of the emptiness of space. I become atten-tive to each inspiration and expiration of breath. My best times are when I'm in the company of nature.

Ignoring the stiffness in my body, I climb the big oak tree that stands sentinel in the middle of the lot. Someone had nailed five wooden pieces of two-by-four blocks up its trunk as steps a long time ago, as evidenced by the rusty nails and weathered gray blocks. The violence done to the majes-tic tree offends me, but I use the steps to make my ascent to the wide cra-dle of the massive lower branches, using one hand to hoist myself up, carefully carrying the figs in the other. Perched securely in the arms of the old tree, I dare to look down. It always surprises me to see how high I can still climb. I sit and eat the sweet contraband, waiting for the dream to begin or end in the gradual graying of dusk.

I have a bird's eye view of the vegetables and flowers below in my back-yard garden, enclosed by the high wooden fence that Ted built. The rows look surprisingly neat and orderly, even though I'd ignored them most of the season. Keeping up the garden had gone from a pleasant hobby to a duty. I had imposed a strict code of conduct on the plants, just as I had on myself in an attempt to please. It was what Ted had wanted, a neat, orderly life and a predictable wife. No weeds allowed. No uncontrollable growth. Now I no longer pretend to hide my mistrust of protocol.

The brilliant reds and oranges of the dahlias are fading in the twilight. I wish I could adorn myself with bright colors like the flowers. Last Christmas, Ted bought me a red cocktail dress. He insisted I wear it to the hospital's Christmas party. Feeling endangered and too visible, I spent most of the evening in the ladies' room.

Owl: *As a child you camouflaged yourself in clothes that matched the river (you belong to the river)—muddy brown after the floods, soft grays and golden beiges that mimicked the marsh wrens hidden in the tall grasses down by the shore. Sometimes you donned greens that matched the colors of moss on rocks or the silver green of willow trees that graced the river banks.*

The vacant lot reminds me of Rose. She had been untamable, a wild weed, defiant of any authority, not budging an inch to conformity. What happened to her in those years that we were separated? Why had she ended up flotsam in the Mississippi River? Had I ever been as wild as Rose? I couldn't remember.

The unclaimed property is a long, narrow plot, sloping down to a shallow stream. Yesterday it rained, and water still stood in the gash of earth. The parched weeds, moistened by the recent rain and then dried again by the sun, smell like freshly baked bread. An unexpected breeze in the stillness brings a toy boat, red hull with white sail, floating by on the water like a dream riding the surface of consciousness. A child has been here, but what child? No children live in the immediate vicinity. As far as I know, I'm the only one in the neighborhood who ever comes over here. A stranger must have come and played while I wasn't watching. I feel protective of my territory. Then I remember. The boat is mine. I had bought it two years ago while on vacation in Paris with Ted. We had been in the Luxembourg Gardens. A small boy was sailing his boat in the fountain. His single-minded focus intrigued me. I had to have a boat just like his. I found one in a little shop on Rue de Vaugirard and hauled it all around Europe. The toy vessel stayed dry-docked in my desk drawer, forgotten until this summer. I'd sneaked it over to the privacy of the lot in June and hid it in the reeds by the hollow in the earth. Whenever it rained I launched it in the water, watching it float in the breeze until it embanked itself in the mud.

From the tree I take aim with a fig at a blue jay dive-bombing a robin's nest.

This place contains an indispensable mystery that presses against some inner wounding. Holding my breath as long as possible, the pressure against my lungs sounds the invisible depths of my longing to recapture an innocence and spontaneity of a childhood that I hunger to remember. Why have I forgotten most of my early years? I seem to remember little before high school. When I'd asked Ted if it were normal for adults to forget their childhood, he'd replied that most people have clear memories of the past, running consecutively like a movie. That surprised me.

A perfume from a different time, another world, blows in on a graceful wind. Ah, the tall angelica plants that border the south edge of the lot. A complexity of smells: violets, wild carrots, and licorice mix with other elusive, sweet odors: fragrant hints of a past I can't hold on to long enough to name. My mind grabs miniature boxes covered with dainty floral fabric, secret boxes stored under lock and key.

Brocade boxes.

Owl: *Granny kept them in her cedar chest in the attic, where her china dolls lived, the dolls with real hair and satin dresses. Granny collected them from exotic ports on her journey around the world when she was young. She wrapped them in silk and put them away in her cedar chest with aromatic herbs in boxes to keep the moths away. She said they would one day belong to you. You found the key in the bottom drawer of her chifforobe. You would wait until the grown-ups gathered themselves around the radio, listening to President Roosevelt report about the expanding war in Europe, then you would crawl on hands and knees (your legs not long enough to span the wide steps to the attic) and release the dolls from their dark, sweet-smelling prison. The dust would make you sneeze, and you would freeze in anticipation of being discovered. You loved to serve them make-believe ginger tea—Granny's favorite— comb their hair, and take off their dainty shoes of real leather and put them on again.*

The breath catches in my throat. I try to retain a vaguely formed image of fading, delicate boxes.

I continue surveillance from my lofty position and wish I'd brought more figs. The concord grapevines that run the length of the north border are heavy with purple clusters of fruit. I think of picking some to take home but know I won't. The vacant lot and its bounty are my secret. If Louise discovered this place was special, she would have the grass mowed and a ramp built so it would be wheelchair accessible.

An owl hoots nearby in the darkness.

A dog barks down the alley, a lonely sound. The fireflies are out. The pressure of the rough bark against my legs and the stinging of mosquitoes bring me begrudgingly back to the present. I climb down the tree trunk, reluctant to go home.

A flash of light fills the sky. Is it dry lightning? There is no evidence of a thunderstorm. Was it a shooting star? Or was it an old memory striking fire from my interior?

Owl: *Granny said that we're all stars. She said the people in St. Louis who were looking up at the sky that night you were born watched as you reentered the earth's atmosphere. She said you lit up the sky, shooting and trailing stardust as you fell. Those who were fortunate enough to be looking up took hope, like everybody does when they see a star or the face of a newborn baby. They are one and the same, Granny said—reminders of who we truly are. One day when our time comes, we'll remember, in the blink of an eye, and we'll turn to light again. That's what Granny said.*

The light flashes again. I see by its steady, sweeping beam that it is a beacon, summoning people to the big top. I remember that the circus is in town. Maybe I'll go all by myself and eat cotton candy.

The wing of a large bird brushes me lightly across the cheek in the dark as I turn to leave, sending little shivers of energy throughout my body. I welcome the gentle, feathery touch.

I cross the alley and step through the garden gate. Locking it securely against the night, I enter my well-constructed house and find my way in the dark to the study. The sweet smell of jasmine fills the room. The blossoms have trusted the night and opened.

Rubbing my cheek where the wild bird touched me, I sit at the desk in the dark and cry.

CHAPTER 4

▼

—Tiny, Kentucky Lake, 1967—

Inside the cramped, one-room shack sat four men around a rickety old card table. One leg of the table was shorter than the other three and had been shored up by an old 1960 telephone directory of Paducah. A bare light bulb hung from the ceiling directly over the table, its hundred watts pushing the heat level to unbearable in the already hellish room.

Two of the men, deputy sheriff George, a wiry little Apache, and Slim, a local fisherman little more than a kid, had stripped down to their boxer shorts. Tiny Moon had unbuttoned his short-sleeved, sheer, white cotton shirt, taken off his leather belt, and loosened the waistband of his blue and white seersucker pants that had been tailor-made to accommodate his girth. The fourth man, Dover, the sheriff of Caggway County, was dressed in a blue polyester leisure suit. Sweat had leaked through his shiny, hot pink shirt and marked the underarms of his pale blue suit jacket with dark blue half-moons. The first two men had sacrificed their shoes to the heat god, but not Tiny or the sheriff. Throughout the night, Tiny had caught the lawman throwing fervent, dart-like glances at his feet. He had instinctively mistrusted Dover from the first handshake and decided he'd better be ready for a hasty escape if need be. Better keep his shoes on. Dover wore well-oiled, ostrich skin Tony Lama boots. They smelled brand-new, but Tiny could tell by the cracks in the leather and the scuffed heels that they'd been around the block a time or two.

The room smelled of unwashed bodies, sour mash, stale cigars, and the remains of the night's dinner of catfish and hushpuppies. The small, oscillating electric fan was on duty but provided little relief from the heat. The whirling blades sounded like a swarm of hummingbirds. It had a mesmerizing effect on the exhausted men, making it even more difficult for them to stay awake. A cloud of smoke hovered above the table, despite the fan's effort to disperse it, as the four men smoked their stogies down to the stubs and laid the stinking, moist turds to rest on the edge of the table, leaving burn marks on the frayed edges. The fine Cubans that Tiny offered as a show of good sportsmanship at the beginning of the game had disappeared hours ago.

Tiny wanted out. He always wanted out when the good cigars were gone. The sweltering heat was torture on his six-foot four-inch frame, stressed already with four hundred and twenty-five pounds of muscle and fat. His bottom was numb from the two hard folding chairs he'd pushed together to cushion his ass.

"I'll raise you two," Tiny said as he bit down on the bitter little stogie. The fat man colonized the cramped space in the room, claiming everything in sight and compressing the muggy air.

"Well, Mr. Tiny, I'll up ya two and call ya," Dover responded to the challenge. The sheriff stood to his height of almost six feet and hesitantly shed his jacket, revealing a gun holster with a forty-five automatic pistol tucked inside. The gun hadn't surprised Tiny. That Dover was so tall had. At first impression he'd thought the sheriff to be a much shorter man, until he stood up. Dover was boxy and carried most of his length from the waist up. He had short arms and legs, and a tic in his neck that caused his head to rhythmically retreat inside his shirt collar.

He looks like a goddamned turtle ducking into his shell, thought Tiny.

Dover sat down and rubbed the stubble on his chin in deliberation. The tic in his neck became more insistent as the stakes were raised. The chin-rubbing gesture looked rehearsed to Tiny. *This guy's too good. The asshole's settin' me up. Dover staged this hideaway rendezvous on the lake to cheat me at my own game.* Tiny knew Kentucky Lake like the back of his hand. Back in the days when he still lived with his wife and daughters, under the guise of family vacations he initiated famous poker parties here for no small stakes, across the lake from this place. *Don't know who he thinks he's foolin', and I knew he was packin' a gun all along. I'll bide my time, wait for a chance to get outta here.* He knew his exit plan must involve strategy rather than swiftness.

It was Tiny's deal. *If I can't stun him now with the deal, I'll know the bastard's cheatin'.* Tiny shuffled the cards with his expressive, lightening-quick hands. They were well-manicured, smooth, big, but not fat. His fingers were long and shapely. He wore no rings to distract him when he dealt. His hands fluttered around the cards like two pink lungs gasping for air in the stinking hot room.

Oh the hell with him. I'll deal him the advantage and use my survival kit to get out of here.

George and the fisherman had folded their cards a little before midnight, cutting their losses. Tiny got the impression they were just waiting for a chance to get out of there without offending Dover.

"You want any cards?" Tiny asked. He knew Dover didn't. He'd dealt the sheriff a royal flush.

"No, I think I'm real good here." The sheriff smiled. He called and laid his cards on the table.

"Well, Dover, looks like you win." Tiny said, in a low, steady voice as he threw down his hand and watched the eager sheriff rake in the winnings on the table. The jerk in Dover's neck caused sweat to fly across the table and into the big man's face.

"George, pour the Tiny Man another drink," Dover insisted. "You'll never find better moonshine this side' the Mississippi."

The laxity with which Dover used Tiny's name made the gambler cringe. It set a tone of mockery and disrespect. *Where do you get off calling me Tiny Man? I never laid eyes on you until yesterday—wished I never did.* He'd had plenty of dealings with hotshots like Dover. There was always one around every corner trying to knock the big man off his throne. A player in Murray had arranged this gig for Tiny. He'd said the sheriff liked to throw around a lot of money and wasn't all that good of a player.

"I gotta go check my lines." The fisherman got up, stretched, and put on his clothes and shoes to leave.

"I'll go with ya. Maybe it'll be a little cooler down by the water." The deputy, Dover's right-hand man, ignored the sheriff's request to fill Tiny's glass with moonshine. He looked thankful for the excuse to escape.

"Hey, Tiny Man, what kind of shoes ya wearin'? I ain't never seen any quite like them. Sandals, ain't they? What kind of dude wears sandals?"

"A dude who wants to stay cool and comfortable. A friend of mine brought these back from Germany for me. They're called Birkenstocks. Can't buy em' here. Somebody ought to sell them, though. They'd make a fortune. Why you so interested in my shoes? I seen you lookin' at my feet all night."

Dover's face reddened. "Oh, I just happen to appreciate a well-made pair of shoes. Got a collection goin'. I keep a stash with me in the truck at all times. I like to change my footwear often. Let's take a break. I gotta take a leak." Dover rose stiffly and headed for the only exit.

Tiny quickly took the survival kit out of his pocket, a red flannel mojo bag prepared for him by a voodoo queen down in New Orleans. It contained a root that looked like a dried up, miniature person named High John the Conqueror (supposed to bring luck to gamblers), a pair of loaded dice (Tiny's own contribution), and a knockout powder the voodooienne had prepared for just such occasions as this. He slipped the little brown envelope out of the bag and poured its contents into Dover's half-full glass of moonshine and Coca Cola. The white powder dissolved instantly. Tiny estimated that the other two men would be gone about thirty minutes.

"Let's play another hand, Mister Tiny Man." The sheriff sat down, shuffled the deck, and reached for the glass of warm brown liquid. He downed it in one spastic gulp. Within five minutes he had passed out cold. Tiny caught him and placed him on the floor, turning his head to the side so he wouldn't choke when the vomiting started.

Tiny heard a scuffling sound from the ceiling directly above him. Looking up he spotted a hole in a beam, so small that it would go unnoticed unless one were looking for it. He took out his pocketknife and ripped up the worn linoleum around the chair where the sheriff had been seated. There it was. A metal pad with electrical wires ran under the flooring, around the base of the wall and up the side of the wall in the kitchen area, hidden by a crack where the wooden planks joined. The old shock-to-the foot trick. A lookout sits directly overhead with an overall view of the players at the table. A code is established and an electric current is sent down through the metal pad into the foot of the cheater, signaling him what cards the other players are holding. *Tryin' to beat me at my own game was he.* In the kitchen area, little more than a sink, Tiny looked up and saw a rectangular wooden door with a metal ring on it. He gave it several whacks with a nearby broom handle.

"You sonofabitch. You better come down now, or I'll shoot you down," Tiny bluffed. He never carried a gun, thought they were bad luck. The wooden hatch was slid aside. A small young man the size of a jockey fell out. He was lobster red.

"Man, I thought I was gonna drop dead up there. You guys don't take many breaks, do ya?" The little man was perspiring copiously. He gasped for air. He looked so relieved to be out of the infernal crawl space that he didn't seem to mind being discovered, until he spotted the sheriff lying still on the floor. He turned from crimson to pale pink.

"Oh Tiny, I'm sorry man. I only did it for the money. I need the cash bad. Don't kill me!"

"You better get your ass movin', boy. Go on, get outta here before I run outta good will."

The man, grateful for the reprieve, pushed open the screened door and ran toward the dawning light, disappearing in the lush vegetation around the lake. Tiny grabbed the wadded bills from the sheriff's bulging pockets, the remaining money on the table, and followed the little man out the door.

Goddamned. Got a flat tire. That fuckin' sheriff must have not wanted me to go anywhere. Wonder what his plans were. Tiny quickly slashed the other three tires on the rented Lincoln he had driven to the lake. He had noticed upon arrival that the sheriff had left his keys in the ignition of his truck, a brand-new two-ton black Chevy, bearing the word SHERIFF in bold gold letters on the side, above the county insignia.

"It's payback time for cheatin' me and givin' me a flat tire, you turtle-necked sonofabitch," Tiny said out loud, shaking his fist. He retrieved a worn leather suitcase from the trunk of the Lincoln and his panama hat from the front seat. He creased the crest of the fine straw and put the hat on his head. It felt soft against his sweaty brow.

Tiny pulled his heavy body up into the driver's seat of the truck's roomy interior; his enormous bottom met the cushioned seat in perfect union. He sighed with relief to be out of the hard little chairs that had threatened collapse all night. The smell of shoe polish and oiled leather turned Tiny's attention to the jump seat. It was filled with shoes, with shoehorns inserted neatly, lined up in rows. *Each to his own.* He took a minute to caress the soft leather upholstery of the seat with his right hand, his dealing hand, and to open the suitcase and take out a brand-new box of Coronas Especiales that he had stashed there. He hadn't shared these with the players. He had saved the best for himself. La Corona: the queen of all cigars. His mouth watered in anticipation of the rich aroma and spicy flavor that tasted like the best coffee and chocolate in the world, with its unique pungency, all in one seven-inch long bundle. He lightly ran his fingers over the cedar box to stir up the odor and smell the fragrance. Grinning, he carefully took the wrapper off of the elegant Havana, removing the bright yellow, black, and white band that distinguished this brand as the Cadillac of premium cigars. He bit off the end and licked it, took the silver lighter out of his pocket, and lit up as he started the engine, pulling the exotic, illegal smoke into his lungs.

Tiny rested his elbow on the open window sill. There was a slight breeze in the air. Soft, hazy light appeared on the horizon. Fish in the lake were starting to feed, making ever-widening circles upon the water.

"Damn, I'm missin' some good fishin'," Tiny said to the world, as the loons across the lake announced the dawn.

CHAPTER 5

▼

Dover was down at ditch number nine, shivering in his birthday suit. He plunged into the deep, cold hole of water, a strip mine pond, sharing it with innumerable species of fish, brown leaches, frogs, other amphibious creatures, plus poisonous water moccasins. He was surfacing for air when he heard his dead brother, Epsen, speak to him through a thick, snotty fog.

"Hey, you little shithead. Let's see how far you can pee with your itty-bitty prick," the muffled, laughing voice said.

Epsen had been two years older than Dover. He'd stepped on a land mine somewhere in Korea at the green age of seventeen. The crushing news was delivered by a representative of the United States Marine Corps on Flag Day. Dover had traveled by train to Dover, Delaware, by himself, a youth of fifteen, to retrieve the remains of the only person he had truly loved, the only person who had ever cared for him. The black body bag that cradled the pieces of his beloved brother was dispensed with no show of emotion by the overworked sergeant on duty in the refrigerated warehouse that day the American flag flew all across the nation. The government hadn't planned for such an overwhelming volume of soldiers coming back in body bags. Dover sat on a cushioned seat in coach while Epsen made the final ride home to Arkansas in a boxcar, the wheels clacking his name over and over against the track. On advice from the preacher back home, the casket remained sealed. The only member of the family to attend the memorial service was Dover. His mother and father were back at the shack they called home, drunk, and his older brothers had scattered as fast as they could when they were old enough to take care of themselves.

Epsen and his two buddies, Clem and Runker, were standing on the shore buck-naked with their penises in hand, standing ready for the contest that would win one of them extra stolen peaches from Mr. Grundy's tree.

"Wait for me. I want in." Dover slipped up the muddy, rocky bank and took his place in line with the other three boys.

"The one who pees the farthest wins," said Epsen. "On the count of three. One, two, three."

Dover's penis was a cornucopia of plenty, spewing forth rich, straw-colored fluid. His stream was magnificent and had the pressure of a fire hose, spanning the far bank of the pond like a bridge of gold.

"I win. I win." Crowds carrying banners with his name on them were cheering, exalting him for his great feat as he circled the stadium with the Olympic torch.

"Boss. Hey, boss, wake up." Deputy George was standing over him with a NuGrape soda in one hand. The other hand was holding a handkerchief over his nose.

Where the hell was he? Smelled like a garbage dump, and flies were buzzing him. He could hardly move, and his head felt like it was stuck in a bucket of putrid pond scum. He was soaked from head to foot with sweat and crusted vomit. He had peed himself and shit his pants.

"Man, what the hell. His head throbbed so bad it was hard to form a thought, and his body felt like it had been beaten to a pulp. He attempted to sit, but his aching head wouldn't allow it.

George was standing by the screened door. "The way I see it, the fat man slipped you something in your drink last night. Knocked you out cold. Cleaned out all the cash and stole your truck. I walked up to the road and hitched a ride back to town and got my truck to haul you home whenever you're ready."

The room became a centrifuge of blazing light and pain, pinning him to the floor and clamping his jaws tight, preventing him from moving or speaking. His last thought before slipping into merciful unconsciousness was how sweet it was going to feel when he stole the big fucker's sandals with the long foreign name. He'd polish them—get rid of all the scuff marks so they'd look brand new. He'd walk in the Tiny Man's shoes. He'd make them fit even if he had to tie them to his feet.

CHAPTER 6

▼

—Ellie, St.Louis, 1967—

The sun is setting, and Louise hasn't come to harass me all day. Jeremy called this morning to say that I was off the hook for twenty-four hours. He plans to take her to the dentist, lunch, shopping, and to the Tivoli this evening to see a rerun of her favorite movie, <u>Now Voyager,</u> with Bette Davis.

The smooth garden hose in my hands feels reassuring. Maybe I have little control over the rest of my life, but I'm in charge come watering time. I turn the hose on my face and body and squeal with delight as the cold water shocks me to wakefulness. I'd dozed off in the hammock under the sycamore tree in the backyard and overslept. It's almost dinnertime. My intention had been to take a catnap and then go into the study and work on the protagonist, who isn't measuring up on the page. I can't seem to hold a clear picture of her in my mind. She has soft edges and spills over into the other characters, as if she were borrowing from their lives in order to define her own.

I walk over to the back fence, open the gate, and glance across the alley toward the vacant lot. The thought is tempting. Instead, I turn to water the neglected garden—what's left of it.

The final crop of green beans had matured and dried on the vine. I have no excuse for not picking them, other than lethargy. I aim the hose at the headless ceramic flamingos the honeymooners brought back from Mexico. They stand sentinel, facing each other, at the entrance to the garden. Their necks had broken shortly after being placed on guard duty. Now after three years, their bright pink bodies and lime green garlands have paled to eggshell. Their leaning in toward each other has become a futile *tête-à-tête*, the gesture an apt symbol of a breakdown of communication and a failed marriage.

I drag the hose over to water the wilted tomato plants. There are enough ripe ones left for a batch of sauce. The basil nearby calls with gustatory fragrance, pleading to blend its spicy leaves with the tomatoes in a simmering pot.

Fresh from sleep, my mind detaches itself, as it is wont to do, and slides down the shoot of water from the hose to lose itself among the pleasing contours of the nasturtiums.

*   *   *   *

Tiny rang the front doorbell. No answer. Ellie's 1960 green Nash Rambler was parked on the street out in front. He'd kept track of her all these years, followed the major events of her life from a distance. The last time he'd seen her was three years ago on her wedding day. He'd parked on a side street by St. Roch's Cathedral with a view of the entrance, and watched her in her white satin gown with its long train descend the steps on the arm of her husband, the good doctor. She looked beautiful. Tiny had been happy for her, relieved she hadn't ended up like Rose.

He didn't know why he'd come to see her now. Why now did he feel brave enough to risk a face-to-face encounter with his daughter? He'd driven all day yesterday from Kentucky Lake in the stolen sheriff's truck and spent the night in a motel in East St. Louis. The day had been pleasantly spent playing poker in the White Horse Tavern on Euclid—an old hangout of Tiny's when he'd called St. Louis home.

He walked the path to the backyard gate with unsure steps. Maybe she was back there, in the garden. How would she respond to his sudden visit, out of the blue, after all these years?

He found his daughter flanked on one side by a row of nasturtiums and by dying tomato plants on the other, standing motionless in a pool of water, unmindful of the gushing stream from the hose she held limply in her hand. She was taller and thinner than he remembered, graceful and lovely. Her long, honey-colored hair was pulled back in a ponytail, matching her suntanned arms and legs. The brown shorts and T-shirt were the same hue as her skin and hair, covering but not hiding her stately elegance. She looked sad, like a lost child.

CHAPTER 7

▼

My father and I watch the crescent moon compete for attention with the yellow globe of the streetlight on the corner. We sit on the front porch together, me on the top step, sideways, with my back propped against the brick pillars, and Tiny in a deck chair facing me. Families stroll by and wave in passing. Others, like us, sit on their porches in an attempt to escape houses that still hold captive the heat of the day. We listen to the chorus of frogs and street sounds, as we dredge the Chianti bottle for its last drops of wine. We'd downed almost the whole bottle with dinner, saving the last to sip on the porch. There had been awkward pauses in the conversation all evening, but the wine and good food helped ease the tension between estranged relatives who have not spoken to each other in twenty years.

"Thanks for cooking dinner. It was a culinary coup," I said. Tiny's spaghetti sauce was legendary. It had been one of the house specialties in the nightclub/restaurant he had owned when the family lived in Cairo. He always made the secret sauce himself, so no one could steal the recipe.

"Are you going to the grave with the recipe? You could at least hand down the secret to your next of kin. I promise I won't tell a soul." Three sentences in a row...the most consecutive ones we'd spoken all evening.

Tiny looks around and pretends to check for someone who might be eavesdropping in the bushes. He puts his hand to the side of his mouth, palm spread out fanlike, as if to conceal his words to all but me and says,

"It's easier than you think. Lots of garlic, dash of vinegar, a few pork chops added to the ground sirloin, and a shot of scotch thrown into the pot while nobody's lookin'."

His voice is deep and resonant—a voice calling me to follow in recurrent nightmares down dark endless hallways, to search for him in countless empty rooms where he had just been. His voice is a blazing meteorite across the night sky of my dreams, tracing my name. Upon waking, the voice becomes an echo, and then an unspoken grief that I can never quite embrace. And now here he is: his presence ordinary, face-to-face, his voice understated in the real world. His voice now brings to mind fairytales by Hans Christian Andersen that he used to read to Rose and me at bedtime. And something less benign, but what? A promise of safety that had somehow been betrayed? I'm confused. It could be the wine. I long to believe my father is trustworthy.

This afternoon when he had wakened me from the trance, out in the garden, I thought at first that I was still in the hammock dreaming. I've tried in the past to hold a picture of him, but his face would constantly change. I'd imagined him as big as the giant in Jack and the Beanstalk, and still growing.

The shock of thick, black hair has turned silver since last I saw him at Rose's funeral ten years ago. I had spotted him peeking through the branches of a magnolia tree at the cemetery, trying to remain unnoticed behind the large pink and white blossoms. The flowers may as well have been trumpets announcing his grand entrance; his vast form could not be confined behind the graceful trees. I was sure that Louise had seen him as well, but neither of us has ever mentioned it. Just as we have yet to talk about Rose's death.

Why has he come to see me now? What does he want from me? I finish off the last drop of wine by holding the bottle straight up to my lips, head tipped back, face to the sky.

Tiny performs a trademark cigar ritual that is pulled from my memory from times past. It reminds me of a dog marking his territory. The way he peels the wrapper from the Havana, sniffs it, bites the end off, and licks the end before lighting up—his front teeth brown with tobacco stains from chewing the stubs. I breathe in the rich smoke, hugging my knees in my characteristic protective gesture. The smoke both disturbs and soothes me.

"How 'bout you? You like to cook?" Tiny asks.

"No. I'm afraid I take after Ma that way. I prefer to grow the vegetables and let someone else do the cooking." I wish I hadn't mentioned Ma. Her sudden intrusion in my thoughts (she had been surprisingly absent from my mind all evening) shrivels my warm expansive mood.

"How is Louise, anyway?" Tiny asks softly.

"She's difficult, that's what she is. Let's not talk about Ma tonight. I don't want to spoil a good evening."

"I was sorry to hear about the accident," Tiny says, remorse in his voice.

I suddenly long for the distance and majesty of Oregon.

I'd run away to the Pacific Ocean five years ago to get away from Louise and to shake the addiction to dextroamphetamine. After college I'd saved money from various jobs, mostly as a grocery clerk, and driven to Oregon where I rented a cottage at Cannon Beach. A good place, I thought, to fall apart by the ocean. I lay in bed—a zombie—for three months, listening to the waves roll in and out against the sand, grateful for the ebb and flow of tides. Without the pills my brain sent no messages to my body to move. When I awoke from a near catatonic state, I haunted the beaches like a phantom in search of a host body to inhabit, in search of something to replace the addiction. I sat in the sand and fed my tears to the ocean.

The ocean saved my life. The energy of big waves had been required to wash me clean. I missed my river, but it had no interest in helping me; it just rolled on its selfish way. The river would have buried me in muck had I stayed, just like it had Rose. Rose had never overcome the dependency, had piled one addiction on top of another. The memory of her helped me stay the course during those months of recovery. I had done it for Rose as much as for myself. It had been my plan to stay in Oregon, forsake my fickle river, live next to the ocean, get a job, and spend the rest of the time writing. I had to come back when the accident happened. The phone call came from Louise's neighbor, Mrs. Setmeir, in the middle of the night.

"I'm so sorry to tell you this dear, it's your mother...the roads were slippery with ice...she never saw him coming...a semi truck ran her straight over the cliff out near Kings Highway," the woman had sobbed. I took the first plane out. At first the doctors weren't sure if Louise would pull through, and when she did they said she was lucky. Only the lower spine had been injured.

Ted was the surgeon who operated on her. She was left paraplegic and needed me. Ted had been a rock to both Louise and me in those difficult days. We started dating and were married a year later. That'd been four and a half years ago.

The fireflies, tiny commas of blinking phosphorescence, are curious about the guest on the porch and seem attracted to the straw of the finely woven hat that lay next to his chair. They circle his circumference as if touring the world.

The night is late, and the traffic on the street has slowed to an occasional bus rumbling by, interior lights illuminating a few lone passengers, reminding me of an Edward Hopper painting. Not many cars drive by. The night strollers have all gone home. Porch sitters are inside houses that have cooled off to a tolerable temperature. An occasional hint of a breeze favors us lingerers. A young man walks briskly by, as the late hour prescribes haste, whistling a tune I recognize but can't name. Tiny takes a harmonica out of his pocket and plays the melody.

"Goodnight Irene," I say.

Tiny's big, graceful hands become animated and take on a life of their own as they assist the flow of the refrain. I watch his hands dance to the music, a front porch fantasia. They are like two Pied Pipers, inviting all to follow him into his world, if only for an evening.

"Must feel good to own your own home, huh? I wonder 'bout that sometimes…what that would be like," Tiny says. He hits the harmonica against his hand to clean out the spittle and puts it in his pocket.

"You and Ma never bought a house, did you?" I ask, although I know the answer.

"Na. Could never make the leap. The thought of it made me feel all boxed in." He shakes his head and pauses. "But sometimes I wonder if we should have." In an instant his eyes glaze over, and he seems to have retreated somewhere deep inside himself.

I remember the story that Granny told me about Tiny's childhood. His was a nomadic heritage, the wandering gypsies of Northern Europe. His father, Ivan Moonsric, came to the United States from Romania at the turn of the century with his young wife and four children in hopes of finding his fortune in a proverbial land where streets were paved with gold. Ivan shortened the family name to Moon upon arrival in St. Louis. After a disappointing period of backbreaking jobs, disillusioned and weary, he wandered off one spring day into a clear, blue sky, never to be seen again by family or friends. This left Tiny (Johnny then), at the age of six, to be the major breadwinner of the family.

Childhood ended abruptly for Johnny when his father departed. He was set to work plucking chickens at the Chicken Dinner restaurant in St. Louis for two dollars a week, with three chickens weekly for the family and all the chicken he could eat while at work. He pulled out feathers back in the kitchen for fifteen hours a day, six days a week. At the end of those long days, he was too tired to walk the three miles to the streetcar line and then another long mile home. At night he slept on a hard canvas army cot in the storeroom.

Later, when I was older, Louise had finished telling me the story of Tiny's childhood. How, whenever it pleased him, the restaurant owner came to the storeroom late at night, when everyone else was gone, and raped the helpless child, leaving an indelible sadness in Johnny's big green eyes. He would cry himself to sleep, Louise had said, alone and afraid every night. On Sunday mornings he would wake before dawn and make the trek home carrying the dead weight of three large chickens wrapped in butcher paper tucked in a burlap flour bag to give to his mother. He was too tired and troubled to play with his two younger brothers. His older brother had already left home and disappeared somewhere in this vast new land of opportunity, just as his father had done. Little Johnny would fall into a deep sleep, secure that no one would molest him for a few hours, before making the long trip back to the feathery prison and more abuse.

After two years, he was promoted to dishwasher and given a nickel a day raise in salary. He stood on a wooden crate to reach the sink. This was his first step up in the world. For five years he washed dishes and polished glasses until they sparkled.

Louise had told me that Johnny walked away one day when he was thirteen and never looked back. He trusted no one, always tried to stay on the move, avoided attachments, and never again in his life ate any creature that sported feathers and flew. Along the way he met a gambling man named Harry who could shuffle a deck of cards in too many ways to count—and do it so swiftly that you would swear his hands had barely moved at all.

Little Johnny Moon was a quick study. This was his ticket out of hell. In a few years, his big, graceful hands with long, supple fingers were so fast that those who watched him shuffle and deal swore they could see tiny sparks of light as he doled out the cards on the table. His admirers said it was worth losing just to watch him in action. His sleight of hand and grasp of the game became legendary in gambling circles. He was the undisputed king in back alleys, taverns, and private gambling parties spanning the length of the meandering Mississippi River from St. Louis down to New Orleans.

In those days he was known as Johnny Lightning, a tall, scrawny kid with a shock of long black hair. Louise said that he got tired of being called skinny and took a Charles Atlas body-building class via the mail. At nineteen his body bulked with muscle. No one dared to bully him around or force him to do anything he didn't want to do.

My father met my mother when he was twenty and she was eighteen. She was a fan dancer in a nightclub in St. Louis. Granny had told me how beautiful she was—that when she strolled by the banks of the Mississippi, the "Old Man" rose in his channel a foot or two, slowing down his flow to linger in the presence of her company before rolling down to the Gulf of Mexico. Johnny Lightning was enchanted. He broke all of his own rules as a rambling man, with dreams of settling down forever with his beauty queen by his side. They were married within a month from the day they met. One year later, Rose was born.

"Then you came sixteen months later," Granny said. "Tiny felt trapped. He'd betrayed the only safe way he knew of being in this world: alone with no attachments." The enchantment with Louise evaporated like ether on a hot day. She became critical of his poker playing. And as the grown woman turned her back on girlhood, fun, and laughter, she begrudged Tiny his playful, happy-go-lucky attitude toward life. She became jealous. Fatherhood was a heavy yoke around your father's neck," Granny said. "For the most part he was shy and uncomfortable around women. He'd been raised only with brothers and didn't understand the more complicated emotions of a woman. He'd mistrusted his mother, who had sold him into slavery to the Chicken Dinner restaurant. Steadily gaining weight after Rose and you were born, he weighed in at four hundred and twenty pounds by the time you were three, earning him the celebrity title of Tiny."

Why has he come back after all these years? Was it just a whim, an impulse? It feels natural, somehow, to be sitting on the porch with him, as if twenty years have not passed by. I'm glad he's here. I want another glass of wine.

"Earth to Ellie. Where were you just then?" I had forgotten the exact contours of his features but have carried deep within me the image of his eyes, a summary of the extremity of sadness, even when he laughed. Now I remember why.

"I was in Siberia, back in my own private gulag. You don't want to know," I say. He sighs and shakes his hands, as if they were numb with old regrets.

"I was just thinkin' you could use a change of scenery. Why don't you pack a bag and come with me?" Tiny puffs his cigar back to life.

My voice takes a detour around a lump in my throat. It sounds high-pitched and childlike. "You want me to go with you? What would we do?" I'm caught off guard by the invitation.

"Come on. It'll be fun. You could use a break from this place. Sometimes fleeing the scene of the crime gives you new perspective. Sometimes it's the best thing you can do. It's always worked for me." He laughs, chewing the brown stub that has gone out again.

"Well, maybe it's the best thing to do when you've burned all your bridges and stolen a sheriff's truck." My attempt at humor sounds reproachful, like something Louise might say. The story of the cheating sheriff, and Tiny's hasty retaliation and retreat had seemed much funnier earlier, while the wine had still been flowing.

This man, my father, has lived flamboyant, incredible stories. I feel like a blank canvas eager to be brushed and splashed with paint.

"What about your job? Can you call your boss and get some time off?"

"Don't have a job. I got fired six months ago." I laugh, and we clink empty glasses in toast. This is the first time I've been able to make light of it. Tiny, of all people, would understand.

Ted had seemed relieved when I told him. He wanted me to stay home and have a hot meal on the table at dinnertime. That's what he said. "A hot meal on the table." Not so much for a busy husband to ask. Most married women I knew stayed home and played the role of housewife, but look at what had happened to Ted's mother. I just couldn't do it—couldn't even give it a Girl Scout's try.

The *Post-Dispatch* was the most widely read newspaper in St. Louis. Dempsey had stuck me on the society page, the purgatory where all women journalists were relegated—especially the good ones. They never got out, despite endless intercession of prayers. Dempsey kept me there with hollow promises of promotion to covering front-page news stories soon. I'd been there for three and a half years.

I did my best to cover debutante balls and tea parties of the famous families of the city while an unnamed war raged far away in the little-known country of Vietnam. I reported accurately on colored feather boas draped around the necks of the elite while Negroes in our own land of the free were being hunted down and hung from trees for fighting for civil rights. Mrs. Answeicher poured today at a tea party for her niece's engagement to Mr. Vanesse. Finger sandwiches with rosettes of radishes were served along with a fine *Beaujolais nouveau* while the land was being raped for profit, and pesticides were being dumped into the oceans.

Too political, Dempsey had shouted when he called me into his office to deliver the severance blow. A distinctive, fetid aroma of warm Limburger cheese, peculiar to his office, had forewarned me of the termination. The malodor had layered over the pervasion of newsprint and ink, smells that usually rattled my bones to alertness. I'd gone too far while covering the Veiled Prophets Ball. Monkey jackets with cozy matching muffs seemed to be fashion's rage this year. "In the forests of a faraway country, endangered animals are being slaughtered to the point of extinction for their fur, while the band played on at the Ball," I'd written.

"I'll go," I say to Tiny. The haste of the decision makes me dizzy. I think about the I-Ching hexagram, the Wanderer, and shiver. I want to get to know Tiny…travel through the territory of my youth with him. To get away from Louise's constant nagging would be worth the trip. There is no reason not to go. I ignore the throaty voice, familiar yet unknown to me, that trills a warning inside my head.

"Go pack your bag, and let's get out of here," Tiny seems suddenly anxious to move on, even though it's after midnight. "I'm glad you decided to come. It'll be good for you to get away from your mother for a while. Besides, a pretty gal like you should be out dancin' and kickin' up her heels."

I know the cliché is meant as a compliment to lighten the mood, but I cringe. I've never seen myself as pretty—not like Rose. She'd been dramatic and bold in her self-presentation, had insisted on wearing bright, primary colors even as a toddler. At twelve, she began exaggerating her lips with bright red lipstick and wore black eye shadow that enhanced her sparkling brown eyes. I was drab next to Rose. I wonder what happened to conquer her feisty spirit and lure her to the river in despair.

"Now? You really want to leave tonight? Don't you want to sleep and then go in the morning?" I start to second-guess my decision.

"There's no time like the present, Miss Ellie," Tiny smiles.

"You always did stir the pot when you were around," I laugh, ambivalent again about joining him.

"Oh yeah?" Tiny has given up on his cigar, mashing the stub to shreds on the wooden porch step and brushing the remains off into the grass.

"I don't remember much about being a child, but I do remember you were always getting Rose and me in trouble with Louise for doing fun things." I sit down again, my body electrified with memory. I want to unfurl and reach for the sky while the core of me contracts like a sea anemone that has been poked by a foreign object. Too much wine and the presence of my renegade father have incited my soul to revolt against the ordinary. Anarchy waves in the air around Tiny like a bright banner.

"Do you remember that time you took Rose and me on a picnic, and Ma got mad at you because you sneaked us out of Sunday catechism class to go with you."

"Your mother was always mad at me about something," he smiles sadly.

"I remember we both had on polished black patent leather shoes and white starched cotton dresses just alike. She always dressed Rose and me alike. Remember? We both hated it." The image is clear, unlike the scraps of fuzzy shorthand notes I usually get. "You took us up to Art Hill by the Art Museum in Forest Park, and we rolled down the hill over and over. I remember getting dizzy, and we got grass stains all over our dresses. And then we jumped in the pond to get the stains out." I am breathless with recall. "Remember?"

"Yeah, I remember. You and Rose decided that if we picked your mother a bouquet of wildflowers she wouldn't be so mad at us. And then I lost my nerve and sent you two in the house to take the heat all by yourselves," Tiny sighs.

"I remember. You went off to play cards with your cronies and didn't come back till the next morning. Rose and I got a spanking, and we were grounded forever." My chest hurt thinking of Rose and how close we'd been back then.

"We used to feed each other oranges and read Raggedy Ann stories in our room when we were grounded. I loved having Rose to myself, captive, but she hated it. She wanted to be out playing baseball with the neighbor boys."

"Yeah, that was Rose, all right." Tiny bows his head. "How'd you know I was off playing cards? You were just a little tick then."

"Because Louise would rant and rave all the time about you playin' cards with those devil friends of yours." Thinking about Ma wilted my enthusiasm to reminisce further.

"It'll be cooler travelin' tonight, and we'll be less conspicuous in the dark. Dover's probably got an APB out on his stolen truck. I figure he's just about recovered from the tonic I gave him. The sooner we can ditch the truck, the better off we'll be."

"Dad, why was Ma so mean to Rose and me all the time? And she was always screaming at you about something."

"I don't know, Ellie." He turns his face from me, but not before I see tears well up. His eyes seem to hold infinities of grief.

"I'm sorry I brought all this up," I say and go inside to call Mrs. Leapy to ask her to water and harvest what is left of the garden and to feed Kitty Karlitos. The big, black tomcat belongs to the whole neighborhood but spends most of his time sleeping in the shade of the sycamore tree under my hammock.

Mrs. Leapy's lights are still on when I pick up the phone to dial. She's a night owl and a busybody. She was probably at the window watching and wondering about the sheriff's truck.

"Are you all right, dear? I saw the sheriff's truck pull up out front."

"I'm fine. Just going on a little trip for a while." I'm sure that will set the woman to blabbing to the neighborhood.

"Will you be gone long dear? Have you told Louise you're leaving?" Her singsong voice brims with suspicion.

"I don't know how long I'll be away, maybe a week. Don't worry, everything's all right." I reassure the nosy woman, but the thought of rumors circulating around the neighborhood about being hauled away in a sheriff's truck amuses me. I hang up with Leapy in mid question.

Louise will be stopping by tomorrow. She has her own key. I scribble a note promising to call from the road. I leave out the part about traveling with Tiny. I go upstairs to pack a suitcase, and when I come down Tiny is standing by the door, hat on head, looking restless to get on the road.

"What about money? I guess I can always wire my bank from the road." I only have twenty dollars in cash.

"Don't worry about money. I've always got some—or know where to get it," Tiny laughs.

I'm on the way out the door with suitcase in hand, when something lures me back into the study. I pick up a tangle of dried snake skins from the desktop. I'd discovered it last spring under a pot of geraniums by the side of the house, an intricately patterned, translucent, entwined ball, a shedding of enormous importance that had been left as a casual gift. A change as extreme as shedding one's skin took either foolish abandon or great courage. The skins would be a reminder that all things are possible, a good omen for the journey.

I feel myself waffling again. The place for a metamorphosis of such magnitude should be a safe and warm one, like the pot of geraniums protected from winds by the wall of a sturdy house, warmed by the sun on the south side—not traveling an open road with someone you really don't know.

I take a deep breath, put the snake skins in my T-shirt pocket, turn on the porch light, and lock the door behind me. If things don't go well, I can always come home. I run down Ma's wheelchair ramp to the truck before I change my mind again. Tiny is waiting with motor running.

My legs are shaking as we pull away from the curb into a clear, star-encrusted night, riding high in a stolen truck with a sheriff probably hot on the trail. With the moon as a prompt, as if it were the natural thing to do, we start singing "Shine on, Harvest Moon," my soprano to Tiny's bass.

Owl: *You sat at Granny's old player piano for hours, the three of you. Rose on one side, and you on the other, with Tiny between you, your legs swinging back and forth...your feet could not yet reach the floor. You touched the ivories, pretending to play, as the keys depressed themselves, as if by magic. He taught you and Rose to sing harmony. "Snow time ain't no time to sit outside and spoon, so shine on, shine on harvest moon." Then, as an after thought, in his exaggerated bass, he sang, just as he does now, "For Me and My Gal."*

You laughed, exuberant in your innocence.

CHAPTER 8

▼

Ellie opened one eye. Nothing looked recognizable or nameable. For a second she thought she was on a different planet. Her head pounded as she pried the left side of her face away from the black leather that seemed to be vibrating.

Honk! Honk! Honk!

Startled to full attention by the horn blast, the world came back into focus. She looked over at the man behind the wheel. It was Tiny. They were in the truck Tiny had stolen two days ago from a sheriff named Dover. The motor was idling. She reached into her T-shirt pocket to feel the snake skins. The tangle was there as proof she wasn't dreaming.

"I'm freezing. Where are we?" She pulled Tiny's seersucker suit jacket around her shoulders. He must have covered her when she dozed off.

The cigar stub in the ashtray sent up a dying SOS, a thin stream of blue-gray smoke. The smell of stale cigar was disgusting. She reached over, crushed out the stub, and rolled down the fogged window to get some fresh air. The faded shell of the moon was a ragged piece of gauze in a sky that was turning quicksilver gray. Shivering, she rolled the window back up.

Honk! Honk! Honk!

"Where's Vigil? He's usually always here," Tiny said impatiently.

He turned on the heat. A blast of warm air filled the truck. Dogs barked—dry, vicious sounds—from behind a high brick wall with a wrought iron gate fashioned in the shape of a running wolf in profile. Painted in bold black letters on the wall was written: BEWARE OF DOGS.

"Where are we?" She stretched and yawned. The rubber band around her ponytail had slipped down and hair fell in her face.

"We're in your old stompin' grounds: Cairo," Tiny said. He rubbed his soft, smooth hands together. They looked cold. "Sure feels like summer is over, don't it?"

"Cairo? What're we doing here?" Then she remembered: the plan was to dump the getaway truck at Vigil's and pick up a different vehicle.

"You were sleepin' the sleep of the dead," Tiny said as he reached over to take out a new cigar from the glove compartment. In the festive mood of last night, she had enjoyed the pungent smoke. Now it turned her stomach. She shook her head in the negative, and he put the cigar back in the glove compartment.

She'd been blasted out of a dream by the horn. The dream had seemed important, maybe because she rarely remembered them. She fished in her purse on the floor for pen and paper to write it down. She felt like Goldilocks caught trespassing on forbidden property.

The dream slowly reformed itself as she quickly wrote down what she remembered.

Flecks of shimmering gold filtered through the branches of majestic trees and gilded the forest floor with dappled light. I was driving a magical car, a red Volkswagen, through an enchanted emerald forest. The car adjusted its size to maneuver between the big trees, getting smaller when necessary for passage. A very important person, a little girl, was sitting in the passenger seat. I couldn't make out who it was. At one point in the journey, fallen Douglas fir trees, giant guardians of the woods like the ones I'd seen in the Northwest, obstructed the path. I told the child that we could go no further. The little girl started to cry. Just then, I saw three grizzly bears; each was wedged between two of the felled trees. They were lying face down on the ground and appeared to be dead. Concerned that they had been wounded and needed help, I got out of the car and walked over to them. One of the bears turned, lifted his head, and roared. "You'd better not come any closer. Don't disturb us. We're hibernating. You'd best leave sleeping bears lie." Terrified, I ran back to the car. I could no longer drive. I handed the keys to the little girl and said, "You've got to get us out of this mess. I can't."

"What ya writin'?" Tiny peered over at the notebook in her lap. She instinctively covered the page with her hands.

As the day broke she could see they were parked in a gravel lot just off Highway 51. Last night's enthusiasm for the road trip with Tiny was gone. She wished she were in her warm, comfortable bed at home. The party was over, and here she was with a stranger. Ma would die if she knew.

Honk! Honk! Honk!

"What's keepin' him. Don't take that long to get out of bed," Tiny said impatiently as he spat out the window. He gave the horn another three quick honks, waited a beat, and gave two more long ones. This signaling gesture was not lost on Ellie.

She imagined her father's life to be full of secret handshakes, espionage, and shadowy disguises—blood oaths taken in abandoned warehouses on foggy waterfronts. His life and whereabouts for the last twenty years had been a mystery to her, leaving her mind free to invent all kinds of illicit plots and intrigues. She fancied he flew by night with bats or vampires.

She'd taken most of her cues about Tiny from Louise—polar opposites. Their minds diverged on every matter of importance. Louise saw Tiny's gambling as self-indulgent, childish, illegal, while Tiny viewed himself as an artist, above the fray of humdrum existence or a regular job. Ellie had formed a belief that he conned innocent people, left families penniless in the streets, begging for bread.

She reached over and turned off the heat. It was hot in the truck now that the sun had risen.

A rare memory broke through the barrier to consciousness. She had been four. They had lived in St. Louis with Granny. She woke up with silver dollars pelting her like rocks. Tiny was throwing money at Rose and her. Finally he dumped the whole bucket of silver coins on them. Rose squealed with delight at the sudden manna from heaven.

"Quick. Hide your money under your pillow. Here comes Ma. She'll take it away from us," Rose said.

"I won't let her take it away. I gave it to you as a present," Tiny said.

"You can't stop her once she gets started. You just get her goin' more," Rose said. She was six years old but understood the dynamics of the family's relationships.

"I don't want your filthy old money." Ellie started to cry and threw the coins on the floor.

"Shut up ya ol' crybaby; she'll hear ya. Here, give 'em to me. I'll hide 'em." Rose scooped the silver dollars back into the bucket and put it under her bed just as Louise stormed into the room.

"How dare you come in and wake up the girls. You with your whiskey breath and bloodshot eyes. Out gamblin' all night and who knows what else. Not even so much as a phone call."

She shooed Tiny out of the room and slammed the door, ending Rose's festive mood and making Ellie cry even harder. They were judged guilty by association and punished for Tiny's indiscretion, confined to their room for the day and given an enema that night.

"Here he comes," Tiny said.

A tall, rangy man who looked to be the same vintage as Tiny stood blinking in the glare of the truck lights. He opened the gate and motioned with a fanfare of the hand for Tiny to drive through. The man wore a red bandana around his long gray hair and had on bell-bottom denim pants and a tie-dyed T-shirt in a sunburst pattern in red, yellow, and blue. A hippy here in Cairo, Illinois. She'd seen pictures on television of this new breed of rebel, protesting America's involvement in Vietnam. They'd gathered at the Haight-Ashbury District in San Francisco this summer. Flower children with their Volkswagen vans airbrushed with elaborate psychedelic colors, flashing peace signs, smiling to the cameras, urging people to "drop out and tune in." She'd fancied joining them but didn't have the nerve.

The man threw a lit cigarette into the gravel and ground it with his boot. He commanded seven barking huskies in the yard to sit and stop barking. They obeyed instantly. Their coats of multiple shades of gray matched the color and luster of the silvery locks of their master. They possessed a wild, vital energy that matched their master's as well. She had the sensation that she'd conjured them all up—even Tiny. They might disappear in an instant—on a whim—like her dreams, into a world exclusive to her, where only they knew how to survive.

"Keep your shirt on Tiny. I thought you was the fuzz. What ya doin' in a sheriff's truck from Caggway County?" Vigil was looking at the official insignia on the side of the truck.

Behind the brick wall was a cemetery of dismembered parts of cars in various stages of decay strewn around the yard. A big, sprawling building made of cement blocks stood in the center of the disorder. The building stirred Ellie to full attention.

"Hi." The man poked his head through the window on the driver's side. His voice showed no sign of irritation or surprise at being wakened so early in the morning. A smile took charge of his bearded face.

"Vigil, you remember my daughter, Ellie? We're traveling together for a while. Thought I'd show her the ropes. Teach her how to hustle," Tiny chuckled.

"I do indeed. I remember you from when you was a little girl. How've you been? Don't get over Cairo way much, do you?" The man stroked his long, gray, cigarette-stained beard.

"No, I haven't been back since Ma and I moved to Paducah. Had no reason to come back, I guess. I do vaguely remember you and this place."

She remembered only disconnected pieces of the past. Thankful that she'd written it down, she'd already forgotten most of the morning's dream. The meaning was waiting to be awakened in a secret woods deep within her mind. Her dream images were toreadors waving red capes, teasing her with hints of meaning, inviting her to rip through the veil of the unknown, to learn some truth about her past held locked inside. She longed to adorn herself with meaningful memories. She would wear them fancifully like colorful clothes that would reflect a certain pizzazz and daring—a distinction of character, a uniqueness of personality that would mark her place in the world. She would wear red if she had substance.

"We ran into some problems an' need your help," Tiny said. He rolled the window down all the way and shook Vigil's hand. "I got into a jam with a sheriff—was forced to borrow his truck here. We need to get rid of it, find somethin' else to drive."

"You drivin' a hot truck?" Vigil laughed and shook his head. He didn't seem that surprised. Ellie suspected he was used to these kinds of negotiations with Tiny.

"Come on in. We'll take care of you." He exhaled tiny bright stars into the cold morning air and motioned them through a wide, sliding garage door.

She sucked in a deep breath. Vigil had turned on a neon sign that hung over the front door. A tilted cocktail glass with the words Tiny's Place in red and pink flashed off and on.

"The old place hasn't changed all that much," Tiny said.

"I had to replace the big oak door with this sliding one so I could get the cars inside to work on 'em," Vigil said.

"You bought this place from my mother after the governor made us close it down," she said.

"Yeah. Your ma sold it to me for a song after your father left." He looked at her and then at Tiny. There was an awkward silence.

"She was anxious to get rid of the place after the trouble started. Yeah," Vigil said rubbing his beard. "I converted it into a mechanic's garage— added that brick wall for security."

Several vehicles stood with their hoods up on the square-patterned, worn, green and black linoleum floor. The building had once been a warehouse. Tiny had remodeled it. There had been fifty tables and chairs surrounding a large dance floor of solid oak planks next to a bandstand.

Her heart beat faster as she remembered dancing with Louise on Saturday nights to live bands. She'd felt like a princess dancing on clouds, her mother's graceful touch leading her lightly around the floor. Louise had been the queen of ballroom dancing. She could make a piece of wood come alive and look graceful. One time, Tommy Dorsey played here. She and Rose were allowed to watch and listen from a back table. They each had the privilege of one dance a night with Louise. She thought of her mother and suddenly missed her, thinking how caged she must feel in her wheelchair.

"I'll show you around." Vigil motioned for her to follow him. An overhead heater blew hot air into the cavernous room, providing welcome relief from the cold morning air. She was still in her shorts from the night before, and her legs were cold.

A double-swinging door led to a spacious, well-equipped kitchen with a display of pots and pans, butcher knives, and cleavers that hung on a stainless steel island across from a massive stove with numerous gas burners and several grills. She remembered when the equipment had been shiny new. A white chef's hat still hung on a hook on the metal island, as if awaiting the return of its owner.

"Well, this is a blast from the past." Tiny shook his head. "I get the feeling that Harry Foo'll walk through the door any minute now, put on that hat, and start cookin'."

"I remember when you went up to Chicago and brought him down here. Nobody around this neck of the woods ever even heard of Chinese food," Vigil said. "He sure was a hot-tempered sonofabitch."

"Yeah, he got mad and fired his kitchen staff every night. I always had to hire 'em back the next day. He was famous in Chicago. I paid an arm an' a leg to get him here. Ellie, you remember Harry Foo, don't ya?" Tiny asked.

"Yes, I do," she said without hesitation—on a memory roll. "He was always following me around and trying to get me to eat those rotten eggs he used to bury in the ground out back. The smell made me gag."

A large walk-in freezer of solid oak was built into the back corner of the kitchen. Puffs of cold, frosty air escaped when Vigil opened the heavy door to demonstrate that it was still working.

"I store deer and ducks in there for the hunters when they come during duck hunting season in the fall. Yeah, Horseshoe Lake, you remember, just outside of town here—hunting Mecca. Makes me a little money on the side. I dress the birds, wrap 'em, and freeze 'em for the hunters to take home. What they leave behind, I make dog food out of. There's usually enough for my dogs, and the rest I sell to local folks," Vigil said.

"Oh no!" She felt her body flinch. "My birds." She remembered the heartbreak she'd felt when the hunters came to kill them. They would come into the restaurant, bragging about how many birds they'd shot.

She'd scream at them, "Killers! I hope somebody shoots you!" Tiny, finally, had banned her from the premises during hunting season.

Owl: *After Granny died and the family moved to Cairo, you counted snow geese every fall and spring for the Audubon Society. Sitting up on the levee with your binoculars, you would call with a loud, steady, landing honk and watch them glide in. Their great white wings slid like snowdrifts in the air, touching down in the bottomlands next to the river.*

"Yeah, ya used to get all upset about the birds bein' hunted. It's a real miracle when you think about it," Tiny said. "Twice a year some of these birds fly as far as three thousand miles or more, north to Alaska and the Yukon to lay eggs at the mouth of the Mackenzie River and even farther north. In the fall, like clockwork, they make a beeline straight down the Mississippi, smack dab through Cairo, and on down to the Gulf of Mexico and South America." Tiny made a sweeping motion in the air with his arms.

"We used to keep live lobster from Maine in this freezer. First place in southern Illinois to serve 'em," Tiny bragged. "Remember, Ellie? Rose used to sneak the lobster home and put 'em in your bed at night. You didn't have a very long memory. You used to fall for that one every time. You'd be so tired, you'd just jump right into bed, and look out! When one of those babies got hold of ya, ya screamed like a banshee." Tiny took a deep breath. "Rose was always doing somethin' like that to you—guess she took after her old man that way, a real practical joker." He shook his head slowly, a tired smile on his face.

She realized that she'd been stingy in her grief—cornered the market on heartaches. Tiny missed Rose, too. Of course he would. Rose had always been his favorite.

The clear memory of Rose and her together—the way they were then, when they had been inseparable—made her loss too great to remember more. She put the memories back into the hidden place and locked them away again. She stumbled out of the kitchen blinded by tears, tripping over her days of youth, huge bears that lay hibernating in the middle of the floor.

She washed her face and changed clothes in the ladies' room to the light that flashed DOLLS on and off in pink neon. Tiny and Vigil were in the storeroom—the room that had remained locked at all times. This had been the notorious back room where gamblers from all over the East Coast had come to wager bets in secret. She knew about the poker games. She'd watched Tiny and the other men go into the back room and not come out for days. Waitresses hoisting giant trays of food and whiskey, were required to give a password before the bolt would be slid back and they were allowed to enter. She had only seen the storeroom door open a few times, after the gamblers had gone home, and the janitor went in to clean up the mess they'd made. It had looked bigger, more mysterious back then. Now it just looked like an ordinary storeroom, much smaller than she'd remembered it. New car parts in boxes were stored on shelves. Old, greasy engine parts were piled in a corner. There was an unmade single bed against the back wall. The big round oak table where the infamous poker games were played for high stakes (sometimes as much as a million dollars it was rumored) was still in its same spot in the middle of the room, piled high with old magazines and newspapers. A lonely, bare light bulb hung down over the table.

Tiny sighed. "We had some good times back here." He walked over to the table and pushed the papers aside and ran his long fingers across the burn marks on the edge. "Me and the boys always laid our lit cigars here. Louise called us barbarians, but old habits are hard to break." Tiny shook his head. "Yeah, those were the good ol' days. Havanas were legal then. You could buy 'em at any newsstand." Tiny took out his handkerchief and blew his nose. He looked tired and old. "You know, gamblin' has always been a big part of things around here. I don't know why they had to go an' make it a crime. Back in the days when Mark Twain rode the steamboats up and down the river, gamblin' was wide open. It still oughta be that way." Tiny made an attempt to laugh. "It's funny. Louise didn't pick on me so much when I had this place. What I did here seemed okay with her, even if I was breakin' the law." He looked down at the floor and chewed on his cigar.

In all those absent twenty years, Ellie had never thought about how Tiny must have felt that day he walked away from this place and his family. She'd always thought that he didn't care. Being here in the old nightclub now felt like a scene from an old movie that had been interrupted. She never knew how it ended. She was watching the ending now.

"There're the bullet holes, up there." He pointed to the evidence, up high in the back wall. "Some goddamn overzealous national guardsman decided to get dramatic."

"What did happen here, Dad? All Ma ever told us was there'd been a ruckus, and you closed the club. Then the next day when we got home from school, you were gone. And I never laid eyes on you again until Rose's funeral. What the hell happened?" They were both crying.

"Well, the governor of Illinois sent the Guard down from Springfield. We were in the middle of a poker game. They busted down the door and started pointin' their guns at us and tearin' up the place. They was smashin' glasses behind the bar and breakin' bottles of whiskey. They slashed the felt on my pool table that I imported from Italy—trashed everything but the kitchen." Tiny made a sweeping gesture with his arms. "The bastards made their point. Why'd they have to go and shoot up my Woody wagon? That car was my pride and joy. They just went out and riddled it, and that was the final straw for me. Somehow it jus' broke my heart. I jus' couldn't stick around here anymore." Tiny chewed his cigar, despite the flowing tears.

"That's it? That's why you left us?" She could feel her face turn hot with anger. "Your old Woody station wagon meant more to you than us! You were angry and disappointed, so you walked out and left Ma to deal with everything."

She ran out of the room. She would leave; maybe take a Greyhound down to New Orleans. She didn't want to go home. She sat down on a stool at the long oak bar with her head in her hands. Vigil came out of the storeroom and patted her on the back.

"Can I get you somethin'? A glass of water or a beer or somethin'? How 'bout a cigarette?" Vigil pulled a pack of Chesterfields out of his pocket and offered her one.

"No thanks. Don't smoke. I'm okay." She wiped her eyes and blew her nose on a Kleenex he offered her. It felt good to cry.

"Your dad's a good man. I know for a fact that he loves you very much. And look here. He finally came back, didn't he?" Vigil was talking in a low, soothing voice. "I was here. I know it broke his heart to leave you and Rose."

"If he loved us so damn much then why did he leave?" She felt calmer now and a little ashamed that she'd blasted Tiny in front of Vigil.

Tiny walked up and put his hand on her shoulder, hesitantly, as Vigil retreated to the kitchen. She shrugged it away and turned to face him. He cleared his throat, opened his mouth to speak, and then closed it again, shaking his head.

"What is it? What do you want to tell me?"

"Look. I'm not good with words. It's hard for me to explain things. An' I'm afraid if I told you why I really left, you'd hate me more." Tiny's hands were knotted into balls, knuckles white.

"I don't hate you. You're my dad. I'm mad at you and hurt that you left, but I don't hate you. Tell me why you left us. I can even understand you wanting to leave Ma. I know she nagged you to death, but why did you cut me and Rose out of your life?" She looked into her father's sad, green eyes. They looked dull and red from lack of sleep. He looked down at the bar.

"I had to leave. That's all. It was the best thing for you and Rose. That's all I know. I didn't want to hurt you. I just hope you can forgive me." Tiny unclenched his fists and reached for the cigar stub he had stashed in his pocket.

"I don't know who I need to forgive anymore. I'm sorry I got mad at you in front of Vigil. I've just had these feelings bottled up for a long time, and I guess they just came out." She needed to know why he really left. She needed to know why Rose had died. She needed to know why she felt so hopeless. Her chest hurt.

"It's okay you got mad at me. Maybe it cleared the air a little, made you feel better. You seem so sad about everything, Ellie." Tiny finally abandoned the dead cigar, laying it to rest in an ashtray on the bar. "Come on.

Let's get this show on the road." Tiny patted her on the shoulder and smiled.

He was right. She did feel better. It was good to get some feelings out, to loosen some of the mortar in the massive stone monument of anger she'd built inside.

Vigil came through the kitchen door, as if on cue, the seven huskies close behind. They lay down in scattered positions around the room, looking like boneless rag dolls, docile and harmless in the light of day. But like her random memories, if provoked, if prodded and poked at, they could turn vicious and dangerous in an instant.

"Let's take a look at this truck." Vigil circled it and kicked a tire on the brand new rig.

"Pretty nice. I'll bet the sheriff's all stove-up about losin' this baby."

The brand-new, no-nonsense 1967 Chevy pickup stood its ground in the converted garage. It squatted square and menacing like a boxer on steroids. Two spotlights, one on either side, gave it the appearance of a grinning frog. A sturdy beam of hardwood was chained across the front bumper. Ellie imagined the sheriff bumping and bullying things around in his big machine.

She took inventory of Dover's belongings in the jump seat. Besides an empty gun rack, there were twelve pairs of shoes and boots displayed neatly on wooden shoetrees. Each pair was shined and buffed with care. Traces of wax and leather still lingered on the shoes and in the air. An uneasy feeling, close to fear, overtook her. The smell was a reminder that the sheriff was a real person, one who coveted his stash of polished footwear and probably missed them. He could be tracking down Tiny this very moment.

"The man's got good taste in shoes." Vigil smiled as he examined the coterie of footwear. "They look to be just my size. I've always had a fancy for fine boots."

"I wonder why he kept them so spiffed up. Most of them don't even look like they've been worn." She counted four pair of Tony Lama cowboy boots, two in cowhide, one in alligator skin, and one well-oiled pair in ostrich hide. There were two pairs of black and white buck suede oxfords, two pairs of steel-toe reinforced work boots, two pairs of leather slip-on deck shoes, and two pairs of loafers, one of turtle skin and the other pig-skin, all neatly arranged with wooden inserts.

"Damn, the man's got good taste." Vigil repeated. He grinned and shook his head. "I wonder why he toted so many pairs of shoes around with him. They ain't even all the same size. Pretty darn near it though."

Tiny laughed. "Maybe the sheriff's got a thing for feet—like a fetish or somethin'. Vigil, why don't you keep the shoes? They're too small for me." He picked up a shoe, smelled it, and caressed the leather. "You take 'em."

Vigil seemed pleased with his newly acquired, stylish shoe collection as he emptied the truck and dumped the pile of shoes behind the bar. Some of the wooden shoetrees fell out and dropped heavily to the floor. He went back to his assessment of the vehicle.

"We could change the license plates, take the lights and ramrod off, and paint over Sheriff and the insignia, but he's still gonna be looking for a '67 Chevy. I tell you what," Vigil said, scratching his head. "I got a Bunny Bread truck out back, just fixed it up. Put a brand new engine in it and a new radio. It even sings a song about the wonders of Bunny Bread. I was fixin' it up for a young fella over in Mound City. He was gonna drive it to San Francisco this summer and "drop out" till his daddy got wind of it and sent him off to military school over in North Carolina. It's got no passenger seat, but, hell, we can yank out that bucket seat on the driver's side and put a big, roomy sofa in there. Give you room to sit right. I'll go get it."

Vigil took a set of keys from a pegboard that held numerous others and went through the swinging kitchen doors. He appeared again, shortly, through the front garage door, driving a big, white square panel truck. It had the head of a big, grinning yellow bunny on either side, with ears erect and the logo BUNNY BREAD underneath the giant heads. Two back doors opened outward to expose a roomy interior, empty of bread racks.

"I was gonna build a bed back here, but I stopped workin' on it when I knew the guy wasn't gonna come git it."

"Look's fine to me," Tiny said. He took two cigars out of his shirt pocket and offered Vigil one. The two men lit up as they circled the truck, blowing smoke at it. It reminded Ellie of some ancient ritual of blessing.

She wondered how men ever made major decisions without cigars in their mouths.

"It's okay. We'll take it." Tiny looked at Ellie as if for approval. "How about an even trade, Vigil?"

"Hell, anything you say, Tiny, is fine with me." Vigil shook Tiny's hand. "She's startin' right up. Sounds smooth." The engine could barely be heard over the loud jingle the truck was singing. "It's Bunny Bread, Bunny Bread. You know it by the bunny on the wrapper. That's what I said, Bunny Bread."

She used to hum the tune to tease Rose when she had a crush on a Bunny Bread delivery boy. Ellie rubbed her aching chest again.

"She's big. She'll be hoggin' the gas. But she'll be comfortable to ride in." Vigil was pleased with the choice. He opened the door on the driver's side and expertly removed the bucket seat.

"'Course there could be a downside to this truck. If Dover gets wind that you're in a Bunny Bread truck, it'll be easier for him to find you. A fat man in a bread truck won't be too hard to spot."

"Do you know Dover?" Tiny asked. "He took office while I was down in New Orleans. I got blindsided by 'em. Should've checked him out better before I played cards with 'em."

"Yeah, I know him. Why'd you think it took me so long to open the gate this morning? I thought it was Dover. I didn't want him to start messin' around with me, even though I'm out of his jurisdiction. I know he's mean and dangerous when he gits crossed. I'd definitely stay out of his way. Junior over near Murray told me the good sheriff was takin' more and more of the profits from his moonshine sales. You know Junior, don't you, Tiny?" Vigil asked.

"Yeah. I buy moonshine from him all the time."

"Junior says Dover's ruthless. You best keep your eyes open for that old cuss." Vigil went outside in search of a front seat for the truck.

"You sure you want to go with me under these circumstances? This could get dangerous," Tiny asked with a worried look.

This would be the perfect opportunity to back out. She could hop on a plane and fly out to Portland, take a real vacation. She wasn't ready to go home and face Louise. The block of ice in her heart that surrounded her feelings about her father was just beginning to thaw. It couldn't be refrozen. She went over and petted one of the dogs.

"Yes. I still want to go with you. Dover won't be looking for a man and a woman. Besides, if he tries to put us in jail, we can blow the whistle on him for cheating." She tried to make light of the situation but was afraid for Tiny.

Vigil came back, hauling a beat-up tomato red sofa in the bucket of his bulldozer. "Help me lift this up, Tiny, and we'll get you all set to ride. Wait, let's put some concrete blocks under this baby and set 'er up some so you can ride higher." Vigil went back outside to get the bricks.

The sofa was covered in a dusty, synthetic material with several wounds that had been bandaged with gray electrical tape. Vigil came back with four blocks and placed two by the driver's seat and two by the passenger's. He and Tiny lifted the sofa up on top of the blocks. The legs rested comfortably on their concrete perches. The width of the truck was a perfect fit. Vigil patted the seat.

"Git on up, Tiny, and let see if it passes muster."

Tiny hoisted himself up into the driver's seat. When he sat down, a puff of dust arose in protest.

"It's comfy. Feels good. It's the right height." Tiny patted the seat next to him, stirring up more dust. "Hop up on your throne, Princess Ellie. Your chariot awaits you." Tiny laughed.

She climbed up and placed her arm behind her head in a Betty Grable pinup pose.

"How do I look in red?"

"Stunning," Tiny said.

"Red is your color. It brings out the green in your eyes," Vigil said as if he had studied the question seriously.

Tiny looked pleased that he finally had a seat befitting his grand bottom. He tooted the horn and started the engine. The Bunny Bread jingle startled the dogs, and they began to howl. Vigil commanded them to stop. He threw some blankets, pillows, and a sleeping bag in the back, along with an old ice chest and a paint-spattered tarpaulin.

Ellie waved goodbye as the dogs stood by Vigil's side in the now warm, midday sun.

"Don't be strangers now, ya'll hear. Stay in touch. I'll keep my ears perked up for any news of the sheriff." Vigil looked down at his feet with a grin. He was sporting a pair of Dover's boots—the ostrich hide ones. They were a perfect fit.

CHAPTER 9

▼

—Dover, Caggway County, 1967—

With chair tipped back and hands behind his head to anchor the tic in his neck, Dover stretched his arms and legs dangerously out of their shell and put his feet up on the desk. He was wearing his favorite Tony Lama ostrich skin boots. He scowled at the boots and wiggled his seething toes. The pig had stolen his only other pair. Those boots were harder to find than tits on a skinny whore. He blinked his slow, thick eyelids in the glare of the midday sun that beat mercilessly through the barred windows, recalling how he'd lucked out getting at once two pair of the highly sought after footwear. He'd done his research, calling all over the tri-state area, finding out what stores carried them, and finding out who'd bought any. Then he'd staked out his prey's home, stalked him for several days, and learned his habits—first eyeballing his foot size to see if it would be worth the effort. He watched and waited all weekend before going in for the kill. Brains. It took brains for this kind of thing. He tapped the side of his head with a short, fat index finger.

He scratched at a rash on his neck until it bled. The goddamned shirts were over-starched again—the stupid cow. He liked a heavy starch in his collar, but this was stiff as a preacher's dick. He unbuttoned the shirt, revealing a tight mass of curly chest hair. He was sweating despite the blast from a big oscillating fan hitting him head on every five seconds.

Every light in the jailhouse was turned on. The sheriff had a need to be in clean, well-lighted rooms, even in the redundant glare of the Indian summer sun. The stupid bitch couldn't understand that. After all these years, she still followed behind him at home, turning off lights as he turned them on. He'd had to belt her again this morning. You'd think after a few black eyes and all those years of marriage she'd learn.

The pork tenderloin sandwich—his favorite—that Deputy George had brought him for lunch was half-eaten. It looked cold and greasy now, like a pig had mauled it with its filthy snout. He cringed, put his legs down on the floor, and leaned forward in his chair, ducking back into his shell. Snakes bite pigs. Dover good boy—not afraid of pig, he reassured himself.

He picked bits of meat and lettuce out of his teeth with his prized coon pick. The fishhook-shaped, polished bone of a raccoon penis served as toothpick and symbol of fraternal superiority—his passport into status of southern white, male, heterosexual, redneck, Christian society. His dominion included everyone and everything that was different than he was.

"You want me to put out an APB on him, boss?" George walked hesitantly into the front office on tiptoe. He stood a body's length away from the sheriff's desk while asking the question, the usual bottle of NuGrape soda in his hand. Mumbling something about a pig's sty, Dover had made him scrub the front office twice already that morning and wipe everything down with Lysol, including the walls.

The sheriff had kept a brooding silence since the incident at the lake three days ago. The deputy had walked the five miles back to town that fateful morning and then drove back with his truck to the cabin to pick up Dover's limp, dehydrated body lying in a pool of vomit—and worse. He'd shit in his pants, thanks to Porky Pig. Dover cringed when he thought of the stench in the cabin. He hated messes, and bodily fluids made him go ballistic. George caught him, totally unhinged, curled in fetal position, reciting his latrine ritual. "Oink, Oink, Oink. Good boy! Good boy! Good boy!" A salute to the forehead with his right hand accompanied every Good boy. George tried to pretend he hadn't seen it, but Dover knew he had. The humiliation was unbearable. He ought to kill the stupid Apache shit of a deputy.

He'd dealt with old wounds around the elimination of waste in his own ways. His mother and father had been poor, ignorant white trash. The mother, crazy and alcoholic; the father, Duffy, meanspirited and addicted to rotgut whiskey. The family had been forced to live in hovels in the backwoods of Arkansas without electricity, running water, or an indoor toilet. Dover's mind, from infancy, had been polluted with fearful memories pertaining to the dark and to necessary bodily functions.

"Git on out thar boy, 'fore I whop ya upside yur haid." The hateful man sat at a makeshift table—a door he'd found at the dump down the road—and spat out a chaw of tobacco on the floor of the small cabin. The seats were long pieces of two-by-fours that rested on pickle barrels cut in half, one on each end of the table. He took a long swig from the bottle of cheap whiskey he was drinking and slammed it down on the table next to a kerosene lamp, which made a circle of light that extended only about two feet from its source. The rest of the cabin was dark.

"Cain't." The toddler stood by the door with his legs crossed, fighting back the tears and the urge to take a poop. He knew if he cried it would only make his father tease him more. He tightened his sphincter muscles in hopes that the urge would go away. He hated the night, with its immense darkness, full of dangerous creatures with voracious appetites and sharp teeth—and pig smells.

"What air ya, a sissy little gurl—frait a' the dark?" His father knew the little boy was terrified to make the long walk down to the outhouse. It had been built a good ways downwind of the house. Duffy Dover sniffed out little Melvin's weakness and poked at it hard, leaving an infected boil in the body of innocence. He picked at it constantly until it became a chronic, festering wound.

"Oh we're gonna cry now ain't we? Well ain't that a pretty sight—jus' like a little sissy gurl."

He sobbed convulsively. If only Epsen could help him, but he knew that would only bring Duffy's wrath down on his older brother. It was futile to call for Old Whore (that's what Duffy insisted the boys call their mother). Dover could make out a lump wrapped in a man's tattered, old overcoat on the cot in the corner. She was asleep. She drank too much of the nasty smelling stuff his father had swilled all day and had gone to sleep before the sun went down.

"Let me tell ya a little bedtime story, son. Once upon a time thar was a skarty-cat, no-good, sissy boy. He was afrait a' the dark. An then thar was these big hungry bears and coyotes waitin' far him to step outside in the dark, and the scariest of them all, the wild pigs."

"No. Don't have ta poo poo." Little Melvin was temporarily delivered from the evil queen of stench that lived in his rectum. The urge went away at the mention of the pigs. He'd heard 'em and smelled 'em out there in the dark, rootin' around, waitin' for him to come out so they could tear him limb from limb. He drew his arms and legs inside himself at the thought and edged his way around the wall of the one-room shanty over to the rusted-out potbelly stove, also a gift from the dump. Epsen was by the stove, sitting on the floor in the dark. He put his finger to his lips as a warning for Melvin not to say anything. Epsen didn't want his father's attention called to him.

"Oink. Oink. Oink. What's that? Why, it's a wild hog down by the outhouse cravin' the taste a' little boy meat." Duffy persisted in his torment of the helpless child as he took another drink of rotgut. The fire had gone out. The boys huddled together, shivering in the dark, not moving or talking. When the snoring started, they knew they were safe for the night. Epsen tiptoed to the cabinet in the kitchen area, quietly opened a drawer, and took out a candle and some matches.

"Come on. I'll walk ya to the outhouse." Epsen was only five, just two years older than Melvin. Epsen was the kindest person in the world, Dover's protector, and the only person he ever really loved.

He'd learned his lessons. The elimination of bodily waste threatened life. The shameful act had to be performed in secret, when Duffy wasn't around. That's when the lifelong, peculiar habit developed. He had to snort like a pig three times before having a bowel movement. Upon completion of the necessary act, he would salute three times, placing his right hand to his forehead, uttering the incantation Good boy, good boy, good boy.

Dover's neck started twitching around the same time. The wrenching tic was a barometer of his volatile emotions. In the early years it measured the intensity of his fears. Later, when he was in grade school, it was an indicator to his classmates that he was angry and they'd best stay out of his way, all of them.

Epsen had been extra protective of his little brother after they'd both been witnesses to their father's rage that had turned deadly. In a drunken fit Duffy had bashed his son Mull's skull in with a piece of firewood, punishment for not scrounging enough wood from the dump for a warm fire one day last December. Mull endured a brain hemorrhage and died after a few days of lying unconscious on the kitchen floor. Duffy forbade Old Whore to call a doctor. He hit Epsen in the face when he'd tried to cover Mull with a blanket. The boy was buried somewhere in the woods without even a marker to bear witness to his brief time on earth.

When Dover turned five, he and Epsen started working summers in the burning sun of the cotton fields to earn enough money to buy themselves each a pair of work boots for the next school year. The importance of wearing new boots the first day of school could not be underestimated. It was essential for self-esteem and the positive regard of one's classmates. By Dover's internal account of all that held value in the world, shoes were tantamount to a steady supply of oxygen to breathe. Shoes signaled one's worthiness in the world. Being shoeless carried with it a stigma of ignorance and poverty, inability to take care of oneself, of not being well-heeled.

One day in the late summer of Dover's twelfth year, he and Epsen had planned to walk into town to each buy a new pair of boots for school. Dover had gone to retrieve his savings, carefully wrapped and hidden in a rabbit hide in the hollow of the big hickory tree down near the dump. He'd been careful not to be seen stashing the money there. Neither Duffy nor Old Whore could be trusted not to steal it for liquor and cigarettes. Dover scooped the leaves out of the hollow of the tree. The rabbit hide was not there.

The hole was empty.

Had he buried it in another tree? He looked around, unable to move or breathe as the reality hit home; the money was gone. His reward for a whole summer of punishing work was gone. Tears filled his eyes and stung his cheeks as he fell to the ground breathless with disbelief.

"I hate the cocksucker." Dover buried his face in the leaves. The tic was smashing his neck against the collar of his shirt. He was paralyzed with loathing for the father who had betrayed him.

"Don't let that ignorant drunk get to ya." Epsen gave him his hand and pulled him up, giving him a brotherly pat on the shoulder—the only person who dared touch him when he was angry. "Come on, I'll buy you a chocolate ice cream soda at Rick's Drugstore."

As they walked into town Dover's anger turned into a cold emptiness that disallowed any possibilities of forgiveness.

They passed the local tavern, and saw Duffy Dover through the window, swilling down shots of whiskey and waving the rabbit skin pouch in the air.

"I'm gonna get even with the sorry bastard. Are ya with me?" Dover asked.

"Yeah. If we do it so as we don't git caught. He'd kill us both if he knew it was us," Epsen replied.

"I know a way. He ain't gonna catch us," Dover said.

Epsen bought a pair of boots with his savings, and the boys loitered around town, making sure Duffy didn't see them. At dusk they walked to the woods and climbed a hickory tree at a cross path, waiting for the drunk to weave his way home in the moonless night. They'd made two sturdy clubs with fallen tree branches. Finally, they heard Duffy coming, coughing and cussing as he swaggered by. He knew his way home even in the dark; he'd walked this route many times, never sober.

"Ready?" Dover whispered, poking Epsen in the side. They jumped down behind Duffy and beat the man senseless with their clubs. The father was unconscious before he had a chance to turn and face the enemy. The man, who so irresponsibly sired them, with no thoughts for their needs, lay bleeding in the night. Dover hoped the wild pigs would come and eat him. Duffy's warm blood felt good on Dover's hands. A peace overcame him as he struck match after match to look at his father's bloody face. Revenge had a sweet taste, like old lady Dickey's stolen honey. He had no recollection in his limited emotional vocabulary for the state of calm he felt. Epsen finally dragged Dover away from the bloody scene.

The boys walked home in silence. Dover wasn't afraid of the wild boars that night for the first time in his life. For several days after the beating, he felt a sense of self-control and euphoria.

Duffy was found the next day by a hunter and taken to the hospital. The doctor had said the large amount of alcohol he'd consumed probably saved his life. He was kept for observation a few days in the poverty ward, and driven home in an ambulance, a quieter, more subdued drunk.

Dover developed one last malignant compulsion. The obsession was born that night in the woods when he struck his father down. The association of owning new shoes and inflicting physical harm was forged in the red-hot foundry of his twisted mind.

It'd begun as petty theft. There'd been no forethought in his acts; his were crimes of opportunity. He knew only that he liked the feeling of power that came over him when he stole someone's shoes. He would enter a victim's home while they were gone and head straight for the bedroom closet, selecting with care the most sturdy or stylish pairs of men's shoes that were there. He would stash the shoes in a canvas bag and hide them in his bedroll in the loft at home. There was little fear of being discovered. His father could no longer climb the ladder to the loft after the beating, and the Old Whore was always too drunk to care. He would take the shoes out and smell them, caress them, and wear the ones that fit, at first only in the privacy of the loft. He stole other small items as well. He had no use for most of the random things he took. He put the loot in the bottom of the canvas bag. When the bag got too full, he dragged it down to the creek and sank it to the bottom. Epsen never asked him about the loot. He sometimes profited in the plunder if it happened to be an item to his liking.

As Dover grew bolder, he wore the stolen shoes to school or walked to town with them on. Wearing the spoils of his conquests made him feel powerful, worthwhile.

As time passed, the stakes were raised in order for him to experience the peace he so craved. A year after Duffy's beating, Dover lied to him and Old Whore. It was his habit in general to never let them know where he was going or what he was doing. He told them he had a job on Saturdays over in Piggot, helping a farmer cut his wood. He stole his father's handgun and wrapped it in a rabbit hide. He'd buried it at the foot of a live oak tree down by the outhouse, being careful to put leaves around where he'd dug the hole.

On these early excursions he used some of his savings from working in the fields around home. He took a bus, sometimes as far as the state line and beyond. He walked around in the finer neighborhoods, watching and waiting for opportunity to present itself, only breaking into houses to steal shoes when nobody was at home. He was disappointed in himself on these occasions, wondering why he even bothered to get on the bus and spend his money to go so far from home for so little reward. He craved more.

One day he rode a Greyhound bus for seven hours to Bowling Green, Kentucky, taking the stolen pistol with him. He followed a man sporting a fine pair of polished leather cowboy boots, complete with western spurs, to his home that evening. They looked to be close to his size. He ascertained that the man lived alone. Dover watched and waited until the time seemed right. Fate made it easy for him; the kitchen door wasn't locked. He covered his face with an old nylon stocking he'd found in a trashcan and quietly entered the house. With gun in hand, he followed the sound of snoring to the bedroom. He saw the boots at the foot of the bed in the moonlight. The man woke up suddenly and turned on the bed lamp.

"Who are you? What do you want?"

The edgy tone of voice and the frightened look in the man's eyes made Dover's body tingle. His days in the woods shooting small animals for food and pleasure had made a marksman of the boy. He raised the gun eye level to the man's face and pulled the trigger. The victim, in his desperate attempt to breathe, made a gasping sound that thrilled Dover. He looked into the bloody face, the face of his father. In a hot glow of revenge, he ran for the kitchen door with boots in hand and bolted down the quiet street into the night.

His euphoria lasted for several weeks before the twitching returned and fear took possession once again, leaving him with no permanent peace. He wore the boots, his badge of courage, until his growing feet could no longer be contained within them. He fed them to the creek in the spring of his fifteenth year—the year Epsen joined the Marines and was killed in Korea.

Dover's life became a flat horizontal line after Epsen's death, punctuated by acts of escalating violence and evolved cunning. By the time he reached sixteen, he enjoyed a solitary, anonymous fame. His heinous deeds were reported in local newspapers all over the tri-state area.

At the age of seventeen, just two years after the pieces of his beloved Epsen's body were brought back home to rest in the local graveyard, young Dover was delivered into the disciplined hands of Marine Sergeant Levon Pitts in Piggot, Arkansas. Duffy hastily marked his signature "X" on the induction papers, as he'd done two years earlier for Epsen. Duffy seemed in a hurry to wash his hands of his youngest son. He didn't even say goodbye.

The Marine Corps and Dover had been a perfect fit. He'd been further tutored in becoming a more efficient killing machine. Although he became a masterful marksman, he never saw combat, much to his disappointment. But he showed a talent in breaking enemy codes and was given top clearance. He loved the feeling of importance his job gave him, the sense of authority he felt while wearing the uniform. He was provided with sturdy shoes that he kept polished to a high shine. His need to steal and kill was abated during this period of high self-esteem.

He was able to hide his compulsive bathroom behavior from his bunkmates by covering his mouth with his hands to muffle the three pig snorts and the good boy incantation. If anyone heard it, they would laugh, thinking he was joking around.

He stayed with the Marines for fourteen years, earning the position of sergeant, and married a Japanese girl while stationed in Hawaii. During this time of stability, he stole three pairs of shoes and murdered only twice.

Dover got up, walked over to the barred window, and looked out. His neck jerked from side to side, a metronome keeping an interior, hateful time.

"No APBs. I'll handle this one myself," Dover said, running his fingers through his thinning hair.

"Don't sound too good for the fat man," George said, frowning.

"Don't worry. I ain't gonna involve you in this. You don't have the balls for the hard stuff."

"I sure don't envy Tiny Moon. He messed with the wrong man this time," George shook his head.

"Well, you ain't seen nothin' yet." The muscles around Dover's mouth jerked in syncopated rhythm with the neck twitch. "Mister Undertaker, you better start makin' a big box for Piggy. That shit-eatin' piece of blubber is goin' to his maker in the style he deserves, in shit-eatin' pieces. No one steals Dover's truck and shoes and gets away with it." There could be no redemption for the humiliation the fat sonofabitch had caused him.

His security blanket against the barefoot days of childhood had been ripped away. Old scars made his bones ache. The thirst for revenge was all he had left, even his favorite pork tenderloin sandwich tasted like dog turds.

"I'll get that motherfucker if it's the last thing I do," Dover promised the glaring, empty room. George had slipped out unnoticed. "The big bastard ain't gonna get very far. Here piggy, piggy, piggy. I'll take your sandals, and then I'll cut out your fat heart and feed it to the hogs with my own hands."

CHAPTER 10

▼

"What say we cruise by the old homestead," Tiny said as he turned left onto Park Place West, not waiting for an answer. "I drive by from time to time when I'm in town."

They were still in Cairo, five minutes from Vigil's garage. The visit to the old nightclub had left Ellie in a mixed state of mind. She'd retrieved some memories, pieces to the puzzle of her life, but she'd never missed Rose so much as now.

They passed by the park with the big sycamore trees, near the aviary that had never caged birds, as far as she knew. It still looked to be a playground for squirrels. She used to carry nuts in her pockets to feed them on the way to school every day.

"Our old house. How old was I when we moved in here? I don't remember."

"You were ten or eleven, goin' on twenty-one. You were an independent little cuss—sat up on the levy after school everyday countin' birds. Your mother was always afraid—you bein' up there alone all the time. She worried about you."

"I know what you're thinking. Ma should have been just as concerned about Rose. Ma let Rose do whatever she wanted." She hated it when she sounded critical like her mother.

"I'm not blamin' your mother for anything. She did the best she knew how. It's me I'm blamin'. If I'd been around, maybe things would 'a been different." Tiny wiped his eyes with his hand. "I was such a jerk back then. Had a hard time stayin' sober sometimes." Tiny's eyes were a kaleidoscope of laments. She wasn't going to comfort him.

The Victorian house by the railroad tracks on Park Place West seemed much smaller than it had in her dreams. The family had moved there from St. Louis after Granny died. She died in her sleep. Ellie had fallen asleep in Granny's bed that night. Granny kissed her goodnight and asked the usual before-lights-out question.

"Where was Moses when the light went out?"

"What?" Tiny asked.

"That's what Granny said every night when she tucked me in, the last thing she said to me before she died. And then I would say, 'Down in the cellar, eatin' sauerkraut.' That's all I remember."

Owl: *When you woke up, Granny's lifeless arms were still wrapped around you. You kissed her cold, silenced lips and said goodbye. She'd been your best friend since Oddy'd left, but you didn't cry because you knew that Granny had gone back to being a star again. You went downstairs to the kitchen where Louise and Rose were eating breakfast and told them that Granny had turned to light again.*

To get out of one of Tiny's gambling debts, he and Louise decided to sell the house and all the stuff in it—even the china dolls in the attic that Granny promised would be Ellie's. That's when the family moved to Cairo so Tiny could open a nightclub and make lots of money. After the move, that's when all the trouble with Tiny started, and Louise made the girls take Dexedrine to slow down the process of puberty, to prevent them from developing large breasts—they ran in the family on Tiny's side, she'd said. Ellie never got a good night's sleep after that, and she supposed it was the same for Rose.

Ellie was disappointed. It was just a house, an empty shell. She'd built it up in her dreams to be a castle full of shadows and demons: a labyrinth of unexpected twists and turns and dead-ends. Her dreams ran on reels like old movies. Only short disjointed scenes, out of sequence, were shown her. The plot of the movie had been cut and thrown on the floor of the editing room of memory.

Owl: *Tiny had been drinking each time it happened. I hated the smell of whiskey on his breath, dreaded his seeking me out. It happened four times, in a period of three months, just before my first menstrual period, after my twelfth birthday. Tiny would come into my room when Louise and Rose were gone. He'd kiss me, stick his tongue in my mouth in a way that made me feel worthless—like an ugly thing, not a person, a piece of trash that no one could ever care about. Then he would unzip his pants and guide my hand down there, into his pants. He would put his penis in my hand and close my hand around it, manipulating my paralyzed hand up and down, faster and faster until his milky juices would come out and he would yell, "Holy Jesus." Then he would tell me not to tell anybody, that I was his secret lover. After he stumbled out of the room, I would run to the bathroom and lock the door. I washed my hands over and over and rinsed my mouth of his whiskey breath with soap and water. But the taste of him and the numbness in my hand, a shameful body part, would linger. I would stay in the bathroom until Louise or Rose would beat with their fists on the door and threaten to break it down if I didn't come out. The priest told me that I'd overreacted, that I would hurt the family if I told anyone about it. Indiscretions happened in the best of families. Tiny hadn't really done anything so bad. He hadn't put his penis in my vagina. Father McDill had said it was best to just put it out of mind and move on.*

I absorbed and buried our pain, to protect you, but we both paid a price. We never trusted anyone again, except maybe Rose and Granny and they're gone. Tiny left and didn't even say goodbye, discarded us like an old, tattered rag doll. You blamed yourself but kept our silence. The testimony of our muteness sat on the dresser in your bedroom, silent witness. The one thing you took with you from Granny's house: the wooden statue of the three monkeys, See No Evil, Hear No Evil, Speak No Evil.

Ellie stood on the sidewalk, glued to the concrete. Tiny honked the horn, jolting her out of the familiar feeling of turning to stone whenever her mind faced a wall it couldn't climb. Saved by the bell.

"I'm hungry. Let's go to Josie's and get some barbecue," Tiny said. "My stomach's growling."

CHAPTER 11

▼

Tiny parked on deserted Main Street in front of Josie's, a place legendary for its barbecued pork sandwiches. It took him several tries. He hadn't quite gotten the hang of driving the bulky truck.

"Let's go see if the food is as good as it used to be. You may remember, I'm the world's authority on barbecue." He was hungry. They hadn't eaten breakfast, and the thought of a meal had a tonic effect. His natural enthusiasm was returning. He'd felt uneasy and helpless when Ellie had stood on the sidewalk, staring at the old house by the park. She'd always been the sensitive one, but look what happened to Rose. How much of their trouble was his fault? What had he done? A little harmless play when he'd been drunk. That was all it was, wasn't it? Hell, he barely remembered anything about it, thought he'd put it out of his mind. Maybe it hadn't been such a good idea to visit Ellie after all these years. It was bound to bring things up again. That's what he'd been afraid of, afraid of hurting her—not in a physical way, he knew that would never happen again, but stir up memories. And then she might hate him if she remembered. That's why he hadn't contacted her before.

They entered a shabby, long, rectangular room with a rough wooden plank floor that looked near collapse and sloped inevitably toward the kitchen.

"The place has gone to hell like everything else in Cairo. Hope the barbecue is still good," Tiny sighed, stepping hesitantly on the slanting floor.

"Hope I don't go through it," he laughed. "Seems like Cairo mimics the ebb and flow of the tides in the rivers out there." He nodded his head toward the channel of water. "The town is either booming or in a state of decay." Tiny wished they hadn't stopped, had driven on to Paducah. It was depressing to see a town that had once held potential for being the crossroads of the Midwest because of the confluence of the two great rivers in such a state of decay. The façade of the old building was crumbling, like the other big brick buildings on Main Street. The hardwood floor, once kept buffed to a shine, was dingy with grime and cigarette burns. The old booths sat shamelessly with their stuffing hanging out. The once-thriving restaurant was empty of customers. He used to have coffee with his cronies here every morning. Muzzy, who'd been murdered by the mob out of Chicago. Little Red Krebbs, still around for a good game of poker. Eddy Dale was doing time for cheating the IRS.

"Looks to be currently in a stagnant drift," Ellie remarked, bringing him out of his reverie.

A sixteen-by-twenty photograph of Mark Twain, autographed by the famous author himself, hung over the antique cash register behind the counter. The restaurant claimed that the famed author used to stop and eat barbecue there whenever he passed by on a steamboat, riding his beloved river. Cairo had been the setting for a scene in Huckleberry Finn. Jim had been headed for Cairo and freedom on his raft, in the story. Tiny recalled that he'd been proud that Mark Twain had chosen his town and his river as the setting for that most enduring story, even though Tiny hadn't read it. He'd always regretted not learning to read until he was in his twenties, something he kept a well-hidden secret. He rarely had time or inclination to read, working his poker route, but he'd promised himself that one day he would read Huckleberry Finn.

"Let's sit out here in the middle of the floor at a table. I can't fit in the booths," Tiny said as he saw Ellie heading for the back booth.

"Okay. I just want to see if I can find something."

His eyes followed her as she slid into an old back booth. She sat very still for a few minutes. He watched her cry. Wished he could comfort her. She came to the table and sat across from him.

"Johnny Max loves Ellie May. It's still there, the heart he carved into the tabletop with our initials on it. He was my first love." She sighed. "I remember how we'd giggle at everything with our heads together and drink fountain cherry Cokes from the same glass with two straws. I wish I could remember more about those times. I wish I could carry those memories in my pocket, wrapped in the snake skins there."

"You got snake skins in there? That's a funny thing to carry around." He laughed and then wished he hadn't. He didn't want her to feel belittled. He wanted her to confide in him, to trust him again. He wouldn't betray that trust ever again, even if it were to cost him his life.

A volley of gunshots sounded nearby.

"What's all the shootin' about?" Tiny asked the waitress.

"Hell, you don't know? The White Hats are shootin' at the niggers, tryin' to scare some sense into 'em. What'll ya'll have?" she asked.

She had a net around her greasy hair and a protruding chin. Two upper front teeth were missing, and she was chewing a piece of gum. She looked like Charlie McCarthy and every time she talked Tiny expected to see Edgar Bergen in the background, pulling the strings that made her mouth open and close.

"Still got good barbecue?" he asked.

"Good barbecue we got. Ya'll ain't from around here is ya? Ya'll don't know 'bout the race riots we been havin', do ya?"

"Race riots, here?" Tiny asked with sarcasm in his voice. Cairo had a long history of prejudice and violence toward its Negro citizens. He remembered the burning of crosses on the levee by the Ku Klux Klan, sparked by an early attempt at integrating the school. Ellie had been a freshman and Rose a sophomore at Cairo High. Most of the public buildings had been segregated, including the library and the swimming pool.

Illinois had been declared a Free State during the days of slavery, but the town's sympathies clearly lay with the South. The townspeople were as unwilling to blend together as were the two rivers that met at their door.

"Some nigger soldier got hisself in jail for goin' AWOL a few weeks ago. He hung hisself in his cell with his belt, and now the niggers and all the civil rights yahoos are up in arms about it, sayin' the cops beat him to death. They been marchin' and carryin' signs and all. It ain't safe to go out on the street." The waitress chewed her gum faster, her wooden jaws working furiously.

"I read about the incident in the newspapers and saw it on television. Knowing the reputation of the police force here, I suspected he was murdered," Ellie said. "I wanted to write about it, but Dempsey had me covering social events."

"Junior, the moonshine man over in Kentucky," Tiny added, "he told me the real version of the story. Said the police beat the poor man to death and then tried to cover their tracks by calling it suicide. The Negroes organized to protest peacefully, and the White Hats started shootin'. Junior wouldn't lie about that."

The waitress came back with two cold sandwiches on white bread—not the good barbeque on a hot bun that he had remembered. The scoop of coleslaw on the plate was runny, with too much dressing. It made the stale bread soggy. Tiny was disappointed. He'd lost his appetite. Bacon and eggs and a soft bed would've hit the spot. He was feeling his age—couldn't go for days at a time without sleep anymore.

"Don't you ever sleep?" She must have read his mind.

Gunshots sounded closer now.

"Let's get out of here," Tiny said. "The barbecue's cold and the bread's stale. The corruption in this town has a way of rubbin' off on ya." He threw a twenty dollar bill down on the table and tipped a finger to his forehead to let the waitress know they were leaving.

"You sure gave her a big tip for such lousy food."

"Yeah, I know, but I always tip big. And I just feel sorry for poor, dumb people like that waitress. Just think how miserable her small-minded life must be," Tiny said. Maybe bringing Ellie to Cairo wasn't such a good idea. Maybe dredging up the past was a mistake. He hadn't thought it out. He was just working from a gut feeling, his usual modus operandi.

CHAPTER 12

▼

Tiny and Ellie drove down Commercial Street. No signs of life. They parked in front of Willie's Pharmacy and got out to have a better look at old landmarks. The crumbling bricks of the buildings were all overgrown with ivy, and most of them wore "Closed for Business" signs. Willie's Pharmacy, where Ellie had worked during her freshman year in high school, was boarded up. A painted, red wooden sign still hung above the front door. She could see broken glass inside where the window had been shattered by rocks or bullets.

Gunshots sounded from down the deserted street, around the corner.

"Let's get the hell out of here," Tiny said. He started walking at a brisk pace toward the truck with Ellie close behind.

"Wish I could remember more about this place," she said, shaking her head.

"Well, some things are best forgotten, I guess. It's time to just move on," Tiny said, climbing into the driver's seat. He started the engine and Bunny started singing, a little too loudly, she thought, in the dangerous silence, broken sporadically by gunshots.

"What things are best forgotten?" she asked. There was a tingle at the base of her spine that rippled up the back and into her head. She was too tired to figure anything out now.

"I don't know. This place gives me the creeps," Tiny said.

The narrow strip of land at the edge of town, near the bridge that spanned Illinois and Kentucky, was where the Ohio and Mississippi Rivers met. It was like a magic trick where they joined. A line of clear blue water from the Ohio seamed with the muddy Mississippi, forming an uneasy pact—much like the citizenry of Cairo. History could be felt in the air and underfoot. This was where General Grant assembled his troops for their journey downriver during the assault on Vicksburg in the Civil War.

Owl: *The muddy old Mississippi is a hard river to be bound to. It doesn't bestow its gifts gently or give up its truths without life-and-death struggles. It stinks of rotting fish and plant life. The oily, treacherous waters are deceptive, deep, and full of strong currents. Its surface, on a windless day, is like murky glass, flat and blindly reflecting back our fears and loneliness. We've seen the river, just on a whim, rip up huge chunks of land and carry them off downstream. Things disappear beneath the surface, taken under by vicious undertows, only to be spat up in new places farther downstream, humbled, yet perhaps stronger for the experience. The Old Man may seem capricious and cruel, but in the end he has his reasons, and he keeps his bargains. You'll see. He always does, in his own way, in his own time, and on his own terms.*

She sucked in the fecund delta air in hopes that it would clear her mind. The broken glass of soda and beer bottles, visible in the thick weeds, reflected flashes of sunlight in the tall grass.

Suddenly, she had a clear memory of coming down here to Independence Park with Rose and one of her boyfriends. They had locked her out of the car while they smooched. Bored and angry at the exclusion, Ellie had stripped down to her panties, jumped into the Ohio River, and swum across. She watched Rose from the Kentucky shore with delight, waving her arms helplessly for Ellie to swim back. She took her time, enjoying Rose's discomfort.

She'd been a strong swimmer in her youth. The thought comforted her. She couldn't have been a zero, without personality. She was at least a good swimmer, a redeeming thought. A breeze from the river caressed her like a greeting from an old friend, carrying with it the scent of Rose's favorite cologne of rose water. She'd stirred up the dead bones of her sister from the depths of the river. Rose's essence eddied around her, a curling vapor, and saturated the air.

"Rose, why did you die and leave me alone? I should have done more to help you." There it was again, that unnamed guilt. The longing to touch her sister and hear her voice seemed unbearable. It subsided into the usual dull ache in her chest as tears ran down her cheeks.

"What's this? Are you cryin'?" Tiny patted her on the shoulder and reached for his handkerchief. She instinctively recoiled from his touch for a second, and then was embarrassed by the gesture.

"It's okay. I need to cry. It's actually good. I need to try and remember things that happened," she said, wiping her eyes with the sleeve of her T-shirt. "Let's go."

She lagged behind for one more look at the river. The waterlogged ghost of Rose edged out into the water and sank as the current carried it south.

She stumbled back to the bread truck where Tiny stood waiting—noted an anxious look on his face—and got in on the passenger's side, glad to be leaving Cairo behind.

Bunny sang his lurid song when the motor started up, followed by a lyrical chant in hi-fi from the local station on the radio—WKRO in Cairo. By the time they crossed the river and touched down on Kentucky soil, the Beach Boys were on a "Surfin' Safari."

CHAPTER 13

▼

—Owl, St. Louis, 1939—

A brooding heat hangs over the afternoon in the big brick house on Watermann Avenue. Granny says we're right in the middle of the dog days of summer. She says they're called dog days because the Dog Star, Sirius, is closer to the earth in August than any other time of year. The air is motionless and muggy up here in Old Mary's bedroom, even though the window and transom are open. Little chance we'll be rescued by a cross draft today.

Old Mary, Oddy's mama, is in her rocking chair, snoring. She looks dried up like an apple doll Rose made in school. She wears pieces of straw in the holes in her ears. Tiny gave her pearl earrings for Christmas, but she said she's saving them for a special occasion—her funeral, Louise says. Oddy and I are in Granny's big rocker, trying to conjure up a breeze.

My Oddy is a large, smooth woman with skin the color of ripe figs. She has a reassuring smell like starched cotton and early morning rain. She's the ground I stand on, my piece of sacred earth. I'd rather be in Oddy's strong arms than anywhere else in the world. The plop, plop of ripe plums falling from the tree in the backyard against the parched earth makes me drowsy, but it's so hot I can't stay asleep for very long. Still, Oddy rocks me like I'm a precious cargo against her heart, both of us sticky with sweat.

I spend most of my time in Old Mary's room. We color together. Rose doesn't like to stay indoors with me. She'd rather be out playing Kick the Can or Mother May I with her friends. She tells Louise to keep me inside because I bother her and her friends. That's all right. I don't want to play with those stinkers anyway. It's too hot.

Louise bought Old Mary and me each a new coloring book yesterday, pictures of animals. Old Mary takes her coloring seriously. She thinks a long time before choosing the page she wants to color. It takes her even longer to choose her sticks of well-worn crayons from the cigar box Tiny gave us to keep them in. She chews snuff and spits brown stuff into a Folgers Coffee can by her chair. Mary is over a hundred years old. She can't see very well, but she struggles to stay in the lines. Not me. I scribble big circles of color that cover the whole page, and I'd rather make a lion purple than the real color Old Mary gets by mixing yellow and brown.

Granny told me that Old Mary's lifelong dream had been to learn to read and write, but she'd been a slave and didn't have a chance to go to school. Granny said that coloring in books makes Old Mary feel like she's doing something close to reading and writing, and that makes her feel important. So at the end of the day, Granny, Louise, Oddy, and I, and sometimes Rose, look at Old Mary's pictures and make a big fuss over them. Old Mary grins wide and shows her gums where teeth had once been. Granny says that the world is full of imperfect people: that sometimes it's a sin what one race does to another and that in Old Mary's case we can only hope that second best will save the day.

Old Mary wakes up and starts humming. Oddy joins in. The creaking of the rocking chairs adds rhythm to the two voices. Although there are only three of us in the room, there is a fourth presence—the song. The humming starts sweet and low at first, then gets fuller and louder, increasing gradually until the emotions behind the sounds can no longer be hushed. All matter in the room comes alive, and in uncanny unison sounds the downbeat, a blow as dire as breath itself. Song is unleashed into voice unfettered. Old Mary's soprano, in harmony with Oddy's contralto, rocks the room.

"Jeeeeeeeesus take me home."

"Sing child!" Oddy says. "Join in on the Lord's joy!"

I add my owl hoots to the mix.

"Ooooooooh Sweeeet Jeeeeeesus, take my hand!" Oddy and Old Mary chant in full-throated warbling: natural songs from wounded night birds singing down the sun. Ancient, matriarchal moans. Souls in rapport sounding the depths of inconsolable rivers, wails of weariness, shouting sorrow for this world and deep longing for another, softer shore.

Old Mary died the winter following that summer of my third year. Wild song stopped. Oddy left our home shortly thereafter for a more lucrative job, operating the elevator at the FamousBarr department store in downtown St. Louis.

I knelt on the couch by the big window that overlooks the busy street in front of our house. I watched Oddy breathe white mist into the snow that fell as she boarded the bus that took her away from me. She turned and waved goodbye from the back window. Granny told me that Oddy was only allowed to ride in the back because she was colored. I wondered if that had anything to do with coloring in books like Old Mary and I used to do. I held my breath for as long as I could and then cried as the bus pulled out into indifferent traffic. My beloved nanny disappeared in a puff of smoke as steamy exhaust assaulted the frozen air.

Several months after Oddy left, my mother felt sorry for me and took me to the department store to say hello to Oddy in the elevator. She was stiff and proper, dressed in a starched, cobalt blue cotton uniform with white collar and cuffs. The strong hands that had nurtured and comforted me since I was born were covered with white gloves. The wings of fingers that I so loved to watch fly at tasks were muzzled like dangerous dogs and silenced, so as not to offend the white clientele. Oddy barely nodded when she saw me, little expression of recognition on her face. She called out the numbers of the floors as the elevator ascended, naming the objects one would expect to find on each floor. As she stopped at each landing, the elevator let out a great gasp of air. Oddy pulled back the heavy brass gate, opened the door, and told the shoppers to "watch your step" as they departed. Her voice sounded tight, cold, and impersonal as she named the wares to the patrons. "Second floor, ladies' shoes and handbags."

We rode up and down as the elevator filled and emptied again. Oddy wasn't allowed to speak to the customers, but why didn't she talk to me, her "sweet white angel". I just wanted her to lift me up in her strong arms and tell me that she loved me. I couldn't stand it any longer. I grabbed her leg and wouldn't let go. I was bellowing like a water buffalo when the elevator descended again to the lobby. It took my mother and a stranger to tear me away from the beloved leg, but not before I managed to rip one of the nylon stockings that Oddy was wearing. I escaped the restraining arms of my captors and ran to hide under a rack of dresses. My gasping cries gave me away, and people were looking at me, a major disturbance in the elite décor of St. Louis's finest department store.

"I'm a little picaninny. I'm a little picaninny," I shrieked. I'd heard little brown girls called that. If it worked for them, it might work for me. If I wasn't white I could go and be close to my Oddy. I kicked and screamed at the enemy when they came and dragged me to the entrance.

The last glimpse I had of my precious nanny: she looked at me from the elevator for a moment, a face in pain, fighting back tears. I guess the cost of salty tears falling on cobalt blue starched cotton was too high a price to pay in a world where merchandise was king and prejudice traitor to the tender heart.

CHAPTER 14

▼

Ellie and Tiny, 1967

They were on higher ground now, in Kentucky. Bunny had just passed the bottom swampland that lies just beyond the bridge from Cairo. Ellie watched fields of tobacco fly by the window. Bundles of large green leaves were drying in the sun on cast-iron metal carts. Leaves in the second phase of drying, with autumn tones of ochre and burnt sienna, hung sticky sweet from gray wooden rafters in open-sided barns. Cut corn stalks drying in the fields gave testimony to the passing of summer. They were a reminder that the season had given a splendid performance this year and was still onstage to make its final bow before the onset of winter. The land felt safe and gentle in contrast to the crumbling decay of Cairo.

"Here we are. My favorite barbecue stop in Kentucky," Tiny said, pulling into the gravel parking lot of Porky's Drive-In. A neon-lit pig with his mouth opening and closing adorned the front of the building.

"We're stopping to eat already?" They were less than an hour away from Cairo, on the outskirts of Paducah.

"Well, we really couldn't eat that swill they served us in Cairo. I'm hungry. I'm testing my theory that the barbecue in Kentucky is superior to the barbecue in Illinois. And this place serves up the best of all. I want you to taste it." Tiny ordered two sandwiches and two chocolate milkshakes without consulting her.

It felt good to be with someone who didn't watch every bite she put into her mouth. The waitress came back with the bag of sandwiches and the drinks.

"Here's yoah shayake," the young girl said. Ellie put her hand over her mouth to stifle a laugh.

"Thank ya'll, and ya'll come agayan," the girl said as she handed the change back to Tiny. He drove away with sandwich in hand, treating the customers and staff of Porky's to a free Bunny Bread jingle.

"May I have a sip of yoah shayake, sir? Laud I do declauh that I have died and gone to hoggy heaven. This barbecue is quite delicious." Ellie rolled her eyes and fanned herself with the greasy brown paper bag. "No doubt about it. This is far better than Illinois barbecue," she said, relishing the delicious, fatty sandwich.

"Ya see, in Illinois the sauce is added after the pig is roasted over a hickory wood fire, and in Kentucky the meat is basted with the sauce while roasting," Tiny expounded.

"Hawuh is it that the people in Kentucky, just minutes across the Ohio Rivuh, have such deep southern drawls? I have nevuh been able to figure that out. I declayuh." She was enjoying her role as a belle. She realized that she had missed the soft drawls of western Kentucky.

Tiny laughed. "Beats me. They go hog-wild with the accent don't they? Real cotton mouths. Soon as ya cross the Cairo Bridge, you'd think you was in Georgia."

"It hasn't changed much in the last fifteen years," she remembered, feeling little nostalgia for the place. Those had been emotionally tough years.

Paducah was a clean, thriving town with wide, tree-lined streets. She'd always liked its location on the Mississippi, Ohio, and Cumberland Rivers. She hadn't lacked for bodies of water in which to swim when she was a teenager, but juggling school and a full-time job in a grocery store left little time to play. She and Louise had moved here the summer before her senior year at Cairo High, three years after Tiny had left them in Cairo. Rose had flown away in the middle of her junior year, keeping with family tradition, with not so much as a goodbye to Louise or her. She had left, impulsively, one night, all dressed up in a black dress and red high-heeled shoes. Ellie had watched Rose dress and spray rose cologne from an atomizer all over her body. She'd told Ellie that she was going out dancing with some sailor she had just met. She never came home.

A beautiful woman with few skills, Louise had worked at various jobs to keep a roof over their heads after the move. She'd worked as hostess in a restaurant at night, and by day she sold silverware door-to-door, dragging Ellie with her whenever she could catch her.

"Once you get your foot in the door, you've won half the battle, then you go for the close," Louise said in her teaching voice. She was a good saleswoman, with a glitzy, showgirl style that people couldn't resist. "You do all the talking at first. You just take control of the floor. Then you let 'em talk. They always want to tell you how hard their lives are. Then you know you've got 'em. You lead 'em to believe that if they buy this silverware, it'll make all the difference in their lives."

It made Ellie nauseous to knock on the doors of strangers. It felt immoral to intrude into private lives, taking advantage of human weaknesses. The dependence on the sale of inconsequential merchandise to pay the rent made her feel like her life was as irrelevant as the silverware Louise peddled. She came to believe that her mother's sales tactics were more underhanded than Tiny's gambling.

"What ya thinkin?" Tiny interrupted her thoughts.

"Nothing really." Bunny was passing a familiar building. They were on the west side of town. "That was Tilghman High. I graduated from there," she said. She hadn't made one lasting friend her senior year. She'd attended classes in the mornings and worked afternoons and evenings, providing little time to make friends in a new school.

"I know. I was at your graduation," Tiny said.

"Really? You were? And you didn't come and say hello to me? How could you do that?" she asked, surprised and disappointed.

"I didn't want to spoil your graduation or upset your mother," Tiny said with regret in his voice.

"I can't believe this. If you only knew how much I wanted you to be there."

"Really? You wanted me to be there? You weren't ashamed of me, didn't hate me?"

"No, of course not. You're my father. I wanted you there," she said.

"I was so proud of you. First one in the family to graduate from high school." Tiny said. He hadn't gone to school.

"Your mother went to eighth grade. She wanted to go on to high school, but her father made her quit after the eighth," Tiny said.

"She never told me that." Ellie was surprised.

"Yeah, he said education of girls was a waste of time. That's when she started dancin' to make a living. Then there's Rose," Tiny sighed and shook his head. "If only she'd stayed in school like you did, she might be alive today. You were always the practical, level-headed one. Rose was the wild child."

"I got drunk with Ma after the cap and gown ceremony," she said defensively, not wanting to be upstaged by her dead sister. She knew she never held a candle to Rose as far as Tiny was concerned.

"Yeah?" Tiny laughed. "You got drunk?"

"We went out to dinner, and Ma let me order martinis carte blanche. I think she got a little wasted too." Although there were only two physical bodies at the graduation dinner, Rose's absence had filled the room with unspoken grief.

"I kept thinking that Rose would surprise me and walk through the restaurant door. I thought she and Mom set it up as a surprise," she said. There was silence. She could feel the air thicken with grief.

"You really miss her, don't you?" Tiny asked softly.

"Yes, I guess I still do. Did you ever see her down in New Orleans?"

"We went out to dinner a few times. The last time I saw her she had the shakes pretty bad. I offered to help her get clean. She agreed, but when I went to get her at her apartment, her neighbor told me that she'd packed up and left town that morning." Tiny looked out at the road, mouth set hard, fighting back the tears.

Ellie wasn't in the mood to comfort him. She wasn't going to let him off so easily. "Were you at my college graduation? I graduated from Murray State with honors. Did you know that? I got a degree in journalism. Rose died just before my graduation." She clenched her fists.

"I knew you went to college. I was so messed up after Rose's death, I guess I forgot your graduation. Here's your old house." Tiny stopped the truck in front of a solid, old brick house in a middle-class neighborhood on a bustling double parkway lined with sycamore trees. He seemed relieved to change the subject.

"I wouldn't have recognized it. I hardly spent any time here except to sleep, don't remember much about it. Dad, how did you know where we lived? Were you spying on us? Did you ever think to knock on the door and say hello?" Angry tears flowed down her cheeks. "Why were you such a wimp with Ma? Why didn't you stand up to her and just come see me if you wanted to?"

"You don't know how many times I tried to get up the courage. I used to drive by every time I was in town. I watched you, all grown-up, come out and get in your car to go to work one day. I almost stopped to say hello that time."

"You knew where I worked?"

"Yeah, you used to work at that twenty-four-hour open air grocery store out on the old Cairo road." Tiny sighed, a sad tone in his voice. "It's all water under the bridge now."

"Is that all you can say? Twenty years wasted. How can you shrug it off so easily?" She felt herself redden and blend into the old red sofa that was the front seat. Tiny's silence fueled her anger. They rode, not speaking, with the radio blaring music from a station in Nashville.

"I hate cowboy music," she said, reaching over and turning it off.

In a secluded, upscale suburban area on the south side of town, Tiny took a right into a circular driveway lined with magnolia trees. He stopped in front of a large, ranch-style house, surrounded by foliage. The shade was a blessed relief from the early afternoon sun. It cooled her anger, but she felt irritable from lack of sleep and smelled like a zoo.

A giant black walnut tree hung its lacy branches over a white picket fence. The tree was alive with squirrels gathering their bounty of nuts for the winter. Several squirrels sat on top of a blue Porsche parked under the tree, cracking the hard inky shells of the black walnuts, dropping them on the shiny blue paint of the new car, leaving black stains.

A petite woman who looked to be in her fifties was on the porch. She was framed by two oversized Corinthian columns, the kind with which the *nouveau riche* adorn their entranceways to impress their neighbors. The front of the house looked like a façade of a movie set. The woman saw them pull up and waved a lace handkerchief in the air, then ran down the path to give Tiny a hug.

"Oh, Tiny, I ayum so glayud yuah heeyah." She was on tiptoe in a pair of flat, black ballerina shoes, trying hard to wrap her arms around as much of the big man as she could manage. Ellie shook her head in a double take. She was tired; maybe she was dreaming. The woman looked as though she had stepped out of the past with a white off-the-shoulder peasant blouse with tiny red roses embroidered around the neck and a flowered peasant skirt with lacy edges of a petticoat peeking out below the long skirt. Bottle black hair was pulled back from her face in a bun in the back. It was adorned with artificial red poppies: one on each side.

"I haven't heard from yu'all, and I've been so worried." The woman took notice of Ellie and grabbed her. She was strong for her size. The vigor and duration of the embrace was surprising. The sweet denseness of the woman's perfume was a direct hit. It had to be Blue Waltz, a dime-store fragrance packaged in a blue bottle and popular among the study hall crowd at Cairo High twenty years ago. Restless boys would lie in wait with squirt guns filled with the cloying, sweet blue liquid. The smell made her dizzy. She stepped back, only to be grabbed again.

"Oh, honey, I know who yuah are from the picture your father showed me of you when you was a little girl." She planted a greasy, soft kiss on Ellie's cheek with her exaggerated red lips.

"You've known my father a long time?" Ellie asked in an unintentionally territorial tone of voice. She waited for Tiny to rescue her from their hostess's enthusiasm, but that wasn't going to happen. She was on her own. He had disappeared inside the house.

"Oh heavens yes. I met your fatha' when I was workin' down South yeahs ago. Back in my heyday. Oh, Tiny forgot to introduce us. I am Ludine Lamar." She extended her delicate, bejeweled hand with a flourish.

Ellie realized that she was staring at the original mold of a living, breathing cliché of a true southern belle with, no doubt, a shady past. She found this endearing and more than a little entertaining.

"Come in, Ellie, welcome to my home. Ya'll must be tired. Would you like something to eat? Or would you like to take a showeh and rest for a while? Laud, it's hot out theyah." Ludine fanned herself and rolled her eyes.

They stood in a spacious, split-level room that served as living and dining room. Dense, ornately carved pieces of furniture stood heavily upon plush, green shag, wall-to-wall carpeting. In the center of the room stood a massive mahogany dining table, its thick limbs deeply carved in figures that looked like devils and saints. Twelve matching chairs of lesser saints and devils were placed around it.

A bouquet of artificial magnolias in full bloom held center stage on the table in a large pewter vase. Keeping with the floral theme, wallpaper with large pink and white magnolias on a green background, busy with buzzing bees and dragonflies, graced the walls. Heavy, textured, red brocade fabric hung in swags over a bay window that looked out on the front yard. The décor might have threatened to upstage this dark-haired, overripe fruit of the South had it not so perfectly embellished her exaggerated personality. Fine Audubon prints of songbirds that Ludine had caged in gilded frames flew atop the busy wallpaper, migrating down a long, thickly carpeted hallway. Propped unceremoniously against the back wall, as though it were an afterthought, was an unlit neon sign announcing that "Madame Lamar: Psychic Reader and Advisor" was open for business.

"What's this?" Ellie asked, intrigued.

"Oh don't mind that old sign. I just keep it around to remind me of the good ol' days. I don't tell fortunes anymore. I used to down in New Orleans, but you know how life goes. I came home to visit my mama. I was born and raised here in Paducah." Ludine stopped to take a breath. "And I met Elmus Trundale and married him right up. I went to church one day with a friend, and Elmus came before the congregation to ask for a healin'. He had cansah, and I just couldn't resist goin' up there and rubbin' that glorious bald head of his. And the rest is history. He did die of the malignancy a short time after our union." Here she stopped and let out a breathy sigh of sadness, "but we did have a short time of lovin' one anotha'. Elmus was a banka', and he left me well off, bless his soul." She rolled her dark eyes upward. "After he died I was just rattlin' around in this big ol' house, itchin' to do somethin' worthwhile with my time, and I was tired of helpin' the ungrateful downtrodden at the church. So I called my boys and offered them the opportunity to game in a safe place. I don't have close neighbors, and none of my church friends would evah suspect anything untoward of me." Not only was her mouth full of cotton, but she loved to spin it and weave it into bolts of cloth.

"They just sleep and eat here while they are in the game. I cook good food for them, and, when the occasion arises," (here she gave Ellie a knowing wink) "I provide them with whoahs so that they may have quality sex." She paused to breathe. "'Course I want the girls to have quality sex as well, so I sometimes try the gentlemen out for them to make sure they are up to par."

"Oh my." Ellie giggled and rolled her eyes in surprise as Ludine poked her in the ribs with her elbow. Where was Tiny?

Come on, let's go in the kitchen. Don't you want somethin' to eat, or a cup of coffee, or somethin'?"

Ludine led the way to enchantment. Sunlight shone through a big bay window, gilding the spacious, clean, homey kitchen with golden light. A large oak table stood under the window with several books related to bird-watching on it. One was opened to a page with a picture of a great horned owl. Ellie felt a shiver of recognition. A pad of paper with names of birds and tally counts behind the names indicated that some kind of bird accounting took place here. Outside in a large, wooded backyard were different styles of birdhouses and feeders. Various birds ate seeds and splashed with delight in a big, concrete basin on a pedestal decorated with cherubs flying up the sides.

"Oh, how wonderful, all the birds!" She was enraptured.

"We get all kinds of birds passin' through heah. Those little yellow finches over theah, they stay in the area all winta long. They turn gray in the winta, and in the spring they get yellow agayun. You have to have a special feeda for them, otherwise you don't really see them much." A red cardinal flew in and perched on the platform of a feeder, preening his brilliance. "Oh my Laud, theyah is an Indigo Bunting!" Ludine exclaimed. "We don't often see those. We know they come through heah, but they don't show themselves often. You must be a lucky charm." Ludine touched Ellie's arm softly. The most intense flash of cobalt blue she'd ever seen flew away, causing an inexplicable ache in her heart.

"I keep track of all the birds coming through." Ludine went to the table and wrote something on the pad. "We're losing some, you know. We need to take care of our friends who flyah in the skyah. You seem to take an interest in birds."

"Yes. I used to count birds for the Audubon Society," Ellie said, sighing in remembrance of her precious snow geese. "Do you ever have snow geese stop by?" She liked this woman.

"Oh, honey, they all stop by heah. This is part of the great Mississippi flyway. The whole Mississippi valley is home to the largest variety of migratory birds in the world." Ludine made an exaggerated sweep with her arm. "It is truly somethin' special."

Ellie thought how appropriate it was for Ludine Lamar to take such an interest in the habits of migratory birds. She played hostess to all kinds of rare and unusual birds of the human species, as well as those that "flyah in the skyah." She was curious about the human breed of fowl that graced Ludine's home. Those, she envisioned, who warbled eccentric, melancholy songs of longing and lust, restless gypsies in search of the next card game down the line. Birds follow fair weather. For them it is instinctual for survival to embark on endless journeys. Is this true of a dwindling number of the human flock as well? Did they inherit the legacy to follow the river? Had the river lore taken hold at a cellular level compelling them to abandon their families, give up all that society holds dear? Was their destiny mandated by instinct rather than free will to follow the meandering snake of the river up and down its uneasy shores in endless ellipses of predetermined flight?

Tiny walked into the kitchen, lighting a cigar. "I called some of the boys. We're gonna have a game if you don't mind, Ludine."

"Oh that's fine with me, honey. That way Ellie and I can have a chance to visit."

"What about the sheriff? Aren't you worried he could find you here?" Ellie was uneasy. She was having trouble adjusting to the rapid change in itinerary. Not that they had discussed a plan of travel.

"The boys ain't heard nothin' about the sheriff lookin' for me, and he don't know about this place. Certainly none of the boys would put Ludine in danger. I don't see what the problem would be. I'm goin' out to park the truck out back in the garage, so it won't be seen from the road. And then I'm gonna take a shower and nap before they get here."

"Come on, honey. Let's get you into a soft, comfy bed." Ludine took Ellie's hand and led her where the pictures of birds migrated down the long hallway to a frilly bedroom done in various tints of pink. Antique dolls rested on satin pillows. Ludine moved the dolls aside, and Ellie crawled in. The shower would have to wait. She was asleep as soon as her head hit the pillow.

CHAPTER 15

▼

The first of the players to arrive was Little Red Krebbs from Cairo, a dapper little man in late middle age, smelling of Wild Root Crème Oil. His carrot-colored hair had a high shine, sides slicked back, and hair draped forward over his forehead. He had dark, beady eyes and was dressed in a double-breasted suit of steel blue-gray. His voice was raspy and flat, like a blue jay's call.

Fats Mahoney from Chicago walked through the door talking. "How youse doin', Miss Ludine, the prettiest girl in Kentucky?" He didn't wait for a response. "Tiny, Tiny, you break my heart. It's been too long my friend." He pumped Tiny's hand while looking at Ellie, winking. "What have we here? A fair-haired beauty if I ever seen one. I'm Chicago Fats, or Fats Mahoney. Take your pick." Fats planted a chain of kisses on her that followed a course from fingertips to elbow. "Ellie, Ellie what a beautiful girlly. See I'm a poet and didn't know it." He laughed with his whole body. He was short and round, a miniature version of Tiny. Chewing gum slightly faster than he talked, he shook his arms and kicked out his legs as he stood and talked, hopping from one foot to the other. He reminded Ellie of a magpie dancing the Charleston.

"Youse two on a father-daughter vacation or somethin'? Why don't you come up to Chicago, and I'll show youse around." He punched Tiny on the shoulder. "Your fatha' is a million dollar man. He's like gold to me, my best and oldest friend, huh Tiny?" He punched him again.

An hour later a tall man with dark hair silvering at the sides landed at the doorstep. Seemingly ageless, he was the most handsome man Ellie had ever seen. Ludine ran to him and gave him one of her long, close, exaggerated embraces.

"How was your flight from Florida, honey? I want you to meet Tiny's daughter, Ellie. She'll be here while ya'll are playin'." It was obvious that Ludine appreciated beauty in the form of the opposite sex when she saw it. Her eyes took on a shine, her accent thickened, and her words dripped honey. "George heah is a champion pool player with a passion for poker. He acquired his nickname from the unique way in which he breaks the stack of balls to open a game. Instead of using the cue and eight ball, he spins the ball with his hand and pockets more points on the opening shot than anyone has evah' done before. Isn't that right, honey?" She gave him another hug and kissed him on the cheek.

"Hi, I'm Spinball George."

"Hello," Ellie said, a little too breathy. She had an almost irresistible urge to dive into the two deep blue lagoons of Spinball George's eyes and never surface. She became aware of her unadorned state. After the shower she'd exchanged khaki shorts and T-shirt for a pair of equally drab faded blue jeans and a gray cotton blouse, her hair pulled back unceremoniously in its usual ponytail. She wished she'd worn makeup—she had a sudden urge to explore Ludine's arsenal of feminine reinforcements.

Spinball George took Ellie's hand and kissed the back of it. The soft touch of his warm lips on her skin made her shiver with unexpected delight.

"How lovely you are, Ellie," he said, holding her gaze.

She could feel her face flush from the attention of this exotic creature but was helpless to stop.

Ludine sensed her discomfort and pulled her away with an excuse that she was needed in the kitchen.

"Don't worry; he has that effect on every female of the species regardless of age, creed, or race. The truth is he is a happily married man and is the least guilty of indiscretion of any of the group. It's good to find a man who makes you feel like struttin' your stuff. Makes you feel alive again, doesn't it? Your father told me that you have just endured a divorce. Is that right?"

Ellie wondered if Madame Lamar could read her thoughts. It felt good to be reminded that she was a woman capable of feeling attracted to the opposite sex after all the months of denial and blame.

The encounter with Spinball George triggered a train of thoughts and feelings that she hadn't often let herself indulge in since the breakup with Ted. Why was it always the burden of the woman in our society to hold a marriage together? Divorce was a brand upon the forehead for all to see that the woman failed the nuptial vows in one way or another. The wife designates herself the guilty party, and her mother and the rest of society follow suit.

"Oh Gawd! There's a scarlet tanager. They're so pretty—those black wings against that stunning red." Ludine went to the table to make a tally mark on the pad. "We better quit talkin' so much and make some sandwiches for the boys. I'll bet they're hungry after travelin'."

So this was Tiny's life. Ellie had wondered about it for so long. She felt as if she were a voyeur hurled into the middle of a Salvador Dali painting where melting objects and people juxtaposed themselves against one another randomly—with no logical order. She bit her lip, ashamed of her feelings. She was jealous of these people who spent more time with Tiny than she ever had in her whole life. It seemed a tasteless joke that Tiny had abandoned her for this, with this cast of characters for companions. She felt cheated of lost years. What would her life have been like if he'd stayed with the family? What kind of person would she have become if he'd given her the attention that he lavished upon his friends? Maybe Rose would still be alive if he had stayed.

After a few hours of sleep, a shave, and a shower, Tiny's enthusiasm for the game had been restored. Good to be here at Ludine's with the boys again, gathered around the mahogany table with the carvings of the devils and saints. Look at them. Even though they'd just arrived, the players were perched on the chairs, nervous, as if ready for imminent flight if a sudden movement spooked them.

Ludine had removed the frilly bouquet of paper magnolias from the center of the table. Three heavy cut large glass ashtrays rested on the polished surface in an attempt to discourage the players, mostly Tiny, from laying glowing cigar stubs on the table's edges. It was a bad habit, one that was hard to break. As proof, the table bore deep scars, and the shag carpet beneath had black-rimmed craters.

"Okay, gentlemen, what's your game?" Chicago Fats said as he broke the seal on a fresh deck of cards. He chewed his gum nervously. "Seven card stud or draw?"

"Let's go with five card draw to warm up," Spinball George said. Astute to even the most subtle of gestures from the players, Tiny saw Spinball glance toward the kitchen where Ellie had disappeared with Ludine. "Is it hot in here, or is it just me?" Spinball removed his blue serge suit jacket and unbuttoned the top button of his shirt.

"Keep your eyes on the game." Tiny frowned. "Don't get any ideas. That's my daughter, you know." *The sonofabitch.*

"Hey, Tiny, I know. It's just—you know. Somehow I never figured you for a family man. All those years we've been playin' together. You never mentioned her." He sighed when he said *her.* Spinball George was a relative newcomer to the group. He'd been a player for about ten years. "Hey, I would never hit on your daughter. She just caught me by surprise is all. A woman like that could have anything she wanted, with that natural kind of beauty." Spinball shook his head, sighing.

She was a beauty. When Tiny had first seen Ellie out in the garden, he'd noticed that his daughter had grown into a mature, beautiful woman. She was elegant, graceful in a quiet way, yet she seemed almost apologetic about her appearance. She didn't seem to have a clue that she was pretty. He chewed on his cigar, uncomfortable with the feelings that Spinball George's attention to Ellie had triggered in him.

"If I may wax poetic," Spinball George hesitated. "It's like all my life I been walkin' around with a bouquet of violets—just waitin' to give 'em to someone like her. But I've already given those flowers away to someone else, and you only get one bouquet to give away. That's the way a woman like Ellie makes me feel. Nothin' personal, Tiny."

Nothin' personal, my ass.

"Enough with the fancy-schmansy poetry stuff," Chicago Fats said. "Let's play poker. High card deals. Draw, my friends." He cut the deck, and they each drew a card.

"Ace. My deal," Tiny said as he shuffled the deck. The new cards felt smooth against his palms, so crisp and cool. They smelled like shellac and dry pine tree bark in the summer. Even though all of the men at the table were familiar with the wizardry of Tiny's shuffle, his legerdemain brought forth sighs of admiration and envy. He was well-aware of the effect he had on his fellow players. The lightning shuffle was part of his strategy. It had a way of stunning the players' minds and putting them into a state of wonderment for a brief moment. This gave Tiny a mental advantage and established his sovereignty as king of the game from the get go.

This was what it was all about, this rush of adrenaline: this thrill that nothing else could touch, not even sex—sitting in company with like-minded friends in deep concentration. They were birds of a feather with one goal in mind, winning the game. Hell, it wasn't about the money. If it were, we would've all packed it in long ago and gotten decent jobs. He felt such satisfaction when he doled out the cards to each player. It was like giving them a gift, a part of him. Here with his friends, nobody asked anything more from him except to play the game the best he could. He was allowed to make mistakes, not like in the game of life. Mistakes could be fatal there. Here, when he wanted out of a game, all he had to do was fold, and nobody jumped down his throat.

Tiny pulled out a new cigar from his shirt pocket, put it to his nose, and breathed in the rich aroma of a tropical island not far off the coast of Florida. He peeled off the wrapper and bit off the end, spitting it into the glass ashtray. He lit the delicious elliptical treat with a silver-plated lighter that'd been given to him long ago by his teacher and mentor, Harry, back when Tiny was still called Johnny Lightening. It was engraved with his initials: J. L.M.

"Okay boys, it's show time. No wild cards. Ante up," Tiny said as he took a long puff and laid his cigar down on the edge of the table. All of the men put five dollars in the pot, earning them the privilege to play. Tiny started the deal to the left. Little Red Krebbs received the first card. Spin-ball George was next. Chicago Fats was to his right. When five cards were dealt to each player, face down, the men picked them up and assessed their hands.

Little Red opened with a twenty-five dollar bet. The betting always started slow and then built. Little Red reached into his shirt pocket and pulled out a Lucky Strike. He lit it and tossed the match into the ashtray. His beady eyes took on a shine as they darted from player to player, not making eye contact.

Tiny chewed his cigar and watched Little Red. *He's got something. Every time he's got a good hand he lights a cigarette to reward himself. And he won't look you in the eyes. Hell, I've played with this bunch so long I can read every little facial gesture. Every move they make means somethin'.*

"I pass," Spinball George said. He glanced toward the kitchen again

Tiny knew that poker wasn't George's game. His skills in poker didn't match his enthusiasm for the game, but Lady Luck seemed to favor him. He was known for winning enormous pots. *Sonofabitch better get his mind on the game.*

"I'm in," Chicago Fats said. He threw twenty-five dollars into the pot.

Tiny dealt him one card. *He could have something here, but I think he's bluffing a little to feel things out.* Tiny blew smoke in Fats' direction.

"Hey youse guys are killin' me here with the smoke. What? Are you tryin' to make me choke to death?" Fats said.

Tiny had a pair. *Nothing to write home about.* He'd stay in the game and see what these guys were up to. He knew Little Red was holding, but he wasn't sure that Fats had squat. In the game of poker, the important thing was to win the pot, and that didn't always involve holding the best hand. Strategy was everything.

"I'm in, and I'll raise the pot to fifty." Tiny discarded and dealt himself three new cards—another pair.

"Hey, Ludine, how about crackin' open a bottle of that fine wine from the cellar. I feel like somethin' smooth," Little Red called in a flinty voice, showing off for the ladies in the kitchen. "How about a 1960 *Côtes du Rhône*? It's not too young—full-bodied, heady, and complex, just right.

Like the beautiful gals sittin' out there watchin' the birds fly by." He winked at Spinball George.

Cocky little rooster. He's got to preen and strut for the ladies. Tiny knew the little prick had something now. *He's tryin' to distract me and Spinball— thinks we'll both lose our concentration.*

Little Red raised, and everyone checked.

"Straight flush," Little Red said as he laid down the five, six, seven, eight, and nine of clubs. The players threw their cards into the middle. Little Red raked in the pot.

"Your deal, Little Red," Fats said, fidgeting in his chair.

"Let's up the ante a little bit. Sweeten the pot to keep things more interesting," Tiny said. He put a hundred dollars down. The other three followed suit. Tiny could afford to lose the first few rounds in order to feel out the players and gather information that could be valuable later on when it mattered, when the stakes got higher. It was all a matter or timing.

CHAPTER 16

▼

Ellie carried the tray with the delicate, long-stemmed wineglasses and the bottle of French wine Little Red had requested, balanced on the palm of one hand. The other hand rested on the side of the tray so she wouldn't drop it, just like the waitresses used to carry the trays at Tiny's Place. She felt stiff and awkward as she placed the tray on the table, trying to remain invisible. She'd been instructed by Ludine not to talk and not to look at anyone's hand. The players considered women in the room bad luck. She bristled at the thought of playing a subservient role to the superstitious gamblers, but Ludine had insisted that she be the one to carry in the tray. Ellie looked down at the table and showed Little Red the label. He nodded his head, and she poured a small amount into his glass to sample.

"Thank you." He swirled the glass vigorously and made a big show of smelling the wine. He carefully put the glass to his lips, making a loud slurping noise as he sipped. Smacking his lips together in approval, he nodded for her to fill the glasses. "That's a good one." Little Red fluffed his feathers. As Ellie turned to leave, the man quickly put a wad of bills into her shirt pocket.

"But I can't take—" She broke the rule of not talking and then made the mistake of looking at the bills in her pocket. All eyes were upon her. She could feel her face redden as she took the money out of her pocket and laid it down on the table next to Little Red.

"No. That's for you." Little Red quickly slipped the bills back into her pocket. His face turned pink as he slicked back his hair with the palm of his hand.

"Thank you." She smiled, embarrassed as she backed out of the room. She hoped she hadn't hurt the little man's feelings. Back in the kitchen, Ludine took the money out of Ellie's pocket and counted it.

"Honey, he gave you a thousand dollar tip!" Ludine laughed and pushed the money on the table toward her.

"I can't take that much money for bringing him a bottle of wine." Ellie felt the way she had when Tiny had dumped the bucket of silver dollars on her bed when she was a little girl.

"Honey, of course you can take it. You would not deny a gentleman the pleasure of sharing his winnings with a beautiful woman, would you? It's just his way of showing his appreciation. It would hurt him greatly if you did not accept." She opened the oven door and took out a ham. The aroma had a stabilizing effect.

"Next time they want something, you go. I feel safer out here in the kitchen." Ellie was watching the birds through the window. She thought of all the mixed messages she'd received from Louise. It was important to be honest and work hard, while at the same time it was perfectly acceptable to lure a rich man into marriage for comfort and security. "It is just as easy to fall in love with a rich man as a poor one," she could hear Louise's voice.

"Those boys in the other room are just that, b-o-y-s." Ludine put a pan of cornbread into the oven. "I'll tell you something about Little Red," she whispered. "He has no flair with the ladies. He brags a lot when other people are around, but he gets tongue-tied and stutters around women when he's alone with one. He may be a winner at cards, but he is no winner with the ladies."

"So you think I should keep all this money so I don't hurt his feelings?" Ellie asked.

"Of course I do. It's a gift. And it's just a gift. He doesn't expect more from you than you've already given. Besides, there is nothing wrong with earning money the easy way, I always say." Ludine gave one of her knowing winks. "As long as it doesn't hurt anybody, it doesn't matter how you get your money. It's part of the game."

Ellie liked Ludine's honesty. She would keep the money. She stuffed her blue jeans pockets, leaving slight bulges on both sides.

Rose had followed in Tiny's footsteps and rebelled against the rules of conformity. Maybe Ellie was next to tread the fallen path, she thought. She surprised herself with how easily moral dilemmas seemed to be resolving themselves in her mind—with the help of Ludine framing the issues into a kinder, if not more convenient, perspective.

"Hey girls, how about some coffee and ham sandwiches? We're starvin' in here." Fats Mahoney called the kitchen staff to action.

For three days and nights, the boys played poker. Five o'clock shadows appeared on sleep-deprived faces like prickly gardens in dry sand. The gradually increasing silences proclaimed the seriousness of the game. Conversation was in low, hoarse tones. Voices were taut, like rubber bands, snapping brief retorts to shorthand questions.

Ludine and Ellie sat at the table in the kitchen and counted birds, busied themselves refilling glasses of whiskey and beer, emptying ashtrays, and making ham and turkey sandwiches or scrambled eggs in the mornings. They hovered around the players like the hummingbirds in the backyard flitted around the red petunias. They took turns napping so that one of them was on duty at all times in case the players wanted something to eat or drink.

"Remember that life is a game," Ludine said when the two of them were in the kitchen together. "You can play it with dead seriousness, or you can play it for fun. All that matters in the end is how kind you were to yourself and others. And you are more likely to be kind if you're havin' fun and keepin' things light."

"Sometimes it's hard to keep things light. Sometimes it's hard to forgive. Especially if you're not sure what it is that needs to be forgiven or who you should forgive." Ellie tried hard not to sound so serious.

"I know it's hard. I don't believe in turnin' the other cheek, but when we hold on to wrongs that we think others have done to us, we're just hur-

tin' ourselves over and over again. We need to first forgive ourselves."
Ludine touched Ellie's hair. It was a mother's touch—one Ellie had longed
for all of her life. "Look at those songbirds out in the yard. They gift us
with their presence and their songs because we don't ask them to be somethin' they're not. We just let them fly away and don't try to hold on."
Ludine paused and took a crystal on a gold chain out of her pocket. "I
have something I want you to have. This crystal will help clear your mind
and remind you to forgive yourself when you get down about things." She
put the chain around Ellie's neck. It felt heavy there.

"Thank you. I feel confused. I know I'm hard on myself and everybody
else most of the time, but what good does it do to forgive myself when I
don't really know what I'm forgiving myself for?" She began to cry.
"There's something that eats at me all the time, and I don't even know
what it is." It was easy to cry with Ludine. She understood.

"The crystal will help you remember. You are going through hard times
right now. You will be led through this darkness. A symbol will lead you to
the light," Ludine said. She got up and went over to a cabinet near the
table. After searching a few minutes, she returned with a name card and
handed it to Ellie. It was inscribed with the name "Madame Duvall" and a
New Orleans address. "If you get down to New Orleans with your daddy,
you will undoubtedly meet Felicia Duvall. Tell her Mother Blackbird sent
you. She's my mentor, and a true psychic counselor." Ludine got up to
pour each of them a cup of freshly brewed coffee.

"So, this "Madame Lamar, Psychic Advisor" hat that you took off so
lightly as a thing of the past is still a part of you. A special gift that you've
developed?" She wanted to know everything about this tiny, aging fortune-teller. Ellie took a sip of the strong black coffee, grateful for the rich
brew. She hadn't realized how tired she was.

"Honey, it's somethin' we all possess if we pay attention to it. It's that
voice inside that people talk about but mostly ignore. When we honor that
voice, it speaks up and tells us the truth about things, no matter how hard
that may be. Knowing the truth is the first step to doin' somethin' about
whatever it is that keeps us down," Ludine said.

Tiny came into the kitchen and interrupted the consultation. "Do you know where the cake tin is?" He asked.

Ludine went to the cupboard and retrieved a silver cake tin polished to a high shine. Tiny went out the back door to the bird sanctuary. The two women watched him through the window, a fishnet in his hands. He dipped the net into a pond next to the birdbath.

"Oh, Laud, he's goin' for the turtle. The game is over." Ludine laughed.

After several scoops, Tiny retrieved a good-sized turtle, thrashing around in the net. It seemed reluctant to leave its watering hole so abruptly. Tiny placed him gently into the cake tin and then hurriedly put the lid on, fastening it in the grooves. He walked through the kitchen and carried the tin into the gaming room by the handle and set it in the middle of the table. Ludine and Ellie broke the rules and followed Tiny. The men, blurry-eyed from lack of sleep, saw the silver dome, and all laughed in relief. They had come to a stalemate, and all seemed tired of the game.

"I'm gonna lift this lid and let this here turtle go. The first man's money the turtle touches wins the final pot. Okay?" Tiny asked.

All chimed their accord. Tiny set the cake tin in the middle of the table and lifted the lid. The turtle sat there on the silver tray, head tucked in his shell. After a few tense moments, his head slowly appeared. Looking around as if deliberating his move, he slowly lurched forward off the silver launching pad and onto the tabletop. He began to travel due south with a firmness of purpose toward Chicago Fats' stash. Then he stopped and made a wide slow turn toward the north end of the table. He landed in the middle of a pile of greenbacks directly in front of Spinball George's seat. He tucked his head back in his shell and stayed there. Ellie smiled to herself. It must be a female turtle.

"Damn, look at that. Even the turtles can't resist this man. How does he do it?" Fats said. He was laughing, but his face reflected his near win of fortune.

The others seemed to take their losses in stride. Only their eyes betrayed the cost. Spinball George raked in the loot and put it into a large canvas bag. Later, when the men had all retreated down the hallway to the bedrooms to get some sleep before leaving, Ludine confided in Ellie that she had estimated there had been around a hundred thousand dollars or more on the table.

Ellie sat alone at the table in the kitchen, drinking coffee, grateful for the solitude and the warmth of the early morning sun streaming through the window. She thought about Ludine and their conversations over the last three days about letting go and not holding on to old grudges. Examples of the lesson were obvious in the gracious way the gamblers had accepted their losses. If only she could let go.

A bluebird that shared his hue with ripe blue plums landed on a feeder in the yard, and Ellie made a tally mark. There were not many marks by the once-thriving breed. She longed to protect the endangered bird, to hold it in the safety of her hands. She watched with aching heart as he flew lightly away into the wide, open sky.

CHAPTER 17

▼

Ellie shivered and hugged herself at the picnic table as she drank the treasured first morning cup of coffee. She was cold despite the wool sweater and blue jeans she'd donned after the storm, the warmest clothes she had brought with her on the trip. Still, she'd rather be outside in the cold, participating in the phenomenon of daybreak at Kentucky Lake, than sitting by the electric heater in the cabin. Tiny had rented the cabin three days ago so they could go fishing together, so he'd said. No telling where he was now. Last night had been hellish, alone in the cabin. A storm had blown up in the middle of the night with lightning and thunder, torrential rain, and high winds. It had terrified her. Rain poured into the open bedroom window, drenching the floor. She awoke to cold raindrops pelting her in the face. It felt like a recurrent nightmare.

The sun took charge of the sky as she watched three spunky gray squirrels gather fallen acorns from the ground, their cheeks bulging with the bounty. Life on the lake was lively after a rainstorm. Fish fed in a frenzy, splashing silvery foam in the water as they circled their breakfast of bugs that were hatching in the early morning light. Dragonflies skittered along the surface of the water like miniature, iridescent helicopters. Little yellow finches with soft angelic voices were scolded by hooded jays. She caught a glimpse of bright red in a nearby tree, adding a perfect triad of primary colors to the tonic symphony of bird colors and songs. A squawking magpie provided the accent points from time to time—like clashing cymbals.

Casualties of last night's storm, tree limbs lay strewn on the ground. She'd listened to them break throughout the long night and thud to the ground in the strong gusts of wind. The storm had not been a dream. It had happened. There had been a dream though—one that had a sense of urgency about it. She'd jotted it down in her notebook when she got up to close the window from the rain. She looked at the scribbled writing in the notebook that lay open on the table. Raindrops from last night had blurred the ink in places, but she could make out most of the words.

A young man wearing what looks like a soldier's uniform from World War II tells me he is twenty-one years old. He's standing in a large bedroom filled with old, priceless furniture. He says that the antiques in this room date back to the days of King Arthur. He stands gazing out of an open window with curtains made of delicate lace, moving slightly in a breeze. There's a four-poster bed in the room covered by a white, gauzy canopy. Across a brilliant red bedspread lies a long dagger. The bed keeps changing locations, sometimes it flies through the air. The soldier looks sad and tells me he's home on furlough, that there is a devastating war going on in the world. A woman comes into the room. The light brightens when she enters, and the soldier stiffens. Even though his back is to her, he senses her presence. This is the woman to whom he is betrothed. I can feel that he's frozen in place with fear and can't turn to face her. She asks him to set the date for the wedding, and he tells her he can't. A storm is brewing outside, and strong gusts of wind are blowing the curtains into a frenzied tango. He knows that if he doesn't set a date for the wedding, she'll kill him with the dagger. She has a perfect right to do so—this is the expected thing to do. I wake up terrified and realize that I am the soldier.

Strange that she should dream she was a man. She'd always felt ill at ease in the land of dreams, a land where shadowy, runaway night horses rode at full speed, knocking down carefully built fences. She fingered the crystal around her neck that Ludine had given her only three days before. It seemed so long ago.

The smell and feel of the air after a cleansing rain on the lake was tonic, and the warmth of the sun gradually trivialized in her mind last night's fear of the storm. Her body begged to differ. She felt like she had been through a battle and wasn't sure whether she had won or lost.

She got up, walked inside the cabin to refill her cup, and sat down at the kitchen table. The cabin hadn't changed much since she'd last seen it, down to the same perennial smell of mildew when the windows were left closed for too long. Her family had come here often when she and Rose were girls, before Tiny left. She noticed the horsehair blooming out of a gash in the old, brown, brocade-covered sofa that stood under the picture window overlooking the lake. The same old floor model Philco radio stood silently in the corner, its big wooden knob inviting her to turn it on.

Owl: *We listened every Saturday morning to fairytales on "Let's Pretend." We would lie on the sofa with Rose, head to feet, and tickle each other's toes. Louise usually managed to find a way to interrupt the program just as it was getting good. We would cry, and Rose would call us big sissy Owl and start a pillow fight with the sofa cushions.*

The cabins were built in the late forties by a friend of Tiny's: Mr. Bliss. Back when nobody bothered about the lake, he'd bought up most of the property on this side of the shore and convinced Tiny to buy in with him. Tiny did, only to lose his share in a card game. Mr. Bliss later sold the property and made a fortune.

Tiny hadn't come back last night or the night before. He'd asked to borrow half of the money that Little Red Krebbs had given her to gas up the truck and check in with some of the local cronies who lived nearby in hopes of generating some action at the table. She gave him the money, but not without protest. She wished she hadn't. Ludine had convinced her that the money was rightfully hers to keep.

Tiny had seemed unconcerned that Dover might look for him at the lake—the scene of the crime. It had been a week, and the sheriff's cabin was on the other side. Kentucky Lake was vast. Its many unpaved roads, hidden by brush and trees, led to privately owned hideaway cabins. It would be hard to find someone here unless you knew where to look.

She poured another cup of coffee. The porcelain cup slipped out of her hands and shattered on the gray linoleum floor. She slammed her fist on the table, tears blurring her vision. Where the hell was he? Had he walked out and left her again like he'd done when she was twelve? She shouldn't have agreed to go on this trip, just when she was beginning to trust him.

She felt fearful of being alone and vulnerable. It was her fault for being so gullible and trusting him. She wished she'd stayed at Ludine's longer. She missed the motherly southern belle and the wild, beautiful birds that she nurtured on their passages through life.

Ellie and Tiny had left the sanctuary of Ludine's home three days ago and driven to the lake to set trotlines, Tiny had said, and rest after the marathon card game.

Rose had always been the one to set trotlines with Tiny. The two would paddle to the middle of the lake. At intervals they would drop fishing line, weighted with a rock for anchor and a white Clorox bottle as a float, to mark the spot where the line was dropped. Every so often the line was inspected for fish. Ellie watched from the shore as the two set out the lines, leaving a trail of white bottles bobbing on the surface. Rose would squeal with laughter as Tiny rocked the boat, tumbling her overboard into the water. Ellie couldn't stand touching the worms to bait the hook and cried when Tiny clubbed the fish to kill them. After they were cooked, she refused to eat them.

Ellie had feigned interest in learning how to set trotlines now to be close to Tiny, but he'd broken his promise and run off, leaving her stranded without wheels and taking half of her money.

She decided to stop worrying, enjoy the solitude and peace, swim, and maybe even write. There was plenty of food. When she was ready to leave, she'd hitchhike back to town and call her bank for money. Things weren't so bad she rationalized. After all, she was an adult now, and Tiny couldn't hurt her anymore than he had. But why did she feel like her skin had been peeled away, with nerves exposed?

She made a fresh pot of coffee and went back outside in the sun to sit at the picnic table. She brushed away a persistent horsefly and peeled off her sweater. It was getting warm. A flock of mallards flew by in formation, following the shoreline of the lake. Some wood ducks waddled by, searching for worms that had tunneled close to the surface of the rain-softened soil. The white throats, black heads, and gray bodies on the background of green grass created a subtle study of colors that longed to be painted on canvas. Two fishermen in a motor boat puttered by and waved.

She went into the cabin to put on a swimsuit and T-shirt, came out, and walked down to the lake, relishing the idea of jumping into the sunlight-bedazzled water. The Mimosa trees along the shore had dropped their large purple pods on yellow ochre sand. An old Smirnoff vodka bottle lay half-buried, a discordant note in an otherwise perfect concerto of colors.

Soft, cool mud oozed between her toes as Ellie waded out slowly into the water, interrupting a blue heron fishing in the shallows. He stood on one foot and then the other. "Sorry, old bird," she whispered.

She swam out to the middle as the lake embraced her like an old friend. She remembered a time when she and Rose had been out in the middle of the lake together, when the motor of their boat had stalled. She could hear Rose laugh as they jumped in the water and took turns pushing and pulling the boat back to shore.

"Two eagles are sittin' on the shore waiting to eat one of us. Which one do they want? It isn't me," Rose laughed so hard she gulped water between words.

"It isn't me, so it must be you." Ellie laughed.

"Rose, you were my best friend in those days. Why did things change? Why did you go away and leave me?" She waited for a response, but all she heard was the cold, gentle water lapping against the shore.

She estimated that it was about a mile to the other side of the lake, a piece of cake.

Revitalized after her swim, Ellie walked up from the lake and saw that the bread truck was parked in front of the cabin. Tiny was back. She sighed in relief.

A fresh bouquet of wild bachelor buttons in a glass jar was on the table. Tiny had washed the dishes and cleaned up the spilled coffee and broken cup from the floor. He sat at the table playing his harmonica. The cabin danced to the homey strains of "Wildwood Flower," always his opening number.

"Where have you been? I've been worried about you." Tiny tapped his harmonica against the palm of his hand.

"Those should have been my lines. Where were you?" She asked, trying to make her voice sound casual. The swim had tempered her anger.

"I'm sorry, Ellie. I got into a game with some old codgers down at the bait store, and you know how it is." He shrugged his shoulders. "But I parlayed that money you gave me back into a thousand. He seemed proud of his accomplishment and wanting of her praise, like a child. "Do you like your flowers?" He looked genuinely contrite.

She hesitated before saying anything. "Bringing gifts can't fix everything."

"I wanted to bring you something," Tiny said.

"Why didn't you just call? You only think of yourself." She regretted the words before they had left her mouth. She sounded just like Louise.

"There's no phone in the cabin, remember?"

"Well, it isn't exactly polite to go off and leave somebody for almost three days and not let them know where you are. You could have driven back and told me. Did you find out any information about the sheriff?" She wanted to be done with the argument and change the subject.

"Well, the guys around here don't know nothin'. So, no news is good news, right? I called Clois Pierce." He looked at his watch. "If anybody knows anything about Dover, he will. Clois is my attorney and friend of many years. I told him we'd meet him in Murray for lunch. Let's check out of here and hit the road."

Ellie sat on the passenger side of the truck, waiting for Tiny to pay and turn in the key. The red sofa felt heavy and hot against her legs and back. It would feel so good to be back in the middle of the lake. She reached over and stubbed out a cigar that Tiny had left smoldering in the ashtray.

Even the cigars he smoked were filled with intrigue. They had been outlawed for five years now, since President Kennedy had placed an embargo on Cuban goods. Tiny had explained that the Corona was the finest Havana made. The wrapper leaf, the *cohiba,* was grown on a plantation called El Corojo, near Havana. It was known as the world's best tobacco farm. The cigars had been hand made by generations of families, men and women who considered it a great honor to sit for hours, trance-like, and roll the exotic cigars. Tiny said he had seen them being wrapped there. He said he paid fifty dollars a cigar on the black market to keep up with his habit. Ellie had observed that he smoked about three a day, sometimes four. And he generously passed them out to friends. He always seemed to have money for smokes, win or lose at cards. He confided in her that there were three places on his route where he could pick up the precious contraband.

Tiny looked tired when he came back and climbed into the driver's seat—probably hadn't slept in the last two days. At least he had shaved. She should have offered to drive but last night's storm, her dream, worrying about Tiny, and the long swim across the lake had worn her out. She wanted a nap.

Bunny broke the peaceful lull over the lake, rudely awakening a gaggle of geese from their midday nap. Honking their disapproval, they walked gingerly across the gravel road and back down to the water.

CHAPTER 18

▼

Murray was a peaceful town in the summer. Most of the college students were gone and wouldn't return for fall term for another week. The central square, lined with big oak trees, was deserted.

Tiny parked the truck in front of Rusty's Café, a no-nonsense big room with large, Formica-topped tables. Every table was filled with old-timers who lunched every day on the sixty-nine cent plate special and caught up on the gossip of the day. The ashtrays on all the tables were crammed with cigarette butts. People smoked between bites of food, blowing out smoke even as they chewed.

"You come here often?" Ellie made a face and held her nose.

"Yep, whenever I come to see Clois. It's still the cheapest place in town and the best," Tiny said. "What? You don't want to go in?" He sounded impatient.

"The heart of tobacco country. Everybody feels it's their patriotic duty to smoke, but I don't know if I'll be able to stand it in there. Why don't you go and talk to Pierce, and I'll meet you later over at the hamburger place around the corner?"

"Please go with me. I want you to meet Clois; he's an interesting old gentleman. I've always wanted him to meet you." Tiny sounded proud of her and disappointed that she didn't want to go inside.

"Okay. I'll hold my breath and go for it," she sighed. "But let's not stay too long."

All eyes were on them—aliens—as they entered the thick, pungent haze and inhaled the polluted air. She gathered that strangers, especially women, were rare at the old boys' lunch club.

Tiny spotted the gaunt man sitting at one of the back tables. He was bent over a newspaper, his rheumy eyes darting rapidly over the print as if scanning for a juicy worm. He appeared to be having a conversation with himself about something he'd just read. He saw Tiny and Ellie and motioned for them to join him.

"Get the plate lunch special," the old man said by way of introduction. "You get catfish or beef, fried corn, stewed tomatoes, green beans, mashed potatoes, a dish of coleslaw, and all the hushpuppies you can eat." He took a deep drag from the cigarillo he held between thin, nicotine-stained fingers.

"Well, old boy, how are you?" Tiny greeted the fragile old man with a handshake and a pat on a bony shoulder.

"That statement, sir, is a paradox." The man peered out through thick lenses. His straggly gray goatee, yellowed by tobacco, resembled the fur-like beard sported by wild turkeys. "If I am old, how can I be a boy? I ask you, sir." The old barrister spoke with a slow drawl and a true southern eloquence, as if arguing an important case of law before a court magistrate.

"Ellie, I'd like you to meet my dear friend and lawyer of many years, Mr. Clois Pierce." Tiny made a fanfare gesture toward the wintry man as he wobbled to his feet and shook hands across the table.

"Honahed to meet you, young lady. I've heard your daddy speak highly of you."

He seemed much like the restaurant he occupied: faded and cigarette-stained, but enduring—distinguished despite his rumpled appearance. He wore a sheer cotton, short-sleeved shirt—riddled with burn holes from cigarette ashes—brown pants, and a white straw hat with a cardinal feather, the state bird of Kentucky, in the yellow hatband. His shirt pockets were stuffed with odds and ends that looked as if they'd been there forever, and the pockets of his wrinkled slacks were equally endowed with a wealth of odd data.

Tiny had explained to Ellie how Clois had gotten him out of jams over the course of many years, most recently with the IRS for income tax evasion. Tiny had a passion for cars and sported a new one every year. Last year he'd bought a Cadillac. When he pulled out a roll of hundred dollar bills to pay in cash, the car salesman became suspicious and alerted the highway patrol. While cruising down the highway a little too fast and a bit inebriated, Tiny was arrested by a state patrolman in Tennessee. He managed to con his way out of jail with some stories and a few portraits of President Jackson stealthily placed in the shirt pocket of the local sheriff. The lawman kept the money but turned him in to the tax collectors. Tiny had lost the Cadillac over in Cape Girardeau in a bet with some local geezers on which direction the birds would fly from a telephone wire.

Clois made a gesture to put out his cigarillo when he saw Ellie make a face.

"I will honah your wishes, young lady, but I will state that tobacco has been good to me. It has put food on ma table all ma life. Ya'll have to endure."

"Judging from the amount of lit cigarettes, I would have to say that you and everybody else in this room owes a lot to tobacco." She coughed.

"I have a present for you, Tiny. I hope you will enjoy it," Clois said.

He handed Tiny a pair of new dice then reconsidered and took them back and gave one die to Tiny and the other to Ellie. He seemed upset that he had only one gift to give.

"Thank you, Mr. Pierce. I'll treasure your gift," she said, smiling through the haze.

"I'll get you another when I go shopping. Do you like coffee mugs, young lady?" Clois seemed pleased.

"Why, yes. I think they are very nice."

Tiny had warned her earlier that Clois had a peculiar habit of giving strange and sometimes inappropriate gifts. He'd developed a daily habit of searching the five-and-dime for odd trinkets. His favorites seemed to be tubes of red lipstick, plastic red roses, boxes of crayons, bubble gum, cards of white mother of pearl buttons, pictures of eagles soaring over pristine landscapes, and, of course, coffee mugs—especially ones with hearts on them. The gifts were doled out randomly to all that crossed his path in the course of a day.

Tiny appeared nervous as he cautiously scanned the faces of the lunch crowd. After a brief show of interest in the newcomers, the patrons turned their attention back to their lunches.

"Dover has jurisdiction over this county. Why did you ask me to meet you here? The sheriff could walk in any minute," Tiny asked, still edgy.

"Don't worry. Dover and his deputy never eat here. They prefer to mingle with a younger crowd. That's why I chose this place. I thought ya'll might appreciate a good meal in safety."

"Thanks." Tiny didn't look totally reassured.

"No one heah would eva say shit to the sheriff if their mouths were full of it. Nobody likes him," Clois said. The old man's fingernails were long and brown with nicotine. His hands shook as he played with his unlit cigarillo.

"Just how dangerous is this man? Last time I was here, Red Foss was the sheriff of Caggway County," Tiny said.

"Well, he was, and that is a mystery yet to be solved. Red died in a hunting accident about five months ago, and first thing you know this Dover shows up and gets himself appointed to the position overnight. Just flew in out of nowhere and stepped right into Red's shoes like they were his very own. Somethin' about it wasn't quite right." Clois shook his head. "Your grapevine must not be workin' well, Tiny. Where've you been?" Clois asked.

"I been mostly workin' my southern route. I been in New Orleans and Biloxi for a good while. Have you heard anything about him comin' after me? Is he gunnin' for me?" Tiny glanced around the room again.

"Dad, you're scaring me," Ellie said.

"Sir, I will have to answer that question in the affirmative," Clois said. "Word has it that you cheated him at cards and stole his vehicle. If there is truth to these facts, I would say you tinkered with the wrong man. He is a mean cougar, both cunnin' and deadly. Rumor has it that he swindled money from the county treasury. Other things I can't put my finger on." Clois ran his fingers through his thin gray hair. "Several prominent men on the mayor's board of directors who opposed Dover on issues of state since his arrival have died in strange accidents. I don't want to point the finger prematurely, but I have my suspicions."

"You don't think he killed them do you?" Ellie didn't like this conversation. Tiny was frowning.

"Like I say, I don't know. I just have a feelin' about him. I know for a fact that he whooped the life out of a poor old Negra man for loitering on the street in front of the courthouse. Took him to jail and beat him like a drum. No one knows for sure what happened to the poor old pud." Clois took a deep breath. "And this man Dover does not eat peanuts. He likes cashews. Got himself a fancy house out on the outskirts of town with some expensive stuff in it. Drives around in fancy cars and sports some fancy duds. Prides himself in always wearing fancy shoes and boots."

"He's spreadin' the rumor around that I cheated him at cards? The sonofabitch cheated me. And when I caught him in the act, I was afraid I wasn't gettin' out of there in one piece, so I drugged him and stole his truck," Tiny said.

The old man's energy was obviously flagging now. His body began to quiver noticeably. He hugged himself as if he were cold, even though the air-conditioning was minimal inside the café. Tiny had warned Ellie that the old man cycled through periods of profound lucidity to extreme confusion and that he may decide to get up and leave suddenly in the middle of a conversation, his usual words of farewell being "I'm workin'." When Tiny once asked him what kind of work he was doing, Clois had answered without hesitation: "Why, sir, I am workin' to get up in the morning, workin' to drive the car, workin' to eat lunch, workin' to shop for gifts, all my life I've been workin'."

Clois turned his attention to Ellie. "Young lady, I am a recoverin' alcoholic. I have been soba' now for thirteen yeahs." The lifelong overindulgence in the local moonshine and old age had obviously taken its toll.

"Well, sir, that's quite a feat. You must be proud of yourself," she said. Tiny had told her that Clois sometimes attended five AA meetings a day. Tiny had sat in on a few with Clois. He would take the floor, thinking he was in a courtroom, and deliver great oratorical speeches to the detriment of the reason for meeting and the time schedule. He would be before a jury arguing a vital defense when several of the members would be surfeited with his eloquent nonsense and escort him to his seat or out to his car.

"Strike first, before this scoundrel attacks." The old man rallied, shaking his head. "Hunt him down like a dog. Familiarize yourself with his intimate habits. Know his fears and his pleasures. What food he prefers to eat, where his favorite haunts are. Attune your senses to his, and enter into his territory. Become one with the jackal. This is your only hope of subduing the enemy."

The man rose on shaky legs to a surprising height of six feet, his face a mask of confusion. Wearing a pair of brand-new loafers, he stood on one foot and then the other, mimicking the blue herons that Ellie so loved at Kentucky Lake.

"Are you leaving?" she asked, not wanting him to go. She liked this man. Tiny seemed to attract lovable, rare birds. The people she knew seemed so ordinary compared to Tiny's confidantes. She'd always been a loner. Rose had been her only real friend.

"I'm workin'. This eagle must soar," Clois said with shaky voice. He looked around the room and flapped his arms in the air as his dry hollow bones took flight, creating a slight breeze in the smoke-filled room. Ellie lifted her hand in a goodbye wave, but he didn't look back.

CHAPTER 19

▼

Bunny turned off Magnolia Street onto Willow Lane, a gravel road that runs along the levee two hundred feet above the Ohio River in Wycliffe, Kentucky. Unpainted wooden shanties lined each side of the road. Weathered gray by the humid river air, they'd been mended piecemeal with odds and ends of cardboard and tar paper in an attempt to firm up their tenuous hold on the earth.

On a nearby porch, six children clad only in white underpants, despite the chilly morning air, played on an old sofa covered in frayed gold brocade. When they saw the Bunny Bread truck, they jumped up and ran inside, screaming for their mama.

Tiny stopped the truck in front of a house partially hidden from the street by blackberry vines—a rhythmic tangle of ochre, reds, greens, and umber against a white fence. The vegetation reminded Ellie of a Jackson Pollack painting.

Yesterday's conversation with Clois had alerted Ellie and Tiny to Dover's capacity for revenge. They wanted to put distance between the sheriff and themselves, but Tiny had been badly in need of sleep after his three-day poker session. They had rented two motel rooms last night near Wycliffe. Now Tiny wanted to talk with Junior, the moonshine man, about Dover before moving on. He had said if anybody knew what the sheriff was up to, Junior would.

Junior's shack stood proud and defiant against the notions of time and wind. Next door, an old, toothless woman dressed in a flowered house-dress with a colorful bandana wrapped around her head sat on the porch in a faded wicker rocker. The old woman rocked and chewed tobacco, spitting out the dark, liquid cud onto the ground. After she spat, she took a big drink of something wrapped in a brown bag, puckered her lips, squinted her eyes, shook her head from side to side, and uttered the words, "Oh Lordy, Lordy."

"We're in luck. Junior's here," Tiny said. A straight-backed cane chair stood on the porch. "If he ain't here or if he runs outta' moonshine, he jams that chair up under the doorknob to let people know not to stop. Sometimes he puts the chair there as a warnin' that the law is watchin'."

"Junior's older brother, Ben, did the bootlegging back in my school days at Murray State." It seemed so long ago—ten years. "Does he still sell it in quart canning jars?" Ellie asked.

"Yeah, that's right. You used to drink that stuff?" Tiny asked.

"I never said I drank it. I just came over and bought it with some of my dorm buddies." Her tastes, even then, were more sophisticated: martinis and scotch. She had only sampled moonshine a few times. "It tasted like burning kerosene. I couldn't swallow it—spat it out." Rumor had it that people went blind on occasion from drinking it. Ellie recalled the wild bashes that were thrown on weekends. The parched roads of the dry county became rivers of white lightening, with young adults rebelling against the inheritance of a repressed nonalcoholic, non-dancing, strict Baptist environment. She'd always been a loner, but she'd gone to a few parties with her roommates. She remembered one night drinking Cutty Sark with an Ag major who had a deep drawl and adorable dimples. They had jitterbugged and joined in on the snaking line of the Bunny Hop at Mama Frogs, a nightclub just over the Kentucky/Tennessee line. Ellie had found herself the next morning in the middle of a lumpy bed in The Dew Drop Inn hung over and alone. She'd had to call her roommate, Pearl, to come and get her. She carefully avoided the agricultural building on cam-pus after that and never saw the boy again. Her first and only one-night-stand.

A face framed itself in the front window for a second. The door opened, and a tall, thin man the color of cocoa stepped out onto the front porch, shading his eyes from the intense morning light.

"Tiny, pull around in the back." He waved Tiny into a lean-to. The house and addendum joined in a symbiotic, united front against final collapse. "What are you doin', Tiny? You oughta know better than to be comin' here. What's wrong with you, man?" His eyes smoldered with anger. He looked up and down the levee, and then his mood changed suddenly and he let out an infectious, musical laugh. "You sure are a sight for sore eyes with your fat self in that bread truck. I heard you were on the lam from the sheriff, but you could've picked a better disguise than a bread delivery boy. Un uh, nobody's ever gonna recognize you with that disguise." He laughed at his own irony.

"Junior, this is my daughter, Ellie," Tiny said.

They stood on the levee behind Junior's house, about a hundred yards above the river, on an embankment covered in blackberry vines, tall weeds, and kudzu. The locusts were warming up with increasing crescendo as the sun rose higher. The Ohio River rolled by, clear and blue, inviting Ellie to climb down the embankment and dive in.

"Nice to meet you." Junior shook her hand hesitantly. "I didn't mean to be rude back there, but Dover's been comin' by here checkin' on me double time lately, and I don't want him thinkin' we're in cahoots. I already got enough trouble with him."

She nodded. "I understand. Nice to meet you. Your reputation precedes you. I hear you sell the best moonshine around." Ellie felt uneasy, anxious to get on the road and be out of the sheriff's jurisdiction.

"Junior, I don't want to cause you any trouble. We'll just go on and get out of your hair." Tiny walked back toward the house and lean-to where the truck was parked.

"I wish I had some hooch to give ya, but I just sold the tail end of it to a college boy from Murray State. School hasn't even started yet, and I can't keep up with the demand. Man, those college kids sure do party. I wonder if their folks know what they do with their money over there at that school," Junior said. "Tiny, you wouldn't be goin' down to Tennessee, would ya?"

"Yeah, we're goin' down through that good state eventually. What can I do for you?" Tiny sounded relieved that he could be of help.

"'Fraid to go down to my daddy's for this week's pickup. I'm supposed to run some hooch down to Memphis for him, but Dover's got that fool deputy of his tailin' me. I'm afraid he'll find out where my daddy makes his moonshine. Dover'd really have us by the balls then."

"He's got his deputy spyin' on ya?" Tiny shook his head in disbelief.

"I'm tellin' ya, that sheriff is mean and up to no good. He used to come by every other week for his payola like Red Foss, the old sheriff, did. And that was okay. I expect to pay somethin' for the law allowin' me to operate. But this guy has upped the ante." He pulled a red bandana out of his pocket and wiped his forehead. "He comes by every weekend and sometimes in the middle of the week, wantin' more money. He's bleedin' me dry."

"Sorry man," Tiny shook his head.

"And that wild Indian deputy of his thinks I don't know who he is, drivin' around all hours of the day and night in the sheriff's Firebird. He looks like some crazy wild bird, drivin' around with the top down in that red muscle machine—thinks I'm too dumb to recognize the car." Junior took a deep breath and went on with his complaints. "Everybody around here knows what the sheriff drives. He's always botherin' somebody bout somethin'."

"I'll do what I can to help out," Tiny said. He gave Ellie a worried glance.

"My cousins tell me he's been cruising by while I'm not here, too," Junior was not finished unburdening himself. "They use this place to practice music. They got a great R and B band goin'—gettin' gigs all over the place. They got one tonight over in Cairo at The Tide Club. It's bad over there, too, for us Negroes. We gotta watch our backs all the time with those White Hats tryin' to kill us."

"I'm sorry to hear that, man." Tiny shook his head again. He looked anxious to leave. "Well, we'll go on now and get out of your hair. How am I gonna find your daddy?" he asked, chewing vigorously on his cigar stub.

"Come on in the house a minute. I'll draw you a map. Tear it up when you're done with it. I don't want anybody knowin' his whereabouts."

They walked through the back door and into the kitchen. The failing structure groaned under the collected weight.

"It's not hard to find if you know your landmarks." Junior drew the map on a clean cocktail napkin that bore the name The Tide Club on it and handed it to Tiny.

The phone rang, and Junior went into the living room to answer.

"Hey, man, talk to me, what's—holy shit! Dover just pulled up out in front."

From the kitchen, Ellie caught a glimpse of a brand new black truck with the word SHERIFF painted on the side in big gold letters. The truck was a clone of the stolen one. Junior hung up the phone abruptly and ran back into the kitchen.

"Quick. Down here," Junior said breathlessly. He dragged the kitchen table about six feet across the floor, pulled back a heavy, worn floral rug, and lifted a wooden lid that was flat with the floor, revealing a ladder leading down into a tunnel. "Get down there—it takes you down to the river. There's an old duck blind down there—hide. Go see Daddy," he whispered. "I'll signal you when the coast is clear."

With pounding heart, Ellie climbed down the ladder. Junior pushed and kneaded Tiny like freshly risen dough until he was stuffed through the opening. She shuddered as she heard the muffled sound of the lid being pulled into place and the table dragged back across the floor.

Ellie had heard about these houses on the levee. History lived within the frail, decaying framework of Junior's moonshine shack. It had been used as a stop on the Underground Railroad. The tunnel led escaping slaves down to the Ohio River where they had been taken across the water to Illinois, supposedly to freedom. Few attempts had been successful.

*   *   *   *

"Junior. You in there, boy? Hows it goin'?" Dover's tone was conde-scending. He knew that Junior and his brothers had all spent a year in a colored college down in Mississippi and were a far cry better educated than he was. It galled him. And more so that Junior played the ignorant Negro act for the sheriff, shuffling his feet and flashing him a big grin full of white teeth.

"I'm fine, Mr. Dover. How's it goin' with you, boss? I'm outta' liquor, and I's about to close and go home. I knows you don't want money, 'cause I gave it all to you yesterday." He avoided meeting Dover's eyes.

"Oh, I just come by to say hello. See how ya'll are doin'. Mind if I come in?" He pushed past Junior and opened the screened door. The old, weath-ered boards of the porch moaned under the heavy, determined tread of his boots.

With great deliberation, as if gathering evidence at a crime scene, Dover inspected the musical instruments that Junior's cousins had left in the liv-ing room: steel guitar, drums, acoustic bass, and trumpet. He walked back through the kitchen and went out the back door. Junior followed him. The hairs on Dover's arms and neck stood at attention when he saw the Bunny Bread truck in the lean-to. He walked over to inspect it, sniffing the air like a bloodhound.

"Cigars!" he said accusingly. "Smell's like Tiny's brand." He opened the truck and found a cigar stub in the ashtray. A half-empty wooden box of the elegant smokers lay on the front seat.

"Don't shit me, boy. These are Tiny's cigars. Where the hell is he?" He grabbed Junior by the front of his shirt and twisted the cotton in a knot, tight around his throat.

"What the hell you talkin' 'bout? I ain't seen Tiny for months. Those cigars belong to my cousins. They bought this truck to haul their instru-ments around in to their gigs." Junior rolled his eyes, faking innocence.

"How the hell can yur jigaboo cousins afford Cuban cigars?" Dover's neck was ticking like a time bomb.

"Well, sir, they doin' real good with their music. They be cuttin' a record soon, make lots a money," Junior said, choking from Dover's stranglehold. He doubled up his fists, but Dover knew he wouldn't risk a death sentence by hitting the sheriff.

"Where's your cousins now?" Dover was angry and disappointed that the truck hadn't revealed more evidence leading to Tiny.

"Oh they's all went home, Mr. Dover. But they be back to load up pretty soon. They got a gig over in Cairo tonight."

"Well, sorry 'bout that," Dover said. His hands didn't want to let go their death grip, but he thought it would serve no purpose to kill Junior. He made a conciliatory gesture of smoothing out the twist in Junior's shirt. "That fat man sure knows how to ruffle my feathers. If you see him, let me know. Ya'll hear? You take care now." Dover did an about turn, spitting on the living room floor as he left.

He got in his truck and pulled down the road, just out of sight of Junior's shack. His plan was to wait until the cousins came to verify that Junior wasn't lying about the truck being theirs. When the truck became a steamy sauna, he got out and paced the levee. He became distracted temporarily by the thought of downing a cold beer over at Ma Pritchett's, but then the thought of Tiny brought him back to purpose. He would stay there until hell froze over if it provided any clues to Tiny's whereabouts.

*   *   *   *

Ellie felt her way forward in the dark, narrow, and damp passageway, recoiling at the touch of the slimy earth that felt like dead, cold flesh. Air was scarce. Tiny groaned as he struggled to squeeze his body forward through the constricted area. His belabored breath on the back of her neck made Ellie's fine hairs stand on end. She felt trapped by the unknown ahead and the heaviness of Tiny behind. Her heart pounded with a claustrophobic fear as she descended the obscure canal that led toward an uncertain birth. She'd had this feeling before, but couldn't remember when. All of her weight condensed and pooled in her knees, pulling her toward the earth. At the same time a phantom, weightless, feather-in-the-wind part of her that she reached out for in her dreams but could never grasp was released from gravity's relentless laws. She sighed with relief as she flew away.

Owl: *Soaring through a soft blue sky, gliding on an updraft through the clouds, estuary and river beneath our wings. We are free.*

The path gradually slanted downward, becoming wetter as they arrived at flat land. Ellie observed the situation, detached from thoughts and sensations as if it were happening to someone else, as if she were a visitor in her own body. She could hear the river nearby. A concrete, circular barrier at the end of the tunnel blocked the entrance. She pushed on it but it didn't move. Tiny managed to squeeze past as she flattened herself as best she could against the wall. He leaned into the barrier and pushed hard. The barricade slowly forced down a bramble of blackberries that grew over the entrance.

Disoriented, she felt as if she'd been somewhere far away. The bright sunlight hurt her eyes. Sucking in the fresh river air, she struggled through the berry vines, scratching her arms and legs on thorns. With Tiny panting and groaning behind her, they forged a path through the tangle down near the water's edge where tall reeds grew and drooping branches of willows reached out over gently flowing water. The incessant, harsh sawing of the locusts was deafening.

The duck blind was well hidden by berry vines; only the open front facing the river was visible. They crawled in on hands and knees over prickly thorns, sweating and out of breath from the hasty retreat.

Her mouth and throat were parched. The pain in her arms and legs where the brambles had ripped the skin brought her back to herself. She'd been terrified and claustrophobic in the tunnel—and not just because of Dover. It had something to do with being in a tight place with Tiny. That was what had triggered the fear. But why? He'd protect her, wouldn't he? That's what fathers do. She felt herself both audience and actress in a play with a treacherous plot. What was Tiny's role? What had caused such terror? And now the performance continues: a dubious reality, a dream within a dream?

They sat in the cramped shelter of the duck blind catching their breaths, watching the inviting water of the Ohio River roll by, for what seemed an eternity.

"The sun must be directly overhead by now, close to noon." Her voice sounded muffled by the screech of the locusts. She hunched down to peer through the cracks of the boards in the back wall to see if there was any sign of Dover or a signal from Junior. Tiny was moaning softly from the physical effort. "Guess we need to stay here for a while," she whispered. It was hard to move in the rickety structure smashed up against Tiny's sweaty flesh. She fought back the feeling of terror by taking deep breaths. She was afraid that, if they tried to move, the old boards would fall apart, exposing them in broad daylight. Horseflies had made an important discovery. They buzzed around the bloody scratches and sweaty skin, occasionally nipping bites of flesh. The sky was a blinding hard blue over the water. Eddies of swirling water, like pockets of subtle new dimensions of space, caught the noonday sun and created fluorescent sprinkles of blinding white light. She wanted to throw her thirsty, throbbing body into the cool water and disappear down one of the miniature whirlpools, like Alice in Wonderland.

"Dad, are you all right? You haven't said a word." She forced herself to speak despite the panic that was again rising in her chest. "Maybe I should swim across to Cairo and call Vigil. What do you think?" She fought the overwhelming urge to jump into the water. It wasn't a good idea to leave Tiny alone. He was still having trouble breathing in the hot, cramped space, and he'd never learned how to swim.

"I think we better stay put until we get a sign from Junior that the coast is clear," Tiny said in a hoarse whisper.

"Dover!" she hissed. The sheriff was pacing back and forth on the levee, occasionally hitching up his pants as if they were too big for him. He stopped and looked out toward the water. Ellie recoiled and then ventured another peek. He took off his hat and wiped his face and head with a white handkerchief. This put an end to any thought of swimming across the river.

"Don't move," she whispered. "He's looking down this way." They sat silent, instinctively holding their breath, as if Dover could hear them above the sounds of the locusts.

"We better just sit here and ride it out till we get a sign from Junior. I don't want to get him in more trouble 'cause of us. He's a good man and so's his daddy, Clarence. I've known Junior ever since he was born," Tiny whispered. "What's Dover doin' now?"

"I don't see him. Maybe he's gone," she said, more nervous because he was out of sight.

Their voices fell silent as the dry shrieks of the locusts, accompanied by the quacking of a flock of ducks, filled the day. The soft sound of the water, like brushes on a drum, provided a subtle background rhythm. The sounds lulled her into a more relaxed, almost drowsy state. Tiny was snoring.

The afternoon was on the wane when Tiny woke up and started singing low, just above a whisper.

"I'll get a line, you get a pole, honey. I'll get a line, you get a pole, babe."

Ellie joined in softly. "Meet you down at the crawdad hole, honey, oh baby mine." She felt a sudden warmth and kindness toward her father. The earlier feeling of panic had passed. Maybe it was the shared status as fugitives that brought on this feeling of camaraderie, maybe the shared song, or both.

"Swing low, sweet chariot, coming for to carry me home." Their voices sounded sweet as the sound floated out over the rippling water and mingled with the songs of nature. They warbled their way through the late afternoon, exhausting their repertoire. Her throat ached with thirst, and her legs had gone numb. She could only imagine how Tiny must feel. He hadn't complained.

The sun had come around and was directly in front of them now, low in the sky. No sign of Dover. The willows along the bank filtered the pink rays of the setting sun through their lacy, weeping branches. Ellie watched the river swallow up the sun and leave traces of gold on the water's surface near the distant Illinois shore. Then the far shoreline became one with the water and sky as night descended. The horseflies went off duty, and the mosquitoes came out to do damage with vigor. The locusts had mercifully abandoned the river stage with the setting sun. The soft croaking of frogs was the starring sound of the night river dance. Tiny and Ellie had finished their third round of "Shine on, Harvest Moon" and stopped singing to listen to the frogs, now joined by crickets. When the fireflies started flickering golden lights, the duo sang a chorus of "Shine Little Glow Worm, Glimmer, Glimmer."

The frogs and crickets stopped singing. Tiny nudged Ellie and put a finger to his lips, warning her not to speak. They heard footsteps rustling in the tall grass. A young colored man appeared from downstream, crouching in the tall grasses. He motioned for them to crawl out and stay low to the ground. Like a grateful banner, Ellie unfurled herself and stood, stretching arms and legs as best she could in a hunched position. Tiny moaned as the man helped him to his feet.

"Are you all right?" he asked.

"Yeah, I'll make it. Just wish I had a cigar," Tiny said.

"I'm Willie, Junior's cousin. He called me and told me to come fetch you when the coast was clear." He shook Tiny's hand and nodded to Ellie. "That cranky-assed sheriff is some piece of work, ain't he? Sat out there in his truck half the day, bakin' in the sun. I got a boat a little ways downstream—bread truck's in Cairo. We'll row 'cross and fetch it."

They tromped through the vines and high grasses close to shore, the beam of Willie's flashlight leading the way, until they came to a rowboat pulled up and hidden in the weeds. Willie reached in and retrieved a water flask and handed it to Ellie. She thought the cool drink of water was all she'd ever need again—she'd never complain about anything ever again—as she felt the sweet liquid slide down her dry throat. She wanted to gulp it all down but restrained herself and handed it to Tiny. She watched as he drank. The ordeal had been hard on the big man.

"Well, it ain't moonshine, but it's the next best thing," Tiny said, handing the flask back to her, winking.

Willie pushed the boat back into the water and motioned for her to get in first. He looked back doubtfully at Tiny and shook his head.

"I'm gonna have to make two trips here. We're not gonna fit all of us in," Willie said.

"I'll swim across." Ellie stood up and peeled down to her underwear, wadded up her clothes, and threw them into the boat. She dove in and felt her parched skin plump out like a sponge in the cool, blissful water, a balm for her cramped muscles, scratches, and mosquito bites.

"I'll stay close to the boat. See you over in Cairo," she said. "I've wanted to do this all day." A gibbous moon adorned the sky and lighted the water in sparkles of silver. She felt free and present in her body like she hadn't remembered ever feeling. Maybe a little underhanded adventure was just what she'd needed. She'd forgotten the incident in the tunnel earlier, when she had become frightened and lost track of time. The boat rode low in the water as Willie labored over the oars, rowing toward the point of land that was Cairo.

An old Dodge Desoto was backed into the boat ramp down on the River road. Two men waited on the shore and blinked a flashlight on and off three times to indicate the coast was clear. One of them saw Ellie in the water and went to the car and brought back a towel. The night had taken on a chill and her teeth chattered. She retrieved her clothes from the boat and stepped behind a tree to change, feeling cleansed and baptized by the water.

"This here's Buster and Marvin. We're all Junior's cousins. We gonna drive you to your truck," Willie said.

They backed the trailer down to the water and loaded the boat, laughing as Marvin related the story about driving away in the Bunny Bread truck with the jingle playing.

"We passed Dover. We was puffin' on those cigars and wavin' out the window to him. He followed us as far as the Cairo Bridge and turned around. The only problem is now I'm addicted to these expensive cigars. Where you get these, man? They ain't even legal." Willie laughed as he passed the box to Tiny. There were two cigars left.

"Take them. I'll send you some more. Small reward for savin' us from Dover." Then, not being able to resist the temptation, Tiny took out the next to the last cigar for himself and lit up.

An unlikely crew, they pulled up behind The Tide Club on First and Commercial in downtown Cairo.

"We'd invite you in to hear us play, but it's probably not a good idea for us to be associated with such notorious outlaws. And besides, no white folk is allowed in there." Willie laughed, but his voice held concern. "You two be careful now. Don't let that sheriff catch ya. Ya'll be hearin' us on the radio soon," he said proudly, as Ellie and Tiny shook hands all around. In the fresh, cool night, Bunny sang his goodbyes as the truck pulled out of the parking lot, headed east back over the bridge and into Kentucky.

CHAPTER 20

▼

Clois's Chevy Super Sport sedan was perched in the parking lot of Buster's Barbecue Restaurant with motor running, its exotic plumage fluffed in anticipation of sudden flight. It was easy for Dover to spot the car by its distinctive markings, crested with a white stripe of paint that ran over the hood and top and down the back door of the trunk. Dover knew that Clois had marked the car in this peculiar fashion so it could be spotted easily. Due to his failing eyesight and frequent bouts of confusion, the old man spent endless hours searching parking lots and side streets for his glaring red vehicle. The white stripe hadn't helped all that much. He had reported it stolen three times in the last month, only to have the sheriff find it in the exact spot where Clois had left it. He'd cried wolf so many times that Dover stopped responding to his calls of distress. Now Dover noticed with irritation, there were still no license plates on the car.

The parking lot was full. Buster's was a popular place for lunch for those who didn't mind driving the few miles outside of town into the pastoral countryside of western Kentucky. Under normal circumstances the aroma of pork roasting over a hickory wood fire wafting out into the bright September day would set the sheriff's mouth to watering. But these weren't normal circumstances. Ever since the incident with Tiny, Dover had lost his appetite. The barbecue smelled like burning rubber tires to him.

Dover had learned of Clois's meeting yesterday with Tiny at Rusty's Café. He had telephoned Clois at his home, a feat that, in itself, was not easy. He knew the old man rarely answered the phone. A friend of Clois's told Dover that Clois had been plagued by unwanted phone calls for the last several years from imaginary dead relatives attempting to lay claim to the family fortune. They would whisper to him in haggard voices, entreating him to give up the gold, that the inheritance he would receive when his hundred and two-year-old mother died belonged to them. These intrusions on his sanity happened with such frequency that Clois had stopped answering his phone. Dover had caught Clois in a rare moment of clarity that morning, and they made a date to meet at Buster's for lunch. Dover had invited Clois to lunch in a friendly manner, not wanting the man to suspect that he was hoping to get some information about what Tiny was doing in Murray, and where the hell he was now.

Clois was in the car with all the windows rolled down. The radio was tuned, full volume, to WSM from Nashville. The resonant, baritone voice of Johnny Cash blasted out in duet with the nasal, spicy whine of June Carter on their latest hit, "Jackson."

Dover was late for the meeting. He'd gotten tied up at the jailhouse. He wasn't sure the old man would even remember to come and was surprised to see him sitting in the car in the hot noonday sun with the engine running instead of cooling his heels in the air-conditioned restaurant.

"Hello, Mr. Pierce." Dover ambled over to the car. He'd worn his uniform today, mostly to look intimidating. The stupid bitch had put too much starch in his collar again; his neck itched. He bent down to look in the window, trying not to sound irritated.

"How ya'll today, sir?" The old man seemed to be unaware of Dover's presence. He sat with his head back and eyes closed.

"I said hello, Mr. Pierce," Dover repeated in a louder, slightly annoyed tone of voice. He didn't know whether the old possum was playing dead with him or fading in and out of one of his authentic spells. He reached across Clois and turned off the blaring radio. "Hello, Mr. Pierce," he said even louder.

The old man opened his eyes and looked at Dover vacantly.

"Do ya'll know who I am, Mr. Pierce?" Dover waved a hand in front of the dazed man's face. He didn't have time for any of the stupid old fart's games.

"Do I know who you are? Do I know who you are, sir?" Clois came to full attention. He seemed poised to launch into one of his long, nonsensical, eloquent speeches. "Why yes, sir, I remember who you are. You are the sonofabitch who has kept me waiting out here for the last half hour." He looked at his watch with a frown on his face. "I'm a busy man. I have important things to do. I can't sit around here all day playin' with myself, waitin' for you. I've got bigger fish to fry," Clois said importantly. "I'm workin'."

"Would ya'll like to go in and have some lunch?" Dover asked, trying to control his temper. He could feel his face flush with a seething heat.

"Hell, no. I don't wanna have lunch. I'm workin'. I've got to go now." Clois put the car in reverse and started backing out of the parking lot with Dover's head still planted inside the window.

The motion caught Dover by surprise. "Hold on there, Mr. Pierce. I just want to talk to you a minute." He was close to the boiling point. Clois had turned the radio back up to full volume, and Dover was shouting above the voices of The Dillards' eulogy to Old Blue. When the old man put the car in forward motion, Dover ducked his head out of the window. He ran back to the truck, still dizzy from the sudden movement. Clois pulled out on the road into the path of a farmer on a slow-moving tractor. The tractor swerved barely in time to avoid a collision. Dover was in pursuit not far behind the runaway car. Clois sped up. He swerved all over the road like a man drunk on the local hooch.

"Stupid ol' fool. I oughta throw his ass in jail and teach him a lesson."

Dover put on his siren and overhead flashing light. Clois ignored the sheriff's entreaty to pull over until Dover ran him off the road and into a deserted cornfield.

Dover got out of the truck and walked over to the vehicle slowly, to gain composure. He scratched at the rash on his twitching neck. A murder of crows was eating the remaining dried kernels of corn from dried stalks in the field. They squawked their apparent anger at the disruption of their noonday meal, flapping their wings aggressively at the intruders as they flew over to perch on a bridge railing. The motor was still running, and the radio was blaring. Dover reached in through the window and turned off the engine. He yanked the keys out of the ignition to avoid another premature getaway and put them in his shirt pocket.

"I just wanna ask ya'll a few questions." He was trying hard to control himself. "I'm not gonna give you a citation for your reckless drivin' if you cooperate with me here. And, by the way, this is your third warnin' about those license plates. You just cooperate and we'll be all right, fair and square, ya'll hear?" He winked at the gentleman, as if to reassure him. He wanted to put his hands around the old geezer's neck and squeeze hard. "I just wanna know if ya'll seen your client Tiny Moon lately. Do ya'll know where he's been keepin' hisself these days? I just got a little business with him is all."

The old man looked blank. A veil of fog had lowered in front of his face. The curtain was going down on this play, either by deliberate device or organic deterioration. Clois reached for his briefcase sitting in the passenger seat amidst a muddle of clutter. He opened the decrepit leather satchel that was held together with duct tape and fumbled with something inside. He looked indecisive and then smiled as though he had made a momentous decision. Dover nervously eyed the briefcase, hand on his gun ready for action.

Clois took something out. He handed Dover a tube of lipstick. "I give you a gift, good sir, as a gesture of our friendship," Clois said smiling.

"Don't play with me, old boy." Dover felt the blood pounding in his head. He took the lid off the lipstick and reached in the window opening and smeared the glossy red grease all over Clois's face. "Where is he? Where's Tiny Moon? Ya stupid old cocksucker." Dover's tic was out of control, directing his head back and forth in jerky spasms. Sweat dripped from his forehead into his eyes, stinging and blurring his vision.

"I don't know, Dover. I don't know." The man shook his head in rhythm with Dover's head. "Ya'll know that I had a nervous breakdown, and I don't remember anything. My memory slipped away slicker than snot on a frozen pond."

Dover grabbed the old man by his shirt, causing an assortment of objects and bits and pieces of paper to fall from the pockets. "Git outta the car. I oughta arrest you for reckless drivin' and impedin' an investigation." The old man felt weightless in Dover's hands as he pulled Clois out of the car and forced him to his full height. The frail, light bones were no match against the powerful and invective wrath of the sheriff.

"Ain't ya'll seen him? You're his advisor, ain't ya'll? Ya'll ain't advised him lately?" Dover hissed. He felt saliva forming at the corners of his lips. He had his hands around Clois's throat and was putting pressure on the old man's Adam's apple.

"Auk—why, yes," Clois choked. "I advised him. Yes, I certainly did."

Dover loosened his hold on the man's throat. "Now we're gettin' somewhere. What'd ya'll say to him?" Dover's hands were shaking. Clois hesitated for a moment and shook his head to clear his thoughts. "I told him to push away. Yes, I told him to just push away from the table." He thought about his response, weighing his words carefully. He seemed satisfied with his response. "Yes, that is what I told him."

"What the hell does that mean?" Dover shouted.

"I advised him to push away from the table, so as to reduce his corpulence. The man is fat because he eats too much." It sounded like a confession of the first order. "Would you not agree, sir?"

Dover's face flushed purple with rage. His hands shook uncontrollably as he resumed his chokehold. The old man gasped for air. Dover knew he was losing control, but he couldn't stop himself.

"Ya'll better be straight with me, old man, or ya'll be sorry. I'll teach ya to mess with me. I'm onto ya'll's helpless senile tricks." Dover shook Clois like a rag doll. Something snapped, and the sheriff felt the fragile old man go limp in his hands. Clois crumpled like a jointed cardboard puppet on a string, his head lolling to the side. *Holy shit! I broke his neck.* Dover felt for a pulse but could detect none. He put the limp body back in the driver's seat and took out his handkerchief to wipe off the lipstick from Clois' face as best he could.

"Damn, if I ain't done it now. Killed the old peckerhead." He went back to his truck and retrieved a brown bag that concealed a pint of Black

Velvet whiskey from the glove compartment. He kept it handy for emergencies of all kinds, as a backup, in case Junior ran out of moonshine. Taking a big gulp, he raced back to Clois's car and poured most of the whiskey in the bottle into the dead man's mouth, watching it dribble out and down the front of Clois's shirt. Dover threw the almost empty bottle onto the passenger's seat. He leaned over the lifeless body and turned off the radio, cutting Hank Williams off in mid rendition of "Your Cheating Heart." He picked up the items off the ground that had fallen out of Clois's pockets. How'd the old fart stuff so many things into these pockets? There was a receipt from a tobacco sale from 1947, old pieces of erasers, the nub of a used pencil, worn and ragged copies of old bank account deposits, a dog-eared map of Montana, a land deed to a farm in Tennessee dated 1935, a small magnifying lens, and a crumpled picture of a young smiling beauty in a nurse's uniform with the inscription, "To C. P., I'll love you forever, Joanne."

Dover took the memorabilia of Clois's life over to his truck and stashed them in his glove compartment. He pulled his truck back up on the road, took a deep breath, and made the call to the coroner's office on his police radio that there had been a fatal accident while he was in pursuit of a reckless driver. "The man ran off of the road and into a cornfield and apparently had a heart attack or somethin'. It smells like maybe he's been drinkin'." He took out his handkerchief and wiped the sweat from his face and neck, absently forgetting that it was full of red lipstick redolent with a concentrate of cheap perfume. He stuffed the crime-laden handkerchief back into his pocket and ran down into the field to wipe away the cloying evidence with dry shucks of corn.

The indignant crows perched on the bridge railing had witnessed the crime. Eager to break their silence, they flew at Dover accusingly. He shook his fists in the air, his head and neck jerking violently, as he whirled around in circles fighting off his attackers. "Git off me, you motherfuckin' birds."

"What's goin' on here, Sheriff?" Ed Judson, the county coroner, walked over to view the spectacle in the cornfield, his face fixed with worry.

"That's Clois's car with the white stripe painted down the middle." He walked over to see his friend, limp as a dishrag, behind the driver's wheel. "That's Clois. What happened to him?" He felt for a pulse and then shook his head. "He's my best friend. We grew up together," he said with a shaking voice. He turned to face Dover. His eyes were narrow slits of accusation. "We've been best buddies since we were kids." He spat on the ground, barely missing one of Dover's well-oiled boots.

"It seems your friend was drunker than a skunk," Dover spat back at the coroner.

Ed picked up the near empty bottle of whiskey and smelled it. "Clois has been sober for thirteen years. If he was to go off the wagon, it wouldn't be with Canadian whiskey. He'd be drinkin' good old corn mash: Kentucky bourbon. I know that for a fact." Dover moved just in time to avoid another wad of spit aimed for his boots. They both looked over at Clois's still body again. He looked jaded, like an effete and weary clown with the lipstick smeared all over his face. I should have left his face alone, Dover thought.

"I don't believe your lyin' ass, Sheriff. I got my eye on you. I'll get to the bottom of this if it's the last think I do."

Dover knew that Ed Judson was suspicious about the car raffle for the children's hospital in Paducah. Dover had pocketed the money. He'd have to rectify that, put the money back in order to fix this bigger mess.

"Don't leave town, Sheriff. I'll let you know what the autopsy shows. You take care now." Ed walked back toward the coroner's van as two ambulance drivers placed the gurney with Clois's body inside.

The crows became silent as all eyes looked upward. An eagle soared higher and higher in slow circles across the hard blue sky. The graceful, outstretched wings drifted on drafts of air, dipping and rising. The bird seemed to be waving down at all below in what looked like a gesture of farewell.

CHAPTER 21

▼

The smell of Lysol assaulted Dover's nose like a blast of hot air from a furnace when he walked through the front door of the jailhouse. He'd gone straight to Ma Pritchett's last night to drink and spend the night with the ladies at Ma's establishment after yesterday's unfortunate accident concerning Clois, and the spooky encounter with the county coroner. He looked at his watch. Two hours late. He was hung over big time.

"Hey, boss. Whew. I'm glad that old-timer got sprung this morning. He was so drunk it made me woozy just breathin' the air around him. And what do you think he did? He puked all over the cell last night and then slept in it. Had to use a gallon of Lysol to get the smell out."

"I don't want to hear your sorry complainin' today." Deputy George's words and the smell of Lysol reminded Dover of his incident with Tiny at Kentucky Lake.

Dover had made George scrub the whole cabin with Lysol. He'd gone through two quarts before Dover was satisfied that it was clean.

"You're in demand today. Where you been? The phone's been ringin' off the hook."

"Who the hell called?" Dover growled.

"Ed Judson. Three times. He says to tell you they want your formal report about that accident with that crazy old man out near Buster's place. He said to tell you to call him as soon as you got in. And the mayor called. He and the city council want to set up a meeting with you—somethin' about the missing proceeds from that raffle for the children's hospital over in Paducah. The phone numbers are on your desk."

Just as he had suspected. He was in doody big time now.

"I don't need no shit today from those peckerheads!" Dover slammed the open palm of his hand down on the desk hard with a thwack. "What the hell do those bastards wanna ask me questions for? I told 'em everything they needed to know."

"I don't know, man. I'm just the messenger. And hey, I found out something you might be interested in. There's a big poker tournament down in Memphis this weekend. I bet that's where Tiny's gonna be."

"Yeah, well then that's where I'm gonna be. If those assholes call again tell 'em I'm out on a case, and I'll call 'em when I have time. Okay? I gotta go now. Cover for me, and I'll catch ya'll later." Dover went through the door, slamming it hard behind him. He jumped in his new sheriff's truck and, without a backward glance, backed out of his reserved parking spot, stepping hard on the gas pedal with total disregard for what or who might be behind him. The tic in his neck betrayed his fury as he shifted into forward gear, scorching the road as he made his getaway.

CHAPTER 22

▼

—Owl, Cairo, 1947—

The melody to "Fur Elise" ran through her head as she walked through the park, kicking up the big, fat, yellow and red leaves that had fallen from the sycamore trees. The graceful forms of the tall trees were silhouetted in charcoal against a pale blue sky, with only a few leaves left in the tops of the trees to dance in the wind. It was a cold morning. Owl could see her breath. She stopped by the big wire-domed aviary that stood in the center of the park. It had never held birds as far as Owl knew, but squirrels could always be seen playing there. She hurriedly emptied her pockets of the walnuts she had brought for them and broke into a trot, pulling the collar of her coat up around her neck and clutching her music books under her arm. She had forgotten her gloves, and her hands ached from the cold. She loved the Saturday morning piano lessons with Sister Mary Leonora. Owl looked forward all week to the hour spent alone with the nun, learning notes and playing scales. She had practiced "Fur Elise" all week on the old upright at home. It was out of tune and some of the keys were missing, but she didn't care. She would have sat all day at the piano, but Louise dragged her away after her allotted hour. Louise said she needed to do other things and be well-rounded. The sounds she could make by pressing down the keys were magical. She could express how she felt by touching the keys— in just the right way with just the right amount of pressure. She looked forward to surprising the nun today by playing the Beethoven piece by heart. She had learned the different keys with their sharps and flats easily.

Today she would finish Book Two of the *John Thompson Piano* series and begin Book Three. Sister had told her that she would be considered an intermediate student after today when she finished Book Two.

She ran up the steps and rang the bell at the front door to the Sacred Heart Parochial School. Owl hopped on one foot and then the other, blowing on her hands to stay warm until Sister Leanora arrived—a small face in a black swish of fabric—to open the massive oak door.

"Hello, Ellie," the nun whispered. The nuns always whispered when they weren't in the classrooms. The wide, long hallway that was so filled with children's voices during the week was silent except for the clicking of Sister's rosary beads and the sound of her square-heeled black shoes tapping on the marble floor. The silence seemed strained and exaggerated in contrast to the weekly hustle and bustle. The music room was sunny and warm with a large bay window facing south. Owl loved this room. It smelled of the fresh roses that were ever present before the statue of the Blessed Virgin Mary, gracing the room with their fragrance.

Owl took off her coat and laid her music books, *Hanon's The Virtuoso Pianist in Sixty Exercises* and her *John Thompson, Book Two,* on the piano stand. She gave the nun six shiny new quarters that were tied in a knot in her handkerchief: the cost of the lesson. The nun took them and smiled, tucking them somewhere inside the sleeve of her copious robe. Owl sat down to play.

"Oh, don't sit down yet, dear," Sister Leonora smiled sweetly. "I have something I want you to help me with first. Let's go down to the laundry room for a while. Sister Mary Estelle is sick today, and I promised I would make sure the altar clothes were ironed for Mass tomorrow."

"But it's time for my lesson. I want to play for you." Owl was fighting back tears.

"Oh, don't worry; we'll get to that later." The nun brushed the back of her hand in the air as if she were shooing away chickens.

Owl's heart sank as she followed the nun to the basement and into the dark, cold laundry room. Owl had been down in this room before—once as punishment for whispering in class. She'd been led down there in disgrace to fold the nuns' thick, muslin undergarments. At the other end of the hall was the big, brightly lit kitchen where the nuns made cinnamon rolls and hot chocolate to serve the children after Mass and on other occasions.

"Now, you crank the handle on this side to the right to lift the mangle, and then you place the cloth in and smooth it down, and then you—"

Owl was too disappointed to concentrate on the instructions. Her mind was with Beethoven and the simple yet beautiful piece he had created especially for Elise.

"And then turn the handle to the left to lower the lid. Ellie, are you listening? Do you understand?"

"Yes, Sister, but what about the music lesson?" Owl's upper lip trembled, and tears fell down her cheek.

"We'll get to that in due time. Remember, no wrinkles now." The nun smiled. "Rejoice in doing the work of the Lord. I'll be down in the kitchen with Sister Althea, making cinnamon rolls for tomorrow. It's the feast of All Saints. I hope you and your family will come to Mass. Tell your parents to come for Communion and then join us in the dining room for breakfast." The nun bustled out of the room.

The parish priest and the nuns were always trying to solicit Owl's help in shepherding her parents to Mass. Owl sang in the choir, and every Sunday would look down from the balcony in hopes she might see them in the congregation below. It had never happened. Rose had managed to avoid the whole business by playing hooky from choir practice and Mass.

There were mounds of rolled, white altar clothes, stiff with starch, waiting to be ironed. The room had no windows. It was dark, with only a dim, naked light bulb hanging overhead. Owl shivered. She wished she had worn her coat. It was cold despite the hot steam that flowed from the mangle whenever Owl pulled the big handle down to flatten the white pieces of cloth. When the lid was up, the machine looked like the menacing mouth of a crocodile waiting to swallow her whole. Moaning sounds came from the pipes overhead. Owl's skin puckered with goose bumps. She wondered if poor souls who weren't good enough to go to Heaven were banished to the laundry room. Their penance for eternity was to be trapped in the pipes. Maybe she would be trapped here, forever in purgatory. Her tears fell and stained the altar clothes.

Sister never came back. After what seemed like an eternity, Owl stood and stretched. She wondered if Sister forgot about her and the music lesson. She walked down the hall to the warm kitchen. The smell of freshly baked cinnamon rolls filled the air. There were trays of them, warm from the oven. The two nuns had their sleeves rolled up, kneading more dough. Three boys two grades ahead of Owl—they were in the eighth grade with Rose—ran around between the long tables playing tag.

"Oh, come in dear. Are you finished with the altar clothes? When you are, I have some tunics for you to iron, and then we'll have a warm cinnamon roll when we're done. We wouldn't want these fine altar boys to be without clean tunics for Mass tomorrow, would we?" Sister chased one of the boys around the table, laughing.

"Why can't they iron their own tunics?" Owl asked. There was a moment of silence.

"Young ladies should be seen and not heard." Sister Althea said, tight-lipped. "Altar boys don't iron their tunics. They are a vital part of bringing the Holy Eucharist to the congregation of sinners."

Sister Mary Leonora escorted a crying Owl back down to the laundry room.

"We'll be done shortly, and then you may have a cinnamon roll."

She brought in another large pile of priestly vestments and tunics, rolled and ready for the mangle. Owl resigned herself to the dreaded task. Rose would have walked out. But then, she didn't give a whoop about anything. Owl cared about the piano lessons.

The smell of freshly baked cinnamon rolls, bright lights, and the promise of a music lesson lured Owl back into the kitchen after she'd finished the ironing.

"Oh, there you are. You must be finished. I've fixed you a cup of hot chocolate and kept a roll warm for you. Thank you so much for helping with the ironing."

"Can we go have the music lesson now?" A bell rang, startling Owl.

"Oh, we don't have any more time today. There's the bell for vespers. I'm so sorry. We'll have an extra-long lesson next Saturday. I have to go, but you stay and enjoy your treat." The nun disappeared, leaving Owl alone in the big basement.

Owl was tired from running the awkward, heavy mangle. She hadn't eaten since breakfast but wasn't hungry. There was a huge lump of disappointment in her throat. She brushed her hand against the cup of hot chocolate, spilling the brown, chalky liquid onto the white tablecloth. "Oh, sorry! Let the precious altar boys clean it up."

When she went back to the music room for her coat and books, it was late afternoon. She sat at the piano and played "Fur Elise" flawlessly to the Blessed Virgin Mary. Then she practiced her scales and played the last two pieces in Book Two. She declared herself graduated to Book Three, then got up and left.

It was getting colder. The air smelled like snow. Owl walked back through the park, kicking hard at the leaves. She was cold but didn't feel like going home. She walked down to Kress's Five & Dime and browsed at the cosmetics counter. A sudden blast of heat from the store made her stomach queasy. She knew that Rose and her friends stole makeup there and kept it in their lockers at school, even though they could be expelled if the nuns found out. She could never imagine herself doing such a thing. Her hand reached out and snatched a handful of lipstick tubes. She slipped them in her pocket. Her face felt hot. She made a beeline for the door, holding her breath until she was outside, running for the park.

It was getting dark, and big, fat snowflakes were falling. She walked over to the aviary. Her squirrel friends greeted her, ready for another nut treat. She took the lids off the lipsticks and threw the opened tubes into the big cage, tossing the lids in as well.

"Here, you stupid squirrels. I hope you choke on these and die!"

She buried her music books in a pile of wet, matted leaves under one of the big sycamore trees. The cold bit into her face and hands. Night fell as rapidly as the snow that was sifting over the ground like powdered sugar over a chocolate cake. Owl could barely see as she ran blindly in an uncer-

CHAPTER 23

▼

—Ellie and Tiny, 1967—

The landscape of Tennessee was colored with tints and shades of reds and browns, a muddy, limited palette. Even the green foliage was grayed with thin sienna washes. It seemed as if a tsunami had swelled the waters of the Mississippi River and broken over the land, coloring everything with its effluence, hardened by time into rosy rock and red soil. The flat, pink ribbon of highway was monotonous, and Ellie drifted in and out of sleep, even though she'd taken a nap that turned into seven hours of deep sleep in the back of the truck.

Sometime late last night after the rescue by Junior's cousins, father and daughter had exchanged the rolling, blue-green hills of Kentucky for Tennessee. Tiny drove until the sky began to catch the first morning light, with Ellie as vigilant lookout. When neither of them could keep their eyes open, they hid Bunny in a deserted tobacco barn somewhere along Highway 51 headed south. It was mid afternoon when they revved up the rabbit again, stopping only to grab a few sandwiches at Bubba's Barbecue, one of Tiny's favorite hangouts—not only for the barbecue—it was one of his cigar pit stops.

"Slow down. There's the red barn with the 'See Rock City' sign."

Ellie was wakened to full alertness, thankful that the wrinkled map Junior had drawn for them yesterday was proving reliable. She watched the big, whitewashed letters painted on the side of the weathered old barn fly by the window. "It says we take the next road to the right, about three miles down from the red barn."

She suddenly realized that she hadn't thought of Louise, Ted, or her state of unemployment since yesterday's narrow escape from Dover's clutches. It felt okay to be faced with a tangible threat, a reprieve from her neurotic afflictions for a while, and just be on the run—with no responsibilities other than to not get caught. Watching the sheriff pace the levee with such determination had made the problem real. The single purpose of mind, their escape, had brought Tiny and Ellie closer together. They were bonded in a covert adventure as fugitives. The intrigue stirred her sense of story; she felt like a heroine in a spy novel. Exchanging one set of problems for another brought up a possibility that she hadn't explored with credibility until now. Life can be played as a game, as Ludine had said, allowing for choice and free will. Life on the road facilitated this state of mind. One could shed one's old skin in Illinois and grow another to suit the climes of the new state. She felt in her pocket for the reassuring touch of the snake skins that she'd brought from home. She and Tiny had been on the road for eight days.

"Take the next road to the right." She came out of her musings to direct Tiny. "Junior said it's easy to miss, so go slow. There it is." She pointed to a side road, little more than a path.

Tiny turned off the highway too fast, causing the boxy bread truck to sway. It lurched its way forward, tearing branches down from encroaching trees and shrubs along the way. Ellie felt sick to her stomach trying to read the directions while the truck bounced and rolled over the rutted road.

"Well, if we ain't in the dreaded bottoms of Tennessee. This is a place I always try to avoid if I can help it," Tiny said with concern in his voice.

A new problem to think about. These swamps next to the Mississippi River were the setting for many a ghost story she'd heard in the past, besides being a rich estuary and home to abundant wildlife. This part of the river valley came with legacies of dark and dangerous incidents. In these muddy shallows, overgrown with pin oak, cypress, and reeds, people had been known to disappear without a trace.

"You can catch malaria down here. I knew a man who hid out from the law here for a few months. Jail would have treated him better. He came out sick with the fever, an' he got bitten by a water moccasin." Tiny shook his head and stopped the truck. "Hand me that Six-Twelve from the glove compartment, would ya." He doused himself with the strong smelling insect repellent and handed it to her. "You better put some on." The metallic smell of the bug repellent, along with the bouncing of the truck as it jogged over the rutted road made her even sicker.

Bunny plowed ahead, grinding in low gear—at times threatening to stall in the damp red earth that in one good rain would turn into boggy, thick mud. The relentless chorus of the locusts was in earsplitting competition with Fats Domino on the radio. He was bellowing to the whole world how he found his thrill on "Blueberry Hill." As much as she loved Fats, the music added to her nausea. She turned off the radio.

The swamp was steamy with heat.

"Goddamned kudzu makes me nervous," Tiny said. He was chewing on a dead cigar butt. "It chokes the life out of all the other plants. They never cut it back in these wild areas." He seemed uncharacteristically irritated. Perhaps lack of sleep in a comfortable bed and the threat of Dover on their heels were catching up to him. "Soldiers brought it back after World War II. Farmers down here call it the Japanese revenge on America for dropping the H-bombs on Hiroshima and Nagasaki," he said. The way in which the menacing vines grew, outlining the shapes of the plants they smothered, looked like hooded ghosts, green Ku Klux Klan members out to do no good.

"Look." She stuck her head out of the window. "There's the tree with the crows that Junior put on the map. He said it was a huge oak tree a half mile down on the left, where the crows go to roost at night." It was not yet dark, but many crows could be seen around the big tree. "Did you know that crows live in families? They have their own separate territories, but at night the families roost together; the gathering is called *murder*," she said, trying to distract Tiny from his somber mood.

"Oh yeah?" He bit down on the dead cigar butt.

"They fly a long way to roost together for safety. Half of a crow's brain, and one eye stays awake while the other eye sleeps. And then they alternate. I have to go to the bathroom," she said, cutting short the crow dissertation.

Tiny stopped the truck by the crow tree. It was a relief to get out and put her feet on solid ground after the constant rocking of the truck. It took a few minutes to steady her legs as she walked behind the tree and pulled down her pants. Several crows cawed at the intrusion. A large, aggressive one dive-bombed her. She could've sworn he was speaking English. It sounded like he said, "Watch out, Clarence." Several other birds joined him in the attack. Ellie ran for the truck as they flew away, repeating and distorting the words in the magnifying lens of the sky. "Watch out, Clarence."

Bunny took to the rough terrain again like a trooper. After awhile, another sign on the map appeared ahead, a crude homemade wooden bridge over a fast-running creek.

"The map says the bridge is reliable to drive across, but I don't know about that," she said dubiously.

"You get out and walk across and tell me if you think those boards can hold me and the truck," Tiny ordered. She crept hesitantly over the bridge, stomping on boards to test their strength as she made her way across. It seemed sturdy. She motioned Tiny across.

A short way down, after the crossing, they came to a slight fork in the road.

"Take a left here and go through the brush for about a hundred feet," she read from the map. They drove until the path ended at a pool of marshy backwater. The kudzu had invaded the reeds and cattails. Even the cypress trees standing in the shallow, brackish water had not escaped the ghoulish enemy.

"It says to walk through the brush to the left, and we'll find a clearing with a building," she read from the map.

They got out of the truck. A few feet beyond the brush was the clearing and an open-sided pole barn that stood a ways from an inlet stream of water. A white beam of wood nailed across the entire upper part of the front of the building read WELCOME TO PARADISE in large blue letters, bold against the white.

A colored man wearing overalls and carrying a shotgun came out from behind the building, the metal of the gun barrel reflecting a spot of sunlight. Ellie froze when she saw the gun. Tiny waved his hand.

"Clarence, it's Tiny Moon."

"Oh hell, Tiny. I thought you was the fuzz." The man propped his shotgun against the building. There was a pronounced limp in his right leg as he slowly made his way over to greet them. He had a lazy eye, giving the impression that he was directing his gaze at something just beyond Ellie, causing her to turn and look behind just as he extended his hand in greeting.

"Hello, Clarence. Nice to meet you." She was afraid she'd called attention to the wandering eye. Clarence spared her any discomfort by ignoring the gesture.

"What brangs ya'll way out here?" He spat out a chaw of tobacco as brown as his skin onto the ground.

"Well, first and foremost, I been missin' that good ol' alley bourbon you make. Nobody makes it finer than Clarence. Everybody knows that."

"Yup, I does make the best tiger sweat round these parts. Ain't that the god's troof." The man chuckled and put his thumbs through the straps of his overalls. "Come on, I'll fix ya'll up. How much the ol' horsey you wantin? Ya knows I don't usually sell it here. My son up in Caggway County peddles it mostly. He be my whippoorwill. Ya'll knows where my son Junior lives, Mr. Tiny. How comes you didn't just git it there?" Clarence seemed to be politely warning Tiny not to make it a habit of tracking him down in the swamp whenever he wanted to buy moonshine.

"I'm afeared dat de long arm of de law gonna finds me back here and um, um, that'd be a bad thang a happen." The man swatted a fly.

"Come on wid me. I'll shows ya'll my setup," Clarence seemed to be addressing Ellie. "Ya gots to git the right mix of corn meal and sugar, and den the rights amount of yeast and malt."

They walked about a quarter of a mile down, following the water, until they came upon Clarence's still.

"The secret to a good brew of hooch is ya gotta cook it at de right temperature once it rots together rail good. And ya gotta use coppa', only coppa' pots and tubing," Clarence explained proudly the proper way to operate a still.

"You know a lawman named Dover?" Tiny finally got to the point of the visit.

"Laud ah God, that man is a greedy devil. He don'ts know where I is, but he shore as hell is a botha' to my son. Sneakin' around Junior's place a business all de time. Takin' half the profits. Laud he sho make this ol' nigga feel unnecessary." Clarence spit out a chaw of tobacco into the grass with a vengeance, as though it was the bad taste of the sheriff in his mouth. "He be tryin' to follow him here all de time. Junior always be tryin' to shake loose of him every time he come back to make a pickup. I gots to go changin' the pickup spot all da' time 'cause a dat greedy man. He ain't out to uphold da law. He be out to hold up poor people who gits in his way." He shook his head. "He be in it to wheedle money out of doze hardworkin' folks likes my son. Too bad he has to go git hisself in charge a' dat county. The lawfolks roun' here is out to close all us cat daddy makers down fer good. Ain't gonna happen though." The man laughed and shook his head again. "Me and my kind, we been makin' the white lightening since slavery days. Ain't nobody gonna shut us down. I be lucky, though, and I gots me a good warnin' system." The old man stopped to catch his breath.

"What kind of warning system you got?" Tiny asked.

"See doze big hickory trees over yona?" Clarence looked in a direction that was hard to follow with his wandering eye. "See doze crows over der? I has taught some of 'em to talk. And then they teaches each other. When someone turns off the main road way back by the roostin' tree, dey hears 'em and de flies over to me talkin' and tellin' ol' Clarence to wake up." Clarence gave three shrill caws aimed toward the trees, and several birds could be heard loud and clear with their responses, "Wake up, Clarence. Watch out, Clarence." "I knowed somebody was comin' up dis road for a long time. As soon as ya'll turned off dat main road they been squackin' for me to wake up. Give me time to hide my makins' and git ma gun ready. I got's plenty of nestin' crows round here 'cause of de cornfield over there." He pointed to a field of dried cornstalks that was surrounded by brush about fifty feet away from the tree. "Dey likes da corn. Ha ha. Dem crows is my friends all right." He grabbed a fistful of dried corn from his overall pockets and threw it out on the ground around the hickory tree. "I keep movin' the fixens' aroun' when doz' revenuers gits too close. I can break down an operation quick as lightnin' if I has to and hide the whole thang." Clarence was silent a minute and then spoke again. "What a fine man like you, Tiny, doin' wid dat old wildcat, Dover?"

"Well, I ran into trouble with him when we played cards together," he said, telling Clarence the story of his hasty getaway.

"Ah yes, Laud. You slipped him some bad panther's breath and then stole his truck. Hah, hah, that shor' make me feel better, you done dat. Good for you, Tiny."

"The main reason I'm here is 'cause Junior asked me to come and tell you he's afraid to come and make the pickup this week. Dover's deputy is followin' him around everywhere he goes. He thinks it's best to lay low for a while. He said to tell you not to worry, he's just bein' careful. He asked me to make the drop in Memphis for you since I'm goin' that way. I kind of owe him a favor."

"Oh, yeah?" The old man motioned them inside the barn with the lofty name, Paridise, and beckoned them to sit.

"He hid us when Dover came snoopin' around, and he could have gotten into more big trouble, so I'd like to return the favor—if you'll let me." Tiny related to Clarence the story of hiding in the duck blind and the cousins in the bread truck outwitting Dover.

"Well, Tiny, I don't want you go gettin' in trouble whippoorwillin' for me. Ya'll in enough trouble with ol' mean man. But de truth is, if I don't git this stuff to the distributor, he gonna be mad at me. They don't like bein' disappointed."

"We'll be glad to do it," Tiny said, looking at Ellie with raised eyebrows as if for approval.

"It's the least we could do for you and Junior." She agreed to go through with the illegal adventure. She liked this independent old man, living his life on his own terms. She liked all of Tiny's friends so far.

"Well, dat all right den. Night's a comin' down soon, so let ol' Clarence fix us a nice meal, and we'll load up the hooch. You two can catnap, and den ya'll be ready for de moonlight travelin'. What you gonna do if Dover be lookin' for ya truck? Ya'll better have a Negro band in there singin' the blues and smokin' cigars." Clarence laughed.

"I wish I knew how serious he is about finding me. From the looks of it, I'd have to say it's pretty serious. What with him hanging around in the hot sun all day. But I think the cousins convinced him that the truck belonged to them. Besides, how's he gonna know I'm in Tennessee?" Tiny seemed to be reassuring himself.

Ellie turned her attention to the interior of Paradise. They sat at a long, makeshift table; a piece of plywood had been laid across two sawhorses, with benches for sitting one on either side, near a wood burning stove. Shelves of mason jars with home-preserved tomatoes, peaches, pickles, green beans, and jams lined one long shelf of a wall. A dozen cages filled with black and white rabbits stood against the far wall. There were bundles of herbs drying from the rafters. She recognized the pungent, minty odor of Pennyroyal, known for keeping insects away. Paradise seemed to be absent of flies. Directly under the rafters was an army cot with a pillow and a wool army blanket. Behind the building was a small wooden enclosure that contained a generator, an old rusty freezer, and a refrigerator of the same vintage. Beyond that was a big vegetable garden, now past its prime, with the exception of a fenced-in area where collard greens grew in every stage of their life cycle, the dark luxuriant leaves displayed dramatically against the rich, red earth. Rhode Island Red roosters and hens strutted around the garden, gleaning the last succulent leaves and seeds from the plants that had bolted and dried in the summer heat. Bundles of cornstalks with the ears still attached were drying under the eaves of the building, next to a bicycle hooked up to a stone grinder. A 1931 rusted-out Ford truck was parked out back next to the garden fence.

Clarence threw some kindling into the firebox of the cooking stove. "I'm gonna fry us up a rabbit and make us some cornbread." He was headed for the rabbit cages when he noticed the look of shock on Ellie's face. She cringed to think of eating the soft, furry wonders with their elegantly shaped ears, like elongated teardrops.

"Maybe we oughta have some a doze red beans dat's on de stove already cookin' real slow. No time to kill a rabbit now."

Ellie looked at Clarence appreciatively.

"How about a little of dis cat daddy?" Clarence poured Tiny and Ellie some moonshine into each of two pint-sized mason jars.

"Thank you. This hits the spot." Tiny took an appreciative sip of the liquor. He was perched precariously on the long, homemade bench at the table. He pulled up a wooden crate beside the bench to help share his weight.

"Here's a tad for you, Miss Ellie. Sip it real slow now if you ain't used to it."

She took a sip, made a face, and coughed. It took her breath away. "It tastes like hot chili peppers," she said hoarsely. Her eyes watered.

"Here, try jus' a little in this Coca Cola." Clarence handed her a bottle of warm Coke. She was surprised to see the bottled soda. It seemed out of place here, an extraneous piece of civilization. She diluted the white lighting by more than half, surprised that she liked the burning, bitter taste.

"I gots some collards growin' out in da garden. Ellie, why don'ts ya go out there and fetch us some?" Clarence handed her a sharp paring knife. "You knows what they looks like, doncha?"

"Yes, I grow collards in my garden. They're my favorite greens." She delighted in the thought of poking around in a garden again. It made her a little homesick. This was the first time that she'd thought of her neglected garden since embarking on this wayward journey. She vowed to call Louise soon.

Ellie cut the dark green leaves, thinking how stunning they would be in a still life painting—juxtaposed against the table's red oilcloth that was printed with multiple images of Jesus with golden halos and arms outstretched in blessing. Clarence told her that he'd ordered it through the mail from a radio station in Memphis that played only gospel music. He'd liked the idea of the Lord blessing his food, right there on the table. She saved some leaves and stems and took them over to the rabbits. Clarence was on the bicycle, pedaling the wheels in place to grind fresh cornmeal for cornbread. Tiny looked relaxed and pleased, his earlier irritation vanished. He put down the ever-present cigar and pulled out his harmonica. The melody to "Wildwood Flower" filled the air. Clarence had started the generator, which provided a noisy resonance for Tiny's melody.

"Don't you get cold sleeping on that cot in the winter?" Ellie asked, intrigued with Clarence's independent way of living.

"Oh, I don'ts ever sleep on dat," he chuckled. "I gots me a real bed over yonna in ma trailer. It's about a quarter of a mile from here, hidden in the brush. If some fool come's lookin' for old Clarence who ain't supposed to be here and they sees the empty bed, they'll go off thinkin' that ol' Nigger run away," he smiled and rolled his eyes.

Clarence went out to the generator-run refrigerator and came back with a piece of salt pork. He put some of it in a pot with some water and the greens. "Ya gots to have plenty of water in dat pot 'cause the pot liquor is the bes' part." He obviously enjoyed cooking and playing the gracious host. He poured the water and cornmeal mixture into a cast-iron skillet that he first rubbed with the rest of the piece of salt pork and set it on top of the wood stove.

"Help me set the table, Miss Ellie, 'cause we's about to have us a feast."

They dined on red beans, home-canned, stewed tomatoes, corn bread, and collards. To top off a perfect meal, Clarence opened a jar of canned peaches, bounty he'd gleaned and preserved from a tree down by the river.

Clarence spat out a chaw of tobacco. "Pick up dat harmonica, and let's see what you can really do with dat thang." He was tuning a steel-stringed guitar. "Go on. Ya do your "Wildwood Flower" thang, and I'll follow ya. Miss Ellie, why don't's ya grab a pot and a spoon or whatever ya wants to make music wid and join in?"

Clarence played chords in harmony with Tiny's melody. After a few choruses of the traditional song, the music spontaneously began to change. The guitar slowed and changed from a three/four to a four/four beat with a strong emphasis on the fourth. Tiny improvised with the use of triplets and a shrill, wavering pitch, answering riffs from the guitar. Ellie played spoons. Before she was aware of what she was doing, she heard her own voice, sweet and steady, mimic the harmonica in a high falsetto wavering pitch and then the guitar in a wide, vibrating glissando.

They played into the night, the music extensions of their own separate sorrows and joys, in a trance-like thrill of abandonment. The harmonies took it all, mixed it up, and for an enchanted time made everything right with the world. Not wanting to miss the jam session, the moon came up high and fast and shone its round, bright, full face—an uncertain beacon in a vast, dark sky.

Clarence was the first to break the spell. "Laud, would you look at the time." He looked at the position of the moon. "That was okay music makin'. Heh, heh, you white folks sure got rhythm. If a body can play music like dat, they's can do anythin'. I always be tellin' my youngins' that when they was growin' up." Clarence and Tiny laughed.

Ellie was breathless and speechless, not yet willing to come back from that space where there was no awareness of time passing, where there were no boundaries that separated the self from others and the music. She remembered how she loved to play the piano as a child. She had taken lessons, hadn't she? She had picked up learning how to read music from somewhere.

"I gots my tractor hidden down in the brush. I'm gonna go get da hooch an' haul it up here. In the meantime, ya'll better git ya some ammunition. Just in case ya need's a distraction to keep doze law hounds at bay. Tiny, you fill up dat bucket with doze big rocks piled up out back, and, Miss Ellie, you grab a couple of doze slingshots I made. I makes 'em so good that one of doze 'ed kill Goliath if aimed at the right place. I uses good, strong hickory wood and strips of ol' inner tube for the slings." Clarence walked into the brush and disappeared.

The sound of the tractor and the smell of diesel fuel brought Ellie out of her rapture. Clarence came back shortly with a drum of moonshine in the basket of the tractor and loaded it onto the bread truck with a dolly, using a board for a ramp. He repeated the task three times.

"Dis' here oughta bring ya 'bout fifteen hundred dollahs apiece. Martel is your man to deal wid. He give you straight cash. Ya'll be goin' over to West Memphis, to a juke joint called the Blue Note over on Eighth Street. It be first mornin' fore you gits dare. Just go to the back door an' whistle like a bird. He live up over the place, so he be dere."

"How will I get the money to you? We'll be headed south for a while. Don't know when we'll be back exactly. Guess I could mail it to Junior," Tiny said.

"Naw don't be mailin' nothin'. I don't trusts da mails. Ya'll just brangs it by when ya'll comes back up dis' way. I trusts you, Tiny. And besides, if ya'll come back, I can hear some more of dat sweet singin' of Miss Ellie's. Yes sir." Clarence winked and shook her hand goodbye. She gave him a big hug, not wanting to leave yet.

They climbed into the truck. Tiny started the engine. Bunny began singing loudly. "It's what ah said. It's Bunny Bread." It was a harsh intrusion in the still, late night air. The sound frightened a large chorus of frogs nearby into silence and the vigilant crows into action. An SOS of "Watch out, Clarence," relayed in waves through the trees.

"Un uh. You ain't goin' nowhere's wid' dat' fool rabbit screamin' like dat." Clarence went back into Paradise and came back with some tools. He popped the hood and yanked some wires.

"Now start dis' fool rabbit up again."

Bunny was silenced. The soft purr of the motor met the late night sounds of the swamp. Frogs resumed their singing. The truck retraced its tracks back over the creaky bridge, going slow over ruts in the road so as not to overturn the burdensome liquid cargo in the back. When they passed the roosting tree, the headlights caught the birds in a glare, startling them into raucous fits of cawing. As the truck pulled out onto a deserted Highway 51, Ellie could hear the crows echoing a warning through the chilly night air.

"Wake up, Clarence. Watch out, Clarence."

CHAPTER 24

▼

The 1966 red Firebird convertible was all muscle and packed a 340 wild-cat engine. The highway was quiet in the early morning hours, except for the man-made package of speed. Four thousand pounds of American steel whirled down Highway 51 at 110 miles per hour. The bird could cruise at 120, no problem. Wrapped around the inner vortex of sound made by the soft purr of the engine, the tires eating up the road, and the radio blasting at full volume, was the powerful force of the wind that greeted the machine head on at top speed. The top was down. Dover couldn't make out the words to the song on the radio, but the steady beat of the drums provided the heartbeat of the tornado. The moon was full and on the other side of high. Dover was dressed to kill in a white leisure suit, his black and white oxfords buffed to a spit-polished, military shine. The hair that he'd carefully anchored down over his bald spot flew wild in the wind. The tic in his neck pulsed with the beat of the drums. His thoughts were a black hole of energy that sucked in everything in their path. Driving fast—just on the edge of out of control—gave Dover a sense of being in charge. Behind the wheel he felt all-powerful; his omnipotence was measured in units of horsepower.

Revenge was the driving force in his life now. He was going to get even with Tiny. And then his life would be saved. He'd take the big man's shoes after killing him and find a way to wear the oversized boats around for a while.

There was no turning back now. He'd hurriedly packed a bag and kissed the bitch goodbye—maybe for good. He'd told her that he was going on one of his "out-of-town shopping sprees." The stupid cow kissed him goodbye with a placid smile on her face. He always came back from his fatal forays with an expensive trinket for her, didn't he? Maybe she was glad to see him go. She never complained when he stayed out all night. She was probably as bored with him as he was with her. There were no children. Dover neglected to tell her before they married that he'd had a vasectomy. It was irreversible, he told her later. After siring two illegitimate children along the way and abandoning them, he decided to play it safe and get himself fixed.

Dover had managed to limit his malevolent compulsions to around once a month since becoming sheriff of Caggway County. Alabama had borne the brunt of his deadly deeds over the past five months since taking office. One of his crimes had gotten a lot of news coverage recently. The police picked up a young man who went AWOL from the Army and charged him with a murder that Dover had committed. Dover and his wife had been watching the news together one night a few months ago when a picture of the suspect flashed on the screen. The wife had turned to him with surprise on her face.

"Lovey Dovey, that man looks just like you. You could be twins," she said.

"Hell, he don't look nothin' like me. He must be fifteen, twenty years younger than me," Dover replied, a little too defensively. The soldier bore an uncanny resemblance to a younger Dover. The man was falsely identified by the victim's widow and convicted on eyewitness testimony—even though all of his alibis checked out. The news picture showed him handcuffed in army fatigues and being placed in a police car to be transferred to the Alabama state prison where he would sweat it out on death row until his execution. Dover felt not a twinge of remorse for sending an innocent man to his death. Hell, he'd done it many times. He considered himself lucky to have escaped a close call.

Dover had made a mistake that time. He'd misjudged the situation. He thought the victim was home alone. He broke into the house, and the man tackled him before he could shoot. In the struggle, the victim pulled off Dover's ski mask before the fatal shot was fired. The wife came out of the bedroom to investigate the noise. She saw a man in jungle fatigues. She saw Dover's face and looked into his eyes. He was going to shoot her, but he hesitated too long. The moment to kill had passed.

He fled the scene. The gun was never found. Dover knew it wouldn't be. He'd worked that part out cleverly. It was his habit to stop at pawnshops in the towns along the killing route and pretend that he was interested in purchasing a gun for target shooting. After finding a suitable weapon, he would pay the price of the gun with cash as a deposit, telling the clerk that he wanted to try it out first to see if he wanted to buy it. He would drive to another town, commit the crime with gloves on so as not to leave fingerprints, and return the gun on the way back home, telling the pawnshop keeper that it did not quite fit his needs. It'd worked for him so far. He would change from his leisure suit into marine fatigues before battle. The uniform gave him courage to face the enemy.

Each time he saw the look of surprised terror on the face of one of his victims, it was like looking into the face of his father.

No evidence from any of the previous crimes had ever been traced to Dover. Now the young man who was charged and looked so much like him could be a problem. What if the pawnshop owner put Dover's face together with the gun he borrowed for the shooting? He'd made his first mistake.

He'd made a mistake with Tiny as well. His original plan had been to meet Tiny, engage him in a game of cards, and then secretly follow him to his different haunts. His plan was for Tiny to lead him to the big money on the table. He'd heard rumors that the gamblers met regularly at secret places—certain nightclubs and private residences all up and down the river route. These men were famous in their field; they had reputations for being the best in the game. He'd heard tales about the size of the winning pots, how they were sometimes upwards of a million dollars. He wanted to play with the big boys. He would discover their hideaways and hold them up at gunpoint in disguise. He rigged up the cheating setup down at his cabin getaway on the lake mostly for sport—to bilk locals that he could con into a game. He would split the pot with the spot man in the crawl space, and they would have a good laugh afterward. His reason for inviting Tiny to the cabin on the lake was to get acquainted, win his confidence, and learn from the master. When Dover saw the stakes were getting high and Tiny was playing serious cards, he got greedy and decided to go for the gold—but it'd backfired. All of the gamblers would know via the grapevine that he, Dover, cheated Tiny Moon and would never invite him into their secret lairs for a game.

And now he was under suspicion for Clois Pierce's death. Damn it! He hadn't meant to kill that daffy old man. A whole chain of events was now set in motion with that fiasco that opened up a can of worms—leading to the former sheriff, Red Foss's, death. Dover knew the county coroner had never been quite convinced that the cause of death had been accidental. Dover had wanted Red's job, so he had ingratiated himself to the sheriff, and they had gone hunting together. Dover made it look like the sheriff had shot himself. He barely got away with that one. And now the city council members may be on to his secret bank account with the money he had stolen from the county coffers after that car raffle for the children's hospital over in Paducah. There wasn't a huge amount in the account, but, over the last five months, it had grown. This was mad money. He'd gone to the bank and closed the account yesterday. Eight thousand dollars, all in Ben Franklins, were in a bag in the glove compartment. He had other accounts with large sums of money in them. One was in Louisiana, one in Mississippi, and one in the Bahamas, with upward of two hundred thousand dollars in each. His wife didn't have a clue. But now he had to worry about the sloppy job of letting his face be seen by the widow. Why should he worry? They already convicted another man for the crime. Dover was free and clear. He just needed to hit the road to think about things. Maybe after dealing with Tiny he would just move to the Bahamas—maybe not even let the bitch know where he was.

After leaving the jailhouse yesterday morning, Dover had closed his bank account, gone home, packed a bag, and kissed his wife goodbye. He spent the day and half the night at Ma Pritchett's with the girls, boozing and whoring. He wanted to travel at night, under a full moon, where he could speed down a deserted highway with no distractions. He needed to clear his mind and make a plan. He was certain he would find Tiny at the poker tournament down at Sal's Place on Beale Street. Dover wasn't sure that Tiny was even aware that he was being hunted down. Dover would catch him by surprise in the middle of a game, take him outside for a ride to a secluded spot at gunpoint, do him in, and throw him in the river. *Snakes bite pigs.* He wondered if Tiny was still driving his stolen truck. It would be a bonus to recover the truck and, most of all, his shoe collection. But what he wanted most of all was that fat fucker's ass.

Dover was oblivious to the increasing traffic as he approached the home of the blues, the city where cotton and Elvis were king, where the Mississippi Delta was said to begin in the lobby of the Peabody Hotel. He had one thought in mind, getting to Memphis and finding Tiny Moon.

CHAPTER 25

▼

It was close to three A.M. when Bunny emerged from the swampland and turned south on Highway 51, headed for Memphis with its illicit cargo of white lightning. Bunny wasn't extolling the virtues of bread anymore. He was outlaw rabbit, silent, armed, and dangerous, with slingshots that could kill a giant. Ellie and Tiny were only a few hours from dawn and Memphis, Tennessee—bone tired.

On a Memphis station, a honey smooth voice announced the next record. B. B. King played his acoustic, steel-stringed guitar and moaned that the thrill was gone. The road was deserted, save for a few big trucks rolling by.

"Would you like me to drive? You could lie down in back and get some sleep." Ellie surprised herself by offering to drive for the first time since they'd left St. Louis ten days ago.

"No, I'm fine. Why don't you take a nap? I'll wake you up if I need you to drive." Tiny relit the stub of his last cigar. She was too tired to protest.

Clarence had enjoyed the cigars so much that Tiny had left the last of them arranged as a bouquet in a canning jar on the table—on the tablecloth of Jesus blessing the world. The smoke from the stale cigar had lost its rich exotic fragrance and smelled harsh and rancid. Ellie had a hangover from drinking too much moonshine, but the pain was worth the price for the intense pleasure the music had given her. She wondered what it would be like to be so uninhibited without the benefit of alcohol.

"Your life is anything but boring, isn't it," she both asked and answered the question.

"I never thought about that one way or the other, I guess. Why? Do you think your life is boring?" Tiny glanced over at her.

"Well, not boring, but it can get bogged down in routine, and trying to do the right thing all the time is tiring, you know. You're so busy sometimes dealing with the mundane things that need to be done, like going to the same old job day after day, that you miss the important things." She thought about her days at the *Post-Dispatch*, writing fluff for the society page. That seemed long ago—another lifetime.

"Yeah, I do know what ya mean. But that ain't for me," Tiny shook his head. "I'm doin' what's important to me. Playin' cards is what's important. When I'm playin', I'm just in the flow. I feel like I'm ridin' on angel wings. There are tradeoffs, but, hell, everything we do in life has a tradeoff." Tiny sighed. "When I start feelin' that where I am is gettin' complicated and sticky, or boring, that's when I just move on. I can't stay in one place too long. When I'm not havin' fun anymore and I get the urge to go, I just do. I guess I've got the old gypsy blood in my veins. I'm just a rollin' stone."

"Doesn't your conscience ever bother you when you think about it?" She knew she'd asked a loaded question, but she couldn't help herself.

"I never think about it too much. God help me if I did."

She realized that this was as close to an explanation as she would get from her father for abandoning his family. She'd noticed things about Tiny on this trip that surprised her, even though they shouldn't have. He really was irresponsible by all of society's definitions. He seemed to be a man of action, with very little introspection. He was self-centered and self-indulgent. He was also loyal and kind to his friends. He seemed to have real affection for them, as they for him. He acted impulsively—like a child—ran away from the messes he created. He thought little about the consequences of his actions after the fact, like stealing the sheriff's truck, abandoning his family, and God knows what else. He seemed to be truly sorry for leaving Rose and her. Didn't he know that intimate relationships always got complicated with the passage of time? He ran away when things got uncomfortable. Is that what she was doing now? Is that what she'd done with Ted? Maybe she was more like Tiny than she'd ever realized. Tiny was more honest than she in his dealings. Could she be honest with herself now? She'd never regretted leaving Ted. She'd never really loved him. She sucked in a breath of fresh air. The honesty made her light-headed. Had she married him in order to get Louise off her back? Well, that hadn't worked, had it? And what about her feelings for her mother? She gave lip service to the word love. She'd made herself numb, zombie-like, rather than admit to the smoldering resentment she felt toward Louise.

"I'd rather be dead than get stuck in a rut," Tiny's voice broke. "I don't ever want to get stuck in the chicken kitchen again."

Louise had told her about Tiny's difficult childhood. The chicken story was prefaced by, "You don't know how good things are for you. Things could be worse. You could have had a hard life like your father, working in the chicken kitchen from dawn until dusk. You're a very lucky girl."

Ellie chose her words carefully. "You must have had a tough time, Dad." This was the first time in her limited memory that Tiny had ever shared his feelings.

"Yeah, well, we all have our tough times." He reached over and touched her shoulder.

"I must have inherited more of your gypsy blood than I thought. I feel more in tune with the world when I'm roaming around. I have to always be creating new people and places in my head, playing make-believe, in order to get through the day," she sighed.

"Then creating stories in your head should be your priority. And don't let your mother make you feel guilty. She's made of different mettle than we are, God bless her soul. I know I've made her life hard. But life's too short to feel guilty about things. That's not a burden I'm willin' to carry."

The world was waking up as Commando Bunny approached Memphis from the north on Highway 51. Dots of cotton in the fields were turning a pinkish color in the rising sun. More commercial trucks were on the road now, headed for the city on the Mississippi River that took its name from the one on the Nile.

"What the hell! I think I just saw Dover!" Tiny shifted into high gear and pushed his foot down hard on the gas pedal, causing the sofa to tip forward. Ellie braced herself against the dashboard with both hands. A red 1966 Firebird was perched next to a gas pump on the left-hand side of the road at a truck stop. Tiny recognized the car from Junior's description, and the driver by the bobbing, turtle-like movement of the head behind the wheel. Dover was looking in the car mirror and combing his hair.

"Damn! What's he doin' here? He's gotta be headed for Memphis," Tiny muttered. He pulled off the highway, turned Bunny around, and parked, hidden in a stand of cottonwood trees with a view of the highway. They watched as Dover started the engine and pulled out onto the highway. When the Firebird flew out of sight, Tiny pulled out on the highway and backtracked to the truck stop. "Let's get some gas and have some breakfast—take a look at this situation over some coffee and food. It's a good thing he was lookin' at himself in the mirror instead of lookin' for us," Tiny said, shaking his head in disbelief.

Ellie thought about the three of them playing out this drama like actors on a revolving stage with ever-changing props. The scene of the moment dubbed "On the Road to Memphis."

Owl: *We are all bright beings missing in action, lost in the dream, and ignorant of our brilliance—Dover no less perfect than the rest of us. Unfinished diamonds forged by the pressure and heat of our own separate lives, each in his/her own way on the road to reclaim her true birthright. Granny says we're fallen stars. She says we'll all take to light again.*

Ellie smiled and looked at Tiny standing by the truck, combing his hair. He seemed to be wrapped in a rainbow of colors.

Tiny put on his sunglasses and peeled a fresh cigar from its wrapper. He hadn't given Clarence all of his cigars. He'd kept some for himself in a stash in the glove compartment.

"Let's go see if we can round up some bacon and eggs. I'm starving," Tiny said, lighting the fresh Corona, a torch in the wilderness. Ellie didn't have the heart to begrudge him a good smoke.

CHAPTER 26

▼

The sun came up fast and glared white hot light on the waking city. The tall buildings of downtown Memphis looked like monuments to Realism, thrown hard against the unrelenting light of the morning sky. They stood in testimony to the sun's no-nonsense promise of another hot, sultry day in the city that sits on the third Chickasaw Bluff, overlooking the Mississippi River. Bunny turned right onto Highway 40 that led down E. H. Crump Boulevard and across the Memphis-Arkansas Bridge to West Memphis.

"Let's get rid of this load. Then we'll come back and stay at the Peabody and get some sleep." Tiny rubbed the two-day, prickly stubble of growth on his chin. "It'll be good to take a hot shower and get some shut-eye in an air-conditioned, luxury hotel. On second thought, I'd better make some phone calls before we go making a grand entrance into the lobby of the Peabody, along with all the other ducks. We need to find out what Dover's doin' in Memphis and where he's goin'. How're you doin'?" He looked over at Ellie. Her eyes felt sore and heavy from lack of sleep.

"I'm okay. I can't wait to go somewhere out of this hot sun and sleep." She squinted in the irritating glare and put on sunglasses. "I've got a headache, and it's hard to stay awake."

"Why don't you get in back and take a nap. I'll wake you up when we get to the Peabody," Tiny said. They were crossing the Mississippi. The horizontal girders of the bridge looked like the wings of giant birds, spread full span in flight, giving the illusion that the truck was standing still and the bridge was flying by. The motion made her dizzy.

"I don't want to miss any of the action." Her tongue felt heavy, and her speech was slurred from drowsiness.

"You're really gettin' into the spirit of the game, ain't ya?" Tiny laughed. "There ain't gonna be any action for awhile. We're jus' gonna deliver our load and then go to sleep."

Ellie was too tired to answer as she drifted off to sleep.

✳   ✳   ✳   ✳

West Memphis was dirty and hazy. Its many gambling spots and juke joints had earned the town the name Little Las Vegas. Tiny turned into a deserted parking lot off of Eighth Street; an unlit neon sign in the shape of a musical note bore the name Blue Note over the front entrance. It looked like a rough neighborhood. Tiny drove around to the back door of the run-down roadhouse. Before he had a chance to get out and whistle like Clarence had told him to do, a man came to the back door.

"Naw, we don't want no Bunny Bread here." He looked annoyed.

"Are you Martel?" Tiny asked, as the man was closing the door.

"Who wants ta know?" The man frowned from behind the screen door.

"Junior from up in Kentucky sent me. I'm makin' a delivery for him. He couldn't make it." Tiny started to get out of the truck.

"Hold it right there, white man. I don't know nothin' about no Junior. You better get on out of here. Go on." He swished the air with his hand as if swatting a fly.

"I'm Tiny Moon, the gambler. Maybe you've heard of me? I play cards down the road sometimes at the Cotton Club. Ask Hewlett. He owns the place. He knows who I am." Tiny stood his ground beside the truck. Most of the club owners in these parts carried guns, and he didn't want any trouble. If he rushed things he could end up at the bottom of the river, with a bullet for his trouble.

"I know who he is." The man hesitated and opened the door wider. "You the man that won all that money contestin' against Big Bones Walker?"

"Yeah, that's me all right." Tiny shook his head laughing.

"Hi, I'm Martel." The man smiled, opened the door, and stepped outside, extending a hand. "Man, you sure can eat. Big Bones took one look at you and knew he was whupped. The way you was puttin' down those steaks and barbecued ribs like they was goin' out of style."

One of Tiny's talents was his ability to eat large amounts of food in short periods of time, winning him the title the "Eating Machine." It usually brought him a considerable pot of money. Tiny was always a favorite to win. People placed bets on the big man, sight unseen, from near and far, trusting his reputation as the top dog to win. Bookies thrived when Tiny ate.

"I had my dollar down for Big Bones last time. But I sure won't make that mistake again. No, sir, I'll slap my money down for the Eating Machine. That your gig tonight?" The man was cordial now. "I ain't heard that you was part of that big shindig happenin' down the street tonight with that guy from Chicago. What's his name, Fat's Baloney or somethin' like that? If I'd knowed that, I could have drummed up more bets," Martel said.

"I didn't know about it. I been out of contact," Tiny said.

"Yeah, they flyin' a bone grinder in from New York City; Little Lester's his name. They say he's a real big eater, bigger than you, they say."

"Never heard of him. He couldn't be that big if I haven't heard of him," Tiny seemed disinterested. "I'm tryin' to tell you that I got a delivery of sweet cat daddy in my truck from Junior. And I'm in a hurry to unload it and go get some shut-eye."

"What's he got a white man deliverin' his stuff for?"

"It's a long story. You got a way to unload this stuff?" The lack of sleep was taking a toll on Tiny's mood. He wasn't as young as he used to be.

Martel went inside and came back with a dolly.

"Let's get this stuff unloaded 'fore it starts gettin' busy around here." He unloaded the barrels and took them to a back storeroom.

"Junior's father, Clarence, said to give me the money, and I'll take it back to him."

"Yes, sir." Martel handed Tiny a bundle of hundred dollar bills in the amount of four thousand and five hundred dollars.

"You'd never know that whiskey was legal in this state, the way the old-timers be drinkin' the white lightning. I guess they got used to drinkin' that stuff when they was young, and ain't nothin' else can come up to that taste in their minds. Besides, it's cheaper."

"Well, thanks, Martel. I might come by tonight and check out the contest." Tiny was halfway out the door.

"You mean you gonna be eatin' tonight?" Martel was excited.

"No, I didn't say that. I don't want to interfere with Fats Mahoney's gig. I may just drop by to watch."

"Come on, man. It's open to anybody who wants to pay the thousand dollar entrance fee. You must be savin' yourself for that big poker tournament down on Beale Street starts tonight. You also the man when it comes to playin' poker, ain't ya?"

"Yeah, well, I just need to get some sleep before I decide which way I'm goin'. Thanks, man." Tiny headed for the door again.

"Tiny, if there's anyway I can talk you into showin' up for this contest tonight, I'll be doin' it, man. Ya know what I'm sayin'? If I know somethin' now, we can arrange more book ahead of time. Make a lotta currency. Know what I'm sayin'? He rubbed his fingers together.

Tiny waved goodbye and walked through the door toward the truck. He changed his mind and walked back to the man, who was watching from behind the screen door.

"Martel, maybe we could help each other out. I need to make a few phone calls first, but how about swappin' vehicles with me for the day? This truck is cumbersome in the city." He put his truck keys on the bar and headed for the telephone.

"You got it, Tiny. I'm drivin' that old beat up brown and white Cadillac out there. It looks like hell, but it runs fine. It's got cold air." Martel seemed pleased that he could help the famous gambling man.

Tiny made a quick phone call and placed a five-dollar bill on the bar to pay for the call. "Thanks for your trouble, man. I'll be back tonight, and I'll be eatin'. You can count on that." He started for the door again and once again turned around. He pulled out the bundle of bills that Martel had just given him in payment for the moonshine.

"Here. Put this all on Tiny to win. Let's go for broke." Tiny handed Martel the wad of money.

"Now you're talkin' my language. The betting starts in one hour. You got in just in time." Martel laughed.

"And here's some money to officially register me as an eater," Tiny said as he pulled the last of his own money out and counted it. "Just made the fee with a little extra to spare." He counted out ten hundred dollar bills and smacked them down on the bar with the flat of his hand.

"Yes sir, this is gonna be a good game tonight." Martel grinned.

I'll win a bundle and give Clarence his money back with interest for good luck, Tiny rationalized as the scorching air outside blasted him in the face.

"Wake up, Ellie. We're gonna take that Cadillac over there so we won't be so conspicuous. I called Fats at the Peabody. I knew he'd be there. He always stays there when he's in town. He and I have a little eatin' gig over here tonight. He's gonna throw the game in my favor, and we'll split the proceeds."

She looked barely awake.

"And I found out why Dover's here. There's a big poker tournament down at Sal's tonight, and I know that fool thinks I'm gonna be there playing."

She awoke to full attention when she heard the name Dover. They retraced their route back across the bridge in the borrowed caddy with the air-conditioner turned on high.

"I gotta get some shut-eye." Tiny looked at his watch. "I have to be back over here in about nine hours. I wonder who the big eater from New York is? He must not be too hot, or I would've heard about him."

Tiny parked the beat-up Cadillac in front of the Peabody and handed the keys to the valet.

They took two adjoining rooms. Tiny slipped the desk clerk a twenty dollar bill with instructions to not give out information should Dover come calling. The clerk was to relay the message to the others following his shift of duty. The staff of the famous hotel knew that Tiny tipped generously and were always glad to accommodate him.

"Wake me when you get up. I want to go wherever you're going. Don't forget me, or I'll be mad at you," she said, barely conscious.

"I promise. You get some rest. We've got a big night ahead of us," Tiny said, yawning.

Tiny was so tired that he didn't bother with a badly needed shower. He turned the air conditioning on high, took off his clothes, and hoped the front desk wouldn't slip up on the wake-up call.

CHAPTER 27

▼

A ramshackle building, the Cotton Club, stood flanked by fields of cotton dense with buds ready for harvest. The building looked like so many other old roadhouses along Eighth Street that connected with Highway 40 going west toward Little Rock: structures made of wood, all with wide-planked porches.

"This is where it all started," said Tiny.

"You mean the blues?" Ellie asked. She was feeling rested and all done up in the only dress she'd packed for the trip, a slinky, peach colored rayon number with spaghetti shoulder straps.

"Yep, blues and barrel house piano. A lot of these juke joints date back before the Civil War. The slaves made up their own songs. They used to get information to each other that way about escapin'. They sang in codes. They would holler to one another and relay songs down the line. That's how it all started. Then after the Civil War, when all the cotton plantations were sold off, most of the colored people were dirt poor and barely surviving. They made up songs about their new kind of misery."

Ellie visualized a colored man in tattered overalls sitting on the porch of the Cotton Club in a straight-backed chair, uneducated and crushingly poor, creating his own music out of weariness and disappointment with a world gone wrong. His fingers gnarled from hard work, playing a steel-stringed guitar, his mojo in the pocket of his overalls for good luck, and a jug of moonshine by his side, wailing his heart out about the woman who left him.

"You look beautiful, Miss Ellie," Tiny said, interrupting her thoughts.

"Thank you. You don't look bad yourself," she said. Tiny was clean-shaven. He smelled of Old Spice and was dressed in a white suit and white suede shoes. His panama hat covered his salt and pepper hair. He was a handsome man despite his size. "Are you ready for the contest?" she asked.

"I'm hungry and ready to eat," Tiny said with enthusiasm. "My stomach's growlin'."

All eyes were on the two of them as they approached the wide porch. Ellie could feel Tiny puff with pride as he took her hand and escorted her up the steps. She felt a peculiar conceit within this rather unconventional context of setting—daughter of the famous Eating Machine. Would this moment be her claim to fame?

The all-Negro audience parted to make way for Tiny and Ellie amid hushed whispers. White people were not allowed in most of the juke joints in West Memphis. Annulments of the rules were granted on the occasion of shared music making or special events. Tiny was a special event.

It was still hot out even though the sun had set. People were fanning themselves with whatever they had that would stir up the air.

"There's Martel from the Blue Note." Tiny pointed out a tall, lean man dressed in a shiny, black acrylic suit leaning on the porch rail with a beer in one hand. His other arm was wrapped around a young woman in a flashy red dress with a big, artificial flower in her hair. He relinquished his temporary hold on the beauty to shake hands.

"How's it goin', Tiny? Did my old beater git you over the river?"

"It was a pleasure to drive, and we sure appreciated the cool air. Thanks, man." Tiny took off his hat and fanned the air around him.

It was a little cooler inside, with big ceiling fans circulating the mixed aromas of cigarette smoke, pulled pork barbecue, and catfish.

Chicago Fats was already there. Ellie could hear his flat, twangy voice even before they walked inside.

"Hey, Tiny, I'm glad youse came, man. And, looky here, with your pretty daughter. Hello, Miss Ellie, good to see youse again." He paced rapidly back and forth, working up a sweat. "That's a million dollah dress you're wearin' tonight, Miss Ellie." He eyed her with a smile of approval and turned to Tiny. "Where's that sucka we gonna outeat? He should'a been here by now." He nervously looked at his watch without slowing his pace. "I called the airport, and they says his plane arrived two hours ago. I'm hungry. I wanna get this show on the road." Fats looked like a man who had never allowed himself the discomfort of hunger pains.

"Relax. It doesn't start until nine. I'm hungry, too." Tiny unbound a new cigar and bit off the end.

"Here, try chewin' on one of these." He handed Fats a cigar, knowing that he didn't smoke. Fats waved his hand in a disgusted manner at the offering.

"Let's go check out the kitchen," Fats said, hopping from one foot to the other. The three walked through the swinging doors. A blast of heat from the bustling kitchen hit Ellie in the face, taking her breath away. Five men wearing white aprons were bent over a big gas stove. The fans overhead worked hard to cool the inferno. Raw whole chickens, hams, and beef steaks were lined up, ready to cook.

"No chickens," Tiny said to the person who looked to be the head chef.

"Theys a big part o' de' food tonight, boss." The man did not look happy to have his menu altered.

"I can't eat chicken. I told Martel that I wouldn't eat chicken or anything that flies. Okay?" Tiny looked pale.

"Okay, boss." The man shook his head, frowning.

They walked out the back door where a whole pig, splayed out on bed springs in a hole in the ground, was being roasted. From a wooden bucket, a mop delivered the luscious tomato sauce that made Memphis barbecue famous throughout the South.

"Do you guys just eat meat in these contests?" Ellie asked, both surprised and disgusted by the amount of food that was being prepared. Who pays for all this?"

"Hewlett over there behind the bar owns this place. He provides most of it. There's a fee to be in the contest. This is big business for him. He books bets and makes some big-time money. As for what we eat, there ain't any rules that say you can't eat other food besides the meat, but you don't want to fill up on stuff like bread or salad 'cause the only thing that counts in the contest is the meat. Remember, the goal is to out eat the other contestants. That's determined by weighin' the meat before each person eats it. That's how you keep tally of who ate the most. It goes by weight."

"How do you know when it's over? When you can't eat anymore?"

"The contest lasts three hours, with a fifteen minute break every hour." Tiny sounded like a gourmand enlightening her about the fine points of dining.

"The contestants can get up and walk around. They can go to the bathroom with a neutral party goin' along to make sure they don't stick their finger down their throat. They're not allowed to use any drugs that would make them vomit or have a bowel movement. They can go outside and walk around for the fifteen minute breaks. My stomach is growlin', and the heavenly aroma from that pig roastin' over there is makin' my mouth water." Tiny was ready for the show to begin.

"Yes, sir, this is a million dollah barbecue." Fats inspected the pig in the ground.

He grabbed the mop and gave it another dousing of sauce, earning a frown from the big man who supervised the roast.

"What about the bones that are left? Maybe some bones are heavier than others?" She was still curious about the rules of this bizarre contest.

"All the bones are weighed after the piece of meat is eaten and subtracted from the total weight. Get it?" Tiny lit a cigar and looked at his watch. "Where is that guy from New York."

"Come over here, Miss Ellie. I want to show you a million dollah trick I have up my sleeve. Guaranteed to work. Nothing in the rules say I can't do it, and it works like a charm." Fats led her over to the parking lot to his rented Cadillac and took a brown paper bag out of the front seat. "I have a very sensitive stomach, so I don't want to smell this yet." He handed her the bag and said, "Here, take a whiff of this. Don't leave the bag open too long. I don't want it to lose none of its appeal." She cautiously opened the bag, estimating that there were about a dozen pairs of dirty socks in the bag. The smell was indescribable. It was Limburger cheese distilled to its essence of characteristic putrid smell, plus some other nauseating odors that were unrecognizable. She carefully handed the bag back to Fats with two fingers.

"That should accomplish what you're after," she said, fighting back an urge to gag.

"My cousin, Al, has a problem with his feet. His wife had to divorce him because of it. You can smell him comin' a mile away. I just have him save up some of these bad boys for me before a contest. Nobody ever suspects I sniff these. So don't say nothin' about it. You know what I mean?" He gave her a knowing wink.

"Your secret is safe with me," she said, wondering about the bizarre scene she found herself in the middle of.

"This little trick kept me outta the Army," Fats confided. "I took my bag and hid it in the men's room when I went for the physical. I kept goin' in there and smellin' the bag and throwin' up. I told them that I always tossed my cookies when I was nervous, and the thought of being in the Army made me real nervous. Worked like a million dollahs. Hell, sometimes I don't even have to smell the bag. Just the thought of it makes me vomit."

Ellie rolled her eyes at Tiny, and he came to the rescue.

"Fats, what've you heard about this guy from New York?" Tiny seemed a little anxious. "I don't want no extra heavy competition tonight."

"Relax. Between the two of us we can eat anybody under the table. You know I got a fast metabolism." Fats patted Tiny on the back for reassurance. "I don't know nothin' about this guy. He's a newcomer. Never heard of him before. He'll take one look at your handsome girth and wet his pants, he'll be so scared. Don't worry, my friend." Fats laughed.

Ellie was perplexed that grown men would jeopardize their health by eating huge amounts of food and wager large sums of money knowing nothing about their competitor ahead of time. Encouraged by the yells and screams of a greedy audience, they would be like fighting roosters in a ring. She felt a wave of nausea at the thought of what the night may hold.

The three were standing by Fats' rented car in the parking lot when a black hearse pulled in, followed by an oversized commercial truck that bore the name TUNNY'S MEATS.

The drivers of the two vehicles got out and walked up to the front door of the Cotton Club, descended the stairs, and then walked around to the back. Walking back to the front of the building, the larger of the two men took off his baseball cap, scratched his head, and put the cap back on.

"I think our best bet is to take the front door off its hinges and use the hydraulic lift to get him up those stairs. No way the hand truck's gonna get that hunk o' meat up those stairs. I think he'll fit without the door." He pulled out a carpenter's tape and measured the width of the door. An increasing number of white faces could be seen in the crowd of onlookers gathered around the front stairs. Hewlett centered himself at the front door.

"What you mean, you gonna take off the door? How much that barracuda weigh? Is he gonna go through my floor if you bring him in here?" He gave a few stomps on the porch floor to demonstrate the precariousness of the situation. The old wooden boards creaked under the attack.

"Once we get him in and put him where he's supposed to go, he'll stay in one spot. He ain't goin' nowhere, that's for sure. He's so big, he can't even walk."

Fats rolled his eyes at Tiny. Tiny chewed his cigar with vigor. The driver of the hearse opened the wide, double back doors of the vehicle to reveal a person lying on a mattress. Propped up on blue satin pillows was the biggest man Ellie had ever seen.

Tiny's jaw sagged. The cigar fell out of his mouth onto the gravel of the parking lot.

"Jesus Christ! That's a monster! How the hell we gonna defeat that sonofabitch? We oughta forfeit right now," Fats said, hopping from one foot to the other as fast as he could.

"Hush," Tiny hissed. "We can't walk out now, man. We'd be dead meat. A lot of people have a lot of money ridin' on us. If they did decide to spare our lives, we'd never be able to work the river route again. Act confident. Everybody's watchin' us." Tiny wiped his brow with his hand.

All eyes were turned to the man in the back of the hearse and the problem at hand: getting him out of the truck and into the building. The driver was operating a forklift that he drove out of the back of the meat truck and down a ramp. He wheeled it over and positioned it in front of the open doors of the hearse, and placed the tines of the forklift carefully under the hand truck that held the mattress with its massive cargo. Ellie heard someone wheezing from inside. The sounds of the man gasping for breath and the soft purring of the hydraulic forklift were all that could be heard.

"I think we got him now." The man driving the forklift began backing away from the hearse with the mattress and its burden on the flatbed of the lift. He wheeled it over to the front stairs. Only six stairs to climb. A feat that a normal person thinks nothing about is an insurmountable obstacle to another, Ellie thought.

The crowd was silenced in the face of such human size.

"I'm gonna lift him up on the porch by the front door, and you go and get the hand truck." The driver wheeled the forklift in close to the stairs and positioned the flatbed directly in front of the opening, now denuded of its door. A ramp was placed over the steps of the porch, and the hand truck was wheeled up parallel to the mattress. It had a steel meat hook attached to the top, shaped like a giant question mark. The man on the mattress reached up for the meat hook, his arms—gigantic hams—hung in the air. He had on a sleeveless T-shirt that could not contain two mountainous breasts that rolled out of the armhole openings. His skin was white and greasy like cold cream, his hands like great white bird wings at rest, wrapped around the steel hook. Tiny's poker face revealed no emotion, but what was left of his Havana that he'd retrieved from the ground was in shreds.

"I wish I'd never started this thing," Tiny whispered in Ellie's ear.

Drenched in sweat and gasping for air, the center of attention was wheeled through the opening, the old, wooden planks of the floor moaned helplessly under the stress of the concentrated assemblage of flesh and steel.

"Back off everybody. Let this man catch his breath." Hewlett took charge of the crowd that had gathered in close around the man. He sat, a vast island of fat, in a small sea, a substantial landmass in danger of being flooded by curiosity seekers. It was hard to tell his age. He looked young. His dull red eyes blinked in the smoke-filled room. Tears fell over the moguls of his hilly cheeks like skiers gliding down snowy slopes onto his T-shirt, wet with sweat. Tiny made his way across the empty sea of space that Hewlett had decreed people-free. He extended his hand.

"Hello there. I'm Tiny. I'll be one of the contestants tonight."

The man made a slight gesture to remove a hand from the meat hook, thought better of it, and nodded his head. "Hi. Glad to finally meet you. We're Little Lester." He managed a faint smile at his own wit, even though the act of speaking seemed to leave him even more breathless.

The trip from New York must have been an ordeal for him, Ellie thought. The man was sweating profusely and smelled of medicated talcum powder.

Fats was the next to approach the mountain. "Hello there. How youse doin'?" He stood with furrowed brow, arms at his side, his body out of character in its stillness.

"How he gonna relieve hisself?" Hewlett asked anyone who cared to answer. The man who drove the hearse answered the question by wheeling in a special portable toilet with a huge seat and placed it next to the hand truck.

Fats leaned across Ellie at the table. He put his hand over his mouth as he talked in a low voice to Tiny. "Don't drink anything, not even a drop of water. Take your time eatin'. Take all your breaks and relax. I'll make a good show and then fold. It's up to you to take this big boy. You can do it, my million dollah man."

Hewlett stood at the front opening where the door had been, collecting a ten dollar cover charge per person. The entrance looked lonely without its door, despite the increasing crowd that was lined up around it, clamoring to get in and view the giant that had just arrived. More and more white faces could be seen as the gamblers and curiosity seekers from Memphis crossed the bridge to witness the event and place their bets. People were lined up at the bar, frantically placing bets on Little Lester to win. Martel made book as fast as he could with a smile on his face.

"This may work to our advantage," Tiny poked Fats in the side. "His odds are goin' down and ours are goin' up. If I take him we could win pretty big."

"Yeah. Look at those suckas. Fame is a fickle mistress." Fats shook his head. He was standing again and jogging in place like a prizefighter.

"Maybe it's time to retire and buy a farm somewhere," Tiny said to Ellie as he watched the people push their way to the crowded bar to get their bets on Little Lester in before the final bell rang.

At nine P.M. on the nose, Martel rang a cowbell and trays of food arrived on cue through the swinging doors from the kitchen. Fats and Tiny sat at a table near Little Lester's bed, both with big white linen napkins tucked under their chins. Ellie sat at the central table with them. Little Lester sat propped up on pillows. A meat scale was wheeled up next to the table with a neutral witness to weigh the meat and the bones. Trays of roasted chicken were brought out.

"I said no chicken." Tiny became pale. He took the napkin from under his chin and threw it on the table. The waiter hurriedly took the unloaded trays back into the kitchen.

"I never eat our fowl friends," Tiny informed the neutral witness. "I thought I made that clear earlier."

Little Lester looked disappointed. Drops of saliva formed at the corners of his mouth in anticipation of the feast of succulent-smelling birds. When the second tray arrived with T-bone steaks just off the grill, juicy and barely cooked, his beady eyes widened, and he smiled, an event that made the circumference of his face increase about three-fold.

"Just the way we like our meat," he said in a husky voice.

The crowd cheered for Little Lester. The plates of meat were carefully weighed for each man and recorded. Blood pooled around the almost raw meat on the heavy white plates. At the ring of the cowbell, the three men set upon the food. Little Lester inhaled the first steak, bones and all. The cracking of the bones in the hushed air sent up another cheer from the crowd for him.

"Hold on there," said the witness. You don't have to eat the bones, man." Lester motioned the man to weigh him another steak. He finished a third steak before he stopped to breathe and let out a great, rolling burp. Ellie noted that Tiny was on his second, and Fats was just beginning his third, commenting with a mouth full of food about the million dollah meat that was being served tonight. Lester racked up ten steaks to Fat's six and Tiny's five by the time the cowbell rang for the official break.

"Saved by the bell." Tiny stood, stretched, and headed for the men's room, his appointed watcher by his side.

Little Lester sat motionless, except for the great heaving of his chest and wheezing noises, as he took in big gulps of the stale smoky air.

Fats went outside to walk around the building accompanied by his witness. Ellie went with them to get some fresh air. She'd been hungry earlier while smelling the food cooking, but when the men started eating she'd lost her appetite and was feeling a little nauseated.

"Just got to focus on you-know-what," Fats said. He winked and poked her in the side.

He's thinking about the smelly socks. She tried hard not to think of them. After a few minutes of strolling in silence, Fats gagged and held his throat. The witness and Ellie watched as Fats heaved his dinner into the grass.

"Man, you ain't supposed to be doin' that." The man looked puzzled.

"You didn't see me stick my finger down my throat or take drugs did you?" Fats wiped his face with a handkerchief. "I just have a very sensitive stomach. Come on. I haven't broken any rules here." He swayed from one foot to the other.

"I'm not sure that's legal, but I guess I have to let it pass," the witness nodded. The imaginary sock sniffing had left Ellie feeling even queasier. She took deep breaths, walking ahead of the other two.

Round two consisted of barbecued pig. People ate and drank as they watched the show, more relaxed now, confident that Little Lester would be the big winner.

Barbecued pork was Tiny's specialty. He gained momentum and had eaten ten racks of ribs to Little Lester's eight and Fats' five by the end of the second hour.

The second break left Little Lester still in the lead but even more breathless. He was beginning to lag. His labored breathing now concerned the crowd. His witness fanned him with a menu and took his pulse, not knowing what to do with the information he had gained from the gesture.

Fats went outside for his usual stroll around the building with his witness and Ellie by his side. The fresh air was a welcome reprieve from the smoke-filled room. She kept walking when Fats went over to the bushes to gift the local wildlife with his second meal.

Ellie circled the building, hugging herself as she walked. Her legs felt heavy, zombie-like. The excitement she had initially felt for the game had turned into humiliation for herself, Tiny, Chicago Fats, Little Lester, and the crowd of people who had placed bets on this twisted and sleazy event. All of them had been swept up in a mob-like mentality. It frightened her. This feeling wasn't new to her. It had grown and matured along with her skeletal framework since childhood.

She had been four. The family still lived in Granny's big house in St. Louis. It was 1940, during the tail end of the Great Depression. Tiny found a job that required he have a car and Granny loaned him the last of her life's savings to buy one. Louise insisted he take the girls with him to keep him on track. Tiny had said, "Come on, let's hit the road, gals."

Rose held Tiny's hand while Ellie rode high on Tiny's broad shoulders, one big hand on her knee so she wouldn't fall off—riding the streetcar to the end of the line, out to Ladue, near the old red brick firehouse, a sense of great adventure in the air. A big tent. Rose said, "Oh yippee, we're going to a circus." There was a crowd of people gathered around a roped-off square, wooden floor. The ground outside the roped area was covered in thick layers of straw. Ellie hoped for ponies. Couples were dancing to music on the wooden floor, some looked like they were asleep as their partners held them up and kept then in motion. From time to time a dancer would fall, crumple like a rag doll to the floor, and people in white coats would come with a stretcher and carry him or her off. People waved money in the air above their heads, cheering and booing. There were no ponies, no circus. Kerosene lamps were lit around the dance floor when night fell. The ghostlike bodies of the remaining couples threw long shadows into the dark around them. Ellie and Rose, cold and hungry, fell asleep in the straw, holding each other.

It was day again when they woke up. The crowd had dwindled to a few hangers-on. Tiny and several others screamed, "Get up! Get up!" when one of the two remaining couples fell to a heap on the floor. Tiny took off the gray fedora hat that he always wore when the season changed to late autumn and whipped it on the ground, stirring up dust from the straw. That was the first time Ellie had seen her father cry. Afterward, at home: the smell of wool blankets, the taste of hot chocolate, eyelids heavy and swollen from lack of sleep and too many tears, Louise's furious voice down the hall screaming at Tiny because he had kept the little girls out all night and lost all of Granny's savings.

Ellie shivered. Fats and his witness had gone back inside. She wished she could stop the nonsense and drag Tiny away, but she knew that was impossible. She took a deep breath and walked back into the hot, smoky nightclub.

Barbecued muttonchops were served for the final hour. When the cowbell rang and the big trays came through the swinging doors, Little Lester rallied.

"It's about time. We're hungry," he said, burping loudly and beating his fists against his ponderous chest.

The crowd whooped and hollered at Little Lester's revival. Ellie wondered for a moment if the whole scene had been staged, if Tiny and Fats were in on the hoax, pretending not to know Little Lester. Maybe they were pretending so the odds would change, and in the end they would split the money three ways.

Little Lester shot out far ahead of the other two eaters. Tiny was eating slow and steady. Ellie looked at the tally board that had been set up by the table. Tiny was behind Lester by seven chops.

"I don't care for mutton," Fats brought up the rear, sweating and gagging. He managed to eat only three chops. Next to come were the baked legs of lamb. Little Lester looked to be a sure win. He devoured six legs to Tiny's two. Fats threw in the towel after only half a leg and went outside just before the problem started.

Little Lester stopped eating. His body began to heave and rumble, like a volcano ready to erupt. He waved his arms back and forth, a leg of lamb in one hand, and the other resting on the meat hook. His mouth was open but no sound came out. His blood-shot eyes bulged in a face that turned bright red, and then a deep maroon color. Tiny was the first to act.

"He's choking!" He went over to the unfortunate man and attempted to lift his body so he was sitting up straight. Ellie followed. She tried to reach her arms around the mass of flesh from behind, but her arms could only go halfway around the monument of fat. "Is there a doctor in the house? Somebody call a doctor!" she heard herself shout out.

Tiny grabbed Little Lester's shoulders and shook him, then pounded on his chest. Tiny was soon out of breath and exhausted from the effort after having ingested so much food himself.

"Let me try." Martel took over, punching the man in the chest with his fists. Gurgles could be heard coming from somewhere inside Little Lester. Martel opened Little Lester's mouth and stuck a finger down his throat in hopes that he would retrieve a bone that was blocking his airway. He felt nothing. Someone at a far table near the dance floor got up and went outside, returning shortly with a leather bag.

"I'm a doctor. I couldn't help but see there was some trouble here."

The doctor opened his bag and took out a stethoscope. He held it to Little Lester's chest, moving it around the mountain of flesh searching for a heartbeat.

"This man is dead." He shook his head, and put the stethoscope back in the bag. A wave of silence washed over the room, followed by a buzz of conversation in low tones.

So the three of them hadn't staged this—Little Lester was really dead, Ellie thought.

"What the hell happened here?" Fats asked. He had just returned from his break.

The gathering was silent. Little Lester's lifeless body was wheeled outside on the meat cart and hydraulically lowered back down the stairs and into the hearse, the same vehicle that had delivered him with high hopes of victory just a few short hours ago.

Martel, Hewlett, and the three neutral witnesses had their heads together at the bar discussing the contest rules when Ellie walked over to get a glass of water. She overheard the men talking. One of the witnesses was shaking his head. "Man, you wouldn't see no Negro be foolish enough to eat hisself to death. Man, oh man."

"The man obviously would have won if he'd lived. So he should be declared the winner even if he be dead," Hewlett said.

"Yeah, but he didn't finish the contest. He didn't go the full time." Martel shook his head.

"If death of a player should occur first, before completion of the contest, then the person in second place wins," Hewlett said. No one seemed inclined to argue the decision. Hewlett walked over to Tiny and raised his right arm in the air, declaring him the victor.

Martel and Hewlett were busy behind the bar, paying off bets. Despite the protests and boos, the crowd seemed to accept the decision of the judges.

"Hey, my man, your odds are lookin' good." Fats smiled furtively, trying not to show his happiness at the outcome. But then his emotions got the better of him and he hopped around and shook Tiny's hand, then he pumped both Ellie's hands vigorously, as if she'd performed as well. "From even money to ten to one ain't bad odds." Fats was shuffling his feet and waving his arms back and forth in a dance of victory.

Tiny collected his winnings. He was passing around cigars like a proud new father when one of Hewlett's bouncers came in and said he'd spotted a red Firebird convertible pull into the parking lot. They had been alerted in case Dover might try to come and break up the party.

"You can drive through the cotton field out back behind the barbecue pit. It takes you over to the Blue Note. Martel threw Tiny the keys to the bread truck.

"Okay. Thanks." Tiny breathed hard from the effort of moving quickly after eating so much food. Ellie worried that he might be next to have a heart attack.

"Come on, give me the keys. I'll drive," she said.

"No, I'm okay. Fats, you better come with us. That bastard might know who you are," Tiny said out of breath. Fats hopped around behind Tiny.

"You go on. We'll take care of this guy, and I'll meet you back over there later," Martel assured the three of them, as they exited through the back entrance.

*   *   *   *

Dover strode up the stairs and stood on the porch facing three big men the color of shiny chestnuts with muscle-bound arms crossed in front of their chests. He wished he hadn't left his gun under the seat of the car. He could hear a band warming up to play inside.

"Can we do somethin' for you, boss?" The biggest of the three men blocked the entrance.

"Yeah. I heard a friend of mine was here tonight. I thought I'd go in and have a look, see if he's still here." Dover tried to keep a casual attitude. He was tired and wanted to get this unfinished business over with.

"Oh, yeah? An' who might that be?" The big man towered over Dover. The other two closed in around him. "If he's white, he ain't in there, boss, 'cause this is an all-Negra joint."

Dover had spent the whole day and half the night tracking down Fat Ass. He had gone to the poker tournament on Beale Street and waited for hours for the big man to make his entrance. He'd lost a lot of his mad money to the professional players. Now he would have to tap into one of his out-of-state accounts for more cash. About an hour before midnight, someone mentioned the eating contest over at the Cotton Club.

"Oh yeah, that's where Tiny'll be. If there's food involved, he'll be there," someone said. Dover had driven over to West Memphis, hopeful he would find Tiny eating. He was not in a mood to be detained now from his goal, but he didn't want to end up in the bushes with missing teeth or worse.

"Look, I don't want any trouble from ya'll. I jus' wanna know if Tiny Moon's in there."

"Like I said, ain't no white man in there. You musta gotten the wrong information, boss."

"Do you mind if I just stand at the door and look in?" Dover's tic was giving him trouble.

"Ain't no door." The men tightened the circle.

Dover was about to haul out his sheriff's badge but decided that wouldn't be a good idea. Besides, he'd left it in the glove compartment, and it would carry no weight with these men. If he caused a scene, it could attract attention from the wrong people, and he might end up on the wrong side of the jail bars. And if he messed with these big boys, he could wind up in the bottom of the river.

"Go on and take a look from here," the man closest to the entrance said.

"You sure Tiny Moon ain't in there?" Dover looked around the darkened room. The dance floor was filled with couples dancing to a mellow jazz number. It was too dark to tell, but it looked like some of the people inside were white.

"Ain't no moon in there." The man closest to the door rolled his eyes.

"Wasn't there an eatin' contest here tonight?" Dover persisted.

"Shoot man, what you talkin' bout? That ain't legal is it? Ain't no eatin' contest in there."

"Well, I guess I'll be goin' now. Thanks anyway." Dover realized that he wasn't going to make any headway here. His face burned with anger as he got in his car and slammed the door. He put his hand to his neck to slow the tic. His tires squealed when he peeled out of the parking lot, cursing.

"Where in the hell is that sonofabitch?" He sped back over the bridge and decided that his best bet would be to go back to the Peabody and lean on the desk clerk to see if Tiny was staying there with the other gamblers. He'd asked the desk clerk earlier about a huge man who may have checked in and was told that no one fitting that description had been seen. Dover was confused. The lack of sleep was taking its toll on his reasoning. If he didn't find Tiny soon, he'd be forced to kill an innocent person just to relieve the tension. He was tired and needed some sleep, maybe he'd just spend the night at the Peabody and resume the search tomorrow. Could he risk being seen? Maybe the law was out looking for him.

CHAPTER 28

▼

Ellie propped herself up on a pillow on the hard metal floor in the back of the truck. Tiny and Fats sat up in front. They were in the parking lot behind the Blue Note. She watched as Tiny counted out Fats' cut of the winnings from the eating contest.

"Hey, we did all right," Tiny said. "Seventeen thousand two hundred and fifty dollars apiece from my initial investment of Clarence's money," he bragged. "I'll give that good man his money, plus a bonus for the loan when I pass his way again," Tiny smiled. They ducked as a car pulled around in back, its headlights blinding them.

"It's just me," Martel said, knocking on the side of the truck. "Dover's gone. He went back over the bridge to Memphis. You folks better stay on this side of the river tonight. The safest place to stay is the most obvious. Go on down the street and park around back of the Piggly Wiggly. A bread truck parked at a grocery store seems right at home there, now don't it?" He seemed pleased with himself. "I can round you up some blankets."

"Thanks, man. We got covers. Thanks for everything. A real pleasure doin' business with you. See you on my next run." Tiny shook Martel's hand.

"Youse don't expect me to sleep in this rig, do youse, when I got a million dollah bed waitin' for me over at the Peabody?" Fats rolled his eyes in disbelief.

"Come on, man. I'll drive you back over to get your car." Martel laughed.

"Meet me tomorrow night, Tiny, in Vicksburg, at the Evening Star. Lots' a high stake rollers gonna be there." Fats rubbed his thumb and fore-finger together to emphasize the largesse of the expected pot. He kissed Ellie's hand and waved goodbye.

It was after midnight when Tiny crawled into the back of the truck. He looked uncomfortable.

The air was chilled, and she could see her breath as she tucked the covers around her chin for warmth. Tiny was asleep, sitting propped up on pillows. He looked old and tired. He was snoring loudly as she drifted off to an uneasy sleep.

"Stop! Stop! Don't come any closer. I can't do it." She was crying when Tiny gently shook her awake.

"Hey, you were having some dream there. Are you all right?" He put his arms around her and gently rocked her back and forth. The sun was already too hot. It shone ruthlessly through the front window of the truck.

"What time is it?" she asked, dazed and unsure of the surroundings.

"It's nine o'clock. I've been up for hours, couldn't sleep." He patted his stomach and grimaced. "It's gonna be another scorcher today. Time for us to get out of Dodge. But why don't you tell me your dream first."

She sat rubbing her head. The light hurt her eyes.

"I've had this dream before. Only the setting was different this time. A young man—a soldier—it's me, and there's a war raging somewhere, but I'm home on furlough to get married. This time I'm in a church, like a big cathedral. It's filled with people. I don't recognize any of them. But I know they are there to make sure I do the right thing. I'm standing at an altar, waiting for my bride-to-be to walk down the aisle. I become petrified with fear, and I can't move. I can't breathe."

She felt her throat closing. She was having trouble telling the dream to Tiny.

"I know in my heart that I'm not capable of going through with this union. The woman starts walking toward me in her long white gown. Her face is covered by an opaque veil. Someone plays the organ. It's a Sousa march. It feels like the march of death for me. If I refuse to marry her, she'll kill me, and all those people in the church will help her. And all of us know that killing me would be the right thing to do. She keeps coming closer, and then I wake up in the nick of time."

She shivered in spite of the sweat that dampened her forehead in the hot, stale air of the truck.

"What do you think it means?" she asked. She couldn't penetrate the dream. There was no passageway. It was a closed window that she couldn't open.

"I don't know. Don't know much about dreams. I never have 'em myself. Maybe they don't mean nothin'." Tiny patted her shoulder as if that was the end of the whole matter and hoisted his body up into the front of the truck and into the driver's seat. He was ready to move down the road.

"I've got to go in the grocery store and use the restroom. I'll be right back." Her legs wobbled when her feet met the asphalt of the parking lot. There was a Nabisco Cookie truck parked next to the Bunny Bread truck. A Pabst Blue Ribbon Beer truck pulled in next to Tiny on the driver's side.

"Hurry up. Let's get out of here," he called to her nervously. She was still too muddled from the dream to move with confident steps.

The store bustled with early morning shoppers. She recognized several of the people from the Cotton Club last night. She hoped they wouldn't recognize her. She was ashamed that she'd cheered Tiny on to victory last night at the expense of another man's life. It reminded her of a scene in a Fellini film or a mob scene involving lions and bloody struggles in ancient Rome. She'd been swept up in the mob mentality.

She looked like a raccoon as she viewed herself in the cracked mirror of the ladies' room. Traces of last night's mascara, caught in a flash flood of tears, were caked around her eyes and on her cheekbones. She felt degraded and wanted to get far away from this place as she brushed her teeth and hurried back out to the bread truck.

They drove into Memphis for a quick look at Beale Street, stopping in a chrome and Formica diner on the corner of Third and Beale for coffee and pastries. After two cream puffs, Ellie felt better. She hadn't eaten since yesterday morning.

"It's been a long time since I've been here," she reminisced. The famous street of blues and rock & roll looked sleazy. There were no musicians out on the street playing. Elvis was in Hollywood making movies. Many of the old hot spots were converted to pawnshops. It saddened her to see the legendary street in such a state of deterioration.

"Let's hit the road," Tiny said, already on his feet before she could finish her coffee.

The radio was turned up to full volume and the truck rocked to Sam the Sham & the Pharaohs' latest hit, "Wooly Bully," as they headed south to Mississippi on the legendary Delta Blues Highway 61.

CHAPTER 29

▼

"Are ya'll travelin' alone, young lady? I couldn't help but notice that you were here in this same rockin' chair last evenin'. May I join you for a refreshment?" An elderly man with a full head of silver gray hair stood beside Ellie's rocker. He could have doubled for the Kentucky Colonel. She'd noticed him last night on the veranda. She motioned for him to sit down in the rocker next to her. He had on a white linen suit and a bolo tie. How perfect was this? She was already in character, sipping her second mint julep and frankly not giving a damn. The liquor had assuaged her anger and disappointment about being left again. Tiny had let her out of the truck at the curb in front of the Magnolia House, a famous antebellum mansion turned hotel, two days ago with a promise to return and take her to dinner that night at his favorite steak house in Vicksburg.

The plantation home had been restored. Corinthian columns graced the entrance. Balconies with intricate grillwork studded the windows like petrified tears flung upward from gallant beaus who had stood below and waited for hopeful signs of love returned from beautiful young maidens dressed in freshly starched white crinolines. The romantic setting and the mint juleps kindled her flare for the dramatic and made her acutely aware of her singular presence. This was the second evening to rock alone on the long wisteria-covered veranda, absorbing the grandeur that once was the old South.

"I would be most delighted to have the pleasure of ya'll's company, sir." She couldn't help it. Her accent ripened like a Georgia peach as it blossomed from her mouth. She took the role with uncanny enthusiasm. Her cheeks flushed like pink magnolias.

She felt cool and elegant in a pale violet rayon sundress with wide straps and a fitted bodice. She loved the way the mid-length skirt ended with a slight flounce—a gesture suggesting playful flirtation. The soft material touched her legs gracefully. She felt like dancing. She'd discovered the dress that morning in an expensive little boutique down on Clay Street. She'd bought new shoes as well—white sandals made of soft Italian leather with a slight heel and cushioned sole that made her feel airborne. She'd never before been so indulgent, spending so much money on clothes.

Ellie could tell that the money Tiny had won from the eating contest had burned a hole in his pocket ever since leaving Memphis. He couldn't wait to get down to Vicksburg and meet Chicago Fats at the Evening Star. He'd dropped her at the curb of the Magnolia House, shoved a fistful of money in her hand, and told her to check in and have fun, buy some fancy duds. She'd worried at first about the money, knowing that some of it needed to be saved to pay Clarence for the delivery of moonshine. But this was a gift to her from her daddy, and she wouldn't worry about anything until tomorrow.

She took a generous sip from the icy drink. Why not spend the money Tiny gave her? Most of it was predestined to sit atop a table in some smoke-filled room, its fate riding on the draw of the cards, an indecisive touch of a turtle's foot, or the random direction in which a crow may happen to fly.

"May I have the honah of buying ya'll anotha mint julep?" The man signaled to a waiter. In keeping with the recreated ambiance of the old South, the waiter was costumed in a flouncy white cotton shirt with a black cotton vest and knickers with long white stockings. He looked hot and tired.

"This humidity's just awful," Ellie said, fanning herself with a plastic fan that had been provided by the management.

"The lady would like another mint julep, and I'll have a shot of Southern Comfort on the rocks, if you please." The old gentleman placed a twenty dollar bill on the table. A gold wedding band adorned his ring finger. His hands were crooked with arthritis and full of liver spots. She wondered what it would be like to have a grandfather. Tiny's father had deserted the family when Tiny was a child, and Granny's husband died before Ellie was born.

"Oh, I couldn't accept a drink from a stranger. What will you think of me?" She turned to the waiter. "Please put this on my daddy's tab, if you will." She'd show Tiny for leaving her again. What hurt the most was that he seemed so anxious to get rid of her, like her existence was of no consequence. His stupid card game came first. Maybe she'd run up a tab and buy everyone on the veranda a drink. The thought wasn't as appealing as the idea of going back to the boutique tomorrow and buying several more pairs of the Italian shoes.

The waiter smiled. He seemed amused at the accent she'd developed over the course of a few hours of rocking on the wide front porch and sipping Mint Juleps. He didn't seem surprised. He was probably used to all sorts of playacting in this theatre, where people paid a lot of money to pretend how romantic the South had been—back in the good old days of slavery and yellow fever. He was probably faking his drawl as well. More than likely, he hailed from Chicago or Cincinnati.

"And what's a beautiful woman like yourself doin' on such a lovely night all alone?" The man took a pack of Salems from his breast pocket and offered her one.

"No, thank you. I don't smoke." She took another giant sip from the big frosty glass. "I'm waitin' for my daddy to come and fetch me for dinnah."

Someone was playing Stephen Foster songs on a tinny and slightly out of tune piano inside the lobby. A woman sang in soprano, "I hear the voices gently calling, Old Back Joe."

Where in the hell was Tiny anyway? Maybe he'd lost all of the money and was ashamed to face her. Maybe he decided he didn't want her tagging along and had just split. He'd certainly left her with plenty enough money to get home. Maybe she'd hop a bus tomorrow and go back to St. Louis. The thought of going back to Louise made her shudder. The third mint julep had been a mistake. Her brain started a slow spin, like a dust devil in a dry field.

When would she learn that she could not rely on her father? He was like the American buffalo, destined to roam the range. He had no more control over his natural inclinations to wander than the animal that grazed the grasslands of this vast country at one time and had come to be an icon of freedom. He could not be domesticated and boxed up into a neat package of conformity and civility. Social institutions cramped his style like a pair of tight shoes. He had to walk free, hoof upon the good earth with no ill-fitting piece of leathery convention between. He cultivated freedom like a crop of rare orchids, nourished it, no matter what the cost in terms of loneliness or detriment to self and others.

"I must go call my mama." She got up from the rocking chair a little too abruptly—the room was circling around her—and extended her limp hand to the old gentleman. He kissed the back of it, tenderly.

"You must excuse me now." She elongated the excuse as she delivered her exit line, unsteady in her expensive, cushioned shoes of Italian leather. "Charmin' to have met ya'll." She felt like executing a smooth glissade across the veranda but settled for a slightly wavering saunter and a backward wave at the old gentleman as she entered the lobby.

The cheery gathering around the piano exaggerated her feeling of loneliness. She bypassed them and made a bee-line to the telephones in the hall.

The receiver felt cool against her ear. She had some difficulty dialing the numbers that were circling in a slow dance around the dial.

"Hi, Ma. How are you?" She slurred the words—couldn't make them come out right.

"Ellie, is that you? Where are you? I was just about to give up on you. I've been sick with worry. Are you enjoying your vacation? I hope so, because things have gone to hell in a hand basket around here. I'm having a terrible time. Jeremy quit, and I've been having an awful time trying to get someone to come in and help me and…

"Ma, I'm in a phone booth, and I don't have much change left. I just wanted to say hello, and let you know that I'm all right." The sound of Louise's voice set off an automatic reaction of guilt. She wished she hadn't called her.

"Where'd you say you were? Why do you have a southern accent? When are you coming home? Your yard looks like hell. I asked Mrs. Leapy's grandson to go over and cut the grass, but he hasn't done it yet. It's so hard to get teenagers to do anything these days. They all think the world owes them a living."

"Ma, I'm down in Missippi." She had trouble pronouncing the slippery ssss. I'm with Dad." Her mouth was made of rubber.

There was an uncharacteristic moment of silence on the other end.

"What? I don't believe it. Tell me you're joking. You're with your father? How did you find that bum? Is he still drinking and gambling? It's a sickness you know. It's an addiction. He needs help. He…"

"Ma, it's okay. We're having a great time." Ellie was close to tears.

"That man is danger to our family. Be careful, he'll ruin your life like he did mine."

She was tired. She wanted only to sleep.

"You listen to your mother, now. You come home as fast as you can. Do you hear me Ellie? Where did you say you were?"

"Misippi." It was easier leaving out the ssss. "I'm going to stay a little longer, and—"

"Why would you ever go looking for a man that walked out on his family without even a goodbye? What did I ever do to deserve this? Did he ask about me? What are you two doing?"

"Ma, really have to go. I'm almost out of time….be home soon. Don't worry."

"Wait. Is he still smoking those filthy cigars? I'll go get a pencil and write down your phone number. Ellie are you there? Ellie?"

Ellie jerked herself awake. She'd heard a soft snoring sound. Had it come from her?

"Bye, Ma."

"Sorry your time is up. If ya'll wish to continue talkin', please insert twenty-five cents now."

"No, operator. I don't wish to continue talkin'. Thank ya'll."

The receiver hung like a dislocated arm from the shoulder of the black box.

The insistent whine of the dial tone brought her back to reality: a harsh, stony prison. She was wide awake. The sound echoed her mother's dry, furious voice, demanding the lion's share of her heart and soul. And Oh, Lord! How she was so much like her sometimes.

CHAPTER 30

▼

"If I ever play cards again, I hope Jesus Christ comes down and picks out my eyeballs," Chicago Fats moaned and rolled his eyes. "He cheated. I know he cheated. But, damn, I just couldn't figure out how." He shook his head in disbelief. "Where the hell did you get this rig to drive, anyway? It makes me want to toss my cookies the way it bounces every time you put on the brakes."

"Hell, man. You'd toss your cookies anyway, as much money as you lost." Tiny released his last cigar from its wrapper. He'd hidden it from himself in the sun visor on the passenger side. Even though the truck was used to hauling around a lot of bread, it wasn't used to so much of it in the front and nothing in the back. The truck bounced up and down at every traffic light stop.

"All I need to make my day perfect is to start barfing. You know I have a sensitive stomach. Go easy on the brakes." Fats had a handkerchief over his mouth. Tiny was putting the brakes on and letting up fast to tease Fats.

"I'm so light I could fly through the window just like the fairy in the Swan's Down Flour commercial." He patted his empty pockets for emphasis. "Who was that guy anyway?" Fats mopped the sweat on his forehead with his handkerchief.

"A nobody. A skinny, snot ass kid from Kokomo, Indiana," Tiny said, lighting up.

"How the hell did he get in the game?" Fats was counting his remaining money.

"There's always a faster and better shark circling the waters waiting to eat us old-timers alive. These young guys are coming up with newer and better ways to cheat, just waitin' in the wings for us to take our final bows. I'm getting too old for this game." Tiny yawned. He longed for sleep. It had taken three nights for him and Fats to lose their entire bankroll at the Evening Star, including Clarence's moonshine money. Tiny knew he'd win it back, but he wasn't looking forward to facing Ellie with empty pockets.

He pulled into Gus's Gas and Soda Fountain down on Clay Street to count his money and plan a strategy to soften the blow of reunion with his daughter.

She was like her mother in some ways, but she was different, too. A lot like him. She had a wild streak like Rose, only she bottled it up. Not that he wanted her to be wild like Rose had been, but it wouldn't hurt her to loosen up a little and enjoy life. You only live once. She was judgmental like her mother, getting all mad and stove-up about something one minute and then the next, Oh, Lord, when she smiled at him—and that laugh was contagious, the little she did of that. He'd wanted to hand her the moon and the stars on a silver platter. Her laugh reminded him so much of Rose. When that girl laughed it was like angels had come down to Earth. It just made you glad to be alive when she was around.

Tiny was lost in yesterday when Fats shook his shoulder.

"Hey. You gonna sit there and cry all day over spilt milk or what?"

Tiny wiped the tears from his eyes, glad to be distracted from his thoughts.

"I've got a grand total of nine dollars and thirty-eight cents. How about you?" Fats asked.

Tiny's recent bulging pocket of bills had deflated to five dollars and twenty cents.

"Well, ain't that wonderful. We got fourteen dollars and fifty-eight cents between us. Not even enough to get into a crap game with the locals down by the dock," Fats said, looking at his watch. "I shoulda' been back in Chicago by now." His rental car had been impounded for parking in front of a fire hydrant at the Evening Star. "I need a couple of Grants to get my car out of hock and gas to get home."

"Let's go in and get something to drink and think this thing over." Tiny wiped the sweat from his brow. After being in an air-conditioned bar for three days, the outside heat felt oppressive.

"What you got in the bag, little man?" Fats walked over to a boy who was sitting on a metal milk crate next to the front door of Gus's Gas. He looked to be nine or ten. He was blond and barefooted with a runny nose. He looked like he hadn't had a bath all summer.

"Barled Goobers." The boy eyed Fats suspiciously.

"Goobers, huh? Where'd you get them goobers?" Fats looked in the bag, feigning intense interest.

"Got 'em at the gittin' place. What's it to ya?" He wiped his runny nose across the sleeve of his T-shirt.

"You gonna give me one of them goobers to taste?" Fats acted like he was going to take one out of the bag.

"Naw. These are mine. Git yer own." The boy held the bag of boiled peanuts to his chest protectively.

"I'm just kiddin' ya. I don't want to take your goobers." Fats almost made the gesture of patting the boy on the head but thought better of it. It didn't look like his hair had seen a swimming hole all summer, either.

"What'll ya have?" A blond man, looking no more washed than his younger version sitting out on the milk crate, asked. A confederate flag was ceremoniously draped over the mirror behind the soda fountain, with a bumper sticker plastered under it, with the warning: "Save your confederate money 'cause the South's gonna rise again".

"Two fountain Cokes and a bag of those boiled peanuts." Fats put up a dollar on the counter. "What's this? A punch board? How much you charge a punch?"

Tiny noticed the stuffed animals and boxes of candy on the shelf above the soda fountain.

"Don't waste your money on that," he advised Fats. "All you'll get if you win is a stuffed animal."

"You boys inerested in somethin' with a little higher stakes, are ya'?" The man lowered his voice to a confidential whisper, even though the three men were the only ones in the store.

"What you got to offer?" Tiny asked with not much interest. He was tired.

The man looked at his watch.

"In about a half an hour, the field workers are gonna be comin' in for their Friday evenin' crap game in the back room. They gits paid Fridays."

"How much does a guy need to start rollin'?" Fat's asked.

"Five bucks a throw." The man said. "Some of these guys are hotshots though. You gotta watch 'em. Thar good."

Tiny and Fats exchanged glances. They both carried loaded dice in their pockets at all times in case of emergencies like this one. When it came to cheating at craps, Tiny and Fats were the champions.

"How about I start with a five spot, and if I win you can come in the game." Fats advised Tiny in a voice meant only for him to hear.

"I'm in." The thought of shooting craps revived the big man's spirits.

The men arrived around dusk, sweaty and tired from a day's work in the hot sun. Some who worked on the docks came up from the river to play, others came from the cotton fields nearby. They cashed their checks and wanted a little entertainment before surrendering their earnings to their wives and debtors. They all filed into the back room where a table was pushed up against a wall that served as a backboard to catch the dice and throw them back on the roll.

Everybody pooled five dollars in the middle of the table. There were five men in the game besides Fats. Each person rolled the dice to see who would play first. The highest roller would start the game.

A big, rough-looking man named Lucas started the game. He rolled a four on one and a two on the other. He had three rolls to hit his point, another roll of six. He crapped out without making his points.

"Dammit, Mammy." He handed the dice to Fats who had strategically placed himself to roll after the starter so he could take the point and have more ante money to stay in the game.

"Come on, baby needs shoes." Fats shook the dice and blew on them.

All eyes were on this newcomer with the gangster accent from up North. Adept at rolling weighted dice and switching when necessary, he rarely got caught. He rolled a five and a two.

"Seven takes the pot." Fats raked in the money that had multiplied to thirty dollars. "Ante up." He rolled again and took the pot on the third roll with a four point. "I think this fat man over here wants to play. Hey mista' if you want to play, I'll spot you a five." Fats handed Tiny a crisp five dollar bill and shook his hand by way of introduction. "I'm Bill. Just passin' through. Good to meet youse."

"Nice to meet you," Tiny mumbled. He frowned at Fats as warning not to carry this charade too far, even though this bunch didn't look to be exactly swift. The owner had seen them walk in together.

Tiny was the next lucky roller. He made his point on the second roll and took the pot. Now that they had enough for a few more antes, they could afford to lose a few rounds to divert suspicion. He lost the next round and handed the dice to a somber looking man with brown teeth and bad breath, who occasionally pulled a bottle of Hadacol out of his overall pockets and took a swig.

"Man, I thought that stuff was outlawed a long time ago." Fats gagged when he smelled the foul concoction. "That smells as bad as cousin Al's socks." He wretched in disgust, his handkerchief over his mouth, as the man swilled the thick brown syrup that looked and smelled like used motor oil.

"Each ta 'is own." The man looked at him with hard, steely eyes.

He rolled a three and a two. On two rolls he made his point and took the pot. The other three men dropped out and left after each losing a round.

"Let's make this game a little more interestin'." Fats suggested. "Let's double the pot, what say?"

"I'm in, man." Tiny primed the pot, hoping others would follow.

The somber man and Lucas followed, giving each other a knowing look that said these suckers don't know who they're playing with. Tiny won on the first roll with a five and a two. He won again with a six and a one. "I'm hot now." He had revived somewhat from his desperate need for sleep. He allowed himself to win one more round, giving him a grand total of one hundred and twenty five dollars, before passing on the dice to the next person down the line, Chicago Fats.

"Baby needs to take me home now." He blew hard on the little red cubes with white dots. Baby took him home with three straight wins, leaving him with a grand total of one hundred and thirty-five dollars. Lucas folded shaking his head in defeat. The somber man with bad breath was ready for more, but Tiny signaled Fats to get out of the game while they were ahead.

Tiny left the building before Fats and pulled the truck around to the front door with the motor running, just in case there was trouble. Fats sauntered out licking an ice cream cone and started walking down the street. Tiny followed him and picked him up on the corner. They drove to the yard where Fat's vehicle was impounded.

"Thanks, man. It's been a real pleasure doin' business with you, as usual, my friend. I got just enough moola to make it to the safety of my front door. You tell that million dollah daughter of yours hello for me."

"Will do." Tiny waved goodbye and turned in the direction of the river. He made two stops along the way: one at Smokey's Famous Barbecue and the other at Rick's Cigar Store on Washington Street. Tiny was disappointed. Rick's was out of Havanas.

It was dark when he arrived at the Magnolia House. He hoped with all his heart that Ellie was still there.

CHAPTER 31

▼

"You gave me two thousand dollars, and now you want what's left of it back?" Ellie wasn't in the mood for this discussion. "I just spent a good portion of it on new clothes and the hotel bill," she said, indignant that he'd wasted all of his money in a card game and now wanted hers. They had left the Magnolia Inn well before sunup. Tiny had been in a hurry to leave. He was out of cigars. His next source would be a little private dealer in Port Gibson.

Bunny traveled along the Natchez Trace, an old wilderness trail that Indians and trappers had used in the old days, before the highway system was built. It was now a scenic highway that stretched from Tennessee through part of Mississippi. There were no restaurants open along the way, and they were both feeling the lack of morning caffeine.

"I wouldn't ask if I didn't really need it for food and gas," Tiny said contritely.

"And for cigars at fifty dollars a crack." Ellie wished she hadn't said it as soon as the caustic words came out of her mouth. She softened her tone. "Why don't we split the rest of the money? That should get us down to New Orleans." She counted out six hundred dollars and handed the bills to Tiny. "Here's your half of what's left. Let's stop for breakfast soon as we find a place; I'm hungry." She was surprised at the authority in her voice.

"I know a great little diner about ten minutes down the road in Port Gibson. They serve homemade biscuits with chocolate gravy." At the mention of breakfast, his natural enthusiasm had returned.

There was a chill in the air. Clouds were gathering diagonally like daggers in a mottled blue and gray sky. As they left the Natchez Trace and followed Route 61 into Port Gibson's Church Street, the morning radio newscast reported that President Johnson was sending more troops to Vietnam to end the conflict.

"See that church over there?" Tiny pointed out on his right. "The chandeliers in there came from the Robert E. Lee steamboat. And the back of the church has a slave galley where they had to sit." The most notable feature of the church was a gold-leafed hand atop a steeple, with its golden forefinger pointed straight toward heaven.

The street was lined on either side with stately live-oak trees, arching over to form a tunnel of shade. "I know why they call this Church Street." Ellie counted eight churches lining the road. "I hope that breakfast you promised me is here." Her stomach growled in anticipation.

"Eggs and bacon comin' right up." Tiny pulled into a big gravel parking lot. A silver diner sat in the middle, an oasis with no name.

A cold wind was blowing. The warmth of the diner and the smell of bacon and coffee were a long-awaited welcome.

"Tiny. It's good to see you. Come on in." A large man wearing a white apron stepped out from behind the counter and hugged Tiny. They looked like two sumo wrestlers in a tight space locked in a challenge.

"Ben, I'd like you to meet my daughter, Ellie," Tiny said, turning to her. "He's the chief cook and owner of this best of all places for breakfast in the world."

The clock on the wall announced that it was a little before eight. The diner consisted of a counter with twelve seats. All were occupied, and several people waited out on the porch to be seated with hands tucked up sleeves and necks scrunched down in collars, surprised by the sudden cold wind. Ellie's mind was fussing with the thought of how Tiny would ever fit his bottom on one of the counter stools.

As if reading her mind, Ben said, "Here, follow me. Come back and eat in the storeroom." The portly man escorted them behind the counter into a larger back room. Being of goodly girth himself insured Ben's sensitivity to the plight of his over-sized customers.

They sat at a roomy, round table with wide, comfortable chairs. The storeroom had shelves filled with commercial-sized canned goods. Trays of biscuits were rising, waiting to be baked, providing a cozy atmosphere.

"I'll have three eggs over easy and sausage, and maybe a little bacon too, and some of those wonderful biscuits that your wife gets up so early to make. And some chocolate gravy," Tiny said.

"I'll have whatever he's having. And some coffee, please," Ellie said, rubbing her hands, glad to be inside where it was warm. A portable radio was playing a rock and roll number by the Yardbirds.

"Turn that crap off. You can't even hear yourself think around here. My son." Ben turned his palms toward heaven and rolled his eyes. "What these kids call music, nowadays. It's a sin. You want grits with that?"

"Yes, indeed," Tiny said with a smile as he took a sip of dark, freshly brewed coffee. The rich, charred taste of chicory reminded Ellie of how close to Cajun country they were.

"Ah. Yes, that's real coffee. The coffee only gets better the farther south you go. Just like the barbecue," Tiny said, smiling.

"Hey, some guy with a jerky neck was in here looking for you yesterday. Said he was a friend of yours. Did he catch up with you?" Ben asked, as he delivered two sizzling plates to the table.

Tiny's smile vanished. "Holy shit! That man is persistent. What did you tell him?"

Ellie's warm feelings of anticipation of the hearty breakfast vanished in an instant.

"The truth," Ben shrugged. "I told him that you haven't been by this way for several months. I take it this guy isn't a friend of yours?"

"He's my worst enemy at the moment. I wonder how he knew to look for me here." Tiny sighed.

"That's easy. He told me. He said he stopped at the filling station down on Church Street and asked the gas attendant where a person would go to get the best breakfast in town. The guy down there told him that he wouldn't find as good a breakfast until he got to New Orleans. That was the exact quote from the gas guy. He was a little strange." Ben shook his head. "He drank a pot of coffee, almost, and ordered ham and eggs with all the trimmings and didn't even touch it. That tic in his neck was scaring customers. My boy was in the back room stocking shelves and he heard him talking to himself in the bathroom, something about being a good boy or somethin'. My son said it sounded like a pig was in there with him, snortin'. I don't know; he just gave us all the creeps."

They finished their meal in silence.

Ben shook his head. "The guy kept insisten' that this place had to have a name. I explained to him that everybody in town knew I was here. Why'd I need a sign out in front? That seemed to make him mad. So I told him he could name the place whatever he wanted, and then stick it wherever he wanted. That really pissed him off. I thought he was gonna punch me. He finally left, squealin' tires out of here in a red Firebird."

"Thanks, Ben. Leave that guy alone if he comes in here again. He's a little dangerous when riled up." Tiny patted Ben on the shoulder. "It was delicious as usual. Say hello to your wife for me." Tiny left a ten dollar bill on the table as a tip. "Hey, if he does comes back in again, you haven't seen me, okay? I don't want him followin' me around."

"Sure thing, Tiny. Nice to meet you, Ellie. Ya'll come back soon, ya hear."

Dark clouds moved rapidly across a slate gray sky. A cold wind whipped from the east. Tiny started the truck and sat in the parking lot a few minutes.

"I'm thinking it truly is time for you to go home. I know we've talked about it before, but this man is up to some evil, I'm afraid. If he's put out an APB on me, none of my informants have told me about it. That must mean he has something other than a legal arrest in mind. I don't like this at all." Tiny turned on the heater and rubbed his hands together.

"I'm worried about what he'll do when he finds you," Ellie said. She couldn't leave Tiny now. The warm air from the heater and the full stomach dulled her mind. She was sleepy in spite of the looming threat of

Dover's unpredictable presence nearby. "Wouldn't things go easier for you if I'm with you when he finds you?" she rationalized.

"I don't know. Everybody says what a tough hombre he is."

"We need to think of a way to get him off your back. First, let's go down and visit Rose's grave. I couldn't go home without doing that. We're so close." Neither of them had mentioned the fact that they were a stone's throw from Rose, but Ellie knew that it weighed on Tiny's mind, as it did hers. "And then we'll talk about a plan of action. Okay?" The thought of leaving Tiny alone with a madman on his heels wasn't an option.

As they drove down Church Street heading south, Ellie turned around to glance at the golden hand atop the gilded steeple of the First Presbyterian Church as it pointed toward heaven. The giant index finger looked as if it were directing traffic upward, in an ever-darkening sky congested with fast-moving cumulus clouds. They drove in silence as Church Street turned into Highway 61 at the edge of town. A blinding rain was beating hard against Bunny's windshield.

CHAPTER 32

▼

The graveyard was deserted except for an old man as brown as the rich earth cutting grass with a hand mower. He had on an old straw hat adorned with faded plastic roses. The rain clouds had dropped their cargo and had moved rapidly to the west. The sun shone hot after the rain, leaving the air heavy and muggy. The mosquitoes were out in full force. Ellie doused her bare arms and legs with Six-Twelve and walked between the rows of graves in search of Rose. A small clapboard church with a wooden cupola stood sentinel over the quiet graveyard. The marble headstones jutting out of the earth looked surreal, like petrified torsos cresting through the ground from the caskets below, desperately attempting to be rescued from anonymity. I'm here, over here. Don't forget me.

She understood in that moment the importance of remembering. Her stomach tightened to face the wave of sorrow that was rolling over her. It was vital to mark the places where bones remained—still tenants of this temporal place. Each being had been remarkable, in his or her own way, in his or her brief period of history. They had each possessed a uniqueness that was kept alive in the memories of those who had known and loved them. When memories faded there would be only the silent deposit of bones left in this place and the marble slabs, impersonal information to strangers: the names of those who had once walked the earth. Why hadn't she made this pilgrimage sooner? Why had she left Rose alone these ten years, unacknowledged and unadorned?

When the coroner's office had notified Louise and Ellie of Rose's death, the only information they had been told was that Rose had drowned in the Mississippi River down by Fort Adams, fifteen miles due west from here, and would be laid to rest in the Woodville cemetery.

From the graveyard hillside, Ellie looked out toward the river and the small settlement nearby. The place had once been a pre-Revolutionary Army fort. The settlement's claim to fame was mostly a literary one. It was the setting for a novel about a traitor, The Man Without a Country, by Edward Everett Hale.

The coroner had called Rose's death suicide by drug overdose and drowning. And that was the end of it. Whenever Louise made reference to her oldest daughter, she would lie to friends, tell them that Rose was away somewhere traveling in another geographical region. Ellie had overheard Louise once tell a neighbor that Rose had married a count and was living in Italy. Ellie was no less guilty than Louise. She had stuffed her feelings into a little box and hidden them away.

The Magnolia trees, like silent mourners, punctuated the rows of graves. Tiny was leaning his cumbersome frame against the trunk of one of them, cooling off in its shade. He wiped his forehead with a handkerchief. Ellie remembered how he'd hidden behind one of the trees at Rose's funeral ten years ago, not wanting Louise and her to know he was there. It had been in the spring, and the trees had been full of blossoms. Now, the branches were bereft of flowers now. Some fallen petals still lay on the ground at the base of the trees, dried and long past their prime, but still sweet enough in her mind to wake the dead. Oh, how she wished!

She noticed that many of the graves were old, dating back before the Civil War. Some of the graves held the remains of children, their markers adorned with cherubs and angels in flight.

She remembered that Rose was on the downside of the hill, overlooking the Mississippi River, meandering snakelike in the distance. The marble headstone was gouged with letters, the simple facts: Rose Moon, Beloved Daughter and Sister, 1934–1957. A dozen fresh red roses in a plastic vase filled with water had been placed on the rectangular mound of dirt before the headstone. Someone had remembered. Red roses had always been Rose's favorite. Ellie looked at Tiny. He had followed her to the grave and stood with bowed head. She could see his big shoulders quaking.

The man with the lawnmower had cut to the top of the hill. She heard the blades of the mower laboring on the steep slope. The old man was sweating. He took a red handkerchief out of his overall pocket and wiped his brow. When he saw them at Rose's grave, he started to go away. She called to him.

"Hello. Oh, hello. I just want to ask you a question." She walked over to the old man, waving. "Do you know who sent these roses?"

"Auh, I dont's know, ma'am." The man took off his hat and scratched his head. "I's jus the yard man." He looked uneasy under interrogation.

"Do they send them often? I noticed they're fresh."

She had to know who this person was that cared about Rose so much to send roses, even after these ten years that she'd been beneath the ground. Maybe it was Rose's true love, never recovered from the loss. Maybe, if she could meet him, he could tell her more about Rose's life after she'd left home. Rose had been a child of fifteen years when she left. Maybe that person would know the circumstances of her death. Rose had written to her only once. Ellie had answered right away, but the letter was returned with "address unknown" on the envelope.

"Yes 'um. I totes 'em out hez on the twenty-third a' each month and replaces the dead ones wid the new. That's whats they tells me to do." The old man turned to walk away, but Ellie reached out and clutched at his shirt.

"Please, you must know something. Please help me."

The ache in her chest was unbearable.

"It's all right," Tiny said to the startled yardman. Ellie couldn't make her hands let go of the man's shirt. Tiny gently pried her loose from the yardman. He left in a hurry, without the lawnmower.

"I send the roses once a month," Tiny said softly. "Yesterday was Rose's birthday. She would have been thirty-three. I have them sent on the twenty-third of each month."

"Oh, I didn't even remember her birthday!" Ellie choked on tears. She fell on her knees and smelled the roses, as if Rose were embodied there in the fragrance. Ellie remembered when they had been little girls. Louise had always made them bathe together. She'd always said that she might as well kill two birds with one stone. Ellie remembered that Rose would raise a fit and wouldn't get in the water until Louise poured a few drops of rose cologne into the tub. And when Rose was older, she wouldn't leave the house without a dousing of rose water behind her ears and on her throat and wrists.

Ellie grabbed the roses out of the vase, unmindful of the thorns that pricked her fingers. She crushed the blossoms to her face, longing to become the sweet odor that Rose so loved and mingle as pure fragrance with her down in the ground. She yearned to sink her body into the earth and be dry bones, lying next to the beloved brittle remains. Ellie couldn't stand the pain in her chest. She wanted to die.

She lost track of time, spreading herself over the grave in a protective gesture, cradling the mound of dirt as if it were Rose's sweet body. Sobbing uncontrollably, her heart finally broke. A mockingbird in a nearby Magnolia tree mimicked the sobs.

Tiny helped her stand. He stood watching with tears streaming down his cheeks. She couldn't breathe. She flew at him in attack, beating him hard with her fists.

"You should have been there. You should have protected us. It's all your fault. She wouldn't be dead if it weren't for you."

"Ellie, stop. Get a hold of yourself." Tiny raised his hands, protecting his head from the blows. She couldn't stop hitting.

"What good does it do to send her roses now? You should've cared before, when it mattered," she heard a voice screaming. "She took us to a doctor who prescribed amphetamines when we were only twelve and fourteen years old, for God's sake, so we wouldn't get fat like you. Never mind the sleepless nights when we felt like climbing the walls 'cause we couldn't get out of our own skins. Where were you to stop her?" She was still lashing out full force with tightly curled fists. Tiny stopped trying to fend off the blows. He stood there, heaving with his own internal earthquake.

"You were never there. You never really cared about anything but your precious card games. Well, look what you've done. This isn't a game." She kicked hard at the mound of dirt. "This is your daughter, and you helped kill her." Tiny grabbed her wrists again. She finally stopped hitting. Her body shook. She could barely stand. Tiny pulled her into a bear hug in his big arms for support.

"Ellie, I'm so sorry. I'm so sorry we lost her," Tiny whispered as he tried to wipe her tears away with his handkerchief.

The yardman had retrieved his lawnmower and gone over to the other side of the graveyard to resume mowing. Tiny helped steady her, leading her back to the truck. He brushed the dirt and grass from her shorts and T-shirt. He opened Bunny's door on the passenger's side for her to get in. Ellie quickly slammed the door shut.

"No, I'm driving now. It's my turn to drive," she said. Her chest still ached with an unbearable pain.

A gathering of crows flew over to an oak tree next to the truck, curious about the human ruckus that had disturbed their peace.

A soft brown deer stood near the entrance, grazing on freshly cut grass. He raised his head and looked at them for a moment with eyes that defined the terms of sorrow. His eyes seemed to say, "This is my yard of constant mourning. I stand my ground." He lowered his head to graze again.

CHAPTER 33

▼

Ellie drove west toward the river through an area of swampy backwater off of Highway 61, driving too fast, on a road that was poorly maintained. The truck hit deep potholes, jostling the two hostage bodies inside. Tiny looked helpless in the passenger seat, without the solace of a cigar. He'd planned to stop in Woodville to replenish his stash of Coronas, but Ellie wouldn't stop the truck.

She'd been hard on him, directing a deluge of pent-up anger toward him. He had red marks on his face where she'd punched him. Where had all that anger come from? She knew it wasn't over yet.

It felt good to be behind the wheel of a truck again. She'd driven big trucks before when she worked for a short time at a commercial tree nursery in Oregon after recovering from the Dexedrine addiction.

Menacing rain clouds were gathering again in a milky sky, and thunder could be heard in the distance.

They hadn't spoken since leaving the graveyard. She was afraid that if she spoke the outrage would once again overwhelm her. Feelings that had been kept dammed up for years, unexpressed, would spill over the floodgates yet another time.

She drove down the levee road and looked for a place of easy access to the water. She found one at a wide bend in the river. The Father of All Waters looked deceptively tame and quiet behind the manmade, sloping concrete walls that lined its banks. It only appeared to slow in order to accommodate the bend in the river. Kudzu vines, clutching all other vegetation by the riverbank in a death grip, pushed its way forcefully out of the cracks in the concrete, almost covering the light gray slabs with a deceptive green. She estimated that the river was about two miles wide at this point.

"Why are you stopping here?" Tiny sounded worried. Without answering, she jumped out of the truck and ran toward the water.

"Rose! Where exactly did you drown? During the graveside service someone had vaguely pointed west to this spot. You could have drowned anywhere above Fort Adams and the current would have carried you down here. I need to know what happened to you, Rose. I need to feel what you were feeling." She was dizzy as she took of her shoes and stripped down to bra and underpants. Tiny wasn't fast enough to stop her. She edged her way down the concrete retainer wall, holding on to the kudzu vines for support. Clutching the crystal around her neck that Ludine had given her, she plunged into the brown, murky flow that descended with seductive quiet toward the Gulf of Mexico.

She'd tasted the muddy water before, she remembered, as a small child up near St. Louis. The water had been clearer there, but the current was just as strong. She and Rose had been on a picnic with Oddy, their nanny. The no-nonsense, wise woman had warned her not to get near the water, but she got too close to the edge. The flow of the current made her dizzy, and she fell in. Oddy had jumped in and grabbed her, just as the current had threatened to sweep her downstream.

"Nobody be dumb enough to step foot in de' Ole Man. He take you home to Jesus way 'fore your time. You 'member dat." The woman spoke now to Ellie in a clear voice, an angel visiting from a lifetime ago.

As she was dragged along the largest river in North America, she could see Tiny, his arms waving high in the air, signaling her to come back to shore. She couldn't. The river swept her downstream into the strong middle current, around the bend, and out of Tiny's sight. She hoped he wouldn't try to rescue her; he'd never learned how to swim. The river smelled of dead fish, the water slippery against her skin. She was quickly exhausted. Fighting the current was futile. She surrendered, drifting closer toward the shore, and being swept farther downstream.

"Rose, are you here? Talk to me. I miss you so much. I need to know what happened to you. What could I have done to help you?"

"I'm here," Rose's clear, sweet, childhood voice said.

Ellie could feel her sister's presence as if it was yesterday, and they were young again, together, in the swirling muddy water.

"I was never strong like you, Owl. You always had something other than this world to fall back on. You always had a source of strength from somewhere deep inside of you. All I had was stark reality. I lived in the illusion of this world, thinking it was the only reality. I had nowhere to go but to drugs. But you, you always knew there was more. Get out of the river, my little Owl, save yourself. You don't have to die in order to learn the truth. You already know. Remember who you are. We are all stars."

Rose was gone.

Ellie swam as hard as she could toward the shore, making little headway, when a vortex of swirling undercurrent pulled her under. All of the air was sucked out of her lungs as she was forced to the bottom where things lay that had never seen the light of day. She felt her body being dragged across the river floor over soft, dead, jelly-like muck. Sharp objects like the bones of ancient ancestors, carved into her chest and stomach. She'd never felt more alive and alert in her pain and terror. She knew if she survived that things would be different. Bottom soil is the richest sowing ground. She'd already given more than enough to the river. If she could go without air long enough, the current would spit her out somewhere. She was dizzy. Her ears buzzed with the pressure of the water, like ten million locusts screaming in her ears. White, sparkling light appeared under the water, surrounding the flotsam of objects that had been sucked under with her.

For an instant she had the sensation that she knew everything about the river. At that moment, she was the world's authority on this body of water. She could have written volumes about it. She understood the patterns of flow—from its many streams and tributaries, to its final descent to the ocean where all things mingled as one. It flowed from the pristine headwaters near St. Paul, a clear fresh stream, to lowlands dotted with marshes and clear lakes, past steep limestone bluffs. It gathered into itself the waters from streams and rivers in Minnesota, Wisconsin, Illinois, and Iowa and met with the flotsam-laden Missouri near St. Louis in the midlands. She knew intimately every fish in every stream. She felt the Missouri flow into the Mississippi as if it were her body, beginning the Old Man's middle journey, following a two hundred mile course to the mouth of the Ohio River in Cairo, Illinois. Beyond Cairo, she could feel the lower river swell to its full abundance and form a meandering of muddy, alluvial sediment as it looped and twisted along its floodplain—leaving in its wake, scars, cutoffs, swampy backwaters, and bayous.

She knew all of its human secrets as well, things that it selfishly took to the bottom to hide beneath its murky water. She knew of land and houses the fickle water washed away, along with lives of those not prepared for floods, and the anguish of sudden death. She knew of those who died at the hands of murderers and thieves to lie buried and forgotten on the dark bottom. She knew all of the river's muddy secrets. The great watery artery of the country carried on its swift and capricious current the alluvium and effluvium of history, with profound disregard for the joys and sorrows of human life. Along its course and beyond, where it joined the ocean, it carried the geological chronicles of a continent.

She was still being dragged along the bottom, unable to rise in the water an inch, when suddenly the river jettisoned her to the surface—as if two strong hands had thrown her upward. She gasped precious air, coughing and spitting out volumes of muddy water like some gargoyle spouting rainwater from a drain. She realized that she was next to the shore. She could feel the concrete wall but couldn't see anything. It was raining hard. The sky and water were the same murky gray. She grabbed a stronghold of kudzu vine on the shore and pulled herself up. She lay in the green vine, never so thankful for the tenacious plant as now. It had saved her life, along with infinite grace, Rose, and a whim of the river.

Tiny jumped into the truck and followed Ellie's bobbing head downstream in the current like a float on a fishing line. He was terrified. It looked as if she was making headway toward the shore when the storm blew in, and he lost all visibility of the river and the shoreline. When a lightening flash illuminated the sky and land, he found his daughter lying on the shore in the kudzu. He held on to the strong vines and climbed down the river wall, hoping the vines would hold him.

"Thank God! You're breathing. I didn't know if you were dead or alive," he choked. "Oh, Ellie, I thought the river had taken you, too. I was so scared. Don't ever do anything like that again." He rocked her shivering body back and forth in his arms.

"It's okay, Dad. I'm okay now."

CHAPTER 34

▼

The nascent morning felt crisp with renewal after last night's rainstorm. Ellie and the birds were the only ones stirring around the Pecan Tree Motel. A wind had blown Camellia and hyacinth leaves into the water from nearby bushes. Ellie shivered and dove into the pool of cold water, the chlorine stinging the numerous scratches on her body. The river had meticulously groomed her, combed her, as if preparing her for a debut. Despite repeated showers and gargling, the smell and taste of the river had become a part of her.

An exaltation of larks on their journey south flew overhead. They dipped down and landed in the crape myrtle tree next to the fence by the pool. The swooping motion initiated a ripple of joy in Ellie's solar plexus like free-falling. She and Tiny had spent the night here on the south side of Baton Rouge. She'd wanted to drive on to New Orleans, even though they were both exhausted, but hadn't put up much of an argument when Tiny insisted they stop for the night. He'd appeared to be more shaken than she by the narrow escape from the hungry river.

They had stopped last night at the emergency room of a hospital on the outskirts of Baton Rouge for treatment of the cuts on her chest and stomach.

"And why would you want to swim in the Mississippi River? There are swimming pools around here." The young doctor sounded suspicious.

"She just wanted to swim in the river," Tiny said defensively.

"I'm not asking you. I'm asking her," the doctor said gruffly.

"It was a stupid thing to do, and I won't do it again," she said to appease the medic.

"You were not trying to kill yourself, were you? In that storm?" the doctor asked.

"No. No I wasn't," she said a little too forcefully. Her motive for jumping in the river, although unclear to her at the time, was clarified in the aftermath. She was desperate to see Rose, to search for answers about her death. Ellie had to go under in search of a lost part of herself. How could she tell the doctor that?

"Nobody in their right mind would swim in that river. I hope you never get that foolish idea in your head again. You hear?" The doctor looked to be the same age as Ellie. He put iodine and Band-Aids on the cuts. The wounds were not deep, little more than scratches. He said she'd been lucky—more like she'd been blessed, baptized by the waters of the river that she'd battled and loved all her life.

She dove under and swam the length of the pool without coming up for air. Her chest was sore, and her lungs ached. She welcomed the sensation. In that moment she felt totally present in her body, for maybe the first time in her memory. She had risen early, put on her swimsuit, and tiptoed out to the pool. She could hear Tiny snoring in the room next to hers. She needed time alone to think about yesterday's events and last night's dream. It was the soldier dream again, only with a positive outcome. She ran the dream through the reels of her mind, straining to remember.

I'm still a young soldier in uniform. Evidently, I've just married the young girl that has been doggedly pursuing me. Vows have been exchanged, and we're standing together behind a long, white table at the wedding reception. Everyone is waiting for us to cut the cake. I'm terrified. I know that I'm not capable of cutting the cake. I keep telling my bride, "I can't cut it. I can't cut it." She takes the big, silver knife out of my right hand and places it in my left. Now you can cut it." We cut the cake together, her hand over mine, and she turns into a rainbow of light.

When she wakened it was as if a weight that she'd carried most of her life had been lifted. She felt young again, lighthearted. She could never remember feeling this carefree, even as a child—what little she could remember of her childhood. Something extraordinary had happened to her these last few days. She was leery about subjecting this interior process to the scrutiny of logic for fear it might shut down some kind of inner urge before it ran its course. Whatever was occurring felt inevitable. Pieces of a psychic puzzle seemed to be falling into place. She felt expanded, as if the narrow boundaries of her life were being pushed out to encompass more than met the eye, more than the logical mind could take in. She thought of the words in the poem, Renascence, by Edna St. Vincent Millay.

> "The world stands out on either side
>   No wider than the heart is wide;
> Above the world is stretched the sky,
>   No higher than the soul is high."

Her heart had expanded: her soul seemed higher.

Last night at dinner she'd told Tiny some of the conversation she'd had with Rose while struggling in the Mississippi. He'd brushed it off as near-death hallucinations until she'd asked him why Rose had called her Owl. Tiny looked surprised.

"Owl was your nickname when you were a little girl. We always called you Owl. Don't you remember?"

The oyster po' boy sandwich she was eating stuck in her throat. "I don't remember Owl. How could that be? Are you sure you called me Owl?"

"Owl was your nickname from the time you could say it," Tiny said.

"Why did you stop calling me Owl?"

"I always called you Owl. I guess one day you must've decided that you were too grown up to be an Owl. When you were around twelve, after I ran away, Rose told me when I saw her down in New Orleans that you stopped answering when people called you Owl. You just pretended she didn't exist. So they started calling you Ellie," Tiny said. "I guess that's why I haven't called you Owl."

"That seems so strange to me. Why can't I remember that?" She scowled.

"Maybe you didn't want to remember Owl. Maybe she had too hard of a time of it." Tiny's face looked heavy and sad. "God knows, you were right—what you said at the graveyard. I was a lousy parent." He pushed his half-eaten plate of shrimp jambalaya aside and shook his head. "It's a good thing I left. Things happened that weren't supposed to happen. I don't know why. I can't figure it out," Tiny said.

"What kind of things? What do you mean?" Ellie was confused.

"Just everything. The kind of atmosphere you grew up in when you were little—around gambling and the nightclub and all, and I drank too much in those days." Tiny's face was pale and sweaty. "I think it's better if we don't talk about it right now. We're tired. Let's just get a good night's sleep."

She'd sensed that the time wasn't right to push him for answers about the past. She'd been too sore and river-weary for any more revelations.

A pigeon at the opposite end of the pool walked back and forth on the concrete, his head bobbing in a beckoning motion. She swam back to the other end and offered her finger. The bird cooed and hopped aboard. He wore a band around his leg with a number on it.

"You must be a homing pigeon. Is that what you are? Do you have a message for me?" she cooed back to the bird softly. He pecked lightly at her hand and then flew up into a camellia bush. He must be a good omen. She thought of Ludine Lamar and the birds that rested in the sanctuary of her yard on their journey. She had landed in Ludine's yard, a respite along the way. Ellie touched the crystal that hung around her neck. It had been miraculously spared from the greedy river. She'd follow Ludine's advice when she got to the Big Easy and look up Ludine's psychic counselor, Madame Duvall. The pigeon looked at Ellie. As if reading her thoughts, he nodded his head from his perch in the camellia bush and then flew south toward New Orleans.

She could hear Tiny playing his harmonica when she walked back to the room after her swim. He was playing the melody to "Wildwood Flower" but with some added licks he'd learned from Clarence. He answered her knock dressed, freshly shaven, Panama hat on head, with an inferior brand of cigar in his mouth. He seemed restored to his usual optimism and eager for breakfast. The smells of fresh tobacco smoke and all-spice aftershave lotion made Ellie smile in remembrance of a time when she was very young—a time when those smells assured safety, protection, and adventure. It was good to reconnect with her father—good to be on this trip that meandered like the river to one inevitable destination: New Orleans.

They headed south with only two stops along the way: one for a box of good cigars and the other for boiled crayfish served in cones of newsprint, along with the best chicory coffee and freshly made beignets in the world, according to Tiny.

CHAPTER 35

▼

Bunny gassed up at Besiboe's Truck Stop while Ellie and Tiny munched on muffulettas.

"New Orleans is the only place in the South where I forget about my search for perfect barbecue," Tiny said. There was excitement in his voice at the proximity to the city famous for its gustatory delights. "They got great barbecue for sure, but there are so many wonderful dishes to choose from." Ever since they'd left Baton Rouge, he'd been describing the delectable treats to the point of salivation. Warm buns straight from the baker's oven were filled with thick mounds of hot roast beef and mozzarella cheese, pickles and olive relish with garlic, marinated vegetables, drizzled with olive oil.

Zydeco, a cross between blues and Cajun music, played loudly on the truck radio. An accordion, guitar, and washboard could be recognized, amidst other instruments that Ellie could not identify.

"What are your plans for the day?" She tried to make her voice sound casual as she took another bite of the muffuleta. She'd memorized the address on the card in her pocket, the one that Ludine had given her: Madame Duvall's address in the French Quarters. Not understanding the urgency that was growing inside of her to visit the acclaimed fortune-teller, she didn't want to appear overly eager. Even though she was concerned that Tiny might laugh at her gullibility, she vowed not to be dissuaded from her mission.

"I thought we'd pay a visit to Madame Duvall and find out whose playin' poker when and where around here. Is there anything special you'd like to do?" Tiny asked.

"You must've read my mind." She sighed with relief. "We must be on the same wavelength. As a matter of fact, I would like to see Madame Duvall. Ludine recommended her. Is she really psychic?"

"Well, she sure puts on a good show. I don't believe in most of that voodoo stuff, personally, but half the population of New Orleans does, and it's made her a rich woman." Tiny laughed. "Let's go. I can eat on the way. Gotta have one more for the road." Tiny unwrapped another steaming hot sandwich from a large bag he had stashed on the dashboard.

"How many muffulettas did you buy?" she asked, laughing. The generosity of food made her feel cared for and secure somehow.

"Just three apiece is all. You never know when we might need them," Tiny winked, his mouth full.

Traffic was stopped at the corner of Rampart and Dumaine for a funeral procession when they arrived in the French Quarter. A casket was being carried down the middle of the street, accompanied by walking mourners dressed in black. A brass band was playing "Just a Closer Walk with Thee" as the somber procession turned down Dumaine, bound for one of the local cemeteries.

Tiny pulled a red flannel bag out of his pocket and took out a dried, wrinkled root that resembled a tiny, shriveled person.

"She gave me this root for good luck. It's called High John the Conqueror, something every Negro gambler and half of the white ones in the South wear on their bodies for good luck in the game."

"Well, look at you—who doesn't believe in that voodoo stuff," she laughed, relieved that Tiny hadn't made fun of her plan to consult Madame Duvall.

"The voodoo people call this bag and its contents a gris-gris. That's when they make you a special mixture of strange things like bones and feathers and special powders that are supposed to help you overcome your troubles. They put it in a bag for you to carry around. Sometimes they make you a black magic gris-gris to get rid of your enemies."

"What's the difference between a mojo and a gris-gris?" Ellie asked.

"Nothing really. You can call it either one. Musicians usually call it a mojo."

"So this voodoo stuff is real? People still really practice it here?" She was intrigued.

"Oh yeah. It's real if you believe in it, and sometimes even if you don't." Tiny turned down Bourbon Street and slowed, looking for a place to park in a block with cars already crammed into every possible parking place.

"What do you mean?" she asked.

"I mean that sometimes the voodoo people take certain actions that make things happen so their clients are convinced that their spells are real," Tiny said.

"Like what kinds of things?" She was beginning to have second thoughts about visiting Madame Duvall.

"Like slippin' poison into someone's food after makin' a big show of sticking pins in a photograph of that person, or burnin' black candles, or takin' some hair from that person and sewin' it up in a cow's tongue and then planting it on the grave of some poor soul in the cemetery and then charging the client a lot of money to make a person disappear—seemingly by casting a spell on him."

"And the client believes it's the voodoo spell? Those things really happen?" She was stunned.

"Oh, yes ma'am. It's not as widespread as it was in the past, but voodoo in New Orleans has been around a long time. The beliefs were brought over from Africa and then the Caribbean with the slaves. It was a big thing here around the turn of the century. They used to have wild voodoo dances over in Conga Square all the time—with live snakes and all," Tiny said.

"Don't they get caught poisoning people and go to jail for murder?" she asked.

"Not usually. They use some kind of plant poison that breaks down in the body before an autopsy can be performed. They are real good at what they do, and they get really rich if people believe they have the power. Even a lot of white people in these parts believe in voodoo. 'Course mostly it's a legitimate, bona fide religion, but it gets a bad reputation 'cause of a few of its practitioners." Tiny circled the block in hopes that a parking space would open up. "I'm not sayin' that it's all a hoax. I've heard of genuine healings. I'm just sayin' that you have to be careful and keep your eyes open, or you can get duped."

"Is Madame Duvall a real voodooienne?"

"She's one of the reigning queens of New Orleans. She claims that she's the great-granddaughter of Marie Laveau: the most powerful and famous voodoo queen of all time in this country." Tiny circled the block for the third time.

"Madame Duvall also goes by the name of Mother Red Hawk. She's a well-stirred gumbo of different races, religions, and beliefs," Tiny said.

"Madame Ellie, Mother Moon to you, is going to use her magic powers to get us a parking place. Go around one more time and don't talk to me while I'm concentrating," Ellie said, closing her eyes. Just as they turned into Bourbon Street again, a car pulled out in front of a small shop with green shutters. The sign above the door read, "Madame Duvall, Public Consultant and Private Advisor."

"Damn, you're good. How'd you do that? You got us a parking spot right in front of the joint." Tiny's eyes widened in surprise.

"It's just a little trick I can do," she said, surprising even herself at the serendipity. "It's no big deal, really. Everybody can do it if they concentrate," she said, only half believing what she'd said.

"What else can you do?" Tiny seemed impressed.

"I don't know. I've never thought much about it. I know who's on the other end of a phone line about half the time." There were other things she knew, like on her wedding day she knew she shouldn't be marrying Ted.

Displayed in the front window of the shop were holy pictures of saints and cheap replicas of statues of the Blessed Virgin Mary and St. Peter that seemed to have been poured from shallow molds, leaving the features of the faces bland and rubbery looking. Along with the familiar Catholic statues were large totem figures carved in wood that looked like they had been charred by fire. The natural charred wood and the simple carvings wedded to create works of art, unpretentious, each imbued with a life of its own, a presence that shouted, "Here I am, deal with me." The images stirred a rich pot deep inside of Ellie.

A tinkling bell over the front door of the shop announced their arrival into a small, dark room. Sweet frankincense, myrrh, and burning bay-scented candles perfumed the air. The aromas reminded Ellie of days gone by, causing a quickening of energy around her heart.

She thought of the dream she'd had a few weeks ago at the beginning of the journey of the three hibernating bears and their entreaty to "leave sleeping bears lie." She tingled with a nascent understanding of the meaning. The first bear had been awakened from his long nap in the murky currents of the Mississippi River while Ellie was fighting for her life, just a few days ago. The physical life-and-death struggle with the waters had changed her, readied her for battle somehow. She knew that she could not only endure the suffering that life presented to her, but now she had an inner strength somehow to overcome most difficulties. The second bear was more indirect in its methods—indicating reparation within her psyche—a feat accomplished beneath conscious understanding. Perhaps the dreams about the soldier struggling to accept his bride were bridging a chasm within her heart and mind. A marriage of some kind had taken place within her. The knowledge both invigorated and terrified her. Here she was in a voodoo parlor in New Orleans. Was she on the verge of awakening the third bear? What would her mother think of all this? Her thoughts were interrupted by Tiny.

"Look at all those weird powders and mixtures." Tiny shook his head. A shelf with herbs, oils, roots and powders in big glass containers lined one side of the wall with labels such as "Love Powder," "Peace Powder," "Gamblers Luck," "Dice Special," "Lucky Lucky Powder," "Get Away Powder," "Easy Life Powder," "Goofer Dust," "Dragon's Blood," and "Black Cat Oil." There was an assortment of votive candles of all colors, mostly black and white, and miniature voodoo dolls in a basket on the shelf. A sign on the desk announced that Madame Duvall was with a customer in the back room and would return shortly.

They heard a door open and shut from within the back room. Shortly thereafter a tall, handsome woman with eyes like wood violets and skin the color of ripe bananas entered the room. She was dressed in a long, gauzy white gown and a purple bandana tied up around her head. Big gold hoops adorned her ears. She looked to be around fifty. A stately hound dog stood by her side. He was muscular with red, white, and black leopard spots and a white chest. His eyes were piercing, the color of a winter sky. He stood guard by his mistress's side with a singular, ferocious focus.

"So ya've finally brought your hija to see me, Tiny. Buholita, I've been waitin' for ya', girl. Ya' may call me Mother Red Hawk." The woman's accent was a mix of Cajun French, Caribbean Spanish, and southern dialect. She emphasized the Spanish words for dramatic effect.

"How did you know we were coming?" Ellie asked, surprised.

"Ludine called you, didn't she?" Tiny laughed at the voodooienne's attempt to be mysterious.

"She did dat. She tol' me ya would come." She took Ellie's hand and put it into hers, palm up. A thrill went through Ellie's skull. "We be goin' in da udder room now, Tiny. You wait out here, and I'll refresh yar High John Root when we come back."

Ellie noticed that Mother Red Hawk wore a crystal around her neck similar to the one that Ludine had given her. Ellie followed the voodooienne behind a red brocade curtain into a candle-lit room, the dog close at heel. White candles on an altar surrounded holy pictures of various Catholic saints, a bowl of holy water, and bones from birds and small animals. Wooden statues that mimicked the larger charred totems in the window of the front room stood vigilant against the walls. A white stuffed dove hung above the altar, its wings spread as if in flight. The odor of incense excited capsules of memories.

"I tell ya da truth, girl. Ya believe me when I tell ya da truth, now. Ya needs some especial fixins'. I gonna make ya' a gris-gris especially for ya' needs." She looked at Ellie with a steady gaze. "Ya have da malaise. Ya've had it since ya was a young girl. Ya have a hole in your soul. We gonna help ya to mend dat hole. Salvador! Ya' go and sit by dis child. Tell me what she needs in her gris-gris ta help her retrieve her animal guide who gonna help her mend de hole and make her whole," Madame Duvall commanded the hound.

Ellie felt herself suddenly bristle with suspicion. This was all a big show intended to extract money from her. She was sitting cross-legged in front of the altar and started to disentangle her legs to get up to leave when the dog came and lay down next to her, resting his head gently on her left knee. His touch had a soothing effect.

As if reading her state of mind, Madame Duvall said, "Ya don't misunderstand me, girl. I'm just here ta help ya ta doin' dis. You're doin' it for yourself. Dat's right. Ya've forgot who ya are, girl. We gonna help you remember. And jus' so you know, we not be chargin' ya no money for dis." The woman took a purple velvet bag from somewhere in her gauzy sleeve and handed it to Ellie. "I've already made dis for ya."

"What's in it?" Ellie asked, matching the woman's steady gaze. She remembered Ludine's words not to judge a book by its cover. She did trust Ludine. She would try to remain open, though cautious.

"Cinnamon, lots of cinnamon. Can't ya smell it, girl? It helps mend holes in your energy field. The gris-gris was blessed by da holy water and run through da flame. It has rosemary oil as well, to help ya remember and marble dust to sprinkle on de front porch for protection against those who think wrongly of ya," Madame Duvall spoke in a singsong voice. The dog growled softly. "And Salvador here is tellin' me to add some things." She went to the altar and picked up some small, delicate bones and the talons of what looked like an owl and passed them once through the flame of a candle. She held them up high in the air and mumbled some words that Ellie didn't understand, and then she placed them in the purple bag. "Here. Wear it next to your heart. Dis will help you, but dis alone won't be enough. Salvador tol' me that ya must do da dance as well."

"What dance?" Ellie asked, alarmed at the thought of what was coming next.

"Da dance we be havin' tonight for ya out on de bayou by my home. Tiny, he'll be dere playin' da cards. You come wid him and do da dance. It gonna be good for you."

With this, the dog and woman rose in unison. She shook Ellie's hand as if a pact had been made. They threaded their way through the red curtain and back into the front parlor where Tiny sat smoking a cigar.

"Ya bring me some of doze cigars especiales?" the voodooienne smiled.

"Of course. You don't think I'd come to see you without them, do you?"

It seemed that Madame Duvall had developed Tiny's rich taste in cigars. He'd said that it was customary to bring the voodoo queen a gift. He handed her a full box of Coronas.

"Let's git ya a new High John Root here. It'll bring ya luck for the game tonight. Ya be a comin' to the game tonight at my place on the bayou. And your hija, she be comin' along wid ya," Madame Duvall pronounced. She went to the shelf of potions and retrieved a root from a big jar.

"Ya better have some of dis Get Away Powder as well," she said as she looked at Tiny and nodded her head knowingly.

"Why the Get Away Powder? Do you know something that I don't?" Tiny looked worried.

"I jus' knows that somebody be wishin' ya evil, and ya needs to counter-attack wid the safety of dis powder on your bein'." She took the root and some of the powder she had measured out and sprinkled holy water over them.

"These must be passed through da flame." She walked through the curtain into the back room. Ellie heard the woman mumble something inaudible. She returned with the items and placed them in Tiny's red flannel bag.

"Now ya be safe from de evil intentions of dis person. Go, and I be seein' ya both tonight en mi casa." She dismissed them with a shooing wave of her hand.

"Well, Madame Moon thought dat was muy interesting." Ellie laughed as she climbed up onto the red throne in the truck, trying to make light of a situation that had left her quaking.

"Yeah. Do you think she knew about Dover?" Tiny was not smiling.

"I think she perceived that someone wished ill of you. I think she may really have some psychic powers. She told me I needed to do the dance tonight. What's that all about?"

"Oh, I understand it's quite an experience. A bunch of people all dressed up in costumes get together and dance around a fire out at her house and get shit-faced drunk and have a good time. Some of them claim that they go into a trance, but I think it's from drinking too much booze. It's pretty harmless really."

"What about her psychic dog? He's the one who picked out what I needed to carry in my mojo bag."

"You're kidding, right? I don't know about his psychic abilities, but he's an endangered breed. He's a Louisiana Catahoula Leopard Hound. There are only a few of them left. They were brought here in the fifteen hundreds by the Spanish to fight against the Indians—fierce war dogs, trained to kill. The Catahoula Indians captured some and crossed them with the native red wolf, creating the breed you see today. Catahoula means 'clear eyes.' You noticed that Salvador has blue eyes?" Tiny asked. "That's why they called them Catahoulas, because many of them have at least one blue eye. Since these dogs were bred in the swamps here, Mother Nature provided them with webbed feet so they can get around in the muck better. I think Louisiana is the only place where you'll find these creatures."

They turned off St. Peter Street onto Chartres, where they encountered the same funeral procession seen earlier in the afternoon. The mourners had unburdened themselves of the casket and shed their somber appearances. Many held colorful umbrellas above their heads, strutting and dancing to the lively sounds of the horns in the band playing "When the Saints Go Marchin' In." Passersby joined in the post-interment celebration, falling in behind the band, swaying their hips back and forth to what Tiny called a "booty bounce." It seemed as if the great Satchmo would appear any minute in the place where he got his start and strut down the narrow streets of the French Quarter blowing his trumpet.

"I know the greatest little oyster bar down by the river. They bring them in fresh from the Gulf twice a day. What say we go and eat a few?" Tiny looked at his watch with a serious expression that made Ellie laugh, as if the time of day had any power in determining when the big man would eat.

Tiny seemed to operate outside of any conventional time zone or normal circadian rhythms. He had no daily routine. Were his idiosyncrasies a rebellion against the norms of society and the mundane life that world implied to him, or was his life on the road something more? He was like the wandering mendicant monks of India: the difference between the two being that he yielded to every impulse rather than denying all earthly pleasures. He followed the practice of hedonism rather than asceticism. Was life for him a single-minded practice of staying in the present moment? She wondered.

They turned off Decatur Street onto Riverfront Park. All of the fine hairs on Ellie's arms and legs stood at attention as she thought about the dance that night.

CHAPTER 36

▼

"Get closer to the receiver. I can't hear you, man." Dover was in a telephone booth on Canal Street. The sounds of traffic made him seethe. A truck went by and honked his horn. Dover shook a fist at the driver.

"I can't get any closer without crawlin' through the phone. Where the hell are you? I can't cover for you much longer." The voice on the other end sounded like it was trying to be loud enough to be heard by Dover but not loud enough to reveal the conversation to the other inhabitants of the jailhouse.

"I'm down in New Orleans. I been followin' Fat Ass—thought I had him in Memphis, and then I heard he was headed south, but my tracks went cold. I need some help." Dover shook his fist again at the traffic. "All these Goddamned gamblers stick together—a tight-lipped bunch." His voice conveyed his frustration.

"You better forget about Tiny and save your own ass, man. There's some bad shit goin' down here as far as you're concerned."

"What's goin' on?" Dover asked.

"I can't talk too much now." George lowered his voice. "They got a substitute sheriff. He's back in the cells talking to a prisoner now, but they've been uncoverin' some stuff about you that don't look too pretty."

"What kind of stuff?" Dover started to sweat, even though it was a balmy seventy-one degrees this morning in the Big Easy.

"Turns out that old man that was killed out by Buster's Barbecue was best friends with the county coroner, Ed Judson. Ed seems to think you had something to do with his death. He's been pushin' the investigation hard. That's for starters." There was a lull in the traffic, and the voice on the other end of the phone. "Then there was a murder down in Alabama and they arrested that guy and convicted him, remember? Well, they've reopened his case. Too many people came out of the woodwork with an alibi for him. They let him go. But it seems they've turned their investigation to you. Now ain't that the craziest thing you ever heard? You and that guy they convicted look like identical twins. And somebody said they spotted a car fitting the description of yours near the scene of the crime. You want me to go on?"

"It sounds like I better keep on moving," Dover laughed, nervously. Things were beginning to unravel.

"Your wife's been callin' here. She says she's filin' for divorce. She's movin' back to Hawaii, she says. They've been questionin' her about a large sum of money that's missin' from the county funds. She's pleadin' the Fifth."

"Hell, let her talk or do whatever she wants. She don't know squat about that money." Dover gave a bitter laugh.

"On the upside, I may have some information about where Tiny might be headed in the next few days. Word has it on the wire that there's a big drug delivery from the Bahamas goin' down in St. Claire's Bayou down in New Orleans. They suspect some voodoo lady and her sons of runnin' drugs in on their shrimp boat. They own their own shittin' bayou. It just so happens that it's also a favorite place of Tiny's to play cards when he's in the vicinity. I've got the address if you want it. A snitch said there's gonna be a big poker game down there tonight."

"Hot damn! You, my friend, are a genius." Dover took a pencil and piece of paper out of his pocket and drew a map, according to George's directions, to the remote bayou.

"You gonna be okay an' all? You got enough money to be on the lam?"

"Hell, yes, I got enough money. Where do ya'll think all those funds went from the children's hospital raffle? Right here in Melvin's pocket, that's where," Dover said.

"Stay in touch. I'll keep you posted about what's goin' down around here. Watch your back, ya'll hear," George said.

"Thanks, man. If ya'll see my old lady, tell her to go fuck herself. Take care of yourself." Dover hung up the phone. Damn, if he wasn't going to miss that little Apache deputy. Dover glanced at the piece of paper with a smile on his face.

I got your big ass now, Tiny Moon.

He strode across the street to Mama Laymoine's for an order of red beans and rice, his appetite restored after a long hiatus.

CHAPTER 37

▼

"How about loanin' me five hundred dollars to get in the card game tonight?" Tiny asked. He looked sheepish. Ellie was driving on a back road somewhere west of the Mississippi and south of New Orleans. After crossing several long waterways, the land had become little more than strips of marsh, broken by mazes of sluggish, brackish water.

"Okay, that seems fair. You've been paying most the bills along the way," she said. You have to rub that root for good luck tonight, because we need money to drive me back up to St. Louis." Ellie felt a melancholy settle into her bones at the thought of parting with Tiny and resuming a life with Louise that now seemed almost unbearable. She wasn't ready to face old problems she'd laid aside for the last two and a half weeks, most notably, her mother.

The road trip had changed her. She was stronger, more assertive. She felt less like apologizing for her existence. The events of the trip and the people she'd met along the way had helped her to see things with new eyes. Possibilities of living in ways that felt more natural and supportive of the pursuit of her dreams had been presented. Here on the road with Tiny there were few mandates from society—or Louise: no expectations to live a normal, uninspired life.

Ellie wanted her own voice to be heard. Was it too late? Had she allowed herself to be silenced forever? Young girls should be seen and not heard. They should sacrifice their dreams and iron altar clothes for the glory of God. Had she internalized her most destructive critics, her mother and the nuns? If she had, could she change? Without Tiny's affirmative presence, could she withstand the naggings of Louise and her unrelenting clichés? Yet there was something even deeper than her hypercritical mother and her upbringing that kept her apart from the flow of life. She sensed there was an injured fledgling inside of her, persistently pecking away at its protective shell.

"Madame Duvall has three sons. They'll probably be at the bayou tonight." Tiny interrupted her thoughts.

Her stomach had been upset ever since the stop at the oyster bar in the French Quarter. She'd eaten too many of the delicious raw bicuspids on the half shell—that on top of the two muffulettas she'd eaten that morning.

"They own their own shrimp boat. The damn FBI thinks they're runnin' drugs, but I've never seen any—all the years I been hangin' out there, unless those weird roots she doles out have drugs in 'em."

"Oh great. I not only have to do a voodoo dance, now I get stuck in the middle of a drug bust to boot." She growled to cover the fear she felt at the prospect of facing off with Madame Duvall.

"I think the Feds are just hasslin' them 'cause they're Negroes. They've got too much money. They've been too successful. White people don't like that. Hell, they own an old plantation on their own bayou," Tiny said.

Ellie pulled into a gas station at Tiny's request. It consisted of little more than a gas pump and a shed with an outhouse in the back.

"This is the last stop before we get to Madame Duvall's, if you want to use the restroom or anything," Tiny said. She thought it wise to take advantage of the offer. It was the only roadside business they'd seen in miles. The mosquitoes bombed her as she ran into the outhouse, doused herself with Six-Twelve, and hastily changed into the peach-colored dress she'd worn to the eating contest. She would wear her new Italian leather shoes to dance in. The thought didn't console her. A feeling of dread overcame her. She was nauseated and just wanted to go somewhere and sleep. Maybe she could make an appearance, dance for a little while, and then slip away and go back to the truck and hide in the sleeping bag. No one would miss her.

"You'd better drive us the rest of the way. I don't feel so good," she said. Tiny was leaning against the truck, blowing smoke at the mosquitoes and fanning them with his straw hat.

Ten miles down a deserted road they came to a bend that turned into a wide, dead-end driveway, lined on either side with live oak trees that met and arched into a cathedral of green.

"Here we are," Tiny said. Spanish moss trailed from branches like banners waving in midair, creating vaporous forms like shadow puppets controlled by a concealed and omnipotent source. The verdant boughs tunneled to a flat, open, graveled space for parking.

"This used to be a pecan plantation back before the Civil War," Tiny said. The only evidence visible of the once agricultural venture was a small stand of pecan trees that bordered the grassy stretch of lawn next to the bayou on one side. The other side was bordered by a long wooden building and an old chicken coop surrounded by Spanish moss-covered cypress trees.

"That old house down near the chicken coop was the slaves' quarters, back in the old days. Hard to believe isn't it?" Tiny shook his head.

"That we had slaves in this country?" Ellie asked.

"Yeah. Some people act like they still should be." Tiny shook his head.

They were not the first to arrive. Seven other vehicles were in the parking lot, including the rented Cadillac that Chicago Fats had been driving just a few days ago in Vicksburg.

"Fats didn't make it home," Tiny laughed.

Their arrival disturbed a flock of pelicans roosting in a mangrove tree down by the water. Their white wings flapped in disapproval of the disruption of their rest. Despite her fear, Ellie thrilled to the sight of so many pelicans in one place.

The bayou was about a football field in length from where the farmhouse stood. The water looked green with algae. She wondered what predators lived in the murky depths.

As if reading her mind, Tiny said, "Don't get any sudden urges to throw yourself in the water for a swim tonight. I know for a fact that this water is full of water moccasins—and Madame Duvall's two pet alligators and their offspring."

There was a large circle surrounded by stones and torches in the middle of a flat expanse of lawn. A young man was in the process of lighting coal oil torches, while another placed firewood in the center of the circle. Suddenly Ellie froze in terror at the thought of dancing inside that circle. She couldn't get enough air into her lungs. Her head spun.

"Just take deep breaths. You'll be all right." Tiny held her upright, patted her firmly on the back, and propelled her toward the lights of the big house.

The sun was gone, and darkness fell swift and heavy like a solid black meteor. The night was balmy. A breeze blew in over the bayou. A young man the color of cinnamon came out to greet them with a showy smile of white teeth. He wore a red and white bandana on his head and a small diamond in his earlobe. He had on cotton pants with drawstrings and was shirtless. His handsome face and stately demeanor resembled that of Madame Duvall.

"Hi, Tiny. It's good to see you again. Everybody's gettin' ready to play cards. Time to laissez les bons temps rouler, my friend." He shook Tiny's hand and waved a hand to Ellie. "Don't worry, lady, things be all right," he said reassuringly.

"Hey, Tiny, my million dollah friend. I rode in on my magic carpet. Youse two surprised to see me?" Chicago Fats came down the driveway to greet them, dancing his unique, birdlike hop. "I found a worthy game back in Memphis after I left you. Never did make it home. Hello, Princess Ellie, you look stunning as ever," Fats said.

Ellie couldn't reply to Fat's greeting: she was hyperventilating. No one seemed to notice.

"How did you do in the game at Memphis?" Tiny asked, chewing the end of his cigar.

"I'm so light I could fly through the air." Fats patted his flattened and empty pockets. "Got just enough to get in the game, but I feel lucky tonight."

Madame Duvall sat on the front porch with Salvador at her feet. She was dressed in a long white gown. Her head was wrapped in a gold silk cloth, which draped around and tucked into a high knot. Ellie's hands shook as she handed the woman a fifth of Old Crow and a fistful of cigars that Tiny had bought for the occasion before leaving New Orleans. He'd told Ellie that it was customary to present the voodooienne with whiskey and good cigars before the ceremony as a show of politeness and respect. Madame Duvall took the offerings in silence. Salvador looked up and let out a low growl.

"Breathe, girl!" Madame Duvall screamed, frightening Ellie's lungs to action. "The gamblers are all upstairs waitin' on ya, Tiny. They are ready to take their chances. And you, girl, are ya ready to take your chances?" She met Ellie's eyes with a steady gaze. Ellie was the first to break the stare. She felt a shiver come over her in the mild evening air. Tiny disappeared into the house. Ellie's heart sank. She was terrified of being left alone with Madame Duvall.

"Ya not be dressed appropriately to do da dance." The voodooienne looked her over.

"Oh, that's all right. I'll just sit and watch for a while. I'm not feeling very well." She hoped she wouldn't vomit on the porch as she sucked in each belabored breath of air.

"Come wid me, girl. Git yourself together. This is not a social affair. This dance is especial para ti. Come wid me." She escorted Ellie into a back bedroom on the first floor of the roomy old house with high ceilings. A red gown of sheer, gauzy cotton was laid out on the bed.

"Here, put dis on. The spirits like red. *Es el colore favorito de los espiritos.* The color of blood lures dem into the circle and makes dem long to be alive again." She commanded her to take off the peach dress and put on the red gown.

"Mira! Que bonita!" She seemed pleased with the fit. "Ya not be wearin' the headdress. Only the voodoo ones sanctified by da spirits wear doze."

Ellie could hear the low, steady beating of drums coming from the direction of the torch-lit circle, beckoning her. Her legs were rubbery. She wasn't sure she could walk.

"Take off doze shoes, girl. How ya gonna dance in doze things? And stop wid your bein' afraid. Why you bein' afraid of your own ghosts? It's other folks' ghosts ya need to be afraid of. Don't ya know dat fear is jus' fun in disguise?" She laughed. Her violet eyes were large and steady as they beheld Ellie's discomfort.

The drums stopped as if on cue as the two women walked out onto the wide porch that faced the water. A screech owl could be heard in the distance from the direction of the bayou. The whole landscape had changed in the short time since Ellie and Tiny had arrived. A fog had descended over the bayou, swift and silent. It lay over the water low to the ground, surrounding the circle, as if conjured up by the call of the conga drums. The steamy vapor lent an atmosphere of illusion to the whole scene, like a stage prop in a magic act.

*   *   *   *

Nobody saw the red Firebird as it turned at the bend in the road. It crept, silent in the dark without the benefit of headlights, guided only by the filtered light of the moon in the thickening fog. Dover wished he'd staked out the place while there had been some daylight left, but he'd made a few wrong turns and gotten lost. George's directions had been vague. Little fart never could get anything right.

Dover got out of the car to have a better look. He was dressed in army fatigues and jungle camouflage. His ostrich skin Tony Lama boots stood out in contrast as they sunk into the marshy soil. He'd left his combat boots at home for the bitch to polish and had forgotten to put them back in the truck. He stepped a few feet away from the car with binoculars in hand. A dog was barking somewhere in the opaque, pearly night. Faint outlines of figures could be seen through the orange filtered light of a window upstairs. People were talking, but he was too far away to understand the conversation. He refocused his binoculars on the parked vehicles by the house but could discern little more than large objects in the dark and dense fog. He inched closer toward the house, hiding behind a hedge of tea roses.

Suddenly he heard drumbeats coming from a place near the water, resonant and vibrant in the misty air. He took a deep breath and exhaled slowly.

This's got to be the right place. Those drums are givin' me the creeps. I hope they're not doin' some weird voodoo crap. I'm not superstitious, but I don't want no part of any black magic baloney. He could hear voices chanting in rhythm to the beat of the drums. Through the thorny branches he saw fuzzy outlines of figures dancing around a blazing fire in a big circle. I wonder if they're doin' a human sacrifice thing or somethin'. Dover shivered. He remembered his lifelong fear of being eaten by wild pigs. Suddenly, he came to an astute attention, every fiber of his being focused on a faint and familiar smell that rode on a hint of a breeze.

Cigar smoke! Fat Ass is here all right. I'll jus' wait out here till the fog lifts, then I'll sneak in there and get 'im. The smell of Tiny's cigars had invaded Dover's unquiet slumber these last weeks and had haunted every waking hour. An imaginary smoke curled around his brain, bearing the smell of burning asphalt. Dover found himself short of breath and gasping for air. He heard a screech owl hoot during a lull in the drumming. It reminded him of his terrible childhood when he'd been alone, outdoors, in the dark. Despite the encouragement provided by the recent piece of olfactory evidence that Tiny might be near, his fear of the dark was taking possession. He patted his loaded pistol for reassurance. He had to pull himself together. He was so close to catching Fat Ass. "Snakes bite pigs," he hissed to the misty night.

*   *   *   *

The gathering of ghostly figures around the outer perimeter of stones parted and made a path for the two women to pass through. Madame Duvall held Ellie's hand firmly, guiding her through the break in the circle. The fire illuminated the flickering shadows of three masculine figures stripped to the waist, striking drums of varying size and shape with their hands. Six other people, indeterminate shadows in the dark, stood at the edge of the circle. Madame Duvall held a scallop shell in her hands with a mixture of burning herbs and essential oils. The familiar fragrances of frankincense, myrrh, rosemary, and sage did not reassure Ellie tonight.

The drums stopped as Madame Duvall stepped into the circle and walked around the circumference of the fire, throwing herbs into the flames and fanning the aromatic smoke outward from the fire with a wing of a great horned owl. She began chanting in a singsong voice.

"Oh guardians of de four directions and up and down, we invoke yur protection and offer ya sage for wisdom and de cleaning of the energy field of dis unhappy child. We bring ya mugwort so dat she may go inta her dreams and follow dem home. We bring ya rosemary to help her come out of de dream, rememberin' all dat transpired dere." She fanned the smoke around her body and then motioned for Ellie to step into the circle. She fanned the aromatic smoke around the younger woman with the owl's wing.

"Great Spirit of da fire dat burns us clean of all our sins, I offer ya dis to drink." From a bottle of whiskey, placed on the ground near the fire, she filled her mouth and spat it out into the flames. She took another long swig and spat it into Ellie's face, the astringent liquid startling her to full attention.

"What ya got to offer de fire, child?"

Without thinking, Ellie reached inside the front of her bra and pulled out the tangle of dried snake skins that she'd been carrying close to her heart since the beginning of the trip. She'd put them in her bra for reassurance. The ball of skins had traveled a long way from under the pot of geraniums by the house in St. Louis to a voodoo ritual by a remote bayou in Louisiana. Without hesitation, Ellie threw it into the fire. "Oh, fire, I give to you a gift, a symbol of courage and faith given me by our snake friends to show me that great change is possible," she heard herself say in a strong, vibrant voice.

Madame Duvall motioned for the others to step into the circle and space themselves equidistant behind her and Ellie. She took a long pull off the bottle of Old Crow and handed it to Ellie to drink. The fiery searing in her throat as she swallowed the whiskey gave her a jolt of courage. She breathed freely again.

Madame Duvall took back the bottle and passed it to the other participants in the circle. She lit two cigars, the ones Tiny had given her, and handed one to Ellie. The voodooienne began chanting again, dancing in small circles as she traversed the circumference of the larger circle.

"Ya mus' do what I do and say what I say," she directed Ellie, puffing on the cigar and blowing smoke in the direction of the fire. Ellie followed her lead, choking on the cigar smoke as she danced around the circle.

"You must call forth the spirit of de owl." She placed the owl wing in Ellie's hand. "Wave de wing to help her to fly to ya. Let her guide ya and speak to ya and den ya must let her fly away, forever, back to her place of restin'. Let her go in peace. Ya only call de owl once in yar life, and den you never mess wid her again. Ya understand what I tell ya?" The woman was circling faster. "Repeat after me. "Buho, Buho sancto, thank ya for yur great large eyes with which ya see all things hidden in da dark"."

Ellie's voice was a faint whisper as she repeated the words of the invocation, fanning the fire with the wing the voodoo woman had put in her hand.

"Speak up, girl, so she can hear ya!" she commanded. "Thank ya far yur silent flight that takes me wid you to the source of de trouble."

"Thank you for your silent flight that takes me with you to the source of the trouble." Ellie followed Madame Duvall's directions, her voice stronger and louder.

Madame Duvall stopped to let Ellie repeat her words to the fire and to take another drink of whiskey. "Thank ya for yur whooo, whooo, whooo that tells to me only de truth," she said.

Ellie repeated the words.

The men began playing the conga drums again. The chant of the two women echoed the rhythm and speed of the instruments. Everyone danced and drank from several bottles of whiskey that were continually passed around the circle. Ellie danced faster and faster as the drums increased in tempo. The fire escalated into a bright circle of heat and light.

Her summons to the owl became a song without recognizable words, a language that she instinctively knew and understood. Her voice traveled through a wide range of pitches, gaining in resonance, as she circled around and around, cued by the increasing tempo of the beating drums.

From the fire appeared a familiar figure, and then another. Beloved Oddy, her nanny who had cradled her in her infancy, and Old Mary, Oddy's mother who'd loved to color and sing with her as a small child. They sang to her in sweet voices that kindled the fires of memory. They danced together once around the circle, one on either side of Ellie. Then they flew away into the top of a nearby cypress tree, over by the chicken coop.

Faster and faster she danced, drenched in sweat. She tucked the long gown up into the waistband of her underpants for more freedom of movement, like she'd done when playing dress-up with Rose in her mother's evening gowns.

Another figure stepped out of the fire with something clutched tightly in her arms. It was Granny! Her embrace was like a time machine that drove Ellie back to her childhood. They chanted in harmony as together they danced one complete circle of the fire. Granny held out her hands and handed Ellie the object.

"This belongs to you, my little Owl. It is your dark legacy. Do with it what you must," Granny said. She flew away, following the flight of Oddy and Old Mary to the summit of the cypress tree.

The hateful object in her arms was heavy. It was the wooden statue of the three monkeys, "Hear No Evil, See No Evil, Speak No Evil." She threw her childhood icon into the center of the fire, remembering her past as she watched the wooden idol burn and char, disintegrating into gray ashes.

From the midst of the ashes, an owl arose and flew straight into Ellie's heart. She felt courage enter her body as she united with the child whom she'd longed to remember all of her adult life. Owl had been with her the whole time, guiding and protecting her on the journey through life. Owl had been the one to carry the shameful secret. Ellie remembered the dream of the three bears. She'd been in the car with a child in the passenger seat.

The child became the driver who led her out of the woods, just as the dream had foretold. The child in her dream had been Owl.

Ellie's childhood played itself out before her eyes. Renewed vitality overtook her as she became an innocent infant, still sprinkled with stardust. She remembered the knowing of self as one with all, then the naming of a separate ego, Owl, the one who watched in silence, never telling secrets. The frightened Owl who flew away in the dark on the wings of the Holy Ghost, to hide deep in the woods of Ellie's unconscious mind. She became again the child who had been rendered deaf, blind, and dumb by a foolish belief in the statue of the disabled monkeys (the symbol of all her misfortune). She had been helpless to end the violations that robbed her of a childhood, the crimes that had been committed by Tiny that ended her innocence and grace. The concealment of the shame she'd suffered at the hands of her father had been a dark secret, a pact that had to be kept no matter what the cost. Those secrets had taken away her memories and her power, had held her at bay from experiencing the world with true emotions—from feeling life in her body and soul. Those secrets had banished her to a barren landscape of disgrace and dishonor. The betrayal had kept her from communion with others, though she hadn't known why. She had turned to stone, had flown away from the world of the senses.

She became a chalice, filled to the brim with hot, righteous rage. She'd given lip service to her anger in the past, but she'd always stopped the feeling by turning to granite. Now the anger was host, allowing the nobility of a white atomic heat to fill her body, righteous and all consuming, scorching her bones. She looked at the gauzy red gown she wore. She had earned the right to wear red—an easy fit now, as easy as cutting the wedding cake with her left hand instead of her right in the last soldier dream.

She fell to the ground, exhausted. The cool, dewy grass doused her smoldering body and mind. She didn't know how long she lay there, unaware of the passage of time. She didn't know when the drums had stopped beating and when the other participants had left. After the anger had burned her clean, she was alone, yet she had never felt so in harmony, so connected to the web of life.

It seemed only moments ago that she had followed Madame Duvall into the circle. The fog had lifted. The moon was on the other side of the sky. It would soon be light once again. Was it her imagination or did she hear an owl hooting up in the top of the tallest cypress tree over by the chicken coop?

CHAPTER 38

▼

Dover was thankful for the dawn. He'd held his place and witnessed the ritual from a ringside position. Slithering over the damp ground, he'd taken a post near the chicken coop behind the cypress trees to get a better view. The party was over. Littered whiskey bottles and smoldering coals from the fire were all that was left.

He didn't know what the big deal about all this voodoo stuff was. It looked like just a bunch of niggers and a white woman gettin' drunk and dancin' around a fire. He was hungry and his body felt cramped. When the fog lifted, he was able to get a good look at the vehicles parked around the house. He saw the Bunny Bread truck. It affirmed what he'd suspected all along—the Bunny Bread truck was Tiny's wheels! Junior and his cousins had been in cahoots to hide the fat man. Wait till I get my hands on those jigaboos. The light was still on in the upstairs windows, and he could see players at the table but couldn't make out their faces. He even thought he heard Tiny laugh a few times. He was so close to dealing out his revenge he could taste it. He would need to make a move soon, before it got too light.

"Hold on here—what's this?" Dover whispered to himself. The big, dark-skinned woman who wore the gold headdress and seemed to be in charge of last night's festivities came out of the house and walked over to the white woman lying on the ground. The big woman was minus her headdress, and her hair was plaited into a long braid that hung down her back. The two were talking. Their voices carried on the morning air.

"Ya all right, girl? Yur daddy send me out to check on you. He be worried about ya. He thought you gone swimmin' in da bayou." The woman's features seemed softer, and her voice was gentler than it had been during the dance.

"I'm fine. Thank you," the white woman said with authority in her voice.

The dark woman touched the other woman's cheek and said, "You've come into your power now, haven't ya." It sounded like a pronouncement not a question. "You may call me Felicia. I'll tell Tiny that ya be all right. Come in and get dry, and I'll make ya breakfast before long. Ya must be hungry." She touched the young woman's arm, got up, and walked back toward the house.

Dover lay on the damp ground listening with open mouth, his heart pounding. Holy shit—Tiny's daughter! What could be better than this? He could twist the knot with a little torture. And damn, but she's not bad lookin', too. Lard Butt would feel real bad if his daughter's pretty face got messed up a little. Dover felt the stirrings of an erection. Hold on just a minute. He needed to think this through and not blow it. He'd almost jumped up and revealed himself in the excitement of discovery. He was soon rewarded for his patience. The Negro woman climbed the porch stairs and disappeared into the house. Tiny's daughter got up and walked down to the water following the bayou, around a bend and out of sight of the house and Dover's hiding place.

The sun was rising, teasing a silent haze over the water. Dover stood and stretched his cramped muscles. Then he made his way down to the path by the bayou, following the row of cypress trees for cover.

*   *   *   *

Ellie needed some time alone to reflect on what had happened last night and recover from the rage she had felt before facing Tiny with the reality of what had happened between them. She felt exhausted, but somehow deliciously attentive to the world around her. Patches of scum on the murky water of the bayou shone like emeralds. The birds sang to her, lauding the wonders of sunrise and letting her in on the secret of where the juiciest worms resided. She mimicked their songs. The energy of the earth beneath her bare feet reassured her. She was at home with both feet on the ground, while at the same time a part of her could soar with birds and touch the edges of infinite space.

She followed an animal path by the shore for some time, careful of the prickly grasses underfoot, when she heard rustling in the grass. She turned to see a man dressed in camouflage. He appeared flat and unreal, like a cardboard recruitment poster for the army. His face was blackened, exaggerating his cold blue eyes. It was almost as if he had arisen out of the slimy water of the bayou, a miasmic shadow. After the extraordinary events of last night, Ellie was not appropriately startled. She thought, perhaps, it was an apparition of some kind to reveal more about her past. Then she saw the neck jerking the head like a mud turtle with no control over its movements. She looked into the face of the man she'd seen pacing the levee at Junior's that day that she and Tiny were trapped in the duck blind.

"Dover!" she snarled, recoiling, ready to strike back, not having the time or inclination to fear.

"Well, hot damn! What have we here? So you're Tiny's daughter. You're sure prettier than he is, ain't ya?" Dover laughed.

Ellie screamed as he rushed at her. He was stronger than she was. Despite her clawing and kicking, he held her in a chokehold from behind, covering her mouth with his muddy hand. He unsheathed a hunting knife which was strapped to his belt and held it to her throat. The steel pressed heavy and cold against her skin.

"Keep your mouth shut, you bitch." He tripped her and threw her down into the thick, marshy grass. "I guess I'm gonna have to teach you and your fat father a lesson. Nobody screws around with Melvin Dover, ya'll hear." He took the knife away from her neck and slashed at the gauzy gown she wore, pinning her body down with his knees and prying her legs apart. His body, wet from crawling through the moist grass, felt heavy and damp on top of her. His hot breath fueled her rage once again.

"No! No! No!" She shouted, gaining strength from the words. "No! No! No! Don't touch me. Don't ever touch me again." She spat in his face. She managed to get an arm free and raked his face with her fingernails.

"Shut up, whore!" Dover put pressure on the blade at her neck, breaking the skin. It stung from the salty sweat that mingled with the blood. Her righteous anger annulled the pain. Blood ran down her shoulder and chest.

Dover laid the knife on the ground to unzip his pants, freeing one of her arms again. She hissed and jabbed at his eyes as hard as she could. He screamed in pain and blindly reached for the knife.

"Okay, you bitch. You're not worth fuckin'. You're gonna die, and then I'm gonna kill your fat daddy."

He was about to plunge the knife into her chest when she saw Salvador running toward them. He flew at Dover, clasping his arm in a vise of strong, razor-sharp teeth and knocking him over. She scrambled up and ran screaming in the direction of the house, running into Tiny and Felicia hurrying toward her.

"It's a good thing somebody spotted Dover's Firebird parked down the road. I knew he was after you when I heard that," Tiny said, out of breath. "Felicia ordered Salvador to run ahead and find you, and we followed him. Are you all right? You're bleeding."

"I'm all right. Hurry. Salvador has him by the arm, but Dover's got a knife."

The dog held tight on Dover's arm. The sleeve of his army jacket was torn to shreds. Dover had dropped the knife in the struggle with Salvador. He was beating at the dog and trying to reach with his free hand into his pants leg for the gun strapped to his leg.

"Salvador, ven aqui!" At Felicia's command, the dog let go his grip on Dover and ran to her side.

Ellie saw the slingshot that Clarence had given them in launching position in Tiny's strong hands, a big rock in the rubber cradle. She watched as Tiny pulled back the bow and aimed. Before Dover had a chance to pull out his gun, Tiny let fly the rock. It hit Dover full in the face, knocking him backward down on the ground. He was crying and moaning. It was difficult to tell how much damage he'd suffered: his face was full of blood.

Ellie felt the blood running down, hot against her neck.

"Jesus, what do we do with him now?" Tiny shook his head in disbelief at what had just happened. "I hate his guts for what he was about to do to you, but I hope I didn't kill him," Tiny said.

"Ya want him to go away and not botha ya no more? I know a way." Felicia had replaced the softer persona of this morning with the fierce Madame Duvall.

"Yeah, I want him to go away and leave us alone. But how are we gonna get rid of him without killin' him? I don't want a murder on our hands."

Ellie could still feel the hopelessness of being pinned down beneath Dover's slimy body and smell his putrid breath on her face.

"Let's jus' take da child closer by the water so we can see how bad he be hurt."

Tiny dragged the near unconscious man to the water's edge.

"Here, jus' put his head down in da water a little bit so we can wash away some of dis blood." Madame Duvall leaned his head backward and dunked it under the water, mumbling some words under her breath, as if performing a bizarre baptismal rite. The green, scummy water quickly became red with blood. "We leave da poor child here now. Nature gonna take care of him."

Dover looked barely conscious. He was moaning and repeating a word that Ellie couldn't understand. It sounded like he was calling someone.

"Epsen, Epsen," he moaned.

Ellie, Madame Duvall, Tiny, and the panting Salvador stood watch over the hateful, unfortunate man's struggle with pain. Ellie wanted to turn and run away but was unable. She watched spellbound as a wide patch of green scum rose up out of the water and engulfed Dover's bloody head, then the shoulders, and the torso. His legs and finally his feet, which sported the Tony Lama boots in which he had taken such pride—his last and only pair—were dragged through the tall grasses to the bayou's edge and disappeared into the slimy green water.

CHAPTER 39

▼

"Ellie, can you ever forgive me for what I did to you?" He was looking down at his graceful hands folded on his lap, swan's wings at rest. It was one of those rare moments that Tiny didn't have a cigar in his mouth. "I know that you remembered what happened to you when you were little. Felicia Duvall told me." His eyes were green oceans of regret.

Ellie pushed her foot down on the gas pedal of Dover's Firebird, accelerating smoothly to eighty, then ninety. The top was down, and the balmy air was filled with haunted marshy secrets, pacts that had recently been made and old ones that had been broken. She wanted no apologies and had no answer to Tiny's question. She felt an overwhelming need to put distance between them to sort out her feelings before any discussions could be possible.

They had left Madame Duvall's a few hours after Dover disappeared into the bayou. It had been Ellie's idea to drive Dover's car to the airport in New Orleans and deposit it in long-term parking. When and if the police looked for him, they would hopefully conclude that he had flown away somewhere of his own volition. Tiny had phoned earlier at Ellie's request and made a reservation for her to fly back to St. Louis that morning.

"We made good time," Tiny said, looking at his watch as she slowed to pull into the long-term parking lot at Kenner Airport. She took a stub from the automatic ticket master and parked in slot C24.

"Are you sure you want to leave like this?" Tiny asked, not making eye contact.

For an instant, when Dover had been on top of her, prying her legs apart, she'd seen Tiny's face. It had been interchangeable with the possessed sheriff's. She'd wanted Dover dead, and at that moment she'd wanted Tiny dead, too. She felt no guilt. She'd stood up for herself: she'd said no. She would have fought Dover to the death. Dover had been an effigy offered up to her rage and guilt, the sacrifice of his life had cleansed her of any feelings at all toward Tiny at this point. She was empty.

She took the key out of the ignition, wiped it clean with a handkerchief, and put it back. She got out and retrieved her suitcase from the trunk, wiping down anything she may have touched.

"I don't know what I'm feeling right now. Everything happened so fast. I don't want to talk about it now." She reached up to touch her neck where Dover had cut her. It ached. After applying a butterfly Band-Aid to stop the bleeding and close the wound, Madame Duvall had brewed up a bitter concoction of herbs and commanded her to drink it down to prevent infection.

Without a backward glance at Tiny, she walked briskly to the bus stop where the bus was loading passengers to transport to the main terminal. She boarded the bus with Tiny shadowing her. They rode in silence, without looking at each other.

"All passengers for Flight 280, departing for St. Louis, board now at Gate C 3." She ran for the boarding gate with Tiny behind, straining to keep up with her. The air-conditioning in the terminal was a cold compress to the throbbing wound in her neck.

She didn't know what to say. A father's expected role and duty was to guard and keep his children free from harm. Tiny had hurled her into the heart of the fire of disgrace at a tender age. And, God help him, his actions may have attributed greatly to Rose's death. And now here he stood. He had rescued Ellie from Dover and from the smoldering ashes of his own betrayal; he had helped her to rise, a charred Phoenix with a renewed capacity, she knew, for proud, sustained flight.

"Look in your suitcase when you get home. I put a little something in there so you can take time out to write," Tiny wanted to smile, but his face muscles couldn't quite make the span. His cheeks were moist with fresh tears. "You didn't ask me how the game went at Madame Duvall's," he said.

"How did the game go at Madame Duvall's?" she asked, attempting to narrow the canyon between them by just an inch.

"I won. Big time." Tiny's face muscles went the distance and smiled.

"Thanks for saving my life. Dover would have killed me, you know," she said, reaching out and lightly touching his shoulder. She felt his muscles tense under the touch.

"It's the least I could do," he said, choking on tears. "Take care of yourself. Say hello to your mother for me." He blew his nose and wiped his eyes.

"What are you going to do now?" she asked, crying with him.

"Well, I'm going to get a plate of beignets, some strong coffee, and buy a good cigar," Tiny said.

"And then what?" She wasn't going to let herself think of how she would miss him, his band of lovable cronies, and the open road. He'd broken a taboo, the most sacred pact between parent and child—trust. She hadn't the option to stay.

"And then I'm going to take a taxi back out to the bayou and pick up the truck. I've become attached to that rabbit. I think I'll keep it."

"I thought you didn't let yourself get attached to things?" She laughed, wiping the tears from her cheeks.

"Some things are worth keeping." Tiny blew his nose again.

"Then where are you going, or do you even know?" She wanted to comfort him but resisted the urge.

"I'm going up to Tennessee to give Clarence his money," Tiny said.

"Tell him I said hello." She felt a sudden sadness that she wouldn't be visiting Clarence again. She touched Tiny lightly on the shoulder and turned to walk away, up the carpeted ramp, before the next deluge of tears flooded her cheeks.

The last image of her father engraved itself on her mind as the airplane left the runway and lifted upward: a giant of a man fanning the air back and forth in a goodbye wave with his supple, big hands, his palms pushing up the sky. Magic lightening hands that dealt the cards too fast for the human eye to see. Hands that had supported and comforted her. Hands that had ripped her out of childhood in disgrace. Hands that had saved her life. She looked down at Tiny's hands. They became lily pads in a blue sky, maple leaves swirling in the wind, and then microscopic amoebas. She understood then that he'd been defiled as a child as she had been. He had perpetuated a legacy of abuse. The crime that had separated them formed them now as islands, brought them together in an unspoken treaty.

She saw the world in a different light as she flew through the sky, defying gravity. A bird's eye view helped change her perspective of appearances and events. Things seemed less than they appeared on the ground and more—seen from a broader, distant perspective. Judgment was suspended at such great heights. While soaring, she understood the importance of illuminating shadows, not pointing the finger in blame.

She looked out of the window as the great silver bird, on its flight north, followed the path of the Mississippi River. The great river wound and turned, a writhing snake, devious in its meandering, yet reassuring in its straightforward determination to deliver its flowing water to the ocean and to guide all of its itinerant children home again.

CHAPTER 40

▼

—Cannon Beach, Oregon, 1997—

A sunny day was a rarity in April, the first reprieve in months from her friend the rain. Ellie relished the soft drizzle that fell for days on end. The rain was sustenance. The constancy of the pit-a-pat on the tin roof of her cabin was grounding and acted as catalyst for the creative spark, chanting steady incantations straight from the Muse.

Just as she was thankful for the rain, she welcomed the coming months of sun and relief from the arthritis that had taken up residency in her aging bones. The intruder had pussyfooted its way into her body slowly over the last few years as her old cat, King Tut, had done, sleeping first on the door step, then coming inside for longer naps by the wood stove each day, and now quite at home, curled up and comfortable by the fire, demanding permanent housing.

The honking of geese lured her outside, away from her computer. She cupped her hand over her eyes and looked high into a brilliant sky to watch them fly in formation. The birds were flying north to their summer home in Canada, a sure sign of sun and warm weather to come.

She glanced over at her woodland garden. It was time to plant the peas and onions, set the tomato plants out, and give the rhubarb a drink of manure tea. The red stalks of the dramatic pie plant poked through the rich, black forest loam, ensuring confidence in the cycles of nature. She felt a rush of excitement at the prospect of another season of gardening.

A gust of wind swept the Douglas fir branches into a lively dance and carried the sweet aroma of flowering woodruff mixed with the smell of the Pacific Ocean, a stone's throw away, to her forest home. The salty, rich odor of the nearby ocean made her think of the river that ran through her veins, the blood that kept her heart pumping. Ellie had proven geographers wrong. The Mississippi did flow west of the Rockies, her body a tributary. And when she remained as only dust, she would be carried in the wind around the globe and home again, to settle in the great river's bottom, that stockpile of history.

Thirty years had passed since the notorious road trip with Tiny along the banks of the Mississippi. She had sold the house in St. Louis and moved to Oregon shortly after the trip. While unpacking after her return, she'd found a manila envelope with seventy thousand dollars and a single red rose inside. No note included. Tiny had gifted her with the spoils of his victory that night on Bayou St. Clair. The inheritance had allowed her the financial freedom to put distance between Louise and her, and to spend her time writing.

She was blessed with a modest success as a writer of children's stories, celebrating childhood every day in her own fashion, cutting and pasting imaginary lives. This writer was inclined to animate all manner of life on earth; plants, animals, and sometimes objects were the heroes and heroines of her stories.

Her desk sat in front of a bay window in her small cabin that looked out on giant firs. In the summer the bark of the majestic trees smelled like chocolate chip cookies.

She still did battle with her inner demons. Occasionally, there were days when she needed a little help—days when the only thing to do was to sprinkle a little marble dust on her door stoop from her gris-gris that Madame Duvall had given her all those years ago to protect her from her enemies, mostly from herself.

Most battles were outer ones now, struggling to preserve the forests from being denuded by clear-cuts, fighting for the life of the oceans.

A hummingbird jetted around her head, attracted by the red scarf she wore and looking for sweet fuel to keep his wings beating. He darted over to the red rose bush she'd planted especially for Rose. The buds were swelling and would soon bloom. She still missed Rose, who would reside forever in a heart that no longer carried the burden of guilt for her death.

Ellie was in the habit of wearing a piece of true red, the color of Rose's lipstick, every day as a celebration—a flag of victory. She needed no reasons to wear red. She was entitled as a citizen of earth to do so. The color complimented her green eyes. She had her father's eyes.

She touched the crystal that hung on a silver chain around her neck and thought of Ludine, as she often did, and all of the people who had graced her path on that life-changing trip with Tiny. With the exception of Chicago Fats, she'd neither seen nor contacted any of them. Madame Duvall had pronounced that one may call forth the owl only once in a lifetime. She had already gotten away with summoning the owl twice. She wasn't going to push her luck. The first summons was a capricious trick, an immature act performed in youth, and the second, a life-saving rescue. She would honor Madame Duvall's request and never call the owl again.

Every year on her birthday, she had received a dozen red roses with no card or return address. The roses had stopped coming seven years ago. She had a dream about Tiny that night before her fifty-fourth birthday, the first time she had dreamed of him since they'd parted at the airport in New Orleans thirty years ago.

In the dream she was on a beach trying to sell paintings that she'd made. People were laughing and ridiculing the work, kicking sand on the canvases. Tiny parted the crowd and stopped the jeering with his presence. He said he wanted to buy all of them. He pulled out a wad of bills from his pocket, in his usual fashion, and grasped the paintings in his big hands, gathering them to him. He disappeared, and she woke up embraced by the smell of his cigar smoke.

Had she forgiven him? She didn't know. She thought of him often and missed him. She felt at ease in her body most of the time. She was able to lay her burden down, only to pick it up again in troubled times. But it got a little lighter each year. Did she love him? Yes. He was her father. She had his green eyes.

She had returned to St. Louis only once since moving to attend her mother's funeral. Louise had softened with old age. She'd come out to visit Ellie several times and managed to keep her criticisms to a minimum. Ellie had looked for Tiny at the service, thinking he would be hiding behind one of the big mulberry trees in the graveyard, but he wasn't there.

Chicago Fats had attended Louise's funeral. He said that he had heard from a sheriff in Caggway County that the search for Dover had been abandoned years ago. The new sheriff told Fats that Dover had been sighted on a beach in Acapulco with a Mexican beauty in one hand and a margarita in the other.

As for Tiny, Fats wasn't sure. He said they had lost touch about seven or eight years ago, when Fats retired from the road. He said he'd heard a rumor that Tiny died in an eating contest down in Biloxi. Big stakes had been involved.

978-0-595-35762-8
0-595-35762-8

Printed in the United States
55505LVS00003B/118

9 780595 357628